THE BARREN WAY

Julie Anne Nelson

young
MOUNTAIN
PUBLISHING

This is a work of fiction. Names, characters, places, and incidents are either products of the author's imagination or are used fictitiously. Any resemblance to actual events or locales or persons, living or dead, is entirely coincidental.

Cover design by: Allison Leonard and Julie Anne Nelson

Young Mountain Publishing
P.O. Box 211061
Columbus, Ohio 43221
www.youngmountainpublishing.com

Copyright © 2013 Julie Anne Nelson

All rights reserved.

ISBN-10: 0985683945
ISBN-13: 978-0-9856839-4-8

For

Sullivan "Sully" Mainor

Ever since I reconnected with your mom, I watched your childhood as it happened, filled with dancing and laughter, family and fun. Almost instantly, you reminded me, with your wacky, fun ways—along with how you look—of my favorite character in this series, a character who always makes my heart smile to write. I was so excited to see you reach his age, to see glimmers of my Dusty in the real world. But now you'll never reach his age; you will always be the boy you were when you left this world. The world misses you, but we understand why Heaven was anxious to have you home.

Thank you, Sully, for reminding me that wacky, fun, courageous superheroes don't just exist in fiction.

Contents

1. Prisons
2. Smiling
3. One Thing
4. Direction
5. Hope
6. Limits
7. Untethered
8. Untold Truths
9. Grey
10. A Sight to Call Home
11. Casting Shadows
12. A Lost Soul
13. Wrath
14. This Desert Life
15. Shades of Yesterdays
16. Hazy
17. Relevant
18. A Portent of Things to Come
19. Tether
20. Lineage
21. Beloved Child
22. Legacy
23. Mostly Dead
24. The Meaning Struggle Gave
25. Try
26. The Nature of Everything
27. Truth
28. Always
29. The Deep East

Strew'd flowers upon the barren way...

—Percy Bysshe Shelley, *The Invitation*

1

Prisons

"*Dearest.*"

Sleep held tightly to Stephanie's mind, just as tightly as Dusty held to her body.

"*Dearest.*"

"Dusty?" Stephanie whispered.

"*Tush, dearest. You don't want to displease me. You don't want me to send you back to your cell, do you?*"

A cold veil draped over Stephanie's consciousness as the truth struck her. Sleep and contentment had smothered memories that should never be forgotten. The demon Ranz's horn-lined face and red and black eyes peered at her from inside her body. "*No, Ranz, I don't want to go back to my cell.*"

"*No?*"

"*You vanished for a little while, Ranz.*"

"*And you filled those moments in your boyfriend's arms, didn't you?*"

Uncertainty blossomed, sending a noxious cloud through her. "*Yes, Ranz. I... love him and you were gone and he was here. I was here. I didn't think you would mind.*" Ranz said nothing, so she stuttered, "*Please, don't punish me again when I didn't know I was doing anything wrong."*

"Who do you belong to, dearest? Who owns your soul?"

Tears—obnoxious and useless tears—fought for freedom. Just a few hours without Ranz in her mind, occupying her body, and Stephanie got lost in Dusty's arms and his kisses. The way he whispered all sorts of wonderful things. The smile only she knew. A few hours of freedom made her prison so much harder to bear.

"You do, Ranz." She paused, knowing without being told the word he was waiting for. *"Forever."*

"That's my girl."

"Are you very angry with me, Ranz?"

"No, dearest. Not at all. But I have a job for you."

Stephanie shuddered, remembering the last thing he'd asked—no, *forced*—her to do. Her empty hand pulsed as though it too remembered the feel of the blade and her ears reverberated with the sound of Morgan's cry.

"Are you certain you aren't craving some time in your cell, dearest?"

"No, Ranz, please no."

"Then what do you say?"

She swallowed over the hope that had no business growing in her heart during her tender moments with Dusty. Her heart wasn't hers to give away. Her life. Her soul. Not her property—*she* was the property.

Stephanie's will rallied inside her gut and she grasped for the one thought that gave her comfort, that instilled in her the knowledge that she could be more with Ranz than she could ever be without him. She put the image in her mind: herself, dressed in gossamer silks, wearing a crown upon her head while millions bowed before her. The Queen of Darienne, maybe even the world.

"Yes, dearest, that is your future."
"Then tell me what I must do next, Ranz."
"There's a blade just out of your reach."
Her nerves spiked. *"Yes?"*
"Take it and run it through the boy's heart."

*

Nightmares. All nightmares. Something in Dunlowe. Something in Cloud City. Something in the place Nate and Darla now lived. Something here. Something so dark, a void growing inside the souls of... not strangers, but friends. Something in the earth below me. Something wrenching through the Source's verdant gift. Something tearing at life and breath and will. Something connected to me somehow.

The earth's agonies ripped through me but my body couldn't take anymore. Couldn't. Not this. Please not this!

Screams tore out of me. Shaking and horror. Horror for innocence lost in the world, or maybe just in my heart.

Finn's voice finally reached me. *"Cecily, just hold on. It will pass. It has to. Please, just hold on."*

His fear lived inside me. Could I die from just screaming? From this pain built on top of so much more? I forced my mouth to shut, burying my face against his chest, but nothing made the tremors subside. The earth felt broken, ready to swallow me, to swallow us all just for the hope of nourishment.

"The earth... the earth... help it," I cried. Words flowed too quickly for me to hold back, words that when smashed together meant nothing. The pain. So much pain. Overpowering everything I was.

"She's not making sense."

I heard the desperation in Finn's voice. I heard Genovan and Morgan. Lille. Bay. Abigail. All panicked. And I was the cause... *again.* Torment wracked through my fragile body bringing forth another scream.

"Cecily, please..."

I couldn't help Finn and that truth broke the remaining slivers of my heart.

"She's burning up," Morgan said. "Lille, can we...?"

"No, that won't help her."

"The water." Genovan sounded calm but I felt that lie. "Let's take her to the sea. We can't fix everything, but we can cool her body."

Finn scooped me into his arms and I cried out. Everywhere he touched sparked with more heat, more agony.

"Give her to me," Genovan ordered.

"Why?" Finn demanded. "You'll hurt her just as much as I will."

"Yes, but it won't kill me the way it is killing you."

I pressed my palm against Finn's chest, wanting him to know I didn't blame him no matter how much he hurt me. I fought to keep my hand connected to him, but the searing of my skin and body felt just as it had when I stood atop the bonfire Pastor Rowe built, leaving me no choice but to rip my hand away and bite my lip to keep from wailing.

A sudden fury rocked through my wounded core. Fury at

the Source.

How *could* she send me back like this? How could *this* be my end—a burden on the lives of my friends and my love? Truly, death would have been a better choice.

∗

Zoe flinched awake, her hands empty, Logan not beside her. Panic flashed and she scrambled to her feet so quickly she swayed. Strong hands caught and steadied her.

"Easy there, miss," the man said.

She squinted at him, blinking a few times to help her dry eyes focus, but with smoke still blanketing the land from a series of fires, blurry was as good as it was going to get. "Where's Logan?"

"We moved him during the night."

"Moved? He didn't... he wasn't..." Her throat choked off her words.

"Don't trouble yourself—he lives. He's a great hero and we took him into the tent—the only one. He didn't want you awakened, but I promised to look after you and be here when you woke."

"Who are...?" Zoe stopped speaking as her mind caught up. Light brown hair. Green eyes. Just a couple years older than she was. "You're Jacoby Duluth from Marsden. You ran Cecily and the sevens out of Dunlowe before the soldiers came."

His face colored and he nodded.

"You came back." Zoe didn't think and lurched forward, hugging the stranger. "It was all over—the soldiers were about to kill us all—but you came back and you brought all of those people with you. Thank you."

Jacoby awkwardly patted Zoe's back until she realized exactly how awkward it was to hug a stranger—only somehow he didn't *feel* like a stranger. Either way, she backed away from him. "Sorry."

With an embarrassed squint, she raised her eyes and found a small smile on his face that was quickly washed away by shame.

"That's quite all right, but I neither deserve your warmth nor your thanks. I won't be having you think I'm a hero or anything like you and your Logan. I'm the reason for this destruction and all I can do is try to make amends."

Zoe took another step back, suddenly wary.

"Miss Crane, please come. See your Logan and then I would have you hear what I have to say."

*

"*Do what, Ranz?*" Stephanie whispered inside her mind.

"*Did you not hear me, dearest?*"

Stephanie's entire body clenched. "*I thought—I mean... I heard you, but you said we could make Dusty your vessel. Why would you want to kill him?*"

Ranz remained very calm. "*What did I tell you to do?*"

"*Sta..ab him.*"

"*Where?*"

"*His heart.*"

A pause.

"*I'm waiting, dearest.*"

Stephanie froze, her insides ice. Ranz could take over her body. Could kill Dusty. Could do *anything* he wanted. He could hurt Stephanie. Steal her body forever and leave her screaming in a cell like Vessel Two and the others. It was a gift to be in the world, one that she had to pay for.

She leaned away from Dusty to grasp the blade handle, praying this wasn't real. Just a test. She could pass a test. *Words*—Ranz's words pressed in: killing an oddity could unleash horrors. Ranz had said that and Dusty was still an oddity, with powers no one could explain. Powers that kept two armies from bringing him down when he'd stood against them and the mystics with the Grey Cloaks behind them.

"*I have the knife, Ranz.*"

"*Bring the blade to his heart.*"

With a trembling hand, Stephanie moved the sharp tip right in front of Dusty's heart, thinking how short a time it was since she rested her head in exactly that spot and how the rhythmic beating of his heart comforted her into a blissful sleep.

Her breath held as she waited for the order, while Ranz's demon mark on her belly throbbed.

"*I could order you to do it, dearest. I could force your body to do it.*"

"*Yes, Ranz.*"

"*I feel just how far we have to go before you are ready to be queen. All your doubts, your scheming—I hear it all. It offends me. If I tell you to pick up a knife and stab someone, I expect it done. No discussion. No insubordination. Compliance. Obedience.*"

Dread piled on more dread. "*Yes, Ranz. What do you want me to do?*"

"*Accept that before this is over, your hands will be covered in blood. You will be a warrior queen. Feared and obeyed.*"

"*Yes, Ranz.*"

"*This boy must be my vessel or he must be killed.*"

"*Yes, Ranz.*"

"*If you fail at this task, you will kill him. Do you understand?*"

"*Yes, Ranz.*"

"*Drop the blade and leave the tent.*"

Stephanie set the blade down though her hand still felt its weight. She quietly stood and hurried out of the tent, grateful to be anywhere but a threat to Dusty.

*

"Follow me, Nathaniel," his goddess said and he followed, hoping he showed his devotion sufficiently enough. His goddess gestured toward a metal cage. "In there."

Nate walked through the opening as she shut the door behind him. He watched as she pricked her finger on a knife and touched the drop of shimmering, silvery, dark blue blood to the metal bars. A flash of blue sparked and the bars seemed to turn to fire. The goddess stepped away, but the bars remained lit. Nate didn't understand, his mind had turned foggy.

"Just wait," the goddess said.

Nate shook his head, rubbing it with his hands, not remembering anything. Then, one by one, images formed in his mind. His mother. His father. Darla. Cecily. Dunlowe. His eyes raised to stare at the demon who had stolen his will, who'd now imprisoned him in a cage.

"Devra," he spat.

"Yes, it is I, your maker."

"My jailer, not my maker."

She smiled, her beauty still intact even though he now had a mind of his own. Tall, regal, dark skin, and deep blue—indigo—hair and eyes. As he stared into her exquisite eyes, eyes that drew him in, he watched them lighten from indigo to sky blue and back again, like the tide coming in and going out. After a few seconds, he cursed, realizing he'd actually gotten lost in her beauty.

Her smile grew. "I am actually both your jailer and your maker, though the cage is a gift to you."

"A gift?"

"I thought you would want to remember your life and who you are. This cage gives you a place to remember. Outside the bars, you will be nothing but a minion unless—"

"Isn't that what you want?"

A flash of vulnerability crossed her face. "You did not choose this prison, just as I did not choose mine, but both of us have to live the lives we were given. If you don't wish to know of your life or the things you do in my service, so be it. I can let you out now if you'd like."

"No, please. Just a little while longer."

Devra nodded.

"Where is my sister?"

"Happy with the other children. They will take good care of her."

"What will you do with us?"

Her voice turned hard. "Anything I like."

2

Smiling

With a desperate and chomping mind, Morgan followed Finn as he carried Cecily to the sea. Morgan fidgeted as she walked, feeling as though she should be doing something... anything. Her hands twitched until Lille took hold of one.

Instantly, Morgan heard singing, the unmistakable songs of the Delphea grove, the place Lille had taken her to when they were still in the Wild Wood. The beginning of the path that led her to this moment when the marks of the Delphea petals lived on her palms, with identical ones on the palms of her *sister*. Not a pretend sister or an honorary one—the trees claimed Morgan to be of their kind, just as Lille was.

Lille smiled at Morgan and nodded, clearly hearing the songs that no one else could.

"Why can't the petals help her? They helped us," Morgan whispered.

"She's not of our blood. They are for us alone." Lille let out a sigh. "I wish you could have met my—*our*—parents."

Morgan squeezed Lille's hand, offering what sympathy she could. Though born in different places in different millennia, Morgan and Lille shared the same horror—murdered parents.

"They are *your* parents, not mine. I've been thinking, in amongst all this craziness, and I think the Delphea trees had to know about your parents."

"They did. They gave me images, but I misunderstood them."

Moonlight peeked at the world as Morgan said, "I figured, but they *knew*, and that's why they did what they did to me, to *us*. The two of us with no family left."

Lille's eyes prepared for rain. "I'm so glad they did."

"Me too." Morgan paused for a few seconds, considering, but curiosity won out. "Lille?"

"Yes?"

"I want to ask you something, but if it is too difficult for you..."

"Ask me anything."

Morgan grimaced slightly. "Who is Reece? When you were weak, you called his name. Who is he?"

Pain rippled across Lille's face and the petals on their hands tingled slightly, just before clouds crossed in front of the moon. "He was the love of my life—the only one. And then he was gone. I would have married..."

As Lille's words became more constricted, Morgan felt like a louse. "I'm sorry—you don't have to..."

Lille nodded. "Thank you. Someday I will tell you everything and then I will finally let him go."

Morgan's thoughts turned to her own love, Oriel, suddenly wishing he hadn't remained at the camp. Lost loves, a new worry.

Morgan and Lille walked for a while and when they reached the sand, Morgan struggled to see the ocean, but the moon now cast only a miser's worth of light and thick fog drifted in from the sea, obscuring everything. Lille's hand remained in hers as they moved carefully toward where Finn stood at the water's edge.

Cecily's whimper hurt Morgan's heart.

Lille's voice whispered through the darkness, "She will make it through this."

"How do you know?"

"Because even broken, she's miraculous. Finn told me she did this to herself to save everyone, including the Source, and to come home to us. We'll find a way to make her better."

"I just hope she survives until morning. This night seems..."

Lille's body tensed and her hand chilled. "Genovan," she called softly, but Genovan's focus was on Cecily, ensuring she was safe while Finn walked into the ocean until her body submerged beneath the cool water.

Cecily's sigh sounded promising, if not for Lille's sudden gasp. Morgan squinted in the direction Lille's eyes were fixed and saw lights appearing over the water as more fog drifted and settled. Lights that were attached to boats. Not much of a glow was needed to see the color of the enemies' clothes—to know that they were grey.

*

Millie heard Cecily scream, a horrible sound that fed the panic that never seemed to rest inside Millie's fragile heart.

"Do you think we should go to her?" Charity asked, while softly brushing her fingers through Millie's hair, just the way Millie's mother always had.

"I don't know. Do you want to? I mean, it's dark out there."

Charity released an unhappy sigh. "If I thought we could do anything, you know I would say *yes*. But we can't. We'd just be useless parts of the crowd worrying about Cecily."

The defeat in Charity's voice caused Millie's shoulders to slump. "Useless."

"I'm sorry. I didn't mean to mope."

"I don't mind. Sometimes moping is the only thing to do."

Charity studied Millie like always, seeing in her an unsolved mystery that no one else cared to notice. "Are you okay?"

"I'm glad you're here," Millie said, giving the same answer she always did when Charity asked.

Charity responded with a smile that showed just an ounce of vexation, but Charity was too sweet to pry with force into places not ready for the light.

Movement at the tent opening brought Millie and Charity to their feet. Stephanie's face appeared between the tent flaps.

"It's you," Charity breathed. "Everything okay?"

Stephanie looked a little distracted. "Yes. Dusty's still sleeping, but I needed some air. Thought I would check on you. Cecily drama still ongoing?"

Tension fixed at the edges of Charity's eyes as she nodded.

"Okay." Stephanie straightened into her favorite princess posture. "You both stay here no matter what happens. I'll keep an eye on things." She flounced away with the same self-importance with which she did everything.

Charity grinned at Millie. "Well, since we were going to do that *anyway*, I guess that's what we'll do."

Charity opened her arms for a hug and Millie leaned into

her embrace, grateful Charity had twelve brothers and sisters and an irrepressible need to nurture.

After changing into their night clothes, they took their places on their sleeping pallets beside each other.

"Will you continue your story?" Millie asked.

Charity's eyes remained closed. "Of course. Where did I leave off?"

"The princess—a nicer one than Stephanie would ever be—had just met her prince and..."

"Right."

Charity wove words into an exquisite tapestry, creating tales Millie could see in her mind almost like they were real. Millie focused with all she was to disappear into Charity's stories, to hide from her own life, her own fears and sorrows. To hide from the dead spirits that had surrounded her every day of her life. In her bedroom in Dunlowe. In her parents' mercantile store. In the worship hall as Pastor Rowe stormed about the sevens and their evil, Millie saw dead faces, haggard and bent in rage, their voices sometimes close and sometimes distant but always filled with hate. Only when holding her cat had they vanished—only then. All the way south in the Wild Wood, the ghosts grew more vivid, more powerful, sometimes blotting out the world so much that Millie lost herself, lost what was real and what wasn't. The ghosts had come for her as never before when she reached the halfway point while crossing the treacherous sea with the beasts—*cararks*—below it yearning to eat her. She'd frozen... and in doing so, had risked Charity's life. They almost died.

Millie shuddered and Charity set a hand on Millie's head and brushed through her hair, soothing without even a thought, not missing even a second of the story. Millie had never told anyone about her ghostly curse. What if they cast her out and she had to wander alone with no Charity, no Cecily, no Dusty or Morgan? To have no companions other than the dead who hated her—that was her true nightmare. A few breaths, combined with reminders that her sisters didn't know anything and simply assumed she was a skittish fool, allowed her to calm as much as she ever could, allowed her to ignore the dead in the tent right now who struggled to scream at her, until finally exhaustion brought silence to her mind and rest to her soul.

*

Zoe followed Jacoby into the tent but forgot him instantly when she saw the pained look on Logan's face, and the worried ones worn by Mindy and Heath, who knelt beside him, their hands held together between them. Logan, Jem, Heath, Mindy, and Zoe—the original members of the Dunlowe Uprising—had all survived the attack. Zoe felt that miracle, but seeing the pallor of death on Logan's face made her wonder if all her miracles had run out.

Zoe lightly touched Logan's feverish forehead and his eyes opened, but their sparkly blue had turned dull. She watched as he forced his mouth to form a small smile, just before whispering something she couldn't hear.

Zoe leaned closer, her ear next to his mouth.

"I think I ate some bad fish," he whispered, his dry lips cracking into a weak grin.

She gave him the smile he sought but knew nothing would hide the terror in her eyes. Zoe glanced up at Mindy. "How is he?"

Mindy's thin fingers lightly patted Logan's head. "I gave him some tea to help break his fever. Mrs. Daye and Mrs. Hardy are searching for more herbs, but I... the wounds are..."

Zoe nodded to stop Mindy's words, her hand gripping hold of Logan's. "Nobody found Doc Forester?"

Mindy shook her head. "He's not here—maybe he was buried in Dunlowe or taken by the soldiers. Nobody knows for sure."

Movement brought Zoe's attention to the others in the tent. Logan's only surviving brother, Mitchell. Mr. Daye. Mr. Kent. Mrs. Rowe. Mrs. Dumphry. Mr. Pollak. Mr. and Mrs. Smyth. Zoe had stared at all of their faces during worship—during a life spent in Dunlowe—but not one of their faces looked the same. Grim. Worn. Broken. The events of the past few days seemed to catch her in their net and everywhere she looked she saw flashes of memories better left behind. And then just one image remained: Pastor Rowe's death... and the look on Jem's face after he had killed him.

"Where's Jem?" she asked, looking at Mindy and Heath.

Heath frowned, his light hair falling into his eyes. "He ran off after the battle. We've looked everywhere, for hours. His dad is still searching. I was just about to go back out and look—Mindy makes me report back... *often*."

"There's no way we killed all of the soldiers—some of them have to be in the woods." Mindy's eyes flashed to Heath. "You are dear to me, Heath. I can't lose you now."

He blushed and leaned to kiss her cheek. "You're not losing me now, or ever."

Logan mumbled something and Zoe leaned in, listening then arguing before letting out a frustrated breath and addressing the others. "I know where he went. Logan wants me to go after him."

"Not alone," Jacoby said from behind her.

"I'll go with you, Zoe" Mr. Daye said.

Zoe allowed her eyes to meet Mr. Daye's. She searched, but surprisingly found no malice even though he had every reason to hate her.

"If you would rather someone else..." he muttered.

"No, I'm grateful for your help."

"If Mindy allows," Heath said, "I'll go with you."

Embarrassment colored Mindy's cheeks. "Yes, go. Keep Zoe safe and all of you come back to me. I'm not ready to lose anyone else, especially when I'm not around to protect you—and to slaughter anyone who would do you harm."

Zoe reached and took Mindy's hand in hers. "Keep Logan safe and I'll keep Heath safe."

Heath laughed. "And the menfolk will hide and wait for you to rescue us."

"Naturally." Mindy kissed Heath just before he stood up.

Mr. Daye and Heath waited while Zoe struggled to force her legs to carry her away from Logan when he looked so vulnerable, not at all like the bear of a man he was.

Logan tugged her to him and whispered, "I'll be here when you get back."

"You better be." She deposited a kiss on his cheek and tried not to think of anything other than getting to Jem and returning. One squeeze of Logan's hand and she was on her feet, facing Jacoby.

"Can what you have to tell wait? It will be most of the day even if we hurry."

Jacoby nodded. "We will await your return, Miss Crane. There is planning to be done and a war to fight. Your opinion will be needed."

Zoe felt the scrunching confusion on her face. "I'm not much—I mean..."

She heard a protest grunt from Logan and an odd smile appeared on Jacoby's face.

"I believe what your boyfriend means is, without you and your friends and what you did in fighting the army, four towns would have ended. Make no mistake, we did our part. We escaped the soldiers and came to fight and die with the people of Dunlowe. Instead, you and your friends gave us all a chance to live and the will to keep fighting. That fight will continue as long as our townsfolk are being held captive by our king. We will await your return."

Awkward silence fell as Zoe honestly couldn't find a single word in her mind until Logan's foot lightly kicked her leg.

"Thanks. We'll be back soon." Zoe turned to Mindy. "Keep him alive—please."

Mindy nodded and Zoe hurried out of the tent with Heath and the father of the girl she'd always hated—only now she couldn't even summon annoyance. Zoe would give anything for Cecily to come back and heal Logan and make all of this go away. But somehow she knew in a world this messed up, Cecily had to have problems of her own and the people of Dunlowe would have to keep fighting without any magic to save them.

*

Stephanie ran because Ranz told her to run. Even with barely any light, she glided over the ground, not tripping or falling, and she wasn't even out of breath.

"You have much power and it grows with use, dearest."

"Is this another power then, Ranz?"

"No, more of the same. You can take the power of beings or objects, including the ground. You absorb energy and your body is already showing it is more than capable of using that power to further our ends."

"That's good, right, Ranz?"

"That's wonderful, dearest. Truly."

Stephanie rushed next to hedges, thinning trees, and over hills on her way toward the water, not at all afraid of the sinking mud that had almost killed her.

"No, that mud could never claim you now, just as it didn't once I had the ability to use your power to save you."

He *had* saved her. That meant something. *"May I ask you something, Ranz?"*

"Of course, dearest."

"Why was it important to know that Millie and Charity were in their tent? And that they would stay there? They are always in their tent. Besides, what do they matter anyway?"

"Do you not like them, dearest? I rather thought you did."

"Of course, I like them. They are my sisters, only they aren't important ones, right?"

Ranz chuckled. *"They aren't your sisters and you are the only important one. Slow down. Go into that grove of trees and watch."*

Stephanie obeyed, moving to the edge of the trees where she

could see the beach. Finn held what was certainly Cecily in the water as heavy fog drifted in, fog that didn't hide much from Stephanie's eyes. Lille and Morgan—holding hands—brought a sliver of rage into Stephanie's bearing. Bay and Genovan stood nearby with Abigail, and a passel of soldiers lingered a few feet away.

"*Watch the water, dearest.*"

Stephanie squinted for a second before using her power to steal the fog's ability to conceal.

"*Well done, dearest.*"

Pride felt nice. Stephanie watched the boats moving through the darkness and saw lights suddenly illuminated just before the boats—hundreds of them—neared the shore.

"*What's happening, Ranz?*"

"*A diversion, dearest.*"

Before Stephanie could think or ask or do anything, trumpets blared. Soldiers moved forward as Finn rushed Cecily back from the shore. Lille released Morgan's hand and reached for her sword, while Morgan pulled a dagger from under her skirt. Genovan held his own blade and stood in front of Finn and Cecily—she the most protected member of their group. Bay looked fierce. They were a small force to take on so great an army, but more soldiers would come.

"*Do I stand with them... or...? What do I do?*"

"*You watch.*"

Stephanie's hands rested on a narrow tree as boats clashed with the sandy beach. Grey Cloaks leapt from them and rushed to fight. Blades crashed. Crossbows pierced soldiers. Stephanie's heart stood still as something pulled at her and the brand on her belly burned *differently*. She realized she was staring at one of the Grey Cloaks, just one. Her eyes wouldn't leave him and she fought the urge to walk out of her protected place... to do *what*? Fight with him? Against him? Everything spinning in her mind gave her no clarity, only questions that seemed less important than feeling wonder at the mysteries of her life now.

More of Darienne's loyal soldiers arrived—including Amanda and Mortimer—and the fighting grew treacherous enough for Stephanie to flinch and gasp as Lille fought for her life. Morgan too, though Oriel, once he arrived, barely let her get in a single jab, shoving her behind Genovan.

On and on they fought until something strange let out a blaring whine and the Grey Cloaks as one, raced back to their boats, some jumping in while others worked together to get the boats beyond the tide. Rowing, they made their way toward the darkness, all of their lights extinguished as the fog became even more like ink spilled on a white page.

The brand pulsed and even in the pitch blackness, far beyond where even she could see, Stephanie still knew exactly where the one Grey Cloak was... and that he was smiling.

3

One Thing

Morgan watched the last of the Grey Cloaks vanish on the water, her breath finally beginning to regain its normal rhythm.

Oriel suddenly stood before her, his hands cradling her face. "Are you hurt?"

She shook her head in his hands, afraid her voice wouldn't hold. His concern washed away and was replaced with such a profound relief that Morgan felt humble. She touched his cheek, drawing a line down his deep scar.

A few soldiers moved closer, holding poles with lit rocks bound to the tops. With the light near, Oriel's teal eyes burned into her.

"Are *you* okay?" Morgan said.

"I am if you are."

"What *was* that?" Lille let out a frustrated grunt. "What's going on?"

Morgan tore her focus away from Oriel... and his eyes, and looked at the other faces around her, the light casting gloomy shadows everywhere. Sounds of pain from the wounded hurt her ears.

"They weren't even trying to win," Bay said. "I mean, they

would have been happy to kill all of us, but... that wasn't their goal."

Finn's face turned to stone.

"What is it, Finn?" Cecily asked, her voice shaky.

Finn's jaw remained tight as he looked at Cecily for a second before turning to Gen. "Why didn't you see them coming?"

"The map—the Commanders aren't healed yet since..."

"Since the surge of power that created me," Cecily said.

"Perhaps. There are patches we can't see. We thought it was Cecily's birth as an immortal that so affected us, but now I wonder if something else is at work. The same chaos that is happening here and probably in the rest of Darienne."

"Finn, what worries you?" Cecily pleaded.

"Gen, can you see the camp right now? Can you see those we left behind?"

Gen focused while Cecily struggled to understand the meaning of Finn's words. A frightening fierceness woke on Gen's face right before he bolted back toward the camp.

This battle wasn't what the Grey Cloaks wanted. They wanted something—or *someone*—left at the camp, unprotected.

Cecily's pitiful cry confirmed Morgan's fears. Morgan ran with the crowd, Oriel at her side, thinking of the most treasured person in the world who had been left behind: Dusty Daye.

∗

Nate stood in his cell, wondering what having a memory was really worth. Hopelessness settled in so quickly. Outside the cell, he had no thoughts. Inside, only torment.

"There is another option," Devra said from where she sat at

her desk, her eyes still fixed on a book. "But I don't think you are ready for it... *yet.*"

Nate considered ignoring her, but even inside his cage and with his mind intact, behaving petulantly before a goddess or a demon seemed beneath him.

Her eyes still down, Devra smiled.

"You can hear my thoughts?"

"I put the mark on your head for a reason."

"Could you always hear my thoughts?"

"Yes."

More defeat wafted into his core. How could he plan an uprising, save Cassa and Jaden's children, get back to Dunlowe, if she could hear his every thought?

"You can't. You are bound to me and my will, and I have need of you. But there is another option, the one your sister chose."

"Darla? What did she choose?"

"To indenture herself to me of her own volition in exchange for the chance of freedom when I no longer have need of her."

"She's a baby—she couldn't make that deal."

Devra finally looked at him, her eyes mocking. "She is no ordinary baby... nor is she a baby any longer."

"What do you mean?"

"She found being an infant challenging and I have no love for the *uselessness* of babies." Her words were hard, but Nate sensed a longing in them. "That is why I leave the children of the *Oades* with their families until the age of five."

"How can you be so cruel? How can you steal their children?"

"You fled Dunlowe, leaving it to a terrible fate to save

yourself. You tried to kill Cecily Daye after you committed to love and care for her. And what you did to Zoe Crane was shameful. Do you really believe you are in a position to stand in judgment of me for doing what I must to survive the life I was given?"

"I never stole anyone's baby," Nate snapped.

Devra's eyes flashed. "*Everyone* is someone's baby, and when you made the calculation to allow Zoe to suffer her fate to protect your own life and family, you cast aside any chance of the moral high ground with me. Besides, you'll be stealing children for me any time I ask."

"As your mindless minion."

"Or as my indentured servant, with a clear mind and purpose, if you choose."

"Why would I choose that?"

"Because it is your only chance of ever being free."

∗

Giant apes with huge teeth troubled Dusty's dreams. He turned over again, careful to keep his eyes very shut, about to fall under the weight of sleep again, when hands grabbed hold of him and shook him.

"What?! You better have a darn good reason..."

"Dusty!"

"What?" Dusty opened his eyes and saw a look of panic on Stephanie's face that instantly forced his brain into action. "What? What happened? What's wrong? Is it Cecily?"

Dusty's eyes came up and he found Cecily weeping against Finn's chest though when she turned toward Dusty, relief filled her eyes. He found the same relief on the other faces in the tent.

"What?"

Stephanie's lips tightened. "We thought..."

"What?" he pressed.

"There was an attack tonight," Morgan said. "We were trying to help Cecily and we were away. The soldiers joined us—we were worried someone might have taken you."

Dusty felt stabbed—well, maybe not stabbed exactly, but ticked off all the same. "Well, if you hadn't gone off with *my* sister without *me*, then you wouldn't have had to worry, would you?" A guilty glow seeped onto Stephanie's beautiful face. "You too?"

She nodded. "Just for the end. I heard trumpets and went to see what was going on. I didn't go far though."

"Far enough to leave me behind." He looked away from her and stared at Cecily. "Are you okay?"

"Better." *Worse* must have been really bad if that was her *better* voice.

A thought registered. "Was I the only one left behind? Like the *only* one?"

"No," Stephanie said. "Millie and Charity were here too."

"And no one worried about them, but you're all worried about me?" Dusty rolled to his feet. "*Whatever.*"

Morgan's brow crinkled as Dusty breezed past all of them on his way out of the tent. Day greeted him and he scowled at its obnoxiously bright light. The battle must have been bad; solemn faces met his as he marched the twenty feet to Charity and Millie's tent.

"Charity? Millie?" he called, expecting to hear their voices, expecting them to be exactly where they should be. But he heard nothing.

Dusty peeked into their tent, still thinking they were probably asleep, and what he found had him hollering to the others as he stared at the wrecked and empty tent. His mouth fell open and shame had his stomach turning. He'd slept through everything, even Millie's and Charity's cries for help.

*

Zoe walked beside Mr. Daye, careful to be quiet, her bow in her hands, an arrow in place ready to be launched in the time it took to pull her arm back. Heath walked about twenty feet ahead, his hand resting on the hilt of his sword and his head moving from side to side as he searched for enemies. For hours, they'd been heading toward the Secret Dunlowe Boys Only Fishing Hole without having seen anyone or anything that shouldn't be there.

Clouds gathered and rain began to fall. Heath turned back toward Zoe, who tilted her head toward some thick foliage that would protect them long enough to see if the rains meant to stay.

Once under the cover of the trees, Heath said, "I'm going to wander around for a bit, make sure we're alone."

"You want me to go with you?" Zoe asked.

Heath shook his head. "You know, the menfolk can actually help once in a while."

"You know we're just kidding—it's not like any of us would have survived without Logan."

Heath let out a worried sigh. "He's going to be all right."

"I know. Call if you need us."

"Will do." Heath walked out into the rain, his posture so

changed from just weeks before. A slightly pudgy boy became a lean warrior so fast.

"I know you don't like me," Zoe said softly. "I know you have no reason to."

Mr. Daye cocked his head. "What are you talking about?"

"I testified against the sevens and Cecily was beaten for it—she could have been killed. I know it was a long time ago, but it still wakes me up at night sometimes, so I know you haven't forgotten. You must hate me—you *should* hate me."

Mr. Daye moved closer, sharing the wide tree she leaned against. "I don't hate you. The town of Dunlowe raised you to be who you were that day. It was *our* fault—for that and so many other things. Zoe, my daughter and son are beyond my reach, and your father and mother..."

"... are gone forever."

The kindness in Mr. Daye's eyes took her by surprise. "How about you let my wife and me look after you?"

Zoe considered, her feelings all tangled. "Only if I get to look after you too."

"Fair enough."

"The whole idea of family has changed, hasn't it? They burned our homes and killed someone or *someones* in almost every family. We're all jumbled up now."

"That's a fact. Look at Heath—he lost three brothers and one sister, not to mention Charity heading into the unknown with Cecily and the others. Even though he has many siblings left, their lives will never be the same. His dad isn't doing well—he may lose his leg, *if* he even survives—and his mom won't eat."

"And yet, he's out here with us, wanting to help Jem." Zoe

thought for a second and then blurted, "I do think having a big family is a good idea. If I'd started with twelve siblings, I wouldn't be..." Fearing sounding like a whiner, she said, "But Logan lives, and he's my family now."

"I know, Zoe—I *know*."

Heath appeared through the shrubs, dirty, wet, and smiling. "The rain let up. Let's go."

After another hour, they cautiously approached the fishing hole, walking up the last hill and winding around the trees.

Zoe pushed through the small branches that smattered her with drops of water and stepped into the secluded camp, finding Jem on the ground weeping with such force that Zoe felt her own heart shudder.

She hurried to Jem, knelt on the ground, and threw her arms around him. "Jem, come on, you'll be okay."

"I killed him... I killed him... I..."

Jem's stammering caused his sobs to choke him and he coughed violently. Mr. Daye helped Jem to sit up and Heath just stood there, hand on his hilt, looking unhappy.

"Son, we've all killed in this," Mr. Daye said. "It's good that it is weighing on you, that taking a life is a horror we should never do. But our world's gone crazy..."

"That's no excuse," Jem said. "I killed him... and I was so glad he died."

Mr. Daye nodded.

"But it didn't bring my mom back... or my brother. It didn't bring Dunlowe back or our homes. And now I just feel empty."

"Jem," Zoe said, brushing his frazzled, wet, red curls away from his face. "We've got a war to fight and you have two little sisters and a dad to protect. And someday, Amanda's going to come back and she's going to be in awe of you and your courage. There's no time for falling down, only time for rising up. Later, I'll come back here with you and cry with you for as long as you want—I promise. But right now, we've got to go. Logan's worried about you and I'm worried about him. And there is a fight coming soon."

"I don't want to fight anymore."

Mr. Daye set a hand on Jem's shoulder. "Then you will build weapons and protect the children... or help the wounded, like Logan. You are a man now, not a boy. There is no more hiding at fishing holes for any of us."

Jem glanced up at Heath, searching his face for something.

"I'm glad you brought us back here, Jem. I wanted to see it again too. We were boys here, you, Logan, Dusty, and me. All those people died and we're still alive—think of that. We need to stick together, through thick and thin. Come on, and quit beating yourself up over Pastor Rowe. He got what was coming to him."

Jem looked around the fishing hole and seemed to make up his mind, dried his face, and stood, reaching to help Zoe up. She took his hand and he pulled her to her feet.

"We'll cry somewhere else, Zoe. I'm never coming back here since I can never be who I was when this was my favorite place in the world."

Jem walked away from the fishing hole without a backward glance and Zoe looked to Mr. Daye and Heath who nodded to her, immediately following Jem. Zoe paused, looking back, seeing the protected nook where the fishing equipment was stored and the trunk where Zoe had hidden her ill-gotten treasures, still not certain why she had stolen from Stephanie Trench. But another Trench pulled her to say goodbye to this place where her love for Logan blossomed and where five kids from Dunlowe became an army.

*

Trumpets blared in the distance and Millie flinched from sleep and pouted. "What now?"

She looked over at Charity groggily emerging from slumber as the pounding of hurried feet sounded all around the tent.

"I don't know, but we don't want to be in the way. We'll be safe here."

"Right."

A quirky grin lit Charity's face. "Besides, Stephanie *ordered* us to stay."

"And when a wanna-be princess orders, we *must* obey." Millie giggled until the twelve dead spirits in the tent registered in her mind and she lowered her head to stare at her hands.

"Don't worry. There are enough brave people around here. Maybe we have a different destiny than any of our sisters. Maybe we will be amazing some day."

"Maybe, but don't leave me, okay?"

"I wouldn't."

"You almost did yesterday. You almost left me to get your head cut off. Don't do that again."

"I'm really, really going to try not to."

When neither of them spoke for a few seconds, Millie realized just how quiet the camp had become. How eerie, and with twelve dead spirits in the tent, *eerier*.

"Maybe we should..." Millie whispered but didn't know what to say, what they should do, only knowing she felt unsafe.

Charity's face showed fear and she reached for Millie's hand but before their hands could touch, the tent flaps flew open and in a sudden whoosh, Grey Cloaks attacked. Millie didn't have a chance to scream before one of them shoved a cloth in her mouth and a bag over her head. She struggled but her efforts were for nothing. They bound her wrists and ankles and threw her over someone's shoulder, her body bouncing roughly as they took her away from the only place she knew in Darienne. The only people she knew. She didn't know if Charity was with her. Or if Charity was even alive.

She didn't know anything.

Nothing.

No—she knew one thing.

Wherever they took her, the dead spirits would follow.

4

Direction

The sun rose but no one got any breakfast. Or lunch. Searching—they were all searching. Well, everyone except for Stephanie, who pretended to search. Mostly, she kept herself busy comforting Dusty, who was very worried about Cecily and the two disappearing sevens, though his concerns for Millie and Charity couldn't touch his focus on his sister. Cecily was *still* the center of everything, even now that she had no power. They all fawned over her, like she still mattered.

"*Aren't you going to ask me, dearest?*"

"*What shall I ask, Ranz, when I know now why you wanted Millie and Charity to stay in their tent? Should I ask if I am to blame for their disappearance? If I'm to blame that they are dead somewhere? I'm not sure I want to know.*"

"*I see.*"

"*They weren't a threat to us.*"

"*Certainly not.*"

"*Would the Grey Cloaks kill them just to kill them, Ranz?*"

"*So now you want to know, dearest?*"

Stephanie thought for a few seconds. "*I'd like to know if they are alive.*"

"*They are.*"

She let out the breath she'd been holding. "*Good.*"

"*Do you want to know anything else, dearest?*"

Stephanie considered but quickly said, "*No, it will just make it harder to hide what I know and to lie to Dusty.*"

"Steph?" Dusty said, squeezing her hand.

"Sorry, what?"

"Everyone's meeting to talk about what's going to happen now. Will you come?"

"Of course." She leaned and kissed his cheek as they walked to where the others had formed a circle in the same place as the night before, when they'd all been together again for the first time since coming to Darienne. Stephanie swallowed down guilt or shame or unhappiness, she wasn't even sure. Millie and Charity were wimps, weaklings, useless, but having them gone seemed wrong, and that she had been part of it—no matter what she told herself—felt awful.

Stephanie's eyes swept over all of the faces. Cecily looked grotesque she was so pale. Morgan and Lille held hands *again* like they were *bestest* friends. Oriel sat behind Morgan, just as he had the night before, but his face was more stern, more possessive, as though losing the two sevens meant Morgan might vanish from his grasp. Stephanie knew exactly how he felt as she glanced at Dusty. Finn kept Cecily resting against him since she would tumble to the ground like a rag doll if he didn't. Genovan and the Commanders lurked nearby. Amanda and Mortimer sat beside each other, and Abigail wore such a look of shock that Stephanie considered moving to sit next to her but didn't. Bay and Keefe, his monstrous friend, were the last to join the circle.

"I am the queen of a broken land and now I am pulled in many directions," Lille said. "I ask for your help in deciding what we do next."

"What's to decide?" Stephanie blurted. "You have to get to Cloud City and be queen. Right?"

Incredulous looks attacked her from every direction.

"What?" she demanded, while Ranz remained silent. "The mystics have a head start already. You think they are done trying to kill you and steal the country from you? They are probably the ones who killed the king and queen. Don't you care?"

Lille winced slightly, but didn't say anything. She just studied Stephanie's face a little too closely for comfort, while Dusty extracted his hand from Stephanie's.

"What?" Stephanie pressed. "I'm not trying to be cruel here, but Millie and Charity were taken to distract you from what you need to do and why you need to do it. I just don't think a queen should make decisions that way."

Lille sat up a little straighter, her eyes cold. "Yes, I know you would be a different kind of queen than I am, just as Daryn would have been. But Daryn is dead. And Stephanie Trench, you will *never* be queen of Darienne. Your place in line for this throne died with Daryn. There is another heir now. If something or someone kills me, that person will rule—not *you*."

Stephanie's face heated and she felt an inner warning by Ranz, but he was still quiet. "I don't care about your throne," she spat, hoping her words sounded less false to the others than they did to her.

"What *do* you care about, Steph?" Dusty asked. "After Cecily vanished, you didn't even seem to miss her or to feel anything.

Millie and Charity are gone, without us to protect them. Don't you even care?"

The warmth in her face turned to fire. "Of course I care, but we have to *think* too. That's what I'm good at. I don't let my emotions get in the way of thinking. If the Grey Cloaks took them, it wasn't because they have a fondness for whiners, it's because they wanted to change our paths. If Lille doesn't go to Cloud City, then they win."

"She's right," Cecily whispered while swallowing, her fingers digging into Finn's arms as pain seized her body.

Stephanie felt Ranz shudder and realized Cecily's destroyed body still hurt him. Without a thought, Stephanie pushed some warmth to her core, seeking to soothe him.

"*Thank you, dearest, you are right. Her fractures radiate so powerfully I can feel them... just in ripples, but it is overwhelming to be this close to her. I might fade away for a bit. Careful with your mouth, but I am not displeased with you so far.*"

"*Thank you, Ranz.*"

Stephanie refocused on the group all staring at Cecily, waiting for her to get hold of her pain so she could continue.

"She is right—even though we don't like that truth. The Grey Cloaks took Millie and Charity for their own reasons and those reasons have something to do with Lille and her rule, since that is what they have been attacking. Millie and Charity have no powers that they want. They tried to kill Morgan because she does have power..."

"But why not me?" Abigail stammered as tears chased each other down her face. "They should have taken me. I can take it, whatever they do, but I hate thinking of stupid, whining

Millie being *hurt*. And Charity—sweet, patient Charity. I feel so horrible."

Dusty leapt to his feet to hug Abigail who sobbed on his shoulder.

"I'm so sorry they didn't take me," she cried.

"I feel the exact same way, Abigail," Cecily said with a rough voice and watery eyes. "Everyone was worrying about me and the Grey Cloaks used that to steal my sisters. I promised to take care of Millie—I didn't do a good job."

Amanda's hand white-knuckled her battle-axe. "We need to stop feeling badly about what *they* did and go out there and kill them and get our sisters back. That's what we need to be doing."

"I like that idea." Dusty brushed the tears off of Abigail's face. "What do you think?"

The sobbing girl nodded and wiped at her snotty nose. It looked like Abigail was going to become the resident whiner now that Millie wasn't around. *Pleasant.*

"But..." Stephanie said, but Lille held up her hand.

"Enough. We know what you want. Cecily, you were saying?"

"There are more choices here than you all know—other things we have to face."

"What do you mean?" Dusty asked.

Cecily closed her eyes for a second and leaned her head closer to Finn's neck.

"Tell them," Finn whispered. "They have a right to know and you shouldn't carry this burden alone."

"Know what?" Stephanie demanded.

Cecily's gaze touched everyone in the circle before coming

to rest on Dusty. "That something terrible is happening in Dunlowe."

"What?" Abigail, Dusty, and Amanda said together.

"I saw things when I was in the Source. Images of places and people. I saw you—all of you—but also our families fighting soldiers who came to destroy Dunlowe. I don't know why the king of Stoughton sent soldiers. I don't know who survived or who... didn't. I saw Nate and Darla as they ran from the soldiers, but they didn't get far; they're prisoners now, somewhere in the Wild Wood, I think. Our home is not safe—our families are not safe. And now Millie and Charity are gone and danger is waiting no matter which path we take." She paused, seeming even more vulnerable as she added, "And our paths won't be the same."

Dusty's face scrunched up. "What? What do you mean?"

Stephanie leaned and reclaimed Dusty's hand, tugging him back toward her. "She means that some of us will go with Lille to Cloud City, while others go after Millie and Charity. And maybe others will go back to Dunlowe, though what we can do about any of that, I don't know."

Dusty looked struck. "Split up?"

Cecily nodded.

"Where are you going?" he whispered.

"I don't matter anymore. I'm just a burden no matter which path I choose."

"No. You aren't."

"It's okay—I am. I can't fight or stand or do anything to help. That is my life now, but there is one path that pulls at me, a path that can't include you."

"What? Why?"

"Finn and I are going to try to find Darla and Nate."

"Why can't I go with you?"

Cecily suddenly looked more like a big sister than she usually did. "Nate and Darla? Dusty, are you really going to tell me that you think your destiny is to save Nate and Darla—or get lost while trying?"

"Well..." Dusty sputtered.

Cecily waited.

Dusty thought for a moment before saying with more conviction than Stephanie approved of, "What if my destiny is to save *you*?"

Their eyes locked onto each other's, a glare that concealed their unspoken battle from no one. Eventually, Cecily's face seemed to close like a door. "I wish you could, but that isn't your destiny. That's no one's destiny. But Finn loves me and will take care of me. And it is time for you to find your own way." Cecily turned to the others, pulling her eyes away from a massively irritated Dusty. "What about the rest of you? Where will you go?"

Amanda held up her axe. "I'm going after Millie and Charity, no matter what. Maybe after, I'll head back to Dunlowe or to Cloud City, but I'm not going anywhere until all of my sisters are free."

"Me, too," Abigail added.

"I follow the redhead," Mortimer said and Amanda smiled up at him.

"I kinda hoped you would."

"I'd like to lend a hand to that fight," Bay said, and Cecily looked surprised. "It won't be easy. The Grey Cloaks were traced to the sea, a place they are better at disappearing in than anyone. There are more than a thousand islands around Darienne and that is where I would guess they have taken Millie and Charity. Hopefully, the Commanders will be able to give us a location soon, but if not, I say we start attacking islands until we have more information."

"I'm in for that fight," Keefe said.

"Morgan?" Cecily asked.

Morgan's face looked torn behind her *stupid* glasses. "I want to help Millie and Charity, but I need to stay with Lille and face the mystics who I am certain are going to try to block her way back to Cloud City. My skills might be really useful, but I hate the thought of..."

"I know," Cecily said. "But our fates are taking us in different directions. Stephanie, you will go with Lille and Morgan?"

"Yes."

"Dusty?" Cecily asked, but Stephanie blurted, "He's coming with me."

"Hey." Dusty pulled his hand away from her. "I'll make my own choice, thank you very much."

Stephanie fought the emotions riling within her.

"*Settle yourself, right now, dearest.*"

"*But he has to...*"

"*Enough or you will be back in your cell and he will be dead.*"

"When do I have to decide by?" Dusty asked.

Cecily looked to Lille, who said, "We will prepare to move out in the morning. First light."

"Then I'll decide at first light."

Stephanie couldn't hide her shock as Dusty stood up and

marched away from the group.

"*Ranz, what does this mean? He might not come with me.*"

"*It means we must work quickly and make him my vessel tonight.*"

*

Nate felt as if he had been smiling for days and days. Time moved differently when he was near Devra, obeying her every wish, sometimes before she even asked. The only disquiet in his heart was the fear that he didn't serve her properly enough, that he didn't do everything perfectly. But when he saw her face looking at his, all that was unsettled within him became pure peace.

He served her in many ways and when she led him to the cell in her room, he was only too happy to go through the opening as she shut it behind him. A flash of blue light later, his feelings of beauty and contentment grew hazy, grew dark, and then... he was Nate again. Trapped in Devra's cage, denied the blissful ignorance of life as her mindless slave.

Nate groaned and lowered his head as the memories pounded his mind and spirit, all of the things he'd done in her service. One terrible memory assailed him, bringing his legs to quiver and drop him to the ground, where he hunched and held his head in his hands.

He had stolen children for her. Three.

A mindless minion.

"How long... was I gone?" he whispered.

"Time doesn't matter here."

"How long?"

"For you, it would have been thirty days. A month to settle

in as my *mindless* minion."

Nate tasted a chill that felt like death and shuddered. "Why did you bring me back to this cell?"

"I missed you."

He glared at her, his mouth open and completely unhelpful.

"What?" Devra asked. "I want you to make the choice, but you weren't ready. Are you ready now?"

"I want to see my sister."

"Make the choice to freely serve me and you will see your sister as much as you like."

Could he make that choice, even for Darla? Not knowing what he did was horrible only when he *did* know. If Devra never put him in this cell, he'd never know who he'd been and all that had mattered beyond this place. He wouldn't know what a failure he was. He wouldn't have to think about Darla, Cassa, Jaden, their children, Cecily, Dunlowe... his mother. He could just fade away from all that was tragic and hopeless.

"I would have thought the chance for freedom would give you hope."

Nate flinched from Devra who stood just on the other side of the burning bars. "I don't believe you mean it."

"But I do. I will free you to follow your destiny when I no longer need you."

"And when will that be? Will my mother still be alive? Will Dunlowe?"

"I don't know, but like I said, time moves differently here."

"I'm your slave whether I am myself or that vapid boy who lives to gush over you. Why do you care so much that I have a mind?"

"The children who serve me aren't under my spell, not past when they leave their villages. They choose to serve me and if you would take the chance, you might come to understand why."

"You brainwash them."

"Maybe, or maybe what I fight for matters, but you can't know that outside the cell, unless you serve me of your own volition."

"Let me see my sister and I will consider it."

She squinted but seemed more hopeful than irritated. Nate heard the sound of running footsteps and turned and saw a little girl, about five, with the greenest eyes he'd ever seen, race toward his cage and abruptly stop. She was bald with familiar marks on her head and an unfamiliar mark on her neck.

"Darla?"

"Would you just agree already so you can join us? You don't even see me when you're a cloudy-heady vapid boy. Come on. Agree to serve Devra and we'll worry about the rest later." She rolled her eyes, as if it were nothing to be here. Already brainwashed.

"*Whatever*. At least I have a brain to use. I'm not hiding from all I've done by choosing to be nothing instead of something."

"What *you've* done? You've been a little girl. You've never done anything to be ashamed of—how could you even understand?"

"Nate, you've done some stupid things. Believe me, I was watching before I was even born, but you're not a bad person. You're my brother. You're good. You saved me and got us away from Dunlowe. Some day we're going to serve our purpose—whatever that is—and I want you to be you and if..." She glanced to Devra, who nodded her consent, and Darla continued, "If you stay stupid and gone, there's a chance one day, you might really *be* gone. Devra doesn't have minions under the kind of control she has with you—that was an accident. She only uses that power in short bursts like with the Oades in the Wild Wood. To stay in that place, it will destroy you. That's why Devra wants you to decide to…"

"I'm staying here. I'm staying *stupid* as you call it. I have no power to do anything but this, so I'm going to take it. Devra wants me to survive and be Nate. No. I'll be nothing. I'll fade away… if only to deny her what she wants."

"Have you forgotten Mom?"

Nate felt struck. "No, have you?"

Darla shook her head. "You were right," she said to Devra. "He's not ready."

"I know," Devra said softly. "I hoped against hope."

"Can we give him a little more time in the cell before we leave for good?"

"Leave for good? Where are you going?"

Darla ignored his questions and stared at Devra.

"If you wish, Darla, but there's not much time. The decision has been made. She's coming and we have to go meet her. It's a very long way."

Darla nodded, her eyes wandering back to Nate.

"Who's coming?" Nate pressed.

Disappointment brimmed in his sister's green eyes, but she shook her head.

Darla raised her hand to Devra, who took it with a sad smile. "I made you dinner, Devra. Should we go and leave Nate to think?"

"Who's coming and where are you going?!"

They studied him, but turned away and walked toward the opening of the cavernous room.

"Who's coming?! Who's *she*?"

They paused and Darla turned to Devra, who nodded. Darla placed the word in Nate's mind as they disappeared beyond the doorway.

"*Cecily.*"

5

Hope

Dusty stomped away from everything and everyone, *wishing* more than really *believing* the others would leave him alone to make this horrible choice. After he was well away from the camp, he turned and found Genovan's familiar face watching him from about fifteen feet behind. Dusty considered running away, but then let out a petulant breath and waited for Genovan to catch up.

Grateful Genovan didn't say anything as they walked together toward the sea, Dusty allowed his thoughts to get twisted back up into the knots that had been driving him crazy.

When he was about to start shouting—possibly whining—Genovan said, "You know I promised you a piggyback ride all the way to the sea and never made good on my promise. Would you like it now?"

A chuckle burped out of Dusty's mouth as he shoved—or attempted to shove—Genovan's shoulder. Genovan didn't budge, but a small smile cracked free on his normally too-serious face.

After his laugh faded, Dusty said, "You know, part of me wants that ride."

"I made a promise, so of course..."

"No, Gen, I don't get to have my piggyback ride, but I still want it."

"Why can't you have it if I'm offering?"

Dusty tried to find the right words, while knowing that words weren't his struggle; reality was. "Because I want to go back to feeling like I'm just a kid who gets piggyback rides, who doesn't have to make big, stupid decisions that could change everything. But I *do* have to make a stupid decision, so I don't get a piggyback ride." He looked at the ground. "I don't get to be a kid ever again."

Gen didn't say anything and Dusty pouted. They reached the forever expanse of sea that made Dusty smile despite himself. Genovan seemed happy, or maybe not happy so much as content, by the water.

After Dusty's legs got tired, he plopped on the beach, shucking off his shoes and running his toes through the sand. Genovan looked around for monsters or Grey Cloaks and then sat beside him.

"How am I going to decide? Choose to go somewhere Cecily isn't? Choose to go where Morgan isn't? Amanda? Millie? Charity? The sevens have been my family and now I'm supposed to make a choice that doesn't include some of them. I don't know how to do that. And Stephanie. She's difficult. She's so far out of my league, but I love her. But Cecily is my family, my blood. And what about Dunlowe? If my family is hurting, don't I have to go back to help them or die with them? And if I do go back, am I going all by myself? I think I would be too afraid to do that."

"I'm not sure what I would do in your situation, since I'm not in it."

"What do you mean?"

Genovan looked stormy and then shook his head. "I don't get a choice. I serve the queen. It is a vow I made and now have to live with."

"But you serve the judge too, right? And Cecily and Finn might need you."

"The Commanders' vow to the royal family supersedes all others, and Lille is vulnerable. Even if she were to order the Commanders to stay with Cecily, we couldn't."

"What about just you then? The Commanders could go with Lille and you could go with Cecily."

"No. Remember what I told you before Cecily returned to us—without my brothers nearby, I am toxic. To do this," he said, touching Dusty's shoulder, "might kill you."

"But they aren't here now," Dusty said.

"Look around."

Dusty scanned the beach and then turned back to the path and trees and saw three Commanders standing nearby.

"I cannot be without my brothers, ever—not without hurting those I most want to help. Except possibly with Morgan."

"Morgan? Oh, right, that toxic dirt thing."

"Yes, but that doesn't matter now. What matters is that I have no choice but to go with my queen, so I must watch Cecily walk away." He let out a hopeless grunt. "Not even walk, be carried away while in a level of pain never felt in this world. I've felt powerless before, but even watching Annisha fall on her sword to enter into this mission was nothing compared to what

I will face tomorrow when Cecily goes beyond my reach."

Dusty sighed. "Don't I have to go with her then? Whether she wants me to or not? Do I really have any more choice than you do?"

"Sometimes love is the most powerful cage there is. But let me say this and you take it however you want: this world is in a troubled time and you are a creature of power, even though we don't understand your power yet. I think your choice should not be about the people you know and care about, but rather the mission that calls to you. We all may die in this, even Commanders—things are changing and if we choose to be guided by survival alone, by holding on to our selfish attachments instead of serving our purposes, then we lose more than each other. We lose the world itself, and people like those in Stoughton don't have a chance."

"It's bigger than any of us, isn't it?" Dusty felt a strange clarity growing within him.

"Yes, it is, and you have a role to play that is yours alone. Don't lose that, no matter how immense the choices and the consequences are."

"Then I guess it's time I become a man, huh?" Dusty stood and brushed the sand off of his butt. "No more time for pouting and wishing decisions didn't have to be made. I've got to face them."

"Good man," Gen said with a smile.

Dusty lowered a hand and pulled—or attempted to pull—Genovan to his feet. Together they walked back toward the camp so that Dusty could spend his last day with most of the people he loved.

*

Zoe saw smoke rising from the camp as soon as she passed the last row of trees, too much smoke. Not from a fire used to cook or keep people warm—this was something different. She kept moving but her brain deserted her when she saw the smoldering ruin in the place where Logan's tent had been. Zoe hurried, with Heath, Jem, and Mr. Daye next to her—Mr. Daye broke away from them to help a crying woman. Chaos lived in the crowd. Newly wounded bodies littered the ground. People held weapons and Zoe felt their panic, but whatever had happened was over. No soldiers remained, except a few dead ones.

But all of that fell away when Zoe saw Mindy standing near the burned-out tent, hunched over, sobbing. Mindy, the warrior who dressed only in her camisole and bloomers to defy the world, looked like a broken, little girl. Weakness and trembling gripped Zoe's legs and she had to slow, so Heath and Jem reached Mindy first.

Heath grabbed Mindy's shoulders, turning her away from the fire. "What is it? What happened?"

His eyes were wild and Mindy's eyes brimmed over with tears. "The soldiers came—we fought, but not hard enough."

Zoe's entire body shook. "Logan?" she choked out.

Mindy's head turned slowly toward her. "We got him out. He's over in the trees... but moving him didn't go well. I don't know... I just don't know."

Zoe turned toward the forest, seeing movement beyond the ridge. "What else happened? What's wrong?"

Mindy looked up at Heath's face. "I'm so sorry."

Heath turned blank. "No, I've lost enough... I've *lost*

enough."

Mindy's fingers lightly touched Heath's face. "They came. They stole people, most of them from Darstel—Nate's aunt and uncle. Some survivors from Kilby. But they also got..."

Heath's face paled even more and he looked at the crowd, but his eyes weren't really seeing. He seemed to be waiting for Mindy to finish, to tell him just how bad things were.

"... they got the rest of your family."

"All of them?"

"Jem," Mindy said, turning to him. "They got your sisters. Your dad tried to save them, but he couldn't. He got hit—hard. I think he's going to be okay."

"*Okay?*" Jem asked. "Okay?! None of us are okay! None of us!!!"

Jem marched away, while Heath stared at Mindy. "All of them? My parents—my dad's leg... how?"

"It was so fast. While we were fighting this huge force, wagons came, but not big wagons heavy enough to be slow. These were fast. They raced in, grabbed everyone they could, before we could get to them."

"And you didn't go after them?" Heath demanded.

Mindy flinched. "They had horses. I could run forever but I never would have caught them. But we'll find them, Heath. We will. We're going north—I don't care what anyone says."

Mindy attempted to comfort Heath, but he stood like a wall and then turned and walked away.

Mindy's eyes filled with shame. "I'm sorry. I should have done better."

Zoe moved closer and hugged Mindy. "You did everything

you could."

"I know you want to see Logan." She paused, setting a hand on Zoe's shoulder. "And you need to tell him—it needs to come from you."

"What?"

"The soldiers took Mitchell, the only brother he has left."

Zoe slumped. "How am I supposed to...?"

Her vision blurred as she stared at nothing. When her eyes focused again, she caught a look of relief in Jacoby's eyes before he went back to helping a man whose shoulder was bleeding.

Mindy tugged Zoe out of her stillness, leading her up the hill to where the wounded were scattered in between wide trees. When Zoe found Logan, he was throwing up... *blood*, while Mrs. Daye and Mrs. Dumphry held him as still as they could. Mindy rushed ahead, grabbing some fabric from a petticoat— not a single woman was going to have petticoats left by the end of this war—and dipping it into a pail. She cleaned Logan's face, while he tried to catch a breath.

Mrs. Rowe called for help and Mrs. Daye and Mrs. Dumphry hurried over to a member of Dunlowe's town council who was clearly going to die.

All this while Zoe stood and watched, her body trapped in a glimpse of the grim future that awaited them all.

"Breathe easy, Logan."

Logan's dull eyes came to rest on Zoe. "It's time to be a leader, Zoe," he whispered. "And do what needs to be done."

Zoe remained where she stood. "What are you saying? What do you mean?"

"You have to leave us—leave *me*—behind. You have to fight, before there's no one left who even remembers Dunlowe."

*

Morgan walked with Lille, their hands joined, mostly because they both enjoyed the singing of the trees. Oriel had gone to help plan for the march south, after ensuring that other soldiers remained close to Lille and Morgan.

"Say it, Morgan," Lille said softly as they entered her tent.

"You said *heir*. You didn't mean..."

"Yes, I did. You are now the rightful heir of Darienne, if anything ever happens to me."

"No, that can't be. It just can't."

Lille pulled Morgan to sit next to her on her sleeping pallet. "The trees ruled Darienne millions of years ago, but they lost interest and chose my family to rule. They chose their heirs when rulers tired of the work and didn't have heirs of their own. They *chose* you."

"But what about Stephanie?"

"What about her?"

"She is Daryn, or *was*."

"Daryn was never going to rule. I don't know what happened exactly but the trees withdrew their support. Her eyes changed color, just as yours have, only hers turned so dark, almost black, the violet smothered completely. Her hair darkened, though she hid it well, but I caught her with the mystics once and saw what she was doing. And now the trees have chosen you. Stephanie may presume to rule one day, but this kingdom is not hers and never would have been."

Morgan rested her head on Lille's shoulder. "Please don't ever die and force me to be queen."

Lille's head leaned against Morgan's. "I said the same exact thing to my parents and to Britton. I'll try to do better than they did."

"Please."

"I'm sorry you have to leave your friends... and Cecily."

Tears pushed at Morgan's eyes, but she held them back. "Me too, but I believe we will meet again. Some day. And just like Cecily climbed onto that rock and surrendered to her part in all of this, I will see this through and maybe, find my own destiny."

Lille picked up Morgan's palm and moved it around, watching the shimmering lavender petal seem to dance. "Yes, we both will... see this journey to its end, wherever that is and no matter what dark road we have to cross to get there."

While Lille told Morgan more about Cloud City and her dreams for Darienne, Morgan rested her free hand on the pocket of her dress, the pocket that held her old glasses, something she'd discovered that she didn't need anymore. The final change of her eye color to violet had corrected her vision, but she still kept her glasses close. Change was all well and good, but Morgan never wanted to forget who she was and where she'd come from even if she one day sat on a throne.

*

Still bound and gagged. Still blinded by a hood. Still terrified. Millie swallowed over her tight, dry throat, wondering what would happen next. What else could go wrong? She'd hidden from as much of the world as she could, but still, it had come for her. Forced her out of Dunlowe. To Darienne. And now onto a boat heading somewhere. The rocking twisted in her stomach, but she fought against being sick and choking to death.

A sharp dip of the boat and something rolled against her back. No, not something—*someone*. A quick squeeze of her fingers and Millie knew she wasn't alone. Charity lived and was with her. Between the two of them, they had no great powers, weren't warriors, just two immortal girls with a bunch of dead, angry spirits stalking them. But still, together was better than alone.

Anything was better than being alone.

*

I'd rested, or tried to, but sleep hid from me behind images of this frightening world, all that I'd seen in the Source, all of the things I'd done, and all of the things I lacked the power to do. Millie. Charity. Would they ever understand why I left instead of helping to save them?

My powerlessness tortured me more than the unending pain. Would they ever understand?

"*They will.*" Finn's voice pulled me from the swirling darkness that lived inside me.

"*If they are alive.*"

"*Don't you think you would feel it if your sister sevens died— that you would just know?*"

"*I'm not sure. You know as well as I do that I am not a seven anymore... and I'm not the only one. Morgan's not either. Did you see her, the changes?*"

"*The new heir to the throne of Darienne. Yes, I saw.*"

"*Will they be able to keep that secret?*"

"*Not for long, but I understand why Lille would try to protect her new sister. Tomorrow will be...*"

"Awful," I said aloud. "Let's not wait until tomorrow. Let's go now. I can't sleep. I can't feel anything but dread."

Finn considered and finally nodded. "As you wish. I'll gather the others, because we certainly aren't sneaking away without proper goodbyes. You don't know—you can't know—what it was like for us seeing you vanish. I fear this is going to feel the same to Dusty... and the others."

"Okay, but I don't think a proper goodbye is going to save any of us from this sorrow. And don't forget, I lost all of you too."

"Yes, my love." Finn kissed my forehead. "You did, but I couldn't feel it, couldn't feel what you were going through when you were in the Source. But I know what I went through, what I lost. You can't feel what is inside me, but believe me when I say that without you, my world had no light, no life, no hope. I was a total failure, bashing around on a battlefield hoping for death. I love you too much..."

"Too much?" I asked.

A sad smile emerged. "Too much," he said with a finality that brought a chill to my heart. "Too much. My love for you has filled my body, leaving little left for me or anyone else. Don't look so worried, my dear. I couldn't leave you, even if I should."

"If I'm not good for you... I could ask Bay to—"

The look in Finn's eyes stopped my mouth. "Don't even think it. I'm not telling you this because I want you to worry or to feel responsible; I just want you to understand that we are together in this. If you die, I *will* die with you. Everything I live for—everything I need is here between you and me. I don't care where we go or what we do, as long as we are together. Forever."

I nodded, but a sick feeling pulsed in my gut. "Forever." The word felt like a sentence rather than a gift.

"No," Finn said. "I'm sorry... my words weren't the right ones. I don't want you to... I wish you could see in my mind. I wish you could know all that I know, all that I am, what I've done. I wish you knew *me*."

Pain gripped at me and my breathing turned to ragged gasps.

"I'm an idiot—you have enough to deal with right now."

When my agony eased, I felt drained of everything, but I managed to raise my hand to Finn's face. "I don't know about all the years of an immortal's life, but I do know you. You are good and kind. Selfless. You love me even with my mountains of flaws, and I love you... no matter what you know or what you've done. Forever."

Finn held me, rocking me in his arms until the uneasiness between us faded. "I'll get the others, and then we'll be on our way."

Finn disappeared out of the tent and I closed my eyes for just a few minutes. A light touch on my hand caused my eyes to open. Bay sat next to me, easing his hand into mine, searching my face to see if he was hurting me.

"Cecily," Bay whispered. "I have so much to atone for in my life. So very much."

"We share that."

"No, you've done nothing wrong."

"I have. You know that, but my penance is alive in this terrible pain inside of me. What is your penance?"

He seemed to consider saying something but stopped himself and changed direction. "That I am letting you go beyond my reach in order to save the sisters you love."

"For me?"

"Always. I know you are with Finn and always will be, but no matter where my path leads, I will always love you and always try to be the man you think I am."

"You give me too much credit. I'm so flawed. What I've done... what I almost did. You don't know."

"But Finn does and he loves you. He's the better man. Remember that when you learn things that might be difficult to understand."

"What do you mean?"

"I mean that life is complicated and immortals manage to muck that up even more. Finn has kept things... he's a—no, never mind; I shouldn't have said anything."

"No, wait, Finn's what? Just tell me. I love him. There is nothing that he or you could say to..."

"He's a good man. I would never let him take you away from me if he weren't. Remember that."

I sensed the uselessness of pushing him to tell, so I ignored the questions and irritation flittering in my mind. "Bay, you are a good man. Remember that."

"Please keep believing that. It gives me hope."

"Hope," I whispered, surprised by the warmth the word brought to my chest, in the subtle lessening of my pain. Just for a second, I felt the power of an idea, a word, a possibility. Hope.

But before I could let it grow, Bay kissed my hand and fled and Dusty stood before me, his face and spirit hollow. And I knew in a way I couldn't understand that my brother and I would face horrors before we were really together again—and when we did find each other, we might be so changed as to be strangers to each other. The sorrow of that gripped me as did the belief that *goodbyes* were a mountain Dusty and I would climb again and again, until they existed forever.

Dusty plopped to the ground and took my hands. "No, Cecily, we'll be fine. We'll never be strangers, not ever. And *goodbyes* are always temporary."

Had I said that aloud? Could he hear inside my mind?

"*Dusty?*" I thought, while he just stared at me.

"Are you okay?"

"Dusty, I love you. I came back for you. I became this weakling for you—I can't believe I'm going away without you after all that."

"You're doing what you have to, just like you always have. You are amazing. And brave. And selfless. I get that now. I didn't before. I hated you for taking the blame in Dunlowe and getting beaten by Pastor Rowe. It shouldn't have been you, but you knew what you needed to do. And you did it, just like you always do. I get it now. And that is why I'm not going to force you to let me go with you. There's something I need to do. I have a mission now, just like you."

"So you've decided then?"

Dusty nodded.

"What's it going to be?"

"I'm not telling you—you're a big sister and all you will do is worry about me. But trust me, I'm going to be okay."

More secrets. If he hadn't been right about me worrying, I would have clobbered him. "Fine."

"Okay. I want to say one thing to you and then I'm heading

out of here as quickly as Bay did, hopefully before I start mewling like a lonely piglet."

"What?"

"Sometimes you get really, really stupid about yourself, and this world doesn't have time for that. We need you strong."

"But I'm not strong anymore."

He pointed at my heart. "Strong in there, not strong like an ox. There's plenty of burly beasts around here. Your strength is in how much you love... me and everyone else. Look what you did to come back—just please, don't leave again. We will see each other again. Promise me."

"I can't promise that."

"Stubborn ox," he grumbled.

I giggled. "Well, *yeah*."

Dusty leaned forward and carefully hugged me, but I latched on, ignoring the pain, and gripped him with all of my might. One last hug with my brother and then he was gone too. The light seemed to fade from the world after that and darkened further when Morgan, Abigail, Amanda, and Stephanie came to make brief goodbyes that were each strange and tragic in their own ways. Weariness claimed me and I slept and when I woke in Finn's arms, I knew we'd left the Downs and were heading along the land bridge that would lead us back to the Wild Wood and all the mysteries that awaited us.

6

Limits

STEPHANIE FELT TWITCHY, standing on a hill with Abigail, Morgan, and Amanda as they watched Cecily carried away in Finn's arms. The two of them looked so small so quickly. Dusty hadn't wanted to watch and was fishing with Genovan, who avoided goodbyes with Cecily like the plague he was.

"Everything has changed." Abigail sounded weird, so Stephanie stared at her, awaiting some stormy-ish outburst.

"Yes," Morgan said softly.

Abigail continued staring north. "Tomorrow you and Stephanie head for Cloud City, while Amanda and I go after Millie and Charity. I feel like something has ended... forever."

Stephanie wished Ranz would give her the script because this conversation felt like a case of hives, but he'd fallen silent with Cecily nearby and hadn't said anything since. At least being far away from Cecily would be helpful to Ranz and he wouldn't bail out at moments like this.

"The sevens have ended," Morgan said.

"Don't say that," Abigail said, her voice sharp.

Amanda switched her battle-axe hand and took hold of Abigail's. "It's true."

"What do you mean?"

"The sevens are over," Amanda said. "Cecily isn't one of us anymore."

"What? You're kicking her out?"

"Of course not, but she isn't. I don't know for sure what she is now, but the bond of the sevens is over. Don't you feel it?"

Abigail frowned and considered, but ultimately shrugged her shoulders. "What about the rest of us? Are we the *sixes* now?"

Amanda shook her head. "I don't think so. I'm with Mortimer. He's my family now—I love you and the others, but the sevens are who Pastor Rowe forced us to be. Now we are coming into our own and making our own choices. It feels sad, but it really isn't. It doesn't mean we don't care or that we don't have enough love for each other, but I think whatever power was in us as a group is gone now."

"Wait—what about when we helped Morgan on the battlefield? We helped her to be strong. Are you saying that doesn't matter anymore?"

"That wouldn't work if we tried it today," Morgan said. "And I'm not completely certain it worked because of any bond with the sevens. I think it had more to do with our gifts. We've all changed."

"No, *you* all have changed," Abigail said. "I haven't. I'm still as angry as I was in Dunlowe. I hate all of this. We are as powerless as we were then."

"Speak for yourself," Stephanie blurted a little too pointedly.

Abigail's face turned into a very pissy-looking mask. "Clearly, I am. Just a few more hours, Stephanie, and you won't have to deal with me anymore... ever."

Abigail stormed away.

"Take it personally then, why don't ya?" Stephanie called while watching Abigail march toward the tents. When she turned back, Amanda stood before her, her battle-axe slightly raised. "May I help you in some way, Amanda?"

Amanda's red curls blew in the breeze and a slightly wild look flared in her green eyes. "Now that the imaginary bond between the sevens is gone, I'd like to share something with you."

Stephanie stood straighter, intending to use her height as an advantage, but realized that Amanda was now almost as tall as she was. "Go ahead."

"There is something very, very wrong with you. You are a hollow creature, Stephanie Trench. Hollow and cold. I wouldn't be you for anything in this world... but then I always felt that way. Careful with your choices, because if you don't grow a heart someday, that empty place in your chest might just fill with evil. I don't want you to end up on the wrong side of this battle—or my battle-axe. I'm just saying."

Amanda walked away to where Mortimer and a few other beasts waited for her; her posture looked like the beasts'. Proud. Defiant. A warrior, not the most daring little girl from Dunlowe anymore. Her words struck, but Stephanie had already made peace with her reality, so let the little warrior spout off now—she'd be bowing later.

An awkward silence encapsulated Morgan and Stephanie. Allies, rivals, sisters, mortal enemies—Stephanie wasn't sure, only being alone with Morgan made the memories harder to fight. That cry in the night. The feeling of the blade.

And then something shocked Stephanie's awareness. Morgan

was pale—not golden anymore. Really, really pale. Paler than she'd ever been and she'd been pale to start with. And her hair. White streaks, just a few, were noticeable in Morgan's dark hair.

"Morgan," Stephanie said, cutting through the quiet between them.

Morgan's face came around very slowly and her wary eyes held Stephanie's. Her wary *violet* eyes. No more of her one green eye and one brown eye—no more glasses even. Her eyes were violet, just like Lille's.

Stephanie's mouth fell open, but no words came.

"*Oh my...*" Ranz breathed.

Stephanie couldn't have said it any better.

*

Nate paced inside his cell. Back and forth. Back and forth. Occasionally, he stopped to scream his lungs out for Darla to come back, for Devra to release him. His throat had long ago turned raw and his stomach grumbled its emptiness. He didn't remember eating anything, not during the entire time he had been with Devra and yet he looked the same as when he'd left Dunlowe.

Thirty days. Gone.

He resumed his pacing as thoughts seemed to chew him instead of him chewing on them. Could he really agree to serve the demon who'd made him? Willingly? And why did seeing the disappointment in Darla's eyes hurt him so much? Why did the prospect of vanishing into simpering slavehood not seem terrible? Was he really just running from the person he'd discovered he was?

Cecily. His memories of her allowed him to stop pacing. Their favorite tree. Her smile. Her flare of defiance at his father. Her willingness to take the punishment, whether it came from a whip or a torch. Cecily, even now after everything, wouldn't want Nate to vanish, to hide from his life under a cloud of subservience. And she very much wanted Darla to be safe.

Like a door opening, Nate saw Cecily walking in amongst the crowd of townsfolk preparing to unleash on the sevens. Cecily begged Nate to hold his screaming sister. "I can hear her," she'd said. "She's trapped in there. I think I can free her." Nate had sent Cecily away, knowing if she did something odd to help Darla, it would mean her death. Even in Dunlowe, Cecily had risked everything for Darla. And suddenly, Nate felt what a fool he was. He was quibbling about the price when he should have been shielding his sister in any way he could. Something he couldn't do without a mind to even stop himself if Devra ever asked him to kill Darla.

Nate shuddered and whispered, "Please, Devra. I submit. Freely. Please let me out."

Darla raced toward the cage, her smile beaming as she jumped up and down. Devra followed, relief in her eyes.

"Approach the bars."

He moved toward Darla who was as close as she could get without touching the lit bars. Devra, standing beside his sister, reached her hand through the opening between the bars and opened her palm.

"Touch your neck to my palm and you are bound to me until I release you."

He closed his eyes, preparing to move forward.

"No. Open your eyes. See me. See this choice. It is yours to make. Victims are people who fight their realities instead of claiming their journeys. Don't be a victim of this. Be present. Do what you can. Fully live your life."

Nate nodded and took the step that would change his life forever. Her hand on his neck singed him, but Darla held him with her eyes and their connection burned with more power than any pain could hold.

The door to his cage swung open and he walked out as Darla leapt into his arms, cuddling against him.

"Thank you, Nate. Thank you," she sobbed.

When Nate's misty eyes met Devra's, he didn't see or feel evil. He felt like he was exactly where he was supposed to be.

✶

Zoe stared at the small fire cooking a dinner of dead horse, as others gathered around her, taking seats in a circle. Logan lay on his litter beside her, seeming to focus very intently on breathing in and breathing out, while Zoe fought the feeling that each of his breaths was a number diminishing every second.

Beyond the flames on the other side of the fire sat Jem, with his dad's arm around him. Five redheaded Payne children reduced to one. The soldiers had even taken Myrtle, the littlest redhead in Dunlowe. Zoe wondered if Jem and his dad were grateful that Amanda was somewhere in the world far away from here, or if they felt betrayed that she and her warrior friends weren't around to help. Mr. Payne didn't look very recovered from his injuries and wobbled a bit, leaning on Jem for support.

Mr. Daye and Mrs. Daye worked to divide up the dinner

and passed around the pieces of cooked meat. Zoe heard Mrs. Daye say, "I'm so glad Bear bolted over the fence when the soldiers came. I couldn't have eaten that wise old dear of a horse for anything."

"Certainly not." Mr. Daye offered a bone with a hefty portion of meat to Zoe.

Zoe shook her head until she felt a soft punch on her side from Logan.

"It's not even slightly fish, Zoe. Eat it."

Zoe scowled and took the bone, holding it lightly not to burn herself, while ripping off a piece of meat to hand to Logan, who shook his head. "If I have to eat, you have to eat."

Logan grimaced and grunted. "I want to eat, and I will eat, but not yet... my belly, ugh."

"If you don't like how this feels," Zoe spat, "I suggest you stop getting shot with arrows."

Logan actually looked guilty and nodded his head.

Zoe let out a rogue laugh and leaned to kiss his cheek. "You are so stupid, Logan."

"I know."

Mr. Pollak, a member of the town council of Dunlowe, cleared his throat. "Dawn is coming. We need to decide what we are going to do. I say, we go back to Dunlowe and start new lives—let all of this go."

"Not a chance," Heath said, standing like a statue next to a tree.

Mindy glanced up at him, clearly grateful he'd come back, but she didn't move toward him.

"They are gone—we have to accept that," Mr. Pollak said.

"That's where you're wrong," Jacoby said. "*You* might be able to accept that, but we can't."

"Death lies to the north," a man from Kilby said.

Mr. Daye took a seat. "You think *death* isn't coming south again to find us? What do you think happened today? They came for us... again. There's no going back."

Mrs. Smyth asked, "What about the wounded? There are so many."

Zoe waited a few seconds, until Logan bumped her again. "Some will stay with the wounded, just the fewest needed to care for them and move them somewhere else as soon as they are well enough. The rest of us are going north. We are going to find our friends, our families, and we are going to make our stand. There is no other choice. No peace for us unless we fight for it."

Everyone sat quietly, no one arguing.

When questions did arise, they involved how many would stay and who would go, decisions Zoe made quietly and carefully, while no one questioned her judgment. A somberness grew as they all sat, listening to the crackling of the fire and grieving each in their own ways.

"There's something you need to know," Jacoby said, his voice low, and Zoe remembered he'd wanted to share something. Had that been just this morning? Jacoby caught her eyes and waited for her to nod. "This is all my fault—all of it."

Tensions flared in the group.

"Why do you say that?" Zoe asked.

"Because I brought this doom on you—all of you, all of *us*. I went to the garrison at Chelton. I told them of the sevens and Dunlowe—of Pastor Rowe leading an army into the Wild

Wood. I am the reason for all of this. I went to them and then they came not just for Dunlowe, but for all of our towns. What they were doing to you, they did to us. Beatings. Interrogations. Rounding up our people and taking them to the north. Trust me, I've paid the price—I lost my wife... and they stole my baby girl. I deserve your vengeance; I deserve death."

Silence gripped them and strangely, everyone waited for Zoe, who said, "You can't have our vengeance and you can't have death—we need every fighter we have."

"Aren't you listening? Didn't you hear what I said?"

Zoe wondered at the way her heart wouldn't let her hate this man who was a stranger, a guilty stranger. "I lied about the sevens. I lied and a good person suffered for it." Her eyes caught Mr. and Mrs. Daye's. "I am so sorry for what I did. I deserve your vengeance. *I* deserve death."

Logan coughed a little. "I chased my sister with a pitchfork, running her out of town when she'd done nothing wrong—more than being a selfish, arrogant, princess impersonator, anyway. I didn't step up when Cecily got blamed for lighting the fires that I lit. I deserve your vengeance. I deserve death."

Zoe set her hand on Logan's and squeezed.

Heath stepped closer to Mindy, kneeling down. "I blamed the woman I love for the attack today, for not doing more than anyone could do. This was my fault. I shouldn't have left. I deserve your vengeance. I deserve death."

Jacoby looked desperate. "Don't you understand? Any of you?"

"Son," Mr. Daye said, "We do understand. We just can't give you vengeance or death, but we will take your life in a different way. Swear to fight for us, to do everything you can to make amends by helping us to find your daughter and all of our loved ones. Help us to change the world."

Jacoby looked near a breakdown that humbled Zoe's heart. He'd faced them and what he did—that took more than most people had in them. "I swear it."

*

"What do I do, Ranz? Morgan is now the heir to Darienne and Dusty—Dusty won't tell me what he is going to do. What do I do?"

"Settle down, dearest. This changes nothing. We were going to kill Morgan anyway. And Lille. It's the only way for you to be queen. And Dusty, well, night is falling, the last night he will ever be free, and when he is in your arms tonight, we will make him our vessel."

"You said you would release him someday."

"That day might as well be forever away, dearest, but I will honor that promise."

"Will it be painful for him?"

"You already know the answer to that better than anyone."

Stephanie shuddered, thinking of the moment Ranz clawed his way into her body and severed her soul. Could she help him do that to Dusty?

"It's that or death, dearest. Now that his sister is away, his will is weakened and there will be no better chance to end the threat of his existence—especially since he doesn't know the limits to his power yet."

"If we do this, he will have to stay with me?"

"He will have no choice but to serve us for as long as we own him."

"*You'll own him, right Ranz? Not me. He can't know that I had anything to do with this.*"

"*If you wish, but I think you will change your mind. You will like power—you always did.*"

"*But how can we be in a relationship if we aren't equals? I mean, if you own us both, then we will be equals, won't we, Ranz?*"

Ranz let out a sigh. "*Dearest, you have never been equals and I feel compelled to tell you something that may be difficult, but I do not wish it to come between us later.*"

Discomfort flared in her heart. "*Yes, Ranz?*"

"*I understand that you love the floppy-haired boy. I understand your feelings. I feel them, but he can never be your future. You will never marry him. Never have children with him. He is not the husband of a queen.*"

"*But he has power, you know that. He could grow into it and become someone powerful enough to be king. Please...*"

"*Dearest, queens rarely choose their husbands. You know that.*"

Stephanie swallowed over the knot that suddenly formed in her throat. Her eyes registered everyone around her, even Dusty returning from his fishing trip. With her eyes locked on his lovely face, she said, "*What are you saying, Ranz?*"

"*I am saying that you are betrothed to your future husband in an irreparable way.*"

"*But Dusty...*"

"*Yes, we have allowed you to continue your love affair out of compassion for you. Your fiancé was insistent that this transition be as kind to you as possible, which is why I am telling you this now, before you make the boy our vessel and are tied to him forever when your love affair has no future and a certain end is in sight.*"

A sob welled up in her heart and she felt like she was choking.

"I should let him go then, Ranz."

"Dearest, I told you, either he becomes our vessel or he must die. I wouldn't ask you to do it, but you would have to lead him to it or go to your cell while I take care of it."

Stephanie covered her mouth to rein in a scream fighting to get free. She spun around and ran toward the sea. Ranz said nothing, didn't order her to return, didn't steal her limbs from her, or force her to fall to the ground. The hurt drove her faster. The cage of her life that she could never free herself from had her racing all the way to the beach. Sand flew as she bolted to the water's edge, not stopping until she was in the sea, wet and screaming. Tears met the ocean and if they could hold the power of her hurt, the sea would have risen a hundred feet.

In her gasping and crying, she sucked in water and began to choke. The weight of her dress pulled her under. Her death flickered at her from the corner of her vision. An escape from this cell. One that would take her away from Ranz. From Dusty. From this choice or the absence of choice. The frightened little girl who'd always hidden inside her, just wanting to be loved, seemed to have the helm of her life and steered her toward the end.

"Stephanie, no. Stop this right now. Take the power from the water. You don't sink. You don't drown. You survive."

"Make me," she spat.

She expected Ranz to take control, aim her for the shore, shove her inside her cell, and torture her until she submitted to this choice. She never would. Never. She wouldn't kill Dusty, couldn't. She wouldn't make him a vessel only to have to follow her orders for the rest of his life while watching her forced to marry someone else. Even Stephanie Trench had limits on what she would and wouldn't do.

"Stephanie, stop this... I'm weak right now. I can't save you. Please, dearest, don't give up. Go toward the shore. We'll work this out. We will. I promise."

His weakness meant her freedom and suddenly she understood how Daryn had gotten free in the only moment she could, in the only way she could. Falling on a sword, just as Stephanie would allow herself to drown. Memories flashed in Ranz's mind, of agony, of betrayal, something Daryn had done to him.

"She almost killed me, just as you may one day, but, dearest, I love you. I always have. Please go back toward the shore. Don't throw everything away when there is so much you don't know or understand."

Blackness dotted her vision. Cold. Hollow. Death.

"Goodbye, Ranz."

7

Untethered

Logan's chest ached, feeling very much like the arrows were still sticking into him. And a feeling—one that seemed to have taken him hostage—refused to let him go. He *should* be dead. These wounds were mortal. He saw all the looks, knew what everyone thought. Zoe had slept for a few short hours against his body, saying goodbye in the only way a warrior girl could. No one expected him to see the dawn. But he did.

He felt like complete crap—worse even—but air came into his lungs and then went out again. Alive and filled with guilt, he watched as the warriors made their preparations to leave while the useless like him did nothing.

"Do you want some water?" Mindy asked.

"Thanks."

Mindy helped him to drink a tiny bit and then tidied up his face like she was a nurturer rather than a butcher of her enemies—he knew she was both, but marveled at the difference.

Logan looked at her, thinking, always thinking these days.

"Say it, Logan. There's not much time."

"I'm not saying that you should give your life for hers, but I would be ever so grateful if you'd look after her for me."

Mindy gently rested her hand on Logan's cheek and looked at him with eyes that gave him solace—she knew *exactly* how hard this was for him. "I was going to do that anyway."

"You know I'm not going to make it, so make sure she doesn't give up when she hears that I'm..."

"Okay, but don't rush off looking for Dunn's mud. I thought you would die the night of the fight and then yesterday and then last night. Maybe it's not your time."

"I hope my time is a million years away, or just one second before Zoe's."

A wistfulness settled on Mindy's face.

"Are things okay with Heath?"

She nodded and frowned at the same time. "He's all about rescuing his family."

"Naturally."

"He's blaming himself. I'm just worried that guilt is going to eat him up and distract him from fighting when the time comes."

"You'll keep him in line—of that, I have no doubt."

Zoe approached them, wearing a wide-eyed expression, a mix of shock and horror.

"What?" Mindy and Logan asked.

"Tell him," Zoe said, as Jem and his dad approached, followed by Mr. Daye and some of the other townsfolk—*rebels*, they should be called now.

Jem's face skewed strangely. "You tell them, Dad."

Everyone looked to Mr. Payne, who seemed much better but still squinted against the light filtering through the leaves. "My boy ran away yesterday because of what he did at the end of the battle... to Pastor Rowe. Of course none of us are judging him at all, but I was part of the burying detail yesterday morning—our work got delayed by the attack and then the grief. We finished our work a bit ago; no matter what we've suffered, the dead deserve a place to rest. Now, I saw Pastor Rowe fall—I know just where he lay. But when the time came to bury him, there was no body. Anywhere. I asked *everyone*."

He paused and let out a weary sigh. "Either that dead body got up and walked away—which after the things I've seen, I can't rule out—or Pastor Rowe is still alive."

∗

The image of Finn walking away, with Cecily's body held tightly in his arms, burned into Bay's mind as he walked over hills and along hedgerows, heading for nowhere, just seeking peace in the only way he knew. Alone. Life and death seemed so random. He and his friends had almost been beheaded just a day before and that would have made sense if not for those who would have died with them. Morgan and Abigail. Charity and Amanda. Lille. Lives worth defending when he would have remained silent for his own.

The gloaming time was upon him as colors burst into the sky inspired by the setting sun. A peaceful moment before the next battles and the next ones. Running, always running, from the decisions he'd made and the things he'd done. The things he'd set in motion before he ever knew who would be hurt by them, before he had to see their faces and care about them.

Bay reached the sandy beach and looked out over the water. Somewhere beyond that vastness was an island where

Grey Cloaks held two frightened girls for reasons beyond Bay's understanding—not that he needed to understand in order to kill to get them back. Having someone to fight for brought clarity. Having a purpose made Bay feel almost okay, but then the awareness of the distance growing between Cecily and him left him bereft.

Cecily's life was a fragile spark. How little would it take for her will to be snuffed out completely? Why had they gone alone when there was no way for Finn to fight any enemies while caring for Cecily? Bay would have gone with them... if they'd only asked.

The waves broke against the shore and Bay broke with them.

A scream to the north ripped through his focus and he ran toward the sound, knowing only that the scream told truth. Agony. Desperation. Hopelessness. Feelings he knew all too well. Could it be Charity or Millie? Could their searches have been called off too soon?

The scream ceased before Bay reached it and he came to a stop, searching for something to guide his way. He stood alone on the beach, empty of life in both directions. His eyes pulled at him and he stared at the blue water, thinking for just a second of disappearing into this sea that looked so peaceful. Bay's eyes locked onto a small movement and the evening sun gave its shine to something gold in the water. Golden hair. Sinking.

Bay sprinted into the surf and dove to reach the falling body before it vanished. He wrapped his arms around the body and pulled it toward the surface as it began to fight him. *Fantastic.* Looked like someone didn't *want* to be saved, but that didn't mean much to him as he dragged her from the water and onto the beach where he fell to the ground under the weight of both girl and very soggy dress. Bay landed on his backside and he held Stephanie for a second before leaning her over so she could choke out the water still threatening her life.

"No, please, let me go back... I won't have this chance again," she cried and coughed.

"Don't worry. Death has a way of finding us no matter what we do."

"Please..."

Stephanie, without her usual haughtiness, seemed fragile beyond Bay's reckoning and he simply held her against him, his arms tight as she sobbed and then settled.

"Why?" Bay asked.

She shook her head and let out an exasperated breath. "*You* already know."

"What do I know?"

"That I'm the most treacherous beast ever to be born in Darienne. Isn't that what you said about me in the Wild Wood? I heard... and you weren't wrong."

"*You* weren't born in Darienne. Daryn was."

"Same difference. Daryn and I are two peas in a very disturbed pod."

For a few minutes, Bay listened to Stephanie's breathing as it quieted, but slight tremors still wracked through her.

"Stephanie," he said quietly as they watched the night sky emerge above them. "You are too strong and have too great a life force to surrender without a fight."

"That *was* my fight and you ruined it. And I'll pay the price for my disobedience." The utter bleakness of her words struck him, but something in her rallied, turned human. "But I don't blame you, even though I'm surprised you would bother saving me. Don't you hate me?"

"Never as much as I hate myself. But maybe redemption is possible for both of us... *if* we live long enough."

Stephanie sighed and actually accepted some comfort in his arms, but abruptly she became stiff and moved away. The look in her eyes was entirely changed when she stared down at him.

"Thank you," she said in clipped words.

Without another word, Stephanie strode toward the camp and Bay rose to follow, curiosity piquing, and empathy growing for the girl he'd once hated enough to kill with his bare hands.

✱

I shouldn't have been so tired. I'd been sleeping for hours as Finn walked across the land bridge, away from the Downs and so many of the people we loved.

"Are you really okay leaving Lille to her fate when she needs you most?"

"We talked about this. Lille understands that our roads have parted."

"Are you tired of carrying me yet?"

"It appears I won't have to much longer."

I looked up at Finn's chin. "Are you planning on dumping me somewhere?"

"No. Look."

I turned my face toward the Wild Wood; standing on the sand just past the land bridge was a flash of chestnut with a white blaze. Bear, my horse. Finn moved faster, feeling how much I wanted to hug my sweet, four-legged friend. As soon as we were clear of the land bridge, Bear trotted the rest of the way toward us, while keeping a wary eye on the water that held the fearful cararks. I certainly didn't blame him. I was just glad I couldn't see and hear everything I once could—couldn't see the cararks with their huge bodies, monstrous teeth, and insatiable need to kill. I didn't hear the screams of those they'd killed echoing in the world for all eternity. Finn heard them, but seemed okay.

Bear came to a stop before us and nuzzled his muzzle against my chest while I hugged his head.

"I missed you, Bear."

He didn't need words for me to know the feeling was mutual.

"Life was pretty dull in Dunlowe without me, right?"

He gave me a look, like he always did, like two-footed creatures couldn't be trusted to take care of themselves.

"You ready for a little weight, Bear?" Finn asked, and Bear held very still while Finn lifted me and set me on his back.

I wasn't strong enough to sit up, so I rested on my stomach, with my cheek pressed against Bear's withers. Even I smiled when I heard my sigh of delight.

"Are you okay?"

"I'm wonderful."

"You are stuck staring at the ground."

"I've seen enough of the trees."

Finn laughed, sounding hopeful. "Yes, Cecily, hopeful. The Source is still looking after you, which makes me even more certain that we are on the right path."

"Or it could have been Laura. And are you really implying that Bear wasn't smart enough to get here all on his own?"

Bear turned to glare at Finn.

"I would never imply anything of the kind." Finn chuckled as he neared the Wild Wood with Bear walking next to him, no rope, no reins, just me on his back, sinking into my memories of home.

*

Blessing. Failure. Neither. Both. Stephanie's mind played with each possibility while still in Bay's arms, her unfortunate and reluctant savior. But he seemed genuine in his care, as strange as that was. Stephanie would have remained there, savoring a few more minutes of relief and sadness. Of truth. She'd told Bay the real story—she *was* a treacherous beast—and in that moment of honesty, she'd felt freer than at any other moment since stepping foot in Darienne.

But the abrupt and harsh ripping of her soul from her body stole her ability to choose to stay with Bay. Ranz at the helm of her body stood up, thanked Bay, and walked away, while knowing they were followed.

Stephanie said nothing, figuring she'd be back in her cell within moments, grateful for the torture that awaited her there. But as Ranz neared the camp, she remained untethered inside her own body and hated it. This awareness of her insignificance was worse than her cell. All she could do was watch what Ranz did, affecting nothing on her own.

Rock fires were lit. Equipment piled and ready to go. Some tents had already been torn down and soldiers slept under the stars for their final night in the camp. As Ranz approached what remained of the sevens, Stephanie really noted how different they looked, how unfinished. Millie and Charity had mostly hid, but their absence felt enormous.

"Have you seen Dusty?" Ranz asked through Stephanie's mouth.

Morgan nodded. "He was looking for you. He's in your tent." She seemed curious about Stephanie's wet hair and clothes, but fortunately said nothing.

Stephanie felt a chill as dark thoughts gathered. Ranz could kill Dusty and all she could do was watch. But Ranz had to know if he did this, Stephanie would be his enemy forever. He'd seemed to care for her once. He'd even warned her about her betrothal so that it wouldn't come between them. Well, Dusty's dead body was something that would never go away and would absolutely be between them—forever.

Stephanie suddenly wished for her benefactor, the one who'd allowed her to stay with Dusty just a little while longer, who'd cared about her feelings. Maybe he could stop Ranz from doing this. If only she knew who he was and how to reach him—if only...

"Hi, Steph," Dusty said with a shallow smile. He looked tired, but there was a calm about him that was new.

"Hi, Dusty," Ranz said.

"How'd you get wet?"

Ranz attempted a smile. "Tripped."

"Are you cold? Do you want me to go so you can change?"

"I'm fine."

Dusty shrugged and hugged Stephanie; Ranz hugged him back, while Stephanie cringed. Dusty tugged on her hand and they sat down together.

"There is something I need to tell you, and I want you to listen before you say anything. Okay?"

Ranz nodded.

Dusty frowned for a second, took a deep breath and let it out. "I'm not going with you tomorrow, and it isn't because I don't want to or that I don't love you. It's because there is something I need to do. I think I have a destiny in all of this and I have to live up to my parents' expectations for me. I have to become a man." His lip quivered. "I'm terrified that we are splitting up, but I love you and I believe that we can make it through everything and meet up again later... and be together *forever*." Dusty studied Stephanie's face. "Well?"

Stephanie felt a jolt in her body, an echo of pain that didn't touch her now that she wasn't attached, but still seemed powerful. Ranz focused intently on something, his power swirling. Stephanie didn't understand until Ranz raised her hand and the demon mark flashed onto her palm as he rammed it against Dusty's chest, connecting with the space near his heart.

Dusty's eyes widened as the power in the brand shocked the life out of him and he collapsed for a moment before his body vanished altogether.

"*Oh my...*" Ranz sputtered before a flash of light seared Stephanie's soul and she landed in her cell.

Stephanie scrambled to her feet, standing at the bars. Vessel Two was in the next cell, his body hunched over on the ground, still blurry to her sight. Stephanie's mouth dropped open when she saw Ranz lying on the floor, his mouth agape, his breathing ragged. And next to him, looking disoriented and unsure, stood Dusty Daye.

8

Untold Truths

Millie woke as her body was lifted, carried, and then handed to someone else. Her fright overwhelmed her control and she whimpered before clamping her mouth shut over the gag still in place. She was set abruptly on her feet and felt the bonds being cut, just before the hood was snatched away. The morning rays blinded her for a few seconds before being blotted out by the sight of a hundred, possibly more, Grey Cloaks. It took a few more seconds for her mind to really take in the sight of the men and women, all wearing thick grey skirts. Their skin held a grey hue and the man in front of her had a mark on his forehead, a strange shape that only he wore.

And just as Millie had known, in amongst the living Grey Cloaks stood the ghosts of the dead, faces hostile and ugly with rage, as though they had never known peace.

"Welcome to you both," the leader said with a strong accent and a cruel smirk.

Millie turned her head and saw Charity just a few feet away. Charity attempted a smile but failed miserably.

Millie quaked and her words squeaked, "Where are we?"

"One of our islands, but it might as well be your prison,

though we need no cage to hold you or rope to bind you now. You are free to roam around the island and make yourselves at home. Everyone has chores here and you will be no different. Work hard and you will be fed. Ask for what you need and if you are good and we are able, it will be given. There is no escape, only enough sea to drown you."

"What do you want from us?" Charity whispered.

"That you accept your fate to reside with us and to help prepare for the arrival of our queen, whom you will serve until such time as she releases you."

"Your queen?" Millie asked.

"The Queen of the Grey Folk."

A man shouted something in a foreign tongue to the leader and in only seconds, the hundreds were back in boats heading out to sea, leaving Charity and Millie to ignore everything else and rush to hug each other.

"We'll be okay," Charity seemed to promise, though Millie heard her uncertainty.

Millie pulled back to look at Charity's face. "Do you think there is any chance our friends will find us?" A war played out on Charity's sweet face that had Millie shaking her head. "No, don't answer."

Charity looked relieved and turned to watch the boats as they grew more distant. Millie leaned her head against Charity's shoulder and joined her in looking at the endless sea. Out there somewhere was Darienne, but Millie was certain they wouldn't find a map or someone to guide their way back to their friends. The dead faces around her grew more vile, screaming and demanding her attention, while she allowed her eyes to grow blurry in an effort to avoid them.

"Are you hungry?" a woman's voice said from behind them, the same strong accent coloring her words.

Millie and Charity both turned, silently nodding.

The woman's grey skin did nothing to hide her beauty. "Follow me."

*

Zoe rested her head against the four inches of Logan's shoulder that weren't in any way damaged, listening to his raspy breathing, each breath seeming like his last. A long pause between breaths had her flinching up to look at his face as he grinned at her and took a breath.

"I'm not so far gone as you think," he whispered.

Zoe snuggled against him. "That wasn't nice."

He tilted his head to kiss her hair. "I know, but you're looking at me as though I'm not looking at you, like I'm already in the ground. I have more fight in me than that. I don't want you leaving thinking I'll go without a hell of a brawl. Or thinking you have to hide the truth from me about my brother."

Zoe sat up, looking down at Logan's face. "I'll get him back—I promise."

"I know you will and as soon as I'm fit enough, I'll catch up. I will."

"Of course, you will." She paused, running her hand along his cheek. "I need to say something to you, to tell you that..."

Logan broke through her words. "So do you think Pastor Rowe's alive or is he some undead creature covered in dirt and decomposing as he grunts and searches for people to eat?"

"Logan!" Zoe whined as she glared at him. "I'm trying to find a way to tell you how much I love you and to say *goodbye* and you're thinking about undead Pastor Rowe nonsense."

Logan let out a painful sounding chuckle. "Save it, Zoe. I know you love me. You know I love you. And we aren't saying *goodbye*. So answer the question."

Zoe's face scrunched of its own accord. "Fine. I'm not so certain he was ever really alive to begin with. And we never did see—and I'm not saying I really wanted to look—whether he had some demon mark like Nate and Darla. He was evil, maybe that lasts longer than one lifetime. But if you see him, try to kill him again to see if it takes this time."

"You do the same."

"Logan, I..."

His hand came up and rested lightly against her mouth. "Please don't. I already feel like the biggest doofus in Stoughton to be letting you go into danger without me there to help you. If it weren't important—if *you* weren't so important—I'd stop you. But this mission is important if we are ever going to have a future worth living, and I want a future with you. I see something you don't—that *you* are important... to more than just me. I see the strength inside you, the strength everyone else feels so much that they listen to you. They'll follow you into anything and you will never let them down. But you have to promise to do everything you can to..."

"I will and so will you. We won't give up, no matter what happens."

"Deal."

Zoe leaned and kissed Logan. Her eyes closed and she

breathed in this moment, hoping it would stay with her long after Logan wasn't around to hold.

When she opened her eyes, she was struck by the love shining at her from Logan's deep blue eyes.

"Marry me, Zoe."

Her eyes went wide. "Really?"

"Really."

Her happiness threatened to gurgle out so she just giggled over a *yes* and sputtered, "You think we can get undead Pastor Rowe to do the service?"

"Absolutely." Logan kissed her... a lot.

Their eyes held each other for a long moment, *their* moment. The entire world of wars, soldiers, kidnappings, and rebellions faded away and Zoe and Logan were the only two people alive.

She leaned and kissed him lightly, whispering, "Don't die."

"You either."

Zoe broke the bond between them that kept her still, like a mighty spider's web, and grabbed her bow and rushed away to join the rebels already heading north.

*

Nate followed Devra into a large cavern where hundreds of teenagers and children lingered, clearly anxious to see their goddess. The Oades' children. So many. His heart ached for all of the parents waiting for word of their survival, while missing almost their entire childhoods. He'd expected, after hearing what Jaden and Cassa said, for the children to be warriors and while they did dress as warriors, their faces were mostly smiles and not at all hard. They moved forward to meet him, welcoming him to the mission.

"Do we go to her?" one young man about Nate's age asked Devra.

"Yes, Brody. She's coming to find us. I knew instantly and others have reported back. We will go to meet her, though the way is long."

"Cecily?" Nate asked.

"Yes."

"Why is she coming here?"

"We don't know."

Nate frowned. "Are you going to hurt her—not that I think you could, but are you going to try?"

"I don't know. That depends on if she will listen, hear our mission, and understand why we do the things we must." Devra turned back to the young man named Brody. "Are we ready to set out?"

"Yes, Devra. All is ready. Most are coming, while the small children remain with the caregivers."

"Wonderful. Thank you for all of your hard work."

Brody beamed at her, bowed, and returned to the others, while Devra turned to Nate. "Are you ready? To see her again? I know how much she hurt you."

"That's not why it will be hard to see her."

"Why then?"

"She'll see my neck. My shame."

Devra looked genuinely confused. "Shame?"

"I'm your slave and nothing more. I'm... *ashamed.*" He looked down, while Darla cuddled against his side.

"I am sorry you feel that way and hope you won't always.

There are reasons for everything, and they will surprise you. But we haven't time for that right now. We must go. She's in the Wild Wood and she's in danger."

"Danger? But she's so powerful."

"Not anymore. You must prepare yourself to find that she has been destroyed but somehow manages to still live."

"Destroyed?"

"The only answers to our questions lie that way. Let's go."

✶

Dusty had known Stephanie wasn't going to take his news well... at all. But that didn't mean he was prepared for her to shock him with some special power. But then she'd drugged him before, so clearly, girls were a dangerous mystery. From the white hot blinding shock, Dusty suddenly stood inside a cave of some sort. A massive and *ugly* demon lay on the ground.

Dusty's stomach went woozy for a few seconds as dizziness overtook him but then faded.

"Dusty!" Stephanie cried and Dusty turned, rushing toward where she stood inside a cell.

"Stephanie, what's happening? Why are you in there? Who's that guy? And did you just shock me?"

Uncertainty leapt upon her face and she babbled, "I... I didn't shock you—I didn't mean to anyway, but... but I..."

"Where's the key? I'll get you out."

"She can't get out," a heavily accented voice said from the next cell.

"Two, what's happening?" Stephanie pleaded.

Dusty sighed. "Two? Like one... *two*?"

Stephanie nodded and looked annoyed.

Dusty pouted. "Well, excuse me, but I still want some answers."

The man in the next cell, who happened to have grey skin and a mark on his forehead, said, "She won't give you answers, but I will."

Stephanie turned anxious. "Two, no, please..."

The demon on the ground with sharp horns coming out of his skin—*gross*—stirred a little causing Dusty to jump, but the big oaf crashed back to the floor, breathing even harder. Dusty ignored Stephanie and Two and searched the room, finding an axe that Amanda would have approved of leaning against the far wall. He walked quickly toward it and returned, holding it over the demon.

"Steph, is he evil? Should I just—you know—whack his head off?"

The grey man gripped the bars. "You'll trap her here forever if you do, and me as well, so if it is all the same to you, I'd rather you didn't."

"Tell me." Dusty snared Stephanie's attention, begging for the truth, but saw in her eyes the guilt of untold truths and a mountain of matching lies.

"Dusty, I love you."

"Then tell me what you've been hiding from me."

"It's not my fault."

"I don't care about blame, just tell me what you've gotten yourself into and how I can help."

Before she could answer, the demon on the ground groaned and his arms twitched. Dusty turned toward the grey man.

"What is he going to do when he wakes?"

The man's grey eyes flashed. "Kill you."

"Right," Dusty said, while trying to remain calm. "How do I get out of here? How do I get you and Stephanie out of here? And anyone else in these other cells?"

The grey man shook his head. "She's trapped, as are the rest of them. Their bodies aren't here. Her body is wherever you came from—how did *your* body get here and you *not* in a cell?"

"She shocked me... or something."

The grey man chuckled.

"What?" both Stephanie and Dusty asked.

"Ranz finally met his match, a being with a soul that cannot be extracted. You are a rare find in this world."

Dusty was about to use the axe on more than the demon. "I don't have time for more mysteries. I need to help Stephanie get free."

"Dusty," Stephanie said, "I can't get free. I'm sorry I didn't tell you... that I lied, but there's no way out for me. But there is for you. You need to get away from here."

Dusty approached her cell, reached through it, and put his hand on her cheek. "I don't understand."

"I know." Tears fell from her eyes and his usually proud girlfriend looked entirely fragile. "Please don't make me say it, just get away from me and away from here. I want you to live and be free. Please."

"But where is here?"

"The middle of the earth," Two said. "A very, very long way from wherever you came from."

Dusty's forehead puckered, maybe permanently. "I won't

know how to get back. How can I leave when I don't know where to go?"

"Take me," Two said. "I'll get you out."

"What?" Stephanie asked. "Is that possible?"

"My body is here. I just have to merge back inside it while Ranz is still out. Please, if we hurry..."

Dusty stared at the quivering demon and then at Stephanie. "I can't leave Stephanie... and certainly not with a demon who might hurt her."

"You have to," Stephanie begged. "You know me; I'll survive *everything*. And this is the fate I deserve. You don't. Take Two and get out of here."

Dusty didn't know what to do but the demon kept grunting and trying to rise and time was running out. He looked to Two. "Are you a Grey Cloak? I mean, you're grey and Grey Cloaks can't be trusted."

"He's a Grey Cloak?" Stephanie asked.

The grey man looked confused. "I don't know... I don't remember."

"Fine. Whatever," Dusty blurted. "But if you are evil, I will kill you."

"Fair enough."

"What do I do?" Dusty asked.

"The wardrobe. The second one. Bring my body here."

Dusty hurried toward the wardrobe and found it locked. "Crap!" Taking a breath, he searched for a key with absolutely no stinking luck. Realizing the weight in his hand was that of an axe, Dusty flushed at his stupidity and took out his embarrassment on the wardrobe. Wood burst before him and he felt for just a moment like a conquering hero until he realized his axe had sliced into Two's still and frozen-looking—and Grey Cloak wearing—body.

"Two?" he said nervously.

"Yes."

"I cut your face... a little. And your arm."

"There's not much time," Two called. "Besides, I'm sure your additions to my appearance are improvements."

Dusty looked at the body, the very tall, broad body. "Are you sure...?"

"Just grab it! Now, Dusty!" Stephanie shrieked.

"Okay, *fine*." Dusty dropped his axe and reached and pulled at the body that was heavier than it looked. A second later, Dusty's legs gave out and he lay sprawled on the ground under Two's body, feeling very, very awkward about the sudden changes in his life.

"Dusty!"

"Steph, shut it. I'm trying!" Dusty pushed and fought his way to turn over. Once over, he hauled his weight and the weight of Two's body as he scrambled onto his hands and knees. From there, he forced himself to his feet, the body draped over his back. Walking like a hunchback, he shuffled, dragging himself and the body to Two's cell. He stumbled at the last second and flung Two's body forward, standing back and watching the body strike the bars and then bounce to the ground with a massive thud.

Dusty cringed as he looked up at Two. "Sorry."

The look, the absolutely entertained look, on Two's face shocked him.

"What?" Dusty asked.

Two shuddered slightly and shook his head just a little, while his smile remained in place. "You just remind me of something I thought I'd forgotten... someone." He seemed to shake off his memory, his eyes drawn to the still-twitching demon. "I need you to put my hand inside the cell."

Dusty grabbed the body's hand and practically threw it in between the bars. It landed with a plop and Two stared at it, his breathing tense.

Stephanie mumbled, "Hurry, he's waking."

Dusty turned toward the demon, still struggling to rise. Dusty glanced back at Two who was holding his own hand as he concentrated. Dusty had a sudden feeling, a strange longing, to go back and choose differently. He should have gone with Cecily... he should never have left Dunlowe in the first place.

Noise broke his thinking and he turned back toward the demon who reached his knees before falling back down.

"You've got to hurry." Dusty's words fell away when he saw Two's empty cell and stared at the banged-up body on the ground whose eyes were open.

Two stared at him, a sad grin on his face. "Thank you."

Dusty extended his hand to help Two to his feet. When Two rose, he swayed and set a hand on Dusty's shoulder rather than touch the bars of his former cage.

"There's one more thing I need to do."

"Then do it," Dusty said.

Two hurried to the desk and grabbed a knife sitting upon it. He rushed back and pulled at his clothes until a dark mark came into view, a mark seeming to have been burned into his flesh. Two clenched his jaw and used the knife to cut through the mark as a grumbled cry came from the demon. With his grey blood smeared on the knife, Two stabbed the blade into the demon's arm.

"What are you doing?" Dusty demanded. "I thought killing him would trap Stephanie."

"He won't die. But he doesn't own me and can't ever again." Two stood up while the demon let out a string of hostile words that sounded a whole lot like curses. "We must go."

"I..." Dusty stammered and moved back to Stephanie who leaned against the bars of her cell while she seized a kiss he was glad to provide.

"I love you. Go."

"Get free of this. I know you'll find a way. Don't give in."

Stephanie nodded, but Dusty saw the resignation on her face. Her eyes flashed to the demon, concern more than fear showing on her face.

"I've made my choice. I've chosen this future and what it will bring me. I can see now that losing you is the price I had to pay to get what I want. But even with that, I will always love you... no matter what. Please, go back to Dunlowe when you get out of here. Do anything but don't go to Cloud City. I don't want you to see..."

The demon lurched to his feet. Two grabbed Dusty and hurled him away, moving to protect him as the demon rose to his full and ginormous height, blood dripping from the horns on his face.

"Now, this won't do."

9

Grey

I HUMMED AS WE CONTINUED, enjoying Bear's warmth and feeling almost okay. Not strong and still in some pain, but the peace in my heart seemed powerful enough to overwhelm the agony.

Bear whinnied at me and I brushed my hand over his chestnut hair.

"You always were a good old gentleman of a horse," I whispered and he turned his head, tapping his muzzle against my arm.

Finn smiled at me. "Are you ready for a rest?"

"Are you kidding—all I'm doing is resting."

"How about something to eat?"

I fought to raise my head off of Bear's back, but Bear snorted his disapproval and I lowered it to rest against him.

"What is it?" Finn asked.

"Does it bother you?"

Finn studied my face. "What? Your thoughts are too fragmented for me to make out."

"That we are going on a journey with no destination, just faith that the Source—and most likely Laura—will ensure we end up where we need to be?"

Finn moved closer, brushing his hand through my hair. "I would go anywhere just to be with you, destination or no. And bringing Bear to you does seem like a very *Laura* thing to do."

I laughed. "It does. She is going to give the Source so many headaches, because she never shuts up anytime she gets something in her head."

Something caught Finn's attention and he looked away.

"What is it?"

When he turned back to me, his face filled with wonder. He nudged Bear to the side a little so that I could see what he saw: a Wild Wood goat peeking at us from behind a tree.

Hope filled me. The Source had repaired what I had damaged and given goats back to the Wild Wood.

I giggled. "You do realize they are going to try to eat me now."

"Absolutely."

*

Stephanie's hands trembled, gripping the bars of her cage, as Ranz rose to his full height, towering over Dusty and slightly taller than Two.

"Now, this won't do."

"Ranz, please," Stephanie begged, but Ranz seemed not to hear her.

Two shoved Dusty out of the way and faced Ranz, fury in his grey eyes. But Two's eyes didn't hold Stephanie's attention, the mark on his forehead did. A mark so familiar to her, she felt it pulsing where it had been burned into her skin.

Ranz studied Two. "You would fight me... *still*?"

"Always."

Dusty's breathing grew choppy, as Ranz and Grey squared off. After a few seconds, Dusty bolted toward where he'd left his axe, grabbed it, and dodged back behind Two, who took the axe out of his hand and held it menacingly toward Ranz.

Ranz seemed amused. "You don't know who you are—you don't even remember your name. I stole that knowledge from you. I stole *everything*. You think you can find your way out of here? That you would even know where home is? Or what you left behind?"

Ranz's words made an impact, but Two simply nodded. "I may not remember my name or who I am... or more than just patches of the life I lived, but I still breathe and dream. I exist. And for the chance of freedom—to discover all those things—I will risk everything."

Ranz looked at Dusty, who peered at him from around Two's shoulder. "And you? You would leave the woman you love in my cage? And do nothing?"

"What can I do?" Dusty asked.

Stephanie's body shook harder. "Don't listen, Dusty. Just get free. Please. Ranz, just let him go. I'll be anything you want. Do *anything* you want. Please! Please, just let him go!"

Ranz turned toward her, his eyes suddenly filled with compassion. He ignored Two and Dusty. He didn't see the tears in Dusty's eyes as he nodded his goodbye and allowed Two to drag him out of the cave. Dusty and Two seemed to not exist to Ranz anymore—but Stephanie did.

Sadness and grief stared at her from Ranz's weary face as he extended his hand to Stephanie, requesting in a way he hadn't before for some solace. She immediately rested her face against his palm.

"Thank you," she cried.

"You were right, dearest. His power is unpredictable, his fate not within the realm of my control. I should have heard you, but more than that, I should have listened to your needs. You need him to be alive in this world. Dearest, I almost lost you—*would* have if not for Bay, which is a debt I have difficulty abiding. I was wrong to drive you to such extremes. Please, dearest, will you forgive me?"

"I do. You let him live. I am yours. I'll marry whomever you want. I'll do whatever you want." She looked up at his face that no longer held any fear for her. "I don't want to be free, Ranz. Not like Two did. You *know* me. You really know me and you accept me. No one would—not even Dusty, if he really knew. No one will ever care about me the way you do."

"One will, dearest, and he will be your king."

"When will I meet him?"

"Very soon."

Stephanie let out a sigh and surrendered everything she was to be what Ranz and her future husband wanted. She would please them, make them proud.

"Of course you will, and here is your chance. I am going to put you back in your body, but I am not strong enough to join you. Tell them Dusty left to follow his sister, that he couldn't handle the goodbyes."

"What happens when he arrives?"

"Lille and her forces will be long gone. Dearest, I didn't kill him, but it is likely these caverns will. The dark time nears—right now, beasts lie in wait, saving their energies for the great conflict. If Two and Dusty are in the caverns when the dark hour strikes, they won't survive. And if they avail themselves of the gateways, they may never be seen or heard from again. I gave Dusty a chance at life, just a chance... for you."

"A chance is enough. He's Dusty Daye—he will surprise you."

"He already has."

"What about Two? Will losing him hurt our plans?"

A strange pride filled Ranz's eyes. "I've spent more than a thousand years trying to obliterate his will." He smiled. "I failed and the consequences may be dire for us, but he earned my respect in a way few do."

"What about me?"

Ranz softly brushed his palm against her face. "Respect is one thing, but love is another, and you have that from me—you are the only one who has in more years than you could comprehend."

A flash lit in her mind and she vanished from her cell, back into her body that still lay inside her tent. Ranz wasn't with her and neither was Dusty. Knowing Ranz would think no less of her, Stephanie curled into the tightest ball she could and wept, knowing her tears would soon dry and her life would continue, but that the bridge toward home had been burned forever.

*

Morning struck after a sleepless night and Morgan gazed at the preparations that continued: tents rolled and packed, soldiers busy everywhere. Bay and Oriel worked together, while Genovan stood like a scarecrow, watching it all from behind an expressionless face. Morgan walked up the hill toward him.

"Can you see her?"

Genovan shook his head. "I know they reached the Wild Wood, but nothing has come into focus since. Blank patches are all that seems to be left of the Commanders' gift of sight."

"I'm glad you are coming with Lille—she will need you."

"Yes."

"I think I'll need you too."

Genovan took his eyes off of the troops to gaze down at her. "I will be there for you and your sister, until she is safely on her throne."

"Thank you, Gen. Now let's go get this goodbye out of the way and get on with things. I still don't know what Dusty decided."

"I don't either, but he's gone."

"What?"

"He's not in the camp and Stephanie was crying."

Morgan stammered a few indistinguishable words and ran toward Stephanie's tent, bursting through the opening. "Where is he?"

Stephanie's red, puffy eyes filled with more tears though her face was already soggy. "He went after *Cecily*. Always Cecily. Never me. He said he couldn't handle saying *goodbye*, so he just left."

Morgan felt her spirit slump as much as her shoulders. She'd really believed he would join Stephanie and in the process remain near Morgan. "Well, I guess we should have known."

"Guess so."

"They are taking down the tents. Come on, let's get out of here."

Stephanie stood, readjusting her haughtiness. "Good riddance to the Downs, I say."

"I agree."

Morgan and Stephanie left the tent that was quickly torn down and rolled, and joined Abigail and Amanda waiting nearby.

"I guess this is it," Abigail said.

Morgan hugged her. "For now."

"Right," Abigail whispered, but sounded doubtful.

Amanda hugged Morgan, made a half-hearted attempt to hug Stephanie which was spurned, and took hold of Abigail's hand.

Amanda stood proudly, red hair flying in the breeze, looking ready for her next adventure. "Good luck." Amanda cast a sideways glance at Stephanie. "You'll need it."

"You too," Stephanie said coldly and walked away.

So much for warm goodbyes.

Morgan prepared to follow when Amanda reached and took hold of her hand, forcing her to remain.

"What?"

"Don't trust her... not even a little."

*

Zoe walked through the woods with the others, all heading north. Birds chirped and danced from tree to tree as they passed. Other animals scurried around, hiding from the humans who'd invaded their land. This was the farthest north Zoe had ever been and she felt the distance deep in her heart. Every step took her away from Logan, Dunlowe, and the life she had known.

She watched the rebels moving as she had ordered, spread out, silent. Every ounce of movement around them seized by many sets of eyes, all watching for the next attack.

Normally, woods this lush and alive would brighten her mood, but memories of the map of Stoughton from her days in Mrs. Dumphry's class had her head hanging down and her focus diminishing. What if it took months to reach the Crownlands? What if they lost more people to attacks when they barely had enough to begin with? What if they never found Heath's family? Logan's brother? Jem's sisters? What if all of this was just a bad ending waiting to be reached?

How could so few people stand up to a king who had unlimited amounts of soldiers?

When Zoe turned to her right, she found Jacoby staring at her, questions in his eyes. "What?" Zoe whispered.

Jacoby shook his head as his expression hardened. He turned his gaze to the north, walking faster and passing her.

Mindy moved closer to Zoe. "He stares at you all the time. Never takes his eyes away for long."

"Yeah."

"Don't trust him. He's a stranger and the one thing we know for certain is that he tried to kill the sevens and their families. And he ratted out the town of Dunlowe to this fate. I know you and Logan are all forgiveness and unity, but if given a vote, I would have chosen differently."

"And done what?"

"Put the sharp point of my arrow right between Jacoby's

eyes. We don't have time for forgiveness—that comes when the war ends, and this war isn't close to ending. We bested some of those soldiers sent to kill us, but the king has more—and we don't have nearly enough. And you..."

Zoe bit her lip. "What about me?"

"You look like you've lost faith. I'll keep fighting until I die—I'm not afraid. I'm not like you, I didn't have much hope to begin with. I was just looking for a satisfying death and then I got wrapped up in a crusade, yours and Logan's crusade. And now I find that I need your belief that we are fighting for something—a chance at a real future, a future that isn't horrible." She glanced at Heath whose eyes were focused on a log he was stepping over and then back to Zoe, stopping her with a light touch on her arm. "I want to believe in a future," she said softly. "I can't if Heath loses his entire *huge* family—he'll never get over it. Charity may never come back. I'm alone. You're alone. Help me make sure Heath never is. Please, Zoe, I need you to believe."

Zoe nodded. "I'll get myself together—I promise. But I need your help with something."

"Please tell me it doesn't involve shiny happy thoughts."

"No shiny happy thoughts."

"Good. What then?"

"A blade, a bow maybe, or a rock—definitely the chance to do violence."

"I'm liking the sound of this already."

✶

Dusty had never liked running. It was something that either meant you were late to school and would get hit with a ruler or, more likely, being chased by monsters. Bad, bad running. And running with the weapons he and Two had stolen was even worse. When Two finally grabbed his arm and forced him to stop, Dusty's legs felt like immovable logs. He dropped his weapons and crashed to the cave floor, panting, until he threw up... all over the place.

"You okay?" Two asked.

"Is it...? Okay...? To stop...?"

"He can't follow us."

Dusty gaped. "Then why have we been running... *forever*?"

Amusement flickered on Two's face. "I just thought we should get some distance. He has many vessels and they could still find us. He can't—he can't leave his cave. It's his prison. Besides, he won't have the strength to do much right now. He needs rest." Two considered. "If he returned her to her body, we *could* kill him to free her. I don't think it's a good idea, but I want you to know that it is a choice we could make."

Dusty moved away from the remains of his dinner and stared at a pool of water that reflected the lit rocks inside the cave walls, just like the lit rocks he'd first seen in the Wild Wood and the Downs. The still water looked peaceful, so he continued to stare at it while a memory, a detail he'd missed, troubled him. Something about the demon's other vessels. But in the end, every memory of Stephanie in her cage smothered whatever pulled at him to remember.

"She didn't want him hurt," Dusty finally said. "She chose her path." He flinched when a tear hit the small pool, followed by another. "She chose... *not* me."

Two sat beside Dusty as still as the water before his tears

inspired ripples.

"Dusty, will you do me a favor?"

"Sure."

"Help me pick a name. I don't remember my own, but I really don't want to be *Two* anymore. I don't want to be just another one of Ranz's vessels."

Dusty looked up at him. "I had a dog named Herbert once."

Two grimaced.

"He wasn't a very good dog," Dusty mumbled. "How about *Grey*? I mean, you're grey and if you pick a normal name, it'll just make things more confusing when you remember your real name." Dusty paused and then added, "I really hope you aren't a Grey Cloak, but I'm pretty sure you are with your greyness and your funny clothes."

Two looked confused and frustrated, as though if he just concentrated hard enough, memories would form... but they didn't. Dusty really thought Two's head might pop off if he thought any harder, so he reached and jostled Two's shoulder.

"I don't know who I am," Two said. "What makes you think that Grey Cloaks are bad?"

Dusty played with the dirt, tossing small rocks into the water. "They've been trying to kill me and my friends for a while now, and they stole two of my friends and took them away to some island. I was going to fight to rescue them, but now I'm here. Maybe this path picked me."

"Maybe. Whatever the reason, I'm grateful fate brought you into my prison. I won't forget the debt I owe for my freedom or for my new name. I will be *Grey*. Thank you."

Grey's gratitude for what Dusty considered dumb luck felt

uncomfortable. "So what do we do next? I mean, if you don't remember your name, how can you remember the way out?"

Grey looked down and muttered, "I might have lied about that."

"Figures."

"Are you angry?"

Dusty shrugged. "Nah. You wanted out of your cage—can't blame you for that. And I was here anyway. I'm glad I'm not alone. So do you know anything?"

"Anything?"

"About anything? I mean, do you know how to fight? You looked pretty comfortable with that axe."

Grey reached and clenched the handle. "Yes, I believe I do."

"Do you mind teaching me? I'm thinking knowing how to fight and find food might be a really, really good idea... soon."

A strange howling reverberated inside the caverns.

Grey patted his back. "Good call."

10

A Sight to Call Home

Bay should have been at the beach with the team going after Millie and Charity, but instead he waited for one moment alone with Stephanie. The group going with Lille had already started out and Stephanie was about to join them when Bay approached her, wrapping his hand around her arm and tugging her away.

"What is your problem?" she demanded.

"Did you hurt the boy?"

"What boy?"

Bay's hand tightened and he pulled her closer. "You are a treacherous creature as we both know, and you will tell me whether you hurt Dusty or I will kill you where you stand."

Stephanie looked affronted but not as much as an innocent person would. She swallowed. "He's alive and he has just as much chance of surviving as we do—maybe more. I didn't hurt him, not physically anyway."

Bay studied her, looking beyond her words for her true meaning. "You set him free, didn't you? Before you do whatever it is you are going to do."

She nodded in answer.

"I'm certain my words are wasted, but it's never too late to make a different choice. No matter how far you walk down this road, you can always choose another one. People forgive... almost anything."

Stephanie nodded, but he saw in her eyes that she was too set on her path to imagine any others.

"Like I said. Wasted words. Goodbye, Stephanie."

"Good riddance." She turned her back and marched away.

Knowing his comrades were waiting, Bay sprinted to the beach and joined the others, staring at the newly constructed boats, awaiting their first touch of the sea. The tide looked rough but not terribly unruly. He glanced at Amanda, Mortimer, Abigail, Keefe, and the forty soldiers joining them.

"That's really the plan?" Amanda asked, making a face at Mortimer. "Randomly attack islands until we find them? This could take a long time."

Bay smiled at Amanda. "It's not like any of us are getting any older."

"True, but there's one thing I want to say. There will be absolutely no hiding me from the battles, leaving me in boats, or any effort to keep me from my destiny. Are we clear?" She looked directly at Mortimer, who grumbled a lot but did eventually concede. "Good."

"What about me?" Abigail asked. "I don't know how to fight."

Amanda studied her face. "Do you want to?"

"I don't know—I guess I won't until I try. You've found your place in all of this. So has Morgan, maybe Stephanie—though I don't think her place is what she *thinks* it is. I'd like to find my place, so I better stop being angry and try some new things."

"The best thing about fighting," Bay said, "is that you can be very angry and still do it very effectively."

Abigail's face reddened unhappily.

"What?"

"I'm not so angry anymore, just sad. Even as weak as she was, being with Cecily again made me feel safe. Being with Millie and Morgan and the others—I was part of something. That's over. And I'm just sad." She let out a sigh. "Sorry, I don't know what's gotten into me, but I can't silence this feeling that the sevens aren't just splitting up for now—that we'll never see each other again, never be in the same place again."

She turned and looked at the sea, while the rest stared at her, not wanting to damage her grieving time. Something she saw in the water had her flinching and taking a step back.

"What is it?" Bay asked.

"Just a bad feeling—another one."

Amanda patted Abigail's back. "Let's just go and find Millie and Charity, fight for them and not worry about the rest right now. We'll be okay. "

With her eyes still locked on the dark water, Abigail whispered, "Or we won't."

"Could I give you a suggestion?" Keefe said, coughing slightly when his voice came out as diminutive as a mouse's squeak, rather than the booming a creature his size was capable of.

Abigail nodded.

"You're looking for the end of your story and you aren't there yet. This time in your life isn't like the others. Change found you. Be open to it. See not the closing of doors as much as their openings. Not knowing your place in this world is a gift. It leaves you open to wonder and adventure in a way having all of the answers smothers. Maybe, just maybe, you will be a seafarer. We'll know in just a few seconds. Doesn't that seem exciting?"

Abigail looked up at Keefe—unafraid of the massive, horned beast—and nodded, but the shadow that seemed to cover her didn't budge. "Yes, thanks." She brushed a few tears away. "Can I ride in your boat?"

"Not sure," Keefe said. "Can I ride in yours?"

"I have a boat?"

"As soon as you claim one."

*

Stephanie walked with the enormous crowd, thousands of soldiers all surrounding their queen, feeling more alone than ever in her life. No Dusty. No Ranz. Silence in her own mind. Morgan and Lille kept near each other, thick as thieves, and Stephanie hated everyone. If only...

No. She wouldn't do that anymore. No more longing for roads that would never be hers. Besides, she had to not care about her former sisters. She might have to hurt them. Soon.

Her brand flared suddenly and she realized that the pain had subsided almost entirely since she'd let go of Dusty and her former life. Even now, it wasn't pain so much as awareness. She searched around the army, looking for what would have made the mark come to life.

With a wave of not unpleasant dizziness, she felt eyes on her from the hedgerows. Stephanie slid her hand over the mark that was back on her belly, feeling the pulsing through her dress. Feeling the connection that no longer felt like a cage.

"*Are you out there?*"

No words came, but the connection grew stronger, as though her readiness to see him brought him closer. And he *was* close. Her future husband. Her king. Her stomach fluttered as butterflies dove and frolicked. He wouldn't be Dusty, but he would be her future, the future Ranz had chosen for her.

Love was all well and good, but allies were everything. And then with another wave, she felt exactly where he was, watching her. The day was too bright for her to rush to meet him, but the night would come.

✶

"What do you think they are doing right now?" Millie asked Charity as they scrubbed grey clothes in buckets near a stream.

Charity didn't look away from her cleaning. "I can't think about them right now."

"Sorry."

"Don't be."

Millie flinched from the dead faces all around them, more than normal, as though this island had seen more death than Dunlowe ever had. "Could you tell me a story?"

"No."

Stung, Millie asked, "Why?"

"It wouldn't have a good ending."

"Why?"

"I'm *out*."

"*Out* of what?"

Charity finally looked at Millie. "Happy thoughts. *Hope*. I've been thinking. We weren't brought here to do laundry. We were taken because we are *harmless*. We were taken to distract the others, the others who *do* have power and purpose, where we have none. The Grey Cloaks knew we would do as we are told, believe them that there is no way out, and just accept."

"What are you saying?"

"I'm tired of just accepting. I'm *tired* of all of this. I don't belong in Darienne; I belong in Dunlowe. I want to go home to my brothers and sisters, and my parents. I have the worst feeling about them right now, especially Heath. I can't explain it, but I think he's having a really hard time, and where am I? Washing my enemies' clothes on an island in the middle of nowhere. The Grey Cloaks think we are too afraid to steal a boat and get out of here."

"We *are* too afraid to…"

"Not any more. You can stay if you want—do what they tell you—but I'm getting out of here even if I don't survive. Better to die than to surrender before even standing up."

"But…"

"Just stay here and do laundry. I'm going to search for a boat."

"But…"

"No more *buts*. I'll be back. I won't leave without giving you the chance to decide to come with me."

Before Millie could say *but* or anything else, Charity ran toward the trees, leaving Millie with her nightmare, alone and surrounded by the angry dead.

*

When the moon stood directly above, Zoe called to those near her, suggesting they take a rest. The message circulated and Zoe watched the shadowy forms of the townsfolk slow and stop, bodies weary, hungry, and tremendously sad. Broken families came together but often separated again, as fears of shared fates drove them to different sides of the group in the hope that if an attack came, some part of their families would survive.

With no family to check on, Jacoby sat next to a log near Zoe. He leaned against it as clouds passed overhead, sealing off the moon's rays like a curtain. Zoe felt unsettled and searched, squinting in the darkness for one face. The dark denied her, but Mindy did not, as Zoe felt the brush of Mindy's hand across her back—Mindy, who managed to move without a sound—as she continued away from Zoe to find a place to watch over the group.

Zoe's feet ached in her ill-fitting shoes and frayed holes in the knees of Logan's little brother's old pants were like open windows for the mild breeze. Zoe stood, feeling lost somewhere between the past and the future. The sounds of scampering animals, an owl's *whooing*, did nothing to silence the memories that rose to attack Zoe.

Her parents. Screaming at her. Voices filled with disgust. Words, so many words. Useless. Ruined. *Worthless*. Knowing what they would think of her, even now, if they were alive, caused her legs to weaken more than the seemingly endless march. Trembling began in her shoulders, as it always did when they screamed and spewed their hate for their only daughter—their only surviving child. Not even their deaths saved her from the ugliness of their words.

"Zoe," Jacoby whispered. "Come sit down. You need to rest."

Zoe swallowed, squinting at him, unsure about everything, especially herself. But she moved toward him and sat beside him.

"You're shaking. Are you cold?"

"It's nothing—I'm fine. Just memories better left in the mounds in Dunlowe."

She couldn't see Jacoby's face but she felt his warmth as his shoulder touched hers.

"I've got some horse jerky left, if you're hungry."

"I thought any meat was better than fish, but horse just grosses me out," Zoe said.

"Do you like horses?"

"Horses were for people with more money than my family had, so I hated them and everyone who rode on them. But when I had a boyfriend with a horse and we galloped over fields, when my hair flew in the wind and I hid my face behind his back to shield my eyes from the stinging—I'd never felt more alive or loved horses more."

"So Logan had horses?"

"Yes, he had horses—the Trenches had everything—but he wasn't the boyfriend I'm talking about. It's weird..."

"What?"

"How life before all of this seems so long ago... and yet, just like yesterday. I've been with Logan for such a short time—and mostly we've killed soldiers and fought for our town—but I know him better than I've ever known anyone. I've seen the truth in him in a way that might never have happened if we'd lived normal lives. I would only ever have been the girl my parents raised me to be."

"And who was that?"

Zoe shuddered. "Never mind. I shouldn't be..."

"What?"

Zoe snapped out of her muddled thinking, remembering her mission. "Boring you with my babbling. Tell me about you."

"Not much to tell."

"I don't believe that. You came face to face with a very angry Cecily Daye and lived to tell the tale." She hoped her tone didn't sound as false to him as it did to her.

The clouds broke apart and light streamed down, revealing a suspicious cast to Jacoby's eyes.

"What do you want from me?" he asked.

"Just to get to know you."

"I doubt that. Besides, there really isn't much to tell. The soldiers killed my wife and stole my daughter. And I'll do anything to get her back. That's who I am."

He glared at her, daring her to say something, while she bit her lip, feeling deceitful and foolish. She'd given away more information than he had—she was lousy at this. Or possibly, he was really good at this. Or, also possibly, he wasn't playing the same game she was playing. Maybe he was just who he said he was... or maybe...

"What was your father like?" Zoe asked to stop her mind from playing chess with itself.

Jacoby did nothing to conceal his shock. "Why would you ask about him?" A pause and distrust stared at her through the moonlight. "Do you know something? Did you know...

about...?"

"About what?"

He stared at her for a long time before he shook his head. "He was just a father... like yours or anyone else's. We should get some rest."

"Would you rather I go somewhere else?"

"No," he said, his voice soft, "I'd really rather you stay."

Zoe rested back against the log, knowing she wouldn't sleep and glad that Mindy wouldn't either, in case Jacoby strangled her while everyone slept. Only she didn't feel fear being near him, but that didn't mean she trusted him either. Too much unknown existed in the crowd now. Jacoby might not be a traitor, but that didn't make him a friend. This many people, so close to danger—someone might betray. At least this way, she could keep an eye on Jacoby, whose breathing became settled as he slept, while Zoe was left to think about fathers and to wish she'd had a different one.

*

Caves aren't cozy. No lie. Dusty listened to Grey's rhythmic breathing, hating him just a teeny, little bit for being able to sleep on the hard ground when Dusty was wide awake and sad and angry and betrayed and maybe, just maybe, *sorry*. Sorry for not seeing that Stephanie had fallen in with bad company. Thoughts tortured him as he wondered how her life had changed so much, all while he'd been around, watching, and sometimes kissing her. She hadn't shared her journey. It would be easy to blame her, and he kinda did, but that didn't stop him from feeling bad and crushed and lonely.

A slithering sound just on the other side of Grey had Dusty slowly moving into a seated position, staring at the space, seeing the lit rocks grow brighter due to his interest, almost like they were living beings themselves. When his eyes adjusted, he leapt to his feet, seeing a snake, a *huge* one, with golden sparkling fangs.

"Grey," Dusty whispered.

Breathing.

"Grey..."

Nothing.

"Grey, seriously, there is a giant snake that's going to eat you!"

Grey's eyes opened and he seemed lost. "Who are you?"

"I'm Dusty Daye. I got you out of your cell and now we're in the caverns and you are about to be eaten by an unusually large snake."

"Right." Grey's hand whipped and grabbed the snake, breaking it in half before it could even move. Grey winked at Dusty. "Dinner?"

Dusty covered his mouth in an effort to keep the contents inside and nodded. Hungry was hungry. Grey used the lit rocks to cook the snake and they ate their fills before Grey stood.

"Let's move out. The sooner we find our way, the sooner we might see the sky. I've missed the sky."

"Are you from Darienne? I thought the Grey Cloaks had been banished or something."

Grey concentrated again and Dusty regretted asking. Grey eventually shrugged. "I don't know, but I remember the sky. I remember when at just the right light, the sky would turn violet.

A beautiful sight. A sight to call home."

Dusty nodded, liking the poetry. They started walking, lights in the rock walls brightening at their approach and then dimming when they'd passed. "So do you want to hear about me?"

"Definitely."

Dusty almost began but then stopped. "First, are you a bad guy? Am I going to regret telling you about me because you will turn on me one day and use everything you know to defeat me in a duel or something?"

Grey chuckled. "I honestly have no idea. Maybe I am bad. Maybe that's why I ended up Ranz's vessel. To be innocent and suffer a fate like that seems cruel. But if I was bad, does that mean I always will be? Or could I choose a different path?"

Dusty considered. "I don't know, but either way, months of walking through the underground seems too long to *not* talk, so if you want to hear, I'm willing to share."

"Please."

"Well, my first childhood memory involved a toad, and he was a mighty fine toad."

*

Resting—all I was good for. Bear lay on the ground next to me, his warm body touching mine, while Finn sat beside me, watching over us. Thinking. I could tell he was thinking.

"I am... about you. And me. I've lived long enough to not bother counting the years and you are just seventeen."

"Just a stupid kid, huh?"

He laughed. "No. I was thinking that all of these thousands

of years I've lived, none of them compare to the seventeen I've spent near you."

"Will you tell me about the years that didn't include Annisha or me, and what you were like when you were my age?"

His face turned dark and he glared at the ground. "I was what I was born to be, filled with rage but believing there was no way out."

"What happened? How did you become *you*?"

"I made my own way out, but not without a cost."

I took hold of Finn's hand and kissed it. "Whatever you did, whatever you had to do to become such a loving person—it had to be right, had to be worth it."

He leaned and kissed me. "You make every price worth paying." His mood lightened. "There is something else I'm thinking."

"What?"

Finn ran his hand through my hair, inspiring giddiness throughout my body. "I think Bear is healing you."

"I do feel a little better."

"*A lot* better since you were burning."

I shuddered, the memory feeling alive in my body, while Bear grunted. "Sorry." I stroked his withers. "Here you are trying to heal me and I go and think about..."

Thinking. Thinking of the pain inspired more pain. Thinking of the burning brought fire to my body. Thinking of Bear brought comfort. Thinking of Finn brought hope. My body might be the weakest on the planet, but it seemed my mind had some of the power my body lacked.

"Bear, I'm going to try something."

"What are you going to do?" Finn brushed my hair away from my face. "You keep doing that, making a decision before I can see what it is. It worries me."

"I'm going to think about things—difficult things—and see if my mind will stretch."

"Why?"

"I just want to know if I am really as diminished as I think. What if I'm not? What if I could…? No, I don't want to hope. I just want to try something."

"Just be careful."

I kissed his palm and took his hand in mine while I kept my other hand on Bear. I thought of Dusty, concentrated on his face, his hair, his smile. But I saw nothing. I thought of Morgan and Lille, Stephanie and Amanda. Charity, Abigail, and Millie. Genovan. All of them, but nothing came and I remained alone with my unhappy thoughts. On a whim, I thought of the barren earth Britton had shown me when I'd left the Source and a sudden flame filled my body, pulsing where my body touched the ground.

Flashes of the barren ground flew through my mind. The image Britton placed, but others. Dry. Dead. Barren. Not like the black earth the Commanders had killed, but deserts stretching for miles. I thought back even further to when Finn had shown me images of his homeland, after Pastor Rowe had scarred my back, and then again when I'd first come to the Wild Wood. I didn't remember desert.

"There is no desert in Darienne," Finn said. "There are the fields of the Downs that go on for thousands of miles. The plains of tall grass stretch just as far, golds of the grass and rich red dirt. And the southern end of the country is all mountains, mountains that stretch all the way to the clouds—to Cloud City which overlooks the sea. No desert. Ever."

I swallowed as I pushed again.

"You're not strong enough."

"You can see my thoughts, Finn. There *is* a desert even if there was never one before. I want to know what it means... I want to know why I can see it, *feel* it."

Both Bear and Finn grunted in roughly the same manner.

"Men," I said with a smile, but my smile faded when I heard the sounds of creatures skittering nearby.

Finn and Bear leapt to their feet—or hooves—while I lay unmoving and infinitely vulnerable. Death serpents. Goats. The Wild Wood's mighty cats and donkey creatures. All creatures I'd seen before when I could fight them. They were much more frightening now that I couldn't.

They moved closer. Finn, his sword drawn, faced one side while Bear pranced in place, ready to use his hooves on any creature who dared to get too close.

One goat stepped closer, his eyes calm, no crazed bloodlust in them. Bear seemed to sense something and calmed, leaning down to smell the much-smaller goat. The ground pulsed under me again, radiating through me. The desert. Devoid of life.

Trees began to moan, but not like they had before. Not like I was a threat to them, but rather, like they saw what I did, a desert expanding, taking all life with it. I reached and touched a tree, and a feeling washed over me. Terror. And then I knew. The barren way was expanding and it didn't matter how far away it was, it could reach us here and kill us all.

11

Casting Shadows

Stephanie's mind drifted as she followed Lille and the thousands of soldiers all journeying south toward Cloud City, the southernmost city in Darienne. The Downs was the northernmost region of the massive country, so Stephanie determined that the walk would take roughly *forever*. Better to let her mind wander back and forth and all around as she avoided the blossoming love between Morgan and Oriel. Envy tasted badly and envying *Morgan*—well, that felt like drinking poison. But Stephanie knew the antidote and wished she could bolt to the hedgerows and meet him: her future husband.

Her fiancé.

Stephanie might not know everything—though she would never admit that to anyone—but she was certain her love affair would be better than any love affair Morgan the *misfit* would find.

As soon as Lille ordered the troops to make camp for the night, Stephanie's heart fluttered and her stomach dropped. With a wave through her body, she felt him near, watching, waiting.

Another hour passed before Stephanie could ditch Morgan

and Lille—and the watchful Commanders—and make her way through the camp. Remembering Ranz's lessons, and missing his voice terribly, Stephanie pulled at her power, focusing, stealing the sight from anyone who might see her, the hearing from anyone who might hear her footsteps. Slowly, deliberately, she walked away from the camp.

With a chill in her gut, Stephanie finally allowed herself to acknowledge the dark power of her gift. She'd stolen energies—sights and sounds—but not lives. Every life of every soldier around her, she could take with barely a thought, just by draining them past what they could survive.

Her feet slowed as she allowed herself to wonder about the man she neared, about the lessons in power he would teach her, and finally, the things he would want her to do—*force* her to do—with this terrible power.

Would he find the lines she wouldn't cross, just as Ranz had? Or would he force her to cross them, not caring about the damage to Stephanie's soul?

She stopped, her breathing choppy. Fear pushed at her, awakening a fierce desire to run back to the life she knew.

"You have nothing to fear from me," he said, from the other side of the shrubs, a heavy accent in his voice, the same accent—the same timber—as Vessel Two.

Stephanie drew in a breath, summoning her courage, her absolute Stephanie *Trenchness*. Power, the word that soothed her, the word this man would understand. Her faith in Ranz brought calm to her heart—*he* had picked her husband, her partner in war and power.

She stood erect as she took the final steps that divided her from her future. All in darkness, wearing his grey cloak with the hood concealing his face, he waited. Stillness existed between them as two rock lights brightened as she neared. She swallowed loudly but didn't stop until she stood before him, looking up at him, seeing nothing but darkness in his heavily shadowed face.

Her hands shook as she reached to push back his hood, to finally see his face. Suddenly her uneasiness grew that she was crossing lines—*his* lines. Maybe she was supposed to just obey him. Her hands flinched away, releasing his hood to fall back over his head.

"Stephanie, I wish for you to be *you*. For you to be comfortable with me. If you would like to see my face, then see it. I expect you to take what you want—just as I will."

With no less trembling, Stephanie raised her hands and pushed back his hood. She drew in a breath as she swooned, her head growing light while her heart pounded and the brand—his brand—tingled. No pain now. Only peace. He was beautiful and frightening... and looked familiar. Very familiar, *very* much like Two. He even wore the same mark on his forehead. But even with similar features, Stephanie felt entirely different about this face, this mark, this man. The grey of his skin drew her in, pulled at her hands until she was caressing his face and then leaning her body against his, her face soothed by the soft fabric of his grey cloak. His arms surrounded her and his heart beat like a war drum. And she cried.

Time failed to matter. Only connection.

As dawn drew close, he said, "You must get back. Is there anything you wish from me? Anything you wish to know?"

She pulled back and looked at him. "Will you love me?"

"I do. I always have."

"But that was Daryn, right? Not me."

His hand tenderly touched her cheek. "How much can a soul truly change?"

Stephanie didn't have an answer and waited.

"We will get to know each other," he said. "I promise."

"Ranz is still gone. I'm not certain what I must do next."

"Watch. Wait. Something treacherous is coming. Know that it is not *our* design—Ranz's or mine. Stay away from it. Our plans may have to wait if the rumors are true."

"What rumors?"

"Something is happening to the earth, something to throw the very fabric of Darienne into the fire. If it isn't stopped, there will be no land for us to rule. And if our seers are correct, nowhere on this world is safe from what is coming. Stay close to the current queen. She will be protected, but know that I will always come for you."

"Will I hear Ranz again soon?"

"Do you miss him?"

She flushed and nodded. "I... don't have anyone else anymore—I mean, you aren't there with me. He is."

"I am glad he is. Glad you've come to care for him. He has always worshipped you."

"Thank you for understanding about Dusty. I... really appreciate it."

"Does he live? Did Ranz...?"

"Ranz set him free. He's somewhere in the middle of the world with the man from the cell next to mine."

"Vessel Two?" he demanded, his voice harsh.

"They escaped together."

"And Ranz let them go?!"

She nodded, wanting to pull away from him, afraid of his sudden intensity. But just as quickly as his anger flared, it vanished and he laughed.

"What?" she asked.

His smile remained, rueful and entertained. "I can see that some fights cannot be put down forever. The shades of the things we've done will always find us and cast their shadows over our future. But we determine our own fates. Looks like you and I both have a war to fight for our power. But then the caverns of the world are deep and the ways out like searching for true goodness in men, almost impossible to find. They may never surface. They may be eaten. And if their hope fades, they will become dwellers of the underground like my forefathers before we were led from the darkness." His eyes grew distant for a second. "I can see that it is as it should be, and it is a fight I look forward to."

Stephanie nodded, unsure what any of that meant or what she should say, and mightily disliking the idea of anything chomping on Dusty.

"You should get back."

She turned away, both grateful and sad to leave him, but sought his face again. "May I know your name?"

"Thorne Greysen, King of the Grey Folk."

*

Nate walked with Devra and her followers through caverns that led to more. Through darkness and light, lit rocks dotting the path no matter where they went. Darla walked beside him, occasionally skipping. He wished for some time to talk to just her, but they hadn't stopped walking in days. How many, he didn't know.

"Time is different here," Devra reminded. "Time in the outside world flows in different directions than within the core of the earth."

"Do you know what happens outside? In Dunlowe?"

"The children tell me. They check on things, including their families."

Nate scowled. "You mean they go near their families but they say nothing to them, give them no comfort?"

"They have no comfort to give, only more sorrow."

"But Cassa and Jaden are good people—you have to know that. Why couldn't you leave them with some of their children?"

The young man called Brody looked at Nate as though he were a bug. "Does he still not know? Can he be that stupid?"

"Excuse me?"

"You're talking about *my* parents—Cassa and Jaden. Do you really think I don't care and that what I do isn't for them? Isn't for my siblings? Isn't for the future of my people and others in the world I have sworn to protect with my life?"

Devra set her hand on Brody's shoulder. "Peace. He doesn't know. There wasn't time."

"He doesn't know?"

She shook her head.

"You could just tell me," Nate spat.

"Don't worry, Nathaniel. You will know soon enough and you will wish that I'd never told you. Some truths are more deadly than ignorance. But you want time with your sister, so wait until the end of the procession and talk together. Don't lose sight of us though. Understood?"

"Yes." After Brody gave him another dirty look, Nate added, "Thank you, Devra."

Darla stopped and waited with him until they were twenty feet behind the crowd who never seemed to tire, or if they did, they didn't pay it much mind.

"They are strong. They are disciplined. They believe."

Nate stared down at Darla. "You believe?"

"Yes—that we are exactly where we are supposed to be. She's not cruel. She does what she must to serve her purpose. Just like you did in risking everything, in leaving Mom, to save me."

"She's a demon and we are slaves."

"We were never free. Never. Father always kept us trapped. I stared at monsters, *really* trapped in a cage, a slave to tortures that I couldn't escape. Until Cecily. You can't really think that Devra is like Father or whoever hurt me."

"But Devra made you. How do you know she didn't do that to you?"

"A victim knows. Why do you think I serve her?"

"What do you mean?"

"I believe the same one who tortured me is the one who hurt Devra, who forced her to do terrible things to survive."

"How did he, she, or *it* hurt her?"

"I don't know, but we will someday."

"If Devra moves to attack Cecily, what will you do?"

Darla shuddered. "I love Cecily."

"I know. I do too, but we may have to hurt her."

"I know."

Darla leaned against Nate and he wrapped his arms around her small body, wishing he had wisdom, *anything* he could give her.

"You do," she said. "You give me everything. You always have." She looked up into his eyes and smiled. "I love you."

"I love you too. Darla, why did you stop talking to me in the Oades' village?"

"Because I knew those moments were the end of my time being a baby. I just wanted to try to be normal for a little while. I'm sorry if that hurt you."

He smiled. "I missed your voice." Nate turned toward the others and found them... gone.

Darla paled in the low light and whispered, "Oh no..."

*

Zoe crawled through the underbrush on her belly, while the surrounding branches sliced her face. She grimaced but kept at her mission. A few more inches and she would know who lit a fire that could be seen for miles. Soldiers most likely—only they would be brazen enough to blare their location to the whole wide world.

She forced her body through the too-small space, fighting the feeling of being trapped, and could finally see the fire and... *children* standing around it. Ten—maybe fifteen—kids, the oldest not more than nine. Dirty, weary-looking children.

Zoe strained to hear what the oldest boy said but couldn't. She thought of Abigail's little brothers, the little warriors who were probably driving Mrs. Dumphry mad. She thought of all of the children—the ones with the wounded, the ones who'd been stolen, and the ones buried in mounds in Dunlowe. For just a moment, she thought of her own brother, Cade, but he'd been gone so long her memories were too pale to see.

But he'd been a boy once, just like these boys, and since no one would know, Zoe allowed herself one moment to imagine that these boys might be brothers with sisters somewhere waiting for them to come home. Even a mean brother like Cade was missed when he was gone.

As Zoe prepared to move, she looked at the oldest boy again. He said something, but his eyes remained on the fire. She squinted, watching his mouth that seemed to be saying the same words over and over again. Words that brought no reaction from the other children. They were all too still, probably just too tired and shocked after all they had been through to behave like normal, squirrely kids.

Zoe couldn't stand it and backed away much less quietly than she had entered. She got to her feet and turned, searching for Heath, but only found Jacoby.

Jacoby stared at Zoe, raising his hands in question.

"It's kids. Alone."

Jacoby's entire body changed and Zoe quickly said, "No babies—your daughter's not..."

Zoe watched her words assault him and had to look away, moving once again toward the children. She found Mindy in her perch in a tree and gestured that she was going into the grove. Mindy nodded, her bow ready.

Zoe walked around trees and through the thick brush until she reached the last row before the fire and the children warming themselves near it. Something caught her foot and she looked down, thinking to see a root, but found a rope instead. She froze as the boy's words finally reached her.

"It's a trap. It's a trap. It's a trap..."

*

Morgan woke with a start. A voice. Urgent. Oriel.

"My queen, they have come."

Lille bolted upright. "What? Who has come?"

"The enemy mystics and the soldiers you sent toward Cloud City. They are moving quickly. We don't know if they mean to attack. The Commanders have moved to meet them, but you know that can't go well. Arm yourself."

Lille was up and changing clothes before Oriel had even made his way out of the tent. Morgan reached and attached her dagger to her calf and quickly put her dress on over her camisole and bloomers. When Lille turned toward her, Morgan studied her face, her fierceness, her absolute readiness to be queen.

"Come," Lille said and both rushed out of the tent and into the morning light.

From the corner of her vision, Morgan saw Stephanie emerging from the hedgerows next to the camp. But the Commanders' chanting silenced the questions in her mind—Stephanie didn't matter right now. Morgan hurried even faster, knowing the Commanders' power was too destructive to be freed.

Lille and Morgan reached the Commanders, seeing what had brought their wrath, the huge army running toward them.

"Genovan, stop," Lille ordered and a few seconds later the

chanting ceased. "We must discover what this is." She turned to Oriel and her soldiers. "Place the bowmen and prepare for an assault, but await my orders. I can't believe all of those soldiers would have turned, no matter what the mystics have done."

The approaching army slowed when they saw the bowmen, and just Ameel, the mystic, floated closer. Duncan and Capria, the Viceroys of the Downs, lingered nearby—the two people who had tried to kill their queen, as well as Morgan and her friends.

"I told you to go to Cloud City, Ameel. It was an order."

"We tried, your highness. But the way is blocked."

"Blocked?"

Ameel looked shaken. "The dirt, the soil, the tall grass... is *gone*. Only desert remains. A desert that kills."

"A desert?"

"We tried to cross it... a mystic and a man. Both vanished, only a puff of smoke remained of their immortal essences."

Lille just stared.

"The desert is expanding—I think it will take all of Darienne before it is through... maybe Stoughton and the rest of the world. The energy is dark and powerful."

"I must see this. We must fight it... together."

"Yes, my queen."

Morgan squinted, not believing Ameel any more than she could throw her, and she really wanted to try launching her. Perhaps from some sort of catapult. Morgan looked to Oriel and found the same doubt and suspicion mirrored in his eyes.

"Form a circle around our queen!" he barked to the soldiers and the Commanders fell in line.

Some soldiers remained to pack the camp, while the rest proceeded toward this desert that the mystics supposedly had nothing to do with.

Stephanie moved closer. "What do you think, Morgan?"

"I don't know what to think... yet."

But that wasn't exactly true. Morgan did have thoughts, just none she would share with Stephanie, who seemed fine without Dusty and had run off alone into the hedgerows. The sister who had become a stranger. But even thoughts of Stephanie couldn't hold sway for long. Words flew through Morgan's mind. Cecily's words... *the earth... the earth... help it.* Nothing Cecily had said made sense that night, but now, the meaning had finally caught up with her words. As did an image that still lingered in Morgan's mind. One of many images that had made a home in her when she'd first gone with Lille into the Delphea grove, the day she'd begun the journey to become the heir to a broken country. She'd seen Oriel's eyes in her visions. Heard her grandfather's words. She'd also seen dry, dead desert ground, with a fallen crown upon it. The crown of Darienne.

Her heart pounded in her chest as she knew now what she hadn't known then: Lille was in danger and if she fell, Morgan would have to take up the crown and fight for a country she barely knew.

*

Crickets. An owl. Bunnies. And Logan. Nature had been Logan's home all through his life, but never had the sounds of the forest seemed more oppressive than when trapped in place as the miles between himself and Zoe grew. Pain stabbed at him, but nowhere greater than in his heart.

"Drink some water," Mrs. Daye whispered and didn't give him a chance to argue before placing the bowl against his mouth. After he had taken a sip, she pulled it away. "You need to rest. You will get strong, and then I have no doubt you will catch up with them."

"It's the same for you, isn't it?" Logan kept his voice low, not wanting to wake the wounded and the children who *could* actually sleep.

She nodded. "My children are beyond my reach. My husband is miles away with Zoe and the others. But we do what we must."

"Thank you."

"No, Logan. Thank you. All I could see was endings. Without you, Zoe, Heath, Jem, and Mindy, we wouldn't have had choices to make. All we would have is the legacy of one man's corruption and the way we let it happen—the victims we became. Thank *you*."

Rustling nearby preceded a disgustingly familiar voice. "I couldn't have said it better myself."

Mrs. Daye tensed, her hand unconsciously gripping Logan, as Pastor Rowe walked out from behind a tree.

*

The fog came in as Bay and his compatriots neared the shore of the first island. Part of the force remained at sea, while the other mounted the sandy beach, leaving a few soldiers to protect the boats. Abigail remained at sea, where she watched the water as though it might be her true enemy. Amanda and Mortimer leapt from their boats and hurried up the beach with Bay. Mortimer's face was more strained than ever to have the redhead with him in battle, but as promised, he did nothing to hold her back.

Mortimer, however, looked downright giddy when the island turned out to be deserted, while Amanda's irritation and upset inspired her to kick her best friend in the shin.

Bay turned away from them and stared up at the moon, casting its light all around them. He felt something... *off*.

"What is it?" Keefe asked.

"Something is wrong."

"With the *moon*?" Keefe's tone clearly implied Bay might be losing it.

"With something..." Bay's eyes strained to see around him. "Bring a rock light over," he called to another soldier, who immediately complied.

With the light, Bay walked up the beach, hearing something growing louder as the sounds of the sea faded behind him. Something sizzled in the jungle terrain. Bay felt suddenly ill as the ground beneath his feet grew hot. He backed away, the pain from the heat still upon him.

Just as Bay was about to shout a warning, Mortimer scooped Amanda into his arms and barreled back to the shore, inspiring the others to follow more effectively than any words ever could. Mortimer set Amanda in the boat and shoved the boat into the water before climbing in with her. All of the soldiers followed, soggy and weary by the time they scrambled into the boats. Once Bay splashed through the water, his feet finally cooled, but he knew without looking that they were covered in welts. From the ground. From the barren earth.

Suddenly the fates of two girls grew to mean less. Not that he cared less, just that he saw with unyielding clarity that greater battles were before him, battles more treacherous than any even he had known. What he wouldn't give to know what Britton in the Source knew about this plague infecting their land. What he wouldn't give... to change the things he'd done.

A gull cried and clouds passed in front of the moon as the soldiers in boats lost their direction.

12

A Lost Soul

WALKING AND WALKING. And walking some more. Dusty had run out of tales for Grey, though repeats of any stories involving Mrs. Dumphry were most welcome. Grey couldn't stop laughing when Dusty described the harpy's glare, her shrill voice, and the way she wielded a ruler like a sword.

While Grey still chuckled, Dusty considered him. He really didn't seem evil, but what if Grey simply forgot to be evil, along with his name and where he came from? And for not remembering knowing much about swords, Grey seemed to be an expert.

"You're considering my possible evil again, aren't you?"

Dusty felt his face redden. "Sorry."

"It's okay. You are alone inside the middle of the earth with me. It's sensible to wonder."

Dusty stopped and Grey turned toward him. "Are you wondering the same thing... about *me*?"

"No. Certainly not."

"Why? I could *totally* be evil."

A grumbling laugh burst free. "Right. The boy who was terrified of his shrew of a teacher is evil—I think not."

Dusty scowled. "Could happen. Could *totally* happen."

"You are unwaveringly good. Be proud of that. I don't remember much about the world, but I still believe you are a rarity."

"Why?"

"You set her free to live her life, no matter what it cost you. You didn't seek vengeance for her betrayals—you wouldn't even now."

Dusty's head lowered and he let out a sigh. "She broke my heart. It won't ever be the same."

"I knew a woman like that... once," Grey said without thinking. "She was everything, but I lost her. I don't even remember how. But I see her face in my mind. Her eyes. The shimmer of mischief alive in them. What I wouldn't give to know her name—I'd give up ever knowing my own if only I could know hers."

Grey got lost in a dark place, so Dusty patted his shoulder. "I don't suppose you'd let me name her Herbert after my dog, would ya?"

Grey gently shoved Dusty and mussed his hair. "Definitely not. Come on, a little farther and we will take a break and spar. I get a turn to pay you back for all the wounds you inflicted on my body when you got me out of that wardrobe."

"Hey now..."

"Gonna cry and hide behind Mrs. Dumphry?"

"*Maybe.*"

Grey's voice changed, growing stark. "Then you better start looking for her now."

"Why?" Dusty didn't wait for an answer before turning

in the direction Grey was staring... at the eyes, the many sets of glowing eyes, attached to wolf-like creatures. Their fangs sparkled in the low light and their growling bounced around the caverns, making them seem like thousands instead of a few dozen. "Ummm, Grey, you haven't taught me to fight yet."

Before Grey could say anything remotely comforting, the wolves leaned back on their haunches and sprang, their eyes never leaving their targets.

*

"What do we do?" Darla pleaded, tugging at Nate. "We promised. She told us to keep them in sight. We've failed."

"Easy, Dar. Come on. Let's just find them, or..."

"Or? What *or*?"

"Or we could run and see if..."

"Nate, no. We promised."

"Like we had a choice, like we would have chosen this. Darla, think. Mom and the destruction of Dunlowe. We could go back and fight for them."

"We did make this choice of the ones we were given. We made a promise. I haven't forgotten Mom and we will get back to her, but that isn't our fight. Not right now. Devra's fight is ours now."

"*Yours*—I still don't know what this fight is."

"But you swore."

"I've betrayed before—I've lied. I've turned on everyone at one time or another."

"Not me."

"Maybe you're next."

She shook her head, her faith pure. "Who do you want to be? Because if you want to be the person I believe you to be, that starts now with Devra's path that will lead us to Cecily."

Cecily's face lit in his mind, bringing clarity and purpose. "Let's find them."

Darla wrapped her hand in Nate's as they hurried through the caverns, their footsteps echoing for miles. When they found no one—heard nothing—Nate's stomach dropped. He'd failed and Darla began to cry, when a stern face met his.

Brody, looking very much like his father just then, scowled. "She told you not to get lost—are you stupid or disloyal?"

Nate considered skipping over stupid and disloyal and moving right into violent, but Darla restrained him.

"Neither. We're just new." Something sparked in her eyes as she stared at Brody. "And your heart is hardly pure enough to be judging us."

Brody looked affronted—though not without guilt and concern showing in his eyes—and turned toward the side passage and walked away, quickly enough that Nate and Darla had to run to catch up. Lights flashed to life as they neared and darkened once they'd passed. Convenient and eerie at the same time.

"You caught up. I'm relieved," Devra said when they neared. "Brody thankfully saw that you weren't with us. The caverns are unstuck in time. You could've been lost forever from me, from us, from the world. You could emerge to a world that has already died. And it *will* die without your help. Please don't lose sight of us again."

A dying world?

Darla nodded to him.

"We're leaving the underground. Prepare yourself for the light."

"But I thought it was far away—you made it seem..."

Devra smiled. "We've been walking for six months in your time, though six months haven't passed in your world. It's been barely a day or two since you came to stay with us."

"Does this mean we are close to Cecily?"

"On the other side of this veil, she will be less than a mile away. You must hold hands with the others so that we all exit at the same time in the same place. Do you understand?"

"Not at all, but I will obey all the same."

"Thank you, Nathaniel, and do try to calm yourself when you see her and what she has become."

Destroyed. That was the word Devra used to describe Cecily. But Nate couldn't imagine it, especially after seeing her levitate the bowmen who had attacked the sevens' families, heal the wounded, and stand with a bearing so proud, like the world belonged to her.

Nate touched—okay, maybe gripped with claws—Brody's shoulder and held Darla's hand as they walked from the strangely lit dark into the brightly lit world.

✳

Morgan had not one memory of what Darienne looked like—*should* have looked like—but that didn't stop the sight of a seemingly infinite desert from stealing her breath. Lille looked like a statue, her shock plain for all to see.

"What is this, Ameel? How?" Lille asked.

"Something is feeding off the land, something without mercy."

"Did you try bringing water?"

Ameel nodded. "The land just sizzled faster."

The ground shuddered and cracks formed, breaking through the still-healthy soil, fracturing the earth. From the rise they stood upon, Morgan saw the world as shattered glass, a web of death in its wake. And then something else...

"Lille, I have to walk into that desert."

"What? No. You heard what Ameel said—the others died."

"Just as anyone who lay upon the earth the Commanders killed should be dead. But I didn't die. I was fine." Morgan leaned closer to Lille. "The trees knew. Knew I had a part to play in this. I have to go into the desert."

Lille gripped Morgan's hand. "No."

"Tell me how we're going to learn anything while standing here gawking as the ground dies. Something is out there. Something that knows."

"No, I forbid it."

"My queen, you must be willing to sacrifice even *me* if it means helping Darienne."

"But we don't know that you won't just die."

Morgan leaned even closer and whispered into Lille's ear, "I saw this. I saw the ground die in the visions the Delphea grove gave me. I heard a voice that told me to trust my heart, not my eyes. I believe in my heart that I can walk on that ground, that it won't hurt me. I must cross this desert and discover whatever I can to help us—to help Darienne."

Lille's eyes showed her surrender though her body remained

rigid. "Alone?"

"You can't be serious!" Oriel spat. "You can't think..."

Morgan released Lille and walked the few steps to Oriel, raising her hands to rest upon his face. "I came back to you once. I'll do it again."

"Not alone."

"Who else could we risk?"

"The Commanders," Genovan said from behind her. "We aren't afraid to die. We will come with you."

"What of Lille and her protection?"

Genovan grimaced and glanced to his queen.

A war played out on Lille's face and she finally shook her head. "The Commanders must remain with me, but Genovan, doesn't it stand to reason that if Morgan could survive your dark earth that she might have an immunity to your toxic nature?"

"It does, my queen."

"Can you map travel to her, to see if she is okay?"

"With my brothers' help, possibly—but that doesn't necessarily mean that the dirt won't kill me and through me, my brothers."

Lille stared at Genovan and then turned to Morgan. "The Commanders are willing to risk for you, so I will give you a lifeline at possibly a very high cost. I can't believe I am letting you..."

Morgan stopped Lille's words with a quick hug. "I will come back, I—"

"No, don't promise. Britton promised. Daryn. My parents. Don't promise."

"Did you see anything about this? Did the Delphea trees

show you this?"

Lille's wide violet eyes shuttered and turned unreadable as she bit her lip and nodded. "I saw you walk out into that desert—that exact desert. I saw flashes of you moving out there, jumpy images that showed you cross over that far ridge, past where I could see."

"You know this is right."

"Right and wrong get all mixed up sometimes," Lille whispered, "because I also saw that this would change things between us somehow. I didn't understand—I still don't."

Morgan took a few seconds to consider. "Let's be right, no matter what it means. Be a good queen and I will see you soon."

Oriel had busied himself creating a pack for Morgan to take, gathering as much water as she could hold and when she turned to him, his eyes stole her will to do this. The scar on his cheek seemed darker as a teal hue colored his face, his unhappiness palpable.

He held the pack and waited for her to approach him. "Conserve this as long as you can. There's food in the pack, but you will need to find more and there may be nothing out there. Morgan, what if...?"

Morgan stood on her tiptoes and kissed Oriel just once. "This is my path, please believe in me."

"I do. I always have."

"Then I will see you soon."

Oriel's faith rallied and Morgan smiled at him as he helped her into the heavy pack, that almost had her teetering over at its weight.

"Better too much than too little," Oriel muttered.

"Right."

Morgan glanced at Lille and nodded, shared a weighty gaze with Genovan and Oriel, and turned toward the desert thirty yards away and already spreading closer. She covered the distance and prepared to take her first step onto the deadly ground before realizing she'd forgotten to say goodbye to Stephanie, forgotten her altogether. And the only emotion she could summon was *concern*... about leaving Lille unprotected from Stephanie. What did that mean?

*

"It's a trap. It's a trap. It's a trap," the boy said, and even though Zoe knew she had bigger problems, she couldn't believe the boy's courage in trying to warn her.

Zoe grabbed her knife to slice through the rope, but the soldiers were already upon her. But they couldn't silence her before she screamed, "It's a trap! Get away!"

The sounds of fighting burst from the woods. Grunts and cries, curses and the clank of blades. Zoe struggled against the soldiers who held her, memories erupting of the soldiers' hands, the king's men who had come to Dunlowe—the men who wanted to take from her something she'd never give willingly. Not to them.

The soldiers held her down. They bound her hands and shoved a gag in her mouth. A heavy man's knee pressed against her chest, his weight growing stronger, strong enough to steal her breath. Why? And then she realized, she was still fighting, hopeless as it was. Still fighting, somehow believing Logan would show up and save her again.

But not this time. This time she was alone.

*

"Greetings townsfolk from Dunlowe," Pastor Rowe seethed, while Logan reached for the knife never far from his grasp.

"He's a demon sent to kill us," Mrs. Daye breathed as she turned to face Pastor Rowe, placing her body between him and all of the wounded.

"Stupid woman—you know nothing of demons." Pastor Rowe chuckled. "You think your dearest little girl will save you?"

Mrs. Daye squared her shoulders. "I don't know, but then, neither do you. You can't be hanging around here in the dark with us if you knew where you were supposed to be... if you had a place in this world. There is nothing here for you, just wounded and the kids. Go away before we..."

The clouds parted and the moon's light shone down, reflecting something gruesome about Pastor Rowe's appearance. Mrs. Daye flinched.

"It is the damnedest thing to wake from the dead, to be denied peace after a long and failed journey." His laugh chilled Logan's bones. "But then I wanted immortality and it is now mine—not the way I thought it would be though."

Crickets chirped and a bunny hopped, while Pastor Rowe seemed distracted. "It is cold, so very cold." He glanced around at the wounded bodies on the ground, some still sleeping while others stared. Logan felt their horror and knew their preparations.

Mrs. Daye took a step back, putting herself closer to the fire, while Pastor Rowe watched her.

"I came for Jem, my murderer. Who knew the boy had it in him."

"He's not here," Logan said before anyone else could react.

"He went with the others. What do you want with him anyway?"

"You're a liar, Logan Trench. I know he's here—I can feel him close. He has something I need."

"What's that?"

"My soul."

13

Wrath

I'D SLEPT FOR A LITTLE WHILE curled in Finn's arms, my back against Bear, who snored as it turned out. But his snoring wasn't responsible for my sleeplessness, nor were the creatures who still surrounded us, most sleeping. They were afraid and for some reason I couldn't fathom, they felt safer near *me*. Me? The weakest girl on the planet, one who only had the power to fail everyone.

What I wouldn't give to have the power—*my* power, the Source's power—back for just a little while to fix things. To be the instrument the Source had dreamed of when she'd given me power no person should have. But that mistake had been righted and now what? What would happen next?

I missed Laura. I missed her laughter that always came at the most inappropriate moments. She was still in the Source with Britton, her love. Was she watching? Could she see me failing to figure out what was happening? Had she really sent Bear to me?

Movement near me drew my attention and I turned, seeing the fluttering of fuchsia butterflies all around the grove. The fuchsia reminded me of a bow Laura had worn in her hair before deciding it looked ridiculous there, something I might have mentioned a few times. The butterflies danced around me, lightening my spirit until I saw something else moving in the darkness, dark shadowy creatures.

"*Finn.*"

"*I see them. Remain still.*"

As if I had any other choice.

"*They might pass us by. Just wait.*"

I felt the hairs on Bear's back raise, but he remained still as more of the shadows came and the animals all around us tensed. All of us, waiting... for something.

"*What happens if...?*"

Finn caressed my face. "*You don't want to know. The Ezias don't normally leave the underground—haven't forever. Something in the world has gone mad, wrecking the order of things.*"

My heartbeat pumped loudly, sounding like a beacon. My breath grew shallow. The shadows screamed and they were everywhere, flying around us, striking against us. The animals bolted but I heard their cries. Bear sprung to his feet, rearing up and striking at the shadowy forms that paid him no mind, continuing to strike against him, just as they slammed into me.

I couldn't move. I didn't want to scream, feeling the need to keep my mouth shut.

"*Yes,*" Finn pleaded. "*Keep your mouth shut. Close your eyes. Try not to breathe. They are looking for a way in... they are looking for bodies to steal.*"

*

Stephanie stood very still watching as Morgan walked toward the desert without a backward glance, without having said *anything* at all to Stephanie. Morgan really didn't care anymore.

Sure, Stephanie had stabbed her and all, but Morgan didn't *know* that. So why had Morgan turned on her? Why did Stephanie care? And why hadn't Ranz come back?

Loneliness burned in Stephanie's heart. Ranz. Dusty. Gone. And Thorne Greysen, too much mystery to be good company at this point. If only Dusty...

No, it didn't matter. Dusty wouldn't love her anymore and she shouldn't love him... but she *did*. She remembered filling almost every page of her journal with stories about Dusty, what he'd done that day, what he'd said, the way he had looked at her, not like she was rich and beautiful, but like she was magical and perfect. Stephanie had never in her life felt as beautiful as when Dusty gazed at her. She'd truly believed that one day he would love her enough that she could trust him with her secret, the one she'd never told anyone, the one she'd denied all these years, even to herself. The one blaring in her mind: she was afraid of who she was and what she might do.

Stephanie shoved those thoughts back, cramming them down inside her, but one rebel thought broke free from her grasp and shouted at her. *"You are just a frightened little girl whose mother abandoned her, who just wants to be loved. No queen here. No princess. A common girl with a simple heart who yearns for a simple life."*

Stephanie shook her head to push the lies out of her mind, only they didn't feel like lies. She thought of her mother for the first time in years, struggling to even remember her face. She'd been beautiful but distant at the end, and then gone. A little girl should have a mother, but Stephanie had pushed that need down, just like every other part of her that craved anything that required someone else to fulfill. No, she took care of herself. Always. But Dusty, for Dusty, she'd grown to believe... he was so good and so kind, and handsome too. But even with his goodness, he wouldn't love her now—couldn't. Not when she'd chosen to be Ranz's vessel rather than stay with Dusty.

Tears shoved at her but she held them in, knowing Ranz wouldn't want her to give any signs that something was wrong. Only something *was* wrong. Stephanie felt herself fracturing, coming apart because she didn't know who she was and her desire to be queen suddenly felt hollow. What if she reached this unreachable and treacherous goal and still no one really loved her?

What if...?

What if... she wasn't *worthy* of love?

"*I love you, dearest.*"

Stephanie's soul sobbed, breathing, feeling relief in the sound of Ranz's voice.

"*I love you, dearest. Thorne Greysen has loved you for thousands of years, loves you, loves Daryn. We will shield you and love you and make you queen. Everyone will love you, need to be near you. You will never be alone again.*"

"*Thank you, Ranz. Thank you. Please, don't leave me.*"

"*Never for long. I am sorry I was gone, but it was necessary. I am stronger now.*"

"*What happened?*"

"*Later. Let's take a moment to see if the desert fries Morgan or if she is indeed as special as she thinks she is.*"

For as harsh as his words were, he didn't seem to want Morgan to die... yet.

"I am foolish enough to hope that she can help with our dying earth problem. We can't move forward with any of our plans until this problem is dealt with—this, the greatest problem our world has known. Thorne didn't know anything about it, did he?"

"No."

"Did you like him?"

"He's a little frightening."

"Those with true power are, and he has fought for everything he has. Sometimes warring tribesmen are frightening, but I assure you, he won't hurt you."

An errant thought filled her mind: Dusty.

"Dearest, I know this wound is fresh and will lessen, but would you like me to remove him from your mind?"

"What do you mean?"

"I can extract every memory of the boy and leave your mind clear to embrace your future, if you'd like. I would never do something like that without your permission."

Stephanie considered for only a second. *"Not yet, Ranz. I'm a little afraid that if you take him away, you might take all of me away."*

"I would never do that."

"No, Ranz, not you, but he's part of so many of my thoughts going back so far. I'm not sure what would be left."

"Then you must make new memories and then we will decide."

Morgan reached the desert and Stephanie expected her to pause, to gather her courage or whatever, but Morgan never slowed. She walked right out onto the desert ground.

"Please," Oriel choked as the entire crowd seemed to hold their breaths. Lille gripped Oriel's hand and Stephanie could see their trembling fear.

Morgan slowed and turned back when it was clear the deadly ground didn't hurt her at all. Morgan waved to the crowd, a strange smile on her face, the smile of a person who knew herself, her worth, and her power. The weakness in Stephanie singed her and she clobbered it, standing straighter, daring her vulnerabilities to show themselves again.

No more. She would be strong. She would be queen. And anyone who dared stand in her way would suffer before her wrath.

"*I drain power from the earth, from others. I could kill, couldn't I?*"

Stephanie felt Ranz's awareness pulse with pride. "*You could take every ounce of life from anyone who stands against you.*"

"*I could drain Morgan's life—this group of soldiers' lives?*"

"*The soldiers—definitely. Morgan, possibly, but you would have to be very strong and unwavering in your goal.*"

"*Unwavering. Yes, I will work on that, Ranz. Thank you.*"

✻

Only a second. Only one stinking second and Dusty was on his back with a wolf drooling on him. *Freaking* drooling. And snarling too, with enormous glittering teeth and really bad breath.

"Grey!" Dusty shouted and something made an impact on the wolf—not a deadly impact, it actually just looked angrier when it growled at Grey who was busy fighting twelve wolves at once, while Dusty had failed with just one.

Dusty struggled to get free but the weight of the massive wolf kept him in place. He thrust his arms at the wolf, attempting to tear at its thick fur. The beast let out a growl and Dusty dropped his hands.

"Grey!"

"Busy just now... *fighting*. What do you want?"

"Help! He's going to eat me!"

"Then fight! Fight for your life!"

Great. *Fight*. He'd already failed, already lost. More drool dripped on his chest as the wolf lowered his head. Instead of ripping through him, the wolf studied him and then sniffed him. The wolf's head dipped lower and smelled his face, his cold nose resting on Dusty's cheek.

"Fight, Dusty!"

The raw concern in Grey's tone caused Dusty to see the real ending he faced. That knowledge brought a strange feeling to his chest, something like steel and fire. Without pausing to think about how stupid it was, Dusty's hand formed a fist and his arm lashed out. His hand bashed at the wolf, knocking him back enough for Dusty to stand.

Dusty looked from his hand to the wolf, just as the beast's lips raised and his fangs dripped. The wolf launched at him, knocking him against the cavern wall. His fangs tore through Dusty's shoulder and Dusty screamed.

"Dusty!" Grey shouted, but Grey couldn't get to him.

Dusty's sight grew blurry as he watched Grey fighting the beasts, but he couldn't do anything except wince and cry as the wolf's teeth continued to tear his flesh. Grey faltered, his blood flowing from many wounds, and he stumbled, barely able to catch himself.

The wolf gnawing at Dusty's shoulder paused and then shuddered and moved back.

"I am so terribly sorry," a voice said before a growl emerged that had the other wolves ending their attack.

Dusty looked into the wolf's eyes, now serious and a bit regretful. "Did you just say something?"

"I am terribly sorry, sir. I didn't know it was you."

Dusty's jaw dropped and he cringed from the pain searing his body. "You can talk?"

"Yes, sir. I wasn't always a wolf—though animals of all kinds have voices of their own."

Dusty heard a thud and turned toward Grey, who had collapsed onto the ground. Dusty shoved the wolf away and ran toward Grey. "Can you help him? Will you?"

"Follow me to the well. The water can heal you both of the bites and our venom."

"Why would you? Why did you stop—I mean, I'm glad you did. But why?"

"I—*we*—do not want to incur your wrath."

"My *wrath*?"

The wolf nodded.

Dusty looked around at the wolves. "Who said I had wrath? I just want to survive and for my friend to survive."

The wolves stared at him, all of their eyes fixed on him, as though he was going to jump up and eat them—as though he was the one with the shiny fangs.

Very quietly, definitely respectfully, the one wolf said, "You *are* wrath."

*

Millie huddled on the ground, believing her tears would run dry at some point, though they hadn't yet. Her arms wrapped around her knees as the angry dead screamed at her louder than ever. She could close her eyes, but she couldn't make them go away. Couldn't do much of anything except hope that Charity would return, but after night had fallen and with dawn just over the edges of the trees, Millie lost heart that Charity would ever come back. She'd probably found a boat and fled this place, leaving Millie alone.

"You're *finally* here," a girl whispered, sounding excited and relieved.

Millie raised her face as a girl brushed through the bellowing ghosts and knelt in front of Millie.

Millie flinched, realizing she could see through the girl, but the girl didn't seem as haggard and hostile as the other dead. She didn't look *dead* at all. She was clearly a Grey Cloak, a pretty one about Millie's age, if the dead had ages.

"I'm not really dead," the girl said with a strong accent, "though not really living either."

Millie had never spoken to the dead before and bit her lip.

"It's okay, Millie. I know it's a shock, but I've been waiting for you for such a long time."

Millie's lip began to protest the pressure of her teeth and she released her control, setting her words free. "How do you know me?"

"I was a *seer* when I was alive. I could see possible futures—mine and everyone else's, though I had the good sense to hide the extent of what I saw. One day, I saw my own death and at whose hands it would come, and I made a plan. You see, I knew of this possibility, that you would come and you would see me and save me, and that you would need saving too. I've waited a long time, watching the living—watching you and your friends, especially a certain young man you know. I can still see the future, but the dead have been my only company until now... which might be why I'm rambling." She looked apologetic and then determined. "The dead aren't all angry, you know, and mostly they are angry with you for working so hard to ignore them when all they want is to be seen and heard."

Millie's mind froze, refusing to accept any more information, and she lowered her head to hide.

"Oh, please, stop hiding. You have a gift that no other has—of course, the dead search for you. You are the only one who can help them—*lead* them." She paused. "It is like penance, you know?"

Millie's head came up. "Penance? What did I do to be punished like this?"

"Not you—Lorelle."

"My former self, the warrior? That's not fair. I didn't do what she did. I haven't killed anyone... and then I had to leave Dunlowe and then I was stolen from my tent and my friends, and Charity left me. I didn't do anything to deserve this!"

The girl looked solemn. "But did you ever do anything to deserve otherwise?"

"What?!"

"Who in your life have *you* ever tried to help, instead of just relying on them to help you? Your friend, Charity, needed your support, your strength, and you gave her none, and now she is lost in the woods, hurt, and can't find her way out. And you sit here and weep for *yourself*."

Millie leapt to her feet. "Charity's hurt?"

"She hurt her ankle. She's lying on the ground, crying right now—needing *you* right now."

"Will you take me to her? Please?"

The girl nodded. "You mustn't tell her about the dead you see or me—not yet. Promise?"

Millie nodded.

"We can still talk inside your head. Okay?"

Millie nodded again, anxious to get to Charity, but then focused. "What is your name?"

"Oona—Oona Greysen, only child of Thorne Greysen, the man who stole you from your tent and brought you here."

"The scary man is your *dad*?"

Oona's eyes filled with sadness that then flashed to fire. "He *was* my father. He was also the man who would have killed me if I hadn't stolen his chance."

"Your *father* was going to *kill* you?"

"He'll kill you too, Millie—he'll kill anyone in the world if his lover asks him to, and *she's* coming home."

*

Zoe woke and instantly wished she hadn't. Aching muscles raged against her. Her wrists, bound above her, felt raw. And the weight of her body, hanging unconscious for so long, strained her shoulders and arms. She forced her legs to take some of the burden and whimpered as her arms cramped when she sought to give them relief.

"How many are there?" a man asked.

Zoe squinted from the candlelight. Finally, her eyes gave her the sight of her captor, a soldier leaning against a table. They were inside a tent... alone.

"A million."

The man moved so swiftly her eyes barely registered it, but her body registered the impact of his fist crashing into her face.

"Tell me. Their names. Their ages. What towns they are from. Tell me everything."

Zoe tasted blood and saw death in the man's cold eyes. "What happened to you... to become *this*?" she whispered.

"What happened to *me*?" His eyes gripped her. "What happened to me? I was pressed into service. Sent to your ridiculous town and watched you kill my brother—he was an artist who never wanted to hurt anyone, which made him easy pickings for you and your lot. You commit crimes against the crown and think you can get away with it."

"What crimes did I commit?"

"You killed the king's soldiers."

"You came to kill us—were we really supposed to just *let* you?"

"We didn't come to kill you. We were supposed to break your spirit and march you to the north, to the Crownlands."

"What then?" Zoe asked. "Try us for treason and kill us?"

He let out a sick laugh. "People are never killed in the Crownlands, though they constantly wish for death."

"Why?"

"You really don't know what is happening here, do you?"

"I have no idea. All I know is that my town was burned,

my parents killed, my friends dead, our townsfolk stolen—even kids—and soldiers came to kill me. I had a chance to fight and I did, but understand something, my brother died a long time ago. Your soldiers killed my parents. I'm the last of my family and I don't care if I die. So torture me if you have to, but I'm never going to tell you *how many. Their names. Their ages. What towns they come from.* I will tell you one thing though—I know the sevens, and when Cecily Daye finds out that you killed all those people, the rebels and I will be the least of your problems."

Zoe enjoyed the look of fear that crossed his face, before brashness took its place. "Those are just fairy stories to scare the weak—I'm not weak."

"But you said it yourself, you weren't a soldier, were you? You were pressed into service; isn't that what you said?"

"Everyone is pressed into service these days, even potters." He scrubbed his hand across his face. "You hicks in the south don't know what's become of this country. Those people dead and buried in your town are luckier than our families stuck in the Crownlands. My brother... was lucky to die, and I think the reason I hate you so much is that you didn't kill me too. You don't know the price for failure—you don't know what this means to those we left behind. My *children*..."

"Then tell me quickly, before my friends show up to rescue me."

He moved closer and Zoe stilled herself, fighting the urge to flinch from him. He placed his hands on her face, his fingers clawing her, causing discomfort more than pain.

"You really are Zoe Crane, aren't you?"

She didn't bother concealing her shock. "How do you know

me?"

"Word spreads quickly, just like hope—you are a brushfire on dry fields, Zoe Crane."

"Tell me what's happening in our country."

"Only if you promise to do something when the time comes."

"What would you have me do?"

"Send me to meet my brother."

*

Bay saw the faces of the other soldiers, the way uncertainty washed over them.

"My sisters still need to be rescued. What are we doing?" Amanda asked, while Abigail added, "Yeah, what are we doing?"

Bay looked over at Abigail in her boat, now attached to his—her eyes still drawn to the deep blue water. What could he say that these girls would understand? What could he say that wouldn't sound like cowardice?

Mortimer let out a sigh. "The lay of the land has changed and we need some reckoning."

Amanda placed her hand on Mortimer's. "Morty, I have to go after them. I can't let hot dirt stop me. This is my fight."

"And where you go, I go, even if we are our own army."

Abigail reached for Keefe's large hand and he steadied her as she climbed into Bay's boat and took a seat right in front of him. "Bay, talk to us. What are you thinking?"

"I'm thinking there's a bigger fight than the one to find and free Millie and Charity, and if we don't try to fight this, they could be gone anyway—they could already be gone. If the island they're on sizzles, they're finished."

"Don't say that," Amanda spat. "Don't even..."

"He's right," Abigail said quietly. "Amanda, we'll go after them, but Bay is right. This isn't about us, it's about the world."

Amanda looked ready to puncture Bay with something sharp. "But where do we go? What can we possibly do about burning dirt? How is that something we can fight? Maybe we could line up and pass buckets up the beach, like when there was a fire in Dunlowe. You think that'll work?"

A gull flew above them—the same gull. Again and again. Bay watched as the bird dashed and dove around them and then seemed to signal them back toward Darienne. Keefe squinted at Bay and Bay wasn't about to confess he was considering taking direction from a bird, so he simply said, "In times of trouble, we support our queen. Darienne is in trouble. We could split up, but I don't think we should. Let's go home and fight for our people and then if the world doesn't end, we'll find the girls. I promise I will search the world over for them—as long as it takes."

Mortimer rested his hand on Amanda's shoulder. "This is soldiering. You don't get your way, you take orders, and stuff down the worries to do what needs doing."

Amanda grunted. "Then take us back to Darienne, but let's make this fast."

14

This Desert Life

Dusty dragged Grey's body—that seemed even heavier with his soul in it—down a corridor that he never would have seen if the wolves weren't leading him. Dusty wished he could turn around and make sure he knew the way back, but with Grey's body draped over him, he simply couldn't. The wolves constantly glanced back, nervously staring at Dusty. Several more turns and long corridors later, Dusty's legs were about to abandon ship.

"Really?" he murmured.

"We are here," the wolf said. "Our den. The water is this way."

Dusty looked around the dark den, wondering if he had just carried Grey into certain death. The dinner that strolls into the fire. Could he have been so stupid?

"Right over here."

Dusty let out a sigh and tugged Grey even farther before he tripped and fell, sending Grey flying and landing with a thud followed by a groan.

"You have absolutely no respect for my poor body," Grey muttered.

"*Whatever.* I could have left you out there, but instead, I've carried you all the way into the wolves' den. Smart, huh?"

Grey chuckled. "With friends like you, I might move back in with Ranz. Any reason why my body won't move?"

"The wolves are venomous, of course."

"Of course." Grey paused. "I would have liked to see the stars... the sky."

Dusty's shoulder smarted as he pulled Grey closer to the water.

"Bathe his wounds," the wolf said. "He will be fine."

Dusty went to work, cleaning Grey's many, many wounds, including all of the damage Dusty had done in freeing Grey from the wardrobe, before getting to his own. The water worked fast. Only a few minutes later, his shoulder looked untouched—too bad his clothes wouldn't repair themselves too. Grey sat up, looking around the den at the wolves.

The main wolf approached. "May we leave? You know the way back, right?"

"I think so, and yes, go."

The wolf considered Dusty for a few seconds. "Sir, if I may...?"

"What?"

"The harvest time nears. Don't stay too long in the underworld. Don't give up finding a way out. You don't belong here."

"Okay, we'll get out as soon as we can."

The wolf bowed his head and led his pack out of the cave, clearly glad to be away from Dusty.

Grey frowned. "How? Why?"

"They think I'm something I'm not. Whatever. Grey, teach me to fight. We can't wait any longer. I'm going to get us killed."

*

Morgan stepped onto the cracked, desert ground, waiting to die but glad to live. Her first step shocked her body, a wave of heat flashed that instantly dissipated. In that instant, the others had died, but why had she lived?

She turned back to wave at Lille, Oriel, and all the others, but their worry fed her own, so she didn't tarry long. Her mission, maybe her reason for surviving so many times when death chased her, called to her and she turned toward the huge expanse.

As Morgan took her first few steps into the desert, she felt something unsettling. Grief. Horrifyingly heavy grief. Grief that infected Morgan in a way the heat hadn't. Her head slumped, but she forced her feet to continue. Tears, that didn't feel like her own, fell and sizzled on the ground. Morgan understood her battle had begun, not against the dryness or the heat but against a sorrow so deep it fought with her, dared her to lay down her burdens and accept the end.

*

Two steps beyond the veil that divided the caverns from the outside world, Nate turned back and struggled to find the entrance, finally seeing a small shimmering outline that would easily be missed. Did these doors exist everywhere? In Dunlowe?

Devra's cry cut short his questioning.

He saw panic flash on her face. "What is it?"

"Cecily is under attack. She can't hold on much longer."

Devra ran, with all of her young soldiers following. Darla's small legs practically flew to keep up, but Nate soon found himself almost at the lead and then in front.

He didn't need Devra to guide him because he heard the strangest shrieking cries that chilled his bones but didn't slow his limbs. When he broke through the brush, he saw them. Cecily. Finn. And Cecily's horse, Bear. All of them surrounded by swirling clouds of thousands of angry dark spirits.

A second later, the clearing took on an indigo hue. Nate turned and saw Devra glowing with a shocking dark light that seared his eyes, causing him to look away.

"Be gone," Devra shouted. "Back to the underworld!"

Her light grew and erupted, inspiring pain-filled howls from the spirits. One more flash and the clearing cleared just as the sun began to light the world. When Nate glanced at Devra, he found her hunched with Brody's arm supporting her.

Nate turned back to Cecily's still body on the ground.

"Careful," Devra whispered. "If they got in, she isn't Cecily anymore."

Nate's brow furrowed as he walked toward Cecily, who might or might not have an evil spirit inside her. Guilt seeped in when he wondered if he'd know the difference—she'd been a bit crabby the last time he'd seen her. Before he reached her, Finn flinched up, every ounce of his focus on Cecily.

"Cecily, are you all right? I can't hear you. *Think* something. *Say* something." Finn's desperation grew as he clung to Cecily's lifeless body.

Bear lowered his head and rubbed his muzzle lightly against Cecily's forehead.

"Is she...?" Nate asked.

Finn didn't look at Nate. "Her body... it doesn't have much

fight left in it, but her soul does. Just give her a minute."

"Finn," Devra said gently. "If she's compromised, you know what has to happen."

Finn rocked back and forth, cradling Cecily in his arms. "She'll be fine. She will... she has to be."

The sun rose and everyone silently watched and waited to know if the dark spirits had won. Darla's hand found Nate's for a moment before she pulled it away and looked to Devra, who nodded to her.

Darla walked across the clearing and knelt beside Finn and Cecily. "May I try? She did so much for me."

Finn appraised Darla, confused at first and then knowing. "Yes, Darla, please try."

Darla moved a bit closer and placed her forehead against Cecily's. A second later, Cecily gasped and looked up, her eyes filled with wonder as she smiled at Darla.

"Well, who became a big girl?"

Darla beamed. "Being a baby wasn't for me."

"That's because you didn't do it right."

Darla leaned forward and was swallowed by Cecily's embrace. "Thanks, Darla."

"Thank *you*, Cecily."

"I'm sorry," Devra said, moving closer, "but we have to know if you're infected."

Cecily studied Devra's face, searching for meaning. She looked to Finn, who then blurted a laugh.

"She's fine, Lady Devra," Finn said in stilted words, fighting against what seemed like embarrassed mirth.

Devra eased.

"How do we know?" Brody asked.

"The Ezias, once they take a body, have access to memories but not humor. They can simulate it, but not generate it—they have no understanding. Finn can hear her thoughts, which were humorous, yes?"

Finn flushed. "Yes, humorous... about..."

"No! Don't tell." Cecily hid her face against Finn's chest.

Finn laughed, holding Cecily in his arms as if life could end and he'd be complete where he was. How could Nate, the slave, compete with that?

"*Their bond is strong, but not unbreakable,*" Devra whispered in Nate's mind. "*He knows everything she is—and she gives fully of herself—but still, he keeps secrets from her. Their story isn't as solid as it appears.*"

Struggling just a little bit, Nate forced himself to say, "*Thank you.*"

Cecily looked to Devra, once her joy at surviving faded. "Thank you for saving us. Now who are you and...?" Her eyes found Nate's and a curious expression crossed her face, while Finn's eyes tightened just slightly. Nate grinned—Devra wasn't wrong. "I came searching for you and Darla, and here you are, saving me."

"You came for us?"

She nodded. "I was sorta dead for a while and had glimpses of those I care about—I saw your marks."

Nate lowered his head, shame burning.

"Nate, don't... we all have them."

"What?" he asked, his eyes meeting hers. "You do?"

"Not the same ones, but yes, we all have our stories and the wounds that come from them. I can't even stand—I'm nothing."

"No," both Nate and Finn said together, while Bear grunted.

"Okay, I'm *something*, but less than I was, even in Dunlowe. Do you know who you are now?"

Nate glanced to Devra and then back to Cecily. "No."

"There wasn't time when he was ready to hear," Devra said. "You were coming and we came a long way to meet you."

"Thank you for that. Now, who are you?"

Finn looked to Devra. "She's Lady Devra Devrile, one of the higher demons, the Keepers, sentenced with the world's care."

"Sentenced?" Cecily asked, gazing at Devra.

Devra wore a hard grin. "We all have pasts, don't we? Finn, let's take her below. I believe the effect will be powerful."

Finn nodded, while Cecily said, "Below?"

"Trust me." Finn kissed her forehead as she melted into him and Nate wanted to retch.

"*Below?*" Nate asked Devra.

"*Trust me*," Devra said, her grin filled with mocking, and Nate knew that a couple kids from Dunlowe had no business trusting any of these immortals.

✳

Logan stared at Pastor Rowe, keeping his focus. "Jem has your soul? How'd that happen?"

Before Pastor Rowe could answer, Mrs. Dumphry bashed him in the head with a branch, sending him sprawling to the ground, while Mrs. Daye took a stick from the fire and hit him repeatedly on the back. Pastor Rowe grunted while falling forward and then raised up. The moment his chest was an open target, Logan sent his blade flying. The knife stuck out from where it *should* have punctured his heart, but Pastor Rowe just flinched, staring at the blade—not dying or crying, just *staring*.

"We seem to have a misunderstanding here..."

Mrs. Dumphry hit him again... and again... and again. But he kept rising, kept *not* dying.

"Mrs. Dumphry," Jem said. "Stop."

She turned around and looked uncertain. "Are you sure? I could keep going."

Logan couldn't help but smile—inappropriately—at her focus and enthusiasm to the task of beating the snot out of Pastor Rowe.

Mrs. Daye patted Mrs. Dumphry's shoulder. "Good work, but I don't think it's helping."

"I don't know about that," Mrs. Dumphry said. "I know *I* feel better doing it." She raised the branch, but Jem stopped her, taking it from her hand and dropping it to the ground.

"What do you want from me?" Jem moved in front of Pastor Rowe, who remained on his knees, Logan's knife still in place.

"You killed me."

"I tried—but clearly, you didn't..."

"You did—*you* killed me. I thought to have a great death, if death found me. But I was certain the deals I made would bring me immortality. I think they have."

Jem looked like he was going to be sick. "Then you must be thrilled—you won. We can't kill you."

"You *did* kill me," Pastor Rowe said, his face revealing a struggle. "Things aren't exactly how I thought they'd be. I wanted eternal *life*, and now I think I've won eternal *death*."

"Then go be dead somewhere else. We don't like you—we hate you, in fact. We lost family members because of you... family members who are gone forever, while you remain, stinking up the place. You are vile. Just go away."

Pastor Rowe grumbled, "I can't."

"What? Why?" Jem pleaded.

"You killed me. I feel compelled to be near you, like I don't have a choice. You killed me and now you *own* me, I guess."

Jem raised his hands, backing away. "No way. Not going to happen. You go. *Anywhere*. But you aren't staying near me."

"I don't have a choice."

Logan squinted at Pastor Rowe. "Does this mean you have to do what Jem says?"

A flash of anger crossed Pastor Rowe's face before a rueful grin settled. "I always thought you were a complete idiot, Logan—not so unlike how I thought about everyone in Dunlowe. But clearly, you aren't nearly as slow as I thought."

Jem looked from Logan to Pastor Rowe. "You have to do what I say? Then go away."

"I can't... that's the one order I can't follow. I'm tied to you. My body brought me here against my will—you think I want to be here, near you? You think I wouldn't leave if I could?"

Jem looked lost.

"Just give him an order, Jem," Logan pressed. "I think this might be fun."

"Stand up."

Pastor Rowe was instantly on his feet, fairly spry for someone in his condition.

"Stand on one leg."

Pastor Rowe's leg raised, and Logan chuckled. Pastor Rowe scowled and a hint of satisfaction appeared in Jem's eyes.

Jem reached forward and pulled Logan's blade out of Pastor Rowe's chest. "Go hug that tree." Jem pointed at a tree twenty yards away. Pastor Rowe immediately complied, while Jem grabbed some rope and followed.

Logan watched as Jem tied Pastor Rowe to the tree and used some extra rope to bind his mouth. When Jem returned, he didn't look even a little amused.

"We've got to figure out a way to get rid of him. I wanted him dead—and I still feel bad about that—but I don't want to be stuck seeing him every day and feeling this hatred in my chest. Sure, he deserves what he got—but I don't."

"Jem, you mind if I go hit him a few more times?" Mrs. Dumphry asked and Jem couldn't help but laugh.

"I think we've done enough for tonight. I just want to get some sleep. Maybe tomorrow I'll let you sink him to the bottom of the nearest lake and see if that gets us free of him."

Mrs. Dumphry set a hand on Jem's shoulder. "I like the way you think."

*

Zoe heard the shouts from the soldiers under attack—Mindy and the others had come.

"Tell me!" Zoe begged. "Tell me what's happening."

"You have to take those children. Promise me you will take them. Don't let them be taken north like the others."

"We'll take them. I swear. What is happening?"

The man pulled away from her and marched across the

tent and back, his hands clenched in desperate fists. "It's torture for my family if I tell, but... but you're *Zoe Crane*. You lead the rebels. Maybe..."

Zoe didn't have the heart to tell him that she was just a girl doing the best she could—not some great leader—but in his frantic pacing, he wouldn't have heard her anyway.

After the fighting grew louder, calls for more soldiers, more weapons, he came back and stood in front of her, looking down on her with hope daring to shine from his dark green eyes.

"The king has gone mad, sees treachery in every direction. He's taken total power, makes every decision about our lives and the lives of our children. He believes that someone is coming to kill him and I pray to Dunn that *you* are that person. Please, Zoe, kill him and free my daughters... my wife. My brother's children. Any perceived slight and our families are taken as slaves. We are forced to serve. Our parents—not even the elderly are safe. There is a ruling class running Stoughton that is more cruel than anyone you've ever met—even Pastor Rowe. Promise me, you won't give up until you reach the Crownlands, until you free our people. Promise me."

"I promise I won't stop until death stops me. Stoughton will be free."

The man reached for his knife and severed the ropes that bound her, catching her when her body gave out. He held her for a few long seconds, her body resting against his.

"My daughters are Ella, Nelly, and Faye Browne. Free them, please. My wife is Haley. Please tell her I'm sorry—tell her I was brave. *Lie*."

Zoe felt the man press the hilt of his knife into her hand.

"No, fight with us. Don't give up."

"They will suffer worse if I betray... better to die." He released her for a moment and she saw the terror and grief in his eyes. "You promised."

Zoe bit her lip, fighting tears. "Tell me your name."

"Allen—Allen Browne."

He pulled her to him, hugging her desperately. "Do it now."

The tent flaps flew open and soldiers rushed in. "Sir, they are everywhere..."

"I will remember your family," Zoe quickly whispered before ramming the blade into his gut, twisting it in the process, ensuring death.

Allen grunted, his mouth still near her ear. "There's a traitor in your camp—he led you to us."

Zoe felt the blood drain from her face, just as surely as the blood fell from Allen's dying body, but she hid her shock and sorrow, shoving Allen's body to the ground. She raised her eyes to meet the soldiers' shocked glares, forcing a smile onto her face. "Yes, *we* are everywhere. Now come and get me."

15

Shades of Yesterdays

"You're getting better!" Grey crowed as Dusty muttered under his breath and rubbed a newly forming bruise Grey had just given him. "Improvement does have a price though."

"I'm getting that," Dusty grumbled.

"We should take a break."

"No. I need to learn. I'm better, but when you suck this badly at something, better isn't much of anything, is it?"

Grey patted Dusty's shoulder. "We're taking a break and you need to not be so hard on yourself."

"You would have died out there, and I would have watched for a while and then died with you." Dusty slumped to the ground, his head in his hands. "This is hopeless."

Grey sat next to him. "Hopeless, huh?"

"Yup."

"Maybe we don't need hope then."

Dusty looked up at Grey. "What do you mean? There is no hope?"

Grey shook his head and looked around the wolves' den. "Hope implies that we care about the ending."

"But I do care."

"And that is what you are stumbling over—and whatever those wolves told you that you won't tell me. Maybe it's okay not to have hope, just to do what we can." Grey's eyes locked with Dusty's. "If it is my time to die, then I will die. You don't have control over that. But you did what you could. You freed me from my cell. Carried me to this den. You didn't let me down by never learning to fight a pack of wolves, something that somehow felt really familiar to me."

"Not your first pack?"

He shook his head. "I don't think so. I think I've spent time in these caverns, *a lot* of time."

"You're remembering?"

"I think I am. I think the water in that pond right there healed more than my shoulder. I think it repaired my mind, somewhat."

"What do you know?"

"I know that time doesn't move right down here. It could be ten years or a few seconds that we've been down here, but we won't know until we leave. And every exit could lead us to another time and another place. I know we could be trapped here forever—maybe that's why Ranz didn't send his minions after us. Though I can't remember what it is, I know we need to be out of the caverns before the harvest comes. I also know that if we don't keep watch on the gateways, we could be trapped any time we leave the caverns, with no way back to the time you lived in or the people you care about."

"And the people *you* care about?"

Grey shook his head. "I still can't remember them."

"So what do we do?"

"Let's practice some more and then search for the exits that are hiding from us. We'll work together, Dusty. We don't need hope. We have a purpose and each other—that's enough."

*

Millie followed Oona as she raced through the tropical forest. Keeping up with a ghost proved difficult enough that her muscles cramped and tears trekked down her face.

"Just a little farther," Oona called. "You really must get in better shape. Much is coming and you need to be ready."

Millie pursed her lips to keep from saying anything she might—or possibly, might not—regret, but all of her irritation faded when she heard Charity's soft whimpers and saw her body lying on the ground, wet from the *suddenly there* and *suddenly gone* rains that seemed common for the island.

"I'm so sorry, Charity!" Millie launched herself at Charity, cradling her as well as a girl who'd spent her entire life being cradled by others could.

"You're here—I prayed you'd find me. What was I thinking? I'm so sorry I left you there... and like that. I had a snit and I'm so sorry. We are sisters, a team. I shouldn't have walked away."

"It's okay. We're together now, and you can be sure, I'm not letting you run off without me again."

"I won't. I promise."

They sat together in silence for a few minutes, while Millie pretended to be Charity and Charity behaved like Millie usually did. It was odd. All the while, Oona stood watching, a wistful look on her face. There weren't any other ghosts around just then, and Millie felt calm in their absence.

"*They are hopeful I will talk some sense into you about them, so they are doing as I asked and giving you some space.*"

Millie had to focus to keep from talking aloud. "*I wish you could convince them to vanish forever.*"

"*And I wish you'd stop being such a pathetic coward all the time and live up to your potential—so we all have things we yearn for.*"

Pathetic coward.

Pathetic coward.

Pathetic coward.

The words looped around in Millie's mind and wouldn't let go. Hurt grew, but with it came honesty, clarity. Oona was being honest in a way Millie's parents had never been. They'd coddled her and allowed her to hide. They'd done the best they could, but had they been right? Charity nurtured. The other sevens ignored or were snippy, but no one had ever said something so cruel and true to Millie in her entire life. Only Oona.

"*Will you always tell me the truth?*" Millie asked, staring at Oona.

"*You have my word—and I promise that means something real. Now, help her up and head for the camp. You need to get something to eat and warm clothes before our journey starts.*"

"*Journey?*"

"*They will be here soon, and we need to be ready.*"

"They *who?*"

Oona smiled. "*You wouldn't believe me if I told you.*"

∗

A maudlin bunch of idiots... everywhere. Stephanie watched Oriel, seeing his melancholy worn like a badge of honor. Lille—

pensive, sad, useless—certainly did not behave like a proper queen. All Stephanie wanted was some time away from this wretched troop of fools, but she couldn't think of any way to leave without being noticed. The brand on her stomach pulsed and she drew in a breath—Thorne was near. He was watching her and wanted her to come to him.

"*Ranz...*"

"*No, dearest, you must do this without me.*"

"*What, Ranz? Do what?*"

"*Your betrothed is trying to teach you. He can't be in your head like I can, but he can still communicate with you and you with him. You must learn from him. I will be around but away. And, dearest, any time you are with him, unless he has need to communicate with me, I will step away and give you time alone.*"

Butterflies, or possibly condors, flapped in her stomach as she felt Ranz vanish, though she still felt the connection, knew him able to hear her if she called loudly enough. Being afraid unsettled her, so she squashed it and concentrated on the pulsing. Four pulses. Two. Three. A small pulse, short, and then long pulses. Like a rapid heartbeat next to a long breath.

A smile formed on her face as she played Thorne's game, learning his code. The pulses were letters, and the patterns became clear.

S. T. E. P. H. A. N. I. E. C. O. M. E. T. O. M.E. N.O.W.

She grinned. But where? She took a step toward the hedgerows, but she felt nothing in the brand. She took a step toward the desert. Nothing. A step toward Lille's tent. Still nothing. Then she turned, facing north, and the brand tingled.

Stephanie loved having secrets. A secret fiancé. A secret

code. A secret destiny. She walked north, making sure to steal the sight from anyone who might be watching. But really, no one was watching her. The Commanders and everyone else had their hands and minds full of the desert tragedy and no room to worry about Stephanie.

With pulses and tingles, Thorne guided her to him and she walked proudly, like his future queen, wanting to show herself worthy.

"Hello," he said, his voice so rich and his accent alluring. His was the voice of a man—a powerful one—where Dusty still wore his boyhood, even though he had changed a lot since leaving Dunlowe.

An ache formed thinking of Dusty, measuring his worth next to Thorne's. It felt cruel and cold, two things Dusty had never brought out in her, but things she needed to be to accomplish all she must do. Thorne didn't want a sweet wife. He wanted a battler. A warrior queen.

"Thorne—should I call you *Thorne*? Or *your highness*?"

Amusement flickered in his eyes, barely changing his face that was still almost too beautiful to look at, a beauty and ruggedness that hurt her in some way. "I am and always will be Thorne to you, and you will be my Stephanie."

She nodded and gathered a breath before continuing. "I still think of Dusty, *often*. I don't mean to be disloyal, but I really do—*did*—love him. I just wanted you to know. Ranz offered to remove him from my mind, but I said *no*... not yet at least." Her words fumbled around and fled from her. "I loved him for as long as I can remember." She glanced down. "Even when I was a little girl, he was always everything to me, even when I couldn't tell him or be near him because of our town's rules."

Stephanie raised her eyes, timidly looking into his, seeing hardness. "I'm sorry."

Thorne's hand moved toward her face and she fought against moving away, still not certain how mad he was or what he might do. "You have nothing to be sorry for. It vexes me that Ranz offered that without consulting me. I will never allow parts of you to be erased. You are you and to be you, you must deal with your feelings for Dusty. It bothers me how deep his hold on you is, but I am still a stranger to you. I have faith you will one day see the value in a man—a *king*—over a boyish youth. But I can't malign him too much because he did have the good sense to love you and to treat you as the princess you always were. But I will treat you as the queen you were born to be."

Stephanie got a little lost, but Thorne brought her back into the moment by stroking her face, his thumb brushing against her lips. Tingles broke forth and her entire body warmed, leaning into him.

His face moved closer and he kissed her cheek as the brand pulsed and her breath drew in. Into her ear, he whispered, "I know how powerful the bond between us is, and it is just beginning. Let the boy hold a part of your mind. Don't fight against it and give it more power. I accept him as part of you. I accept that Ranz has access to thoughts I can't reach. But I will have what they won't, what no one else will. I will have you as my wife, my partner, this lovely body mine to cherish and know as no other man will."

Stephanie felt her head growing light as Thorne's arms encompassed her, holding her weight, keeping her from falling as everything about her got lost in him. All at once, she dared to take what she wanted and kissed him, the passion between them too overwhelming to rein in. His kisses seemed to burn, to singe inside her mind, sending flames through old thoughts, the shades of yesterdays and the days before. A newness emerged from the wasteland. Her place wasn't in the past—Lille had told her that once. It was in the present and the future. It would come from looking ahead, always seeing her direction.

And her direction was Thorne.

Stephanie Greysen, Queen of the Grey Folk and all Darienne.

*

Zoe stared at the three soldiers who looked less like monsters and more like men who were just as trapped as Allen by a brutal king and a fallen country. But she had to shove those thoughts away. They were soldiers who had to kill or capture her, or their families would pay the price. Better they die than fail.

Better *they* die—better *she* live to honor her promise to Allen, to Logan—she told herself, but even as she lunged for them, using her knife to tear their flesh, using her teeth and her legs, grappling in close quarters as she had never done before, she felt a part of herself dying. Hating her enemies had made murder possible, but her hate fell away with the knowledge of Ella, Nelly, and Faye Browne. Families living through desperate times, forced to tear their countrymen apart rather than go after the king who brought them to this horror.

Her eyes blinked, tears fell, as she stood in the middle of the tent looking at the three dead soldiers on the ground. She didn't flinch when Allen let out a small gasp and touched her ankle with his bloody hand.

"You *really* are Zoe Crane."

She knelt beside him. "I will never forget your Ella, Nelly, and Faye." She leaned and kissed his forehead and held his hand while he took his last breath. His eyes remained open, but their light had gone out.

Zoe felt her body trembling and hoped her legs would hold her as she stood, coming face to face with a ragged-looking Jacoby.

Jacoby's face wore such relief that Zoe could do nothing but stare until he rasped, "Come on, we have to go."

"The children?"

Jacoby nodded. "We've got them. Let's move."

*

I leaned into Finn's embrace as he lifted me. Once standing, he kissed my forehead, probably wishing to focus or even silence the scattered thoughts whisking and chattering around my mind. Nate was *here*, just a few feet away, looking so different, so mysterious. Darla, too, and she was a little girl, not a baby, though just weeks before she'd been that baby with white eyes who'd inspired the townsfolk to turn on the sevens. And Lady Devra with her stunningly beautiful eyes that changed colors as she stared... and her very, very constricting dress that accentuated curves that had made me giggle. I'd imagined myself in a dress like that and still chuckled at the thought, laughing into Finn's chest.

But all too soon, a dark shadow passed over my lighter thoughts, thoughts that attempted to shield me from reality. The

Ezias had almost found a way in—one small surrender and I would have lost myself completely.

One thought had kept me strong, but it didn't seem like the right thought. I didn't fight for Finn or Dusty. Bay or my sisters. Lille. My parents. I fought for the Source's mud. The Ezias would have denied me an ending, the chance to heal the scars from this life and the last. I'd been lying to myself for a while, hoping I could convince Finn to believe my deception, but I felt the Source's mud calling me. And becoming so breakable now seemed like a gift. The Source wouldn't have to destroy my soul now. I could just die and be at peace.

"*I'm sorry, Finn.*"

Finn's jaw clenched and he sent a dagger-laden expression at Nate, who looked back at us as we followed the others, while Bear kept pace beside me.

"*You were right that the Ezias wouldn't have given you that ending. You would have been captive in your body, until it was consumed. Removing the Ezias is something few can attempt and even then, it's usually deadly. I'm glad you fought for your chance to return to the* mud, *if not for me and for our love.*"

"*I'm sorry.*"

"*You already said that,*" he spat.

I cringed—being this close, this vulnerable, while he held a grudge against thoughts I couldn't control or hide from him made me feel like a captive already. "Nate," I called.

Nate instantly turned and walked toward us, surprise in his eyes.

"Would you mind carrying me for a little while? Finn *surely* is tired of this burden."

Finn looked deadly. "Cecily, no."

An order?

"I'd be honored to carry you." Nate's smile widened, while Bear blew snot at him which he dodged quite effectively. Nate studied Finn as he moved closer, seeming to prepare for impending violence.

"*Cecily.*"

"*Give me to Nate, and think about the sky or the dirt or the world ending, but get out of my thoughts for a little while. I won't be ashamed for thinking that being this weak, this useless, is any kind of life. Not for you—not when you can stand and run and live thousands of years. Give me to Nate, if you care about me at all.*"

Nate watched us, seeming to know a war was fought in the silence between us. Finn stepped toward Nate and gently handed me to him. His hands remained near until he was certain Nate had a good hold on me. Nate immediately turned and followed the others, leaving Finn and Bear.

I heard a grunt and smiled, knowing Bear had kicked Finn. Well done, old friend.

Nate said nothing for a little while, but as we walked his expression softened. "I like you in my arms, Cecily. I know you are with *that*—whatever he is—but you feel right just where you are."

I didn't want to agree and hurt Finn more, but I felt what Nate did. Memories. More good than bad. "Tell me everything that happened in Dunlowe," the chicken in me said.

He winked at me, knowing I was dodging, knowing what I was feeling, knowing a part of me that he could know because we had been humans together. We had shared what seemed like a lifetime of love. I fought the urge to run my fingers along his naked scalp, covered in mysterious and *attractive* designs. I felt the yearning for him that I thought—I'd been so certain—had died.

Nate told me everything. My relief at hearing that my parents were alive when Nate fled had me resting my face against his chest. Then he told me the words that made me cry—that my father had been the one to stand up for Nate and Darla. He gave them the chance to survive and might have given his life because of it.

I told Nate everything about my journey. About cararks. The Source. Laura and Britton. The pain. Dusty and the end of the sevens' bond.

Darla's hand rested on my hand. "We're going underground now. Don't be scared. This will be good."

"Bear? Will he be okay?"

"Of course," Lady Devra called. "Everyone touch."

Bear caught up with us and I looked over at him. His eyes were wary, as he lowered his head onto Nate's shoulder as Nate cringed, just as we crossed through the veil and entered the inside of the world.

∗

Dusty and Grey walked near the walls of the caverns long enough that Dusty began to believe there were no exits—no ways out of the middle of the earth. And who the heck decided that there should be a middle of the earth in the first place? That was just plain stupid. Life should be lived outside the world's core, with fresh air, green grasses, and puffy clouds.

His hand, that had been running along the wall, hit some free space and he stopped abruptly enough that Grey ran into him.

"Sorry. What is it?"

Dusty stared. "It looks like rock, just like the rest of the walls, but there's nothing there."

Grey ran his hand along the wall and watched as his hand drifted into the empty space. "Good job! Shall we see where we end up?"

As much as Dusty wanted to see blue sky more than anything, he felt a tightness in his chest about taking this path. But his mouth, with pride attached, said, "Sure. Lead the way."

Grey studied him, his friendly grin in place, clearly seeing through Dusty's totally false bravado. "We'll stick together. Keep your hand on my shoulder, just in case."

"In case of..."

"Just in case."

"Right."

Grey drew his sword and Dusty pulled his dagger, resting his non-dagger-holding hand on Grey's shoulder, feeling puny next to the massive grey man. Together, they walked down the hidden corridor all the way to the end where a shimmering fabric-looking surface blocked the way.

"Okay, here goes. Look behind us, no matter what is in front. We need to be able to get back in here."

"All right," Dusty said.

Grey stepped through the exit and Dusty looked behind, memorizing the sight of the tree they had emerged from, but his focus quickly faded at the sound of Grey attacking something that snarled. Like really, really snarled in a decidedly intimidating way.

When Dusty turned away from the entrance, his eyes got stuck on the massive beast twice Grey's size that had chomping sharp teeth on *both* of its heads and something oozing all over his skin. Gross and yikes.

"I'm thinking this isn't where we want to be," Dusty muttered.

"Good call. Get us back in there while I keep fighting."

"Yeah..." But when Dusty turned back, the tree was gone, and with it, their way out.

16

Hazy

Zoe fought her way to the rest of the rebels, beside Heath and Jacoby, Mr. Daye, Mr. Pollak, and so many others. Mrs. Hardy rushed the children along, while Mindy used her bow to kill everyone in their way. All through the fighting Zoe felt a tidal wave of emotion growing and growing, and the moment she stopped running, the moment they were far enough away to gather their breaths and rest, she looked to Mindy.

"I need a minute. Watch over them." Not waiting for an answer, Zoe bolted from the group, racing through the woods, glad for the darkness that matched her soul.

A fallen branch tripped her and brought her crashing to the ground, scraping more places than could register, as she cried into the moss-covered dirt. Breathing in ragged gasps that had her lungs protesting, her body stuttered through the grief choking her. So much death. So much. Everywhere she looked.

Her hands, her face—covered in blood and mud. She'd never get clean. And the one person who could make her smile, could bring her hope, was miles away, maybe dead.

The truth, the real possibility that she might never see Logan again, gripped her like a plague. What if at the end of all of this—when she was nothing more than the butcher of men and women trapped by circumstances into being her enemies—there was no happy ending for her? What if Logan succumbed to his wounds? What if he was dying right this moment?

The images flashed through her mind. The sight of Logan being shot with so many arrows that it made no sense that he had survived as long as he did. The sounds of his breathing. The dullness of his eyes. Her mind conspired against her and she sobbed even harder.

"You really are Zoe Crane."

Allen's words. The proof of her identity came in the bodies littering the ground. Zoe Crane was a killer.

A hand rested on her back and she flinched up, knocking the hand away before she even saw who had come for her.

Jacoby. Again.

"What do you want?" she spat.

Faced with her venom, he quietly said, "To see if you are all right."

"Why do you care?"

He studied her face, his green eyes catching the moonlight, reminding her so much of Allen that she shuddered, her body trembling uncontrollably. "You're not all right." Jacoby moved toward her, wrapping her in his arms and holding her tightly.

A distant voice reminded her that Jacoby might be the traitor, but for this moment, she didn't care if he was, not even if he killed her.

"Let it out. You've held it in for too long." His words, rough and deep, rumbled in his chest, words she felt on the side of her face that rested against him. "You lost your brother, your mother... and *your* father. But you found something else—you found love. You found that life moves on, no matter how gruesome it is. Logan is still out there, and he needs you to live as much as you need him. We must continue... until there is nothing left to fight for."

The tiny tyrant inside her sought to regain some pride and shove her pain away, deny this stranger the chance to help her, but with death and grief so near, she gave in, sobbed against him, allowed his arms to hold her body together. To keep her from breaking.

"You continue for your daughter," she whispered after her tears ran dry.

"Yes... for Emmaline."

"We can't let her reach the Crownlands."

Jacoby pulled away and stared at Zoe, moving his hand under her chin so that he could place her face in the path of the moon's rays. "What do you know?"

"The children—*all* of us—were meant to be taken to the Crownlands and sold into slavery."

"No," he breathed. "She won't even remember having been born free... and loved."

Zoe nodded in his hand. "I think that's the point."

"Please, come with me. We have to tell the others. We have to make a plan, and you need to know what we decided while you were gone."

Zoe saw how hard Jacoby worked to control the desperation growing inside him, the images assailing him of his daughter raised as nothing but a slave, never knowing love or warmth, never knowing she was everything to her father. That she had a father who would slaughter half the world, do whatever it took to make her safe, even if he didn't survive.

He simply couldn't be the traitor… unless he'd made a deal to sacrifice Zoe and the others to save his daughter. He could—he *would*—do it with a clear heart. But the only way to know was to get closer, to rely on him, to draw him in. She had to know, so she nodded to him and together they walked back to the others, passing the tree Mindy lurked behind, always watching over Zoe as she'd promised.

*

The sun beat down on Morgan's body and she felt her skin growing more taut. Swarms of birds and bugs flew, some frantically, searching for places to land, their worlds having changed while they were in flight. Her steps grew more unsteady as she continued, feeling slivers of the death that had killed the others but that didn't fully reach her. Not fully, but she was far from okay as she continued, with no landmarks that mattered anymore. Only the sun and it ravaged her.

Her mind, singed by the never-ending heat, betrayed her, sending visions that weren't real. Mirages of not just pools of cool water, but of people she'd loved. Some whom she'd lost. Cecily kept showing up, smiling, hopeful, strong, carrying the power that could save the world. Morgan rushed to her the first time, feeling confident that something had happened, something had restored her. But when Morgan reached her, Cecily vanished.

Morgan's parents appeared and vanished in the exact same way, leaving Morgan weeping on the dry ground, until she forced herself up and her feet to keep moving. One by one, visions came and went, leaving Morgan more lost in this desert than just her location. Her mind, the thing she had always relied on, became hazy, as hazy as the glare over the desert. Reality and imagination merged and after hours and hours—how many she would never know—she began to wonder who she was and why she had come here. Her pack grew heavy, so she left it behind, not remembering why it was important.

Morgan seemed to see stars... and Oriel. She seemed to remember things beyond the scope of this life. The scar on Oriel's face—somehow she knew she had caused that scar. Places appeared in her mind, rooms she had known. The burned remains of a Delphea grove. More stars, these she could see through a massive device that made millions of miles away seem near. And with a terrible shudder, she saw the bloody, beaten body of Dusty Daye. The image wavered, like looking at someone across a bonfire, the heat blurring everything, just as the desert heat blurred Morgan's mind.

Morgan knew she'd made a mistake in coming here. She shouldn't have done this, shouldn't have believed she could overcome a power so great. She was still new to her powers—powers that could only help her to disappear forever in this dry prison—and wasn't ready for this test.

She stumbled to the ground the moment her belief in herself faltered. She wasn't a princess, had no business near a queen—she was still the girl who everyone forgot. Not someone with a great purpose. Dry gusts came and carried away the proof of her passing, until her body was an island in a seemingly endless dead sea.

All turned quiet; the birds had fled. Her cheek rested against the chafed ground and she closed her eyes.

"I'm not the person I thought I was," she whispered. "Or maybe I am."

Shade suddenly covered her and she sighed, attempting to sink deeper into the unyielding ground.

"You are exactly who I raised you to be," a voice said, a familiar voice, one straight out of a memory.

When Morgan opened her eyes and looked up, she found a man squatting next to her, blocking the sunlight that gave him a halo and shaded his face too much to make out.

But she didn't need the face when she had the voice. Another mirage, this one seemed so real... even more real when her grandfather reached down and patted her face.

"It was worth it, Morgan, everything I've done and everything I will do—don't ever doubt it."

*

Crap. Crap. No really, *crap*.

"Grey!" Dusty screamed. "I can't find it! I can't find the way out!"

Grey lunged at the monster whose mouths snapped at him. "That's not very helpful."

"I don't think you get how serious this problem is."

Grey stabbed at the beast. "Oh, I think I have an inkling."

"Grey, it's really gone. The doorway. The tree. It's gone."

Grey dodged the beast's left head, almost sending Dusty to the ground. "Busy... but thanks for clearing that up."

Dusty looked back and the tree was still *gone*, like really, really not there. "Grey..."

Grey grunted and stumbled as one of the heads made contact and tore at his shoulder. Grey blood splattered Dusty's face as he turned.

Dusty slumped. Not *again*.

While the beast stopped to savor Grey's flesh, Grey looked at Dusty, his eyes fiercely burning. "Use your weapon. Let's fight together... till the end."

Grey's calm through his pain inspired calm in Dusty, who nodded, and felt something in his gut as he held his sword. A strange kind of certainty. His chest didn't burn like it had when that crazy power had come out of him when his friends were about to get killed. This was something different—something that could be worried about later. For now, Dusty stepped out from behind Grey, distracting the beast's focus away from his wounded friend. He raised his sword, while grabbing his dagger with his left hand, and let out a battle cry that almost made him sound like a worthy fighter as he charged into the fray.

*

Stephanie lay on the ground on a soft blanket in Thorne's arms. He kissed her, held her, caressed her, and for all of it, Stephanie's mind and body seemed to have disappeared except for the pleasure he brought her. Her worries faded, her memories too.

But something felt familiar about Thorne's touch, something strange that brought her mind back to her. This shouldn't feel so familiar. She'd never been in his arms before and his touch was entirely different than Dusty's. Dusty touched her with a reverence, a request. Thorne touched her as though he had the right, that she would not deny him, that she *couldn't* deny him.

Stephanie felt Thorne's care for at least the idea of who she was. He was committed to giving her pleasure, not just taking his own. She felt that, believed it. But there was something wrong here, something like a dream that skirted the edges of her memories. Something to make her pause... and to pull away from him.

"What's wrong, Stephanie?"

"It's just too much... all of it. I've been away a long time. I should get back."

Thorne seized her hand. "Tell me. You weren't thinking of *him* while I..."

Stephanie shook her head. "I'm not thinking of much when you touch me. You kind of steal my mind."

A cheeky smile flashed across his face. "Then why would you want to get back?"

"Out here with the moonlight and you, I fear we might go too far. I'm not your wife yet, and I have no interest in being a woman who..."

He raised his hand, thankfully stopping her words. "I wouldn't want that for you... even if I do yearn to go *exactly* too far. The pleasure I will show you is like none you have known..."

Thorne continued talking while images formed in her mind, imaginings of exactly what he was saying, exactly what he would do, and feeling somehow that he had already done it. A chill brought ice to her veins. Something wasn't right, but he couldn't know that, so she listened as he sought to woo, but her core had turned cold.

He seemed to sense the change in her and his words faded.

"Later, Thorne. Let's talk about this later. I need to get back."

Confusion filled his grey eyes, along with surprise. She saw his confidence waver. He was so certain about himself that her reaction stumped him. Stephanie kept her smile hidden on the inside, but liked the feel of it. She'd wanted to please Ranz and her future husband, but all this being predictable and accommodating really didn't fit. Being controlled really didn't suit her, strange as that was in her present circumstances.

Even knowing that Ranz would peruse her thoughts later didn't scare her because something flickered in her mind, a truth she could own. Both Ranz and Thorne needed *her*. Ranz could wear her body but it would only be a matter of time before he was found out, and cast out. He could use her power on everyone, but there were others with powers who would stop him. Besides, she'd seen the toll his possession took on him; she'd seen him weak.

Yes, they both needed her and she liked being needed, being important, but she didn't like being used.

"Thorne, this is an arranged marriage and I don't have the option to say *no* if I want to get what I want. Why are you trying to woo me?"

Thorne's brow furrowed and his eyes took on a violent glow.

Her heart fluttered but Stephanie Trench still lived inside her and she held herself still and glared right back at him. "You think you can frighten me into a quivering mess and that I'll do what you want? You and Ranz made some deal for me. You both branded me. But I am part of this too. I've made a deal too, to go along with this, because I want to be queen. I'm finding my way in all of this. I'm learning about my new life. And I do want to get to know you—*you*, not just your lips. After we are married, you will have my body when and *if* I say so, but it is still my body, unless you want Ranz to take over and be amorous with him, and he's not that pretty."

Thorne looked sufficiently horrified and Stephanie felt relieved that that terrible option wasn't something any of them wanted.

"Stephanie, I…"

"You've been cavalier in love before, but I've only ever been loved by a boy who really and truly *loved* me. I can see the difference, feel it. It's time for you to get to know me, because I'm not Daryn—I don't want to be Daryn. I've never met her and I never will. I don't want to just be some shadow of a dead person who is trapped married to a man who doesn't love, know, or care who I am."

"Stephanie, I…"

"We're done here. I'll see you later." Stephanie enjoyed the flummoxed look on his face, the product of meeting the real Stephanie Trench.

But she didn't remain to enjoy his bafflement, and marched back toward the force hanging around the edge of the expanding desert that might prove to be a bigger problem than her own love life. *Might.*

*

Bay didn't want to say it—really didn't want to think it—but it was staring him down and he had no choice but to flinch.

"We can't go to the shore. Not here." With Bay's words, the others in his boat looked toward the beach—the shore that they had originally started from, the shore where Bay had saved

Stephanie from drowning herself, the shore that had become desert.

"Well, I'll be..." Mortimer muttered, his hand protectively placed on Amanda's shoulder.

"This doesn't mean they are all gone, right?" Abigail asked, having remained in the boat with her sister seven.

Amanda let out a worried huff. "We don't know what it means for our friends, but we know what it means for us. We can't get back from here, and we might be safer remaining on the water." She looked to Bay. "What will the desert do to this water—I mean, underneath the sea—if it spreads?"

Bay pointed to the shore. "See the water steaming?"

"Yeah."

"If the desert keeps expanding, it will drain the sea and we won't be able to hide here. If we go north and then get onto land, there's no guarantee the desert won't kill us."

Amanda looked determined. "Let's stay on the water then, and head south. See if we find life there... anywhere. We can always go north to the Wild Wood if we just need to get on land at some point."

Bay nodded, agreeing with her assessment, while hoping she was shielded from his own. A weight pressed on his heart as he imagined Cecily burned. Morgan. Dusty. Finn. Oriel. Lille. Darienne. To think it had come to this, and he still didn't know if his crimes had something to do with it. They could, he supposed, but still chose to doubt that anything he had done could lead to something this momentous and horrifying.

How could the Source allow this to happen? Send Cecily back to a world that was dying? It didn't make sense—none of it made any sense.

17

Relevant

Jem stomped back into the camp, followed by Mrs. Dumphry, both of their faces covered with a hefty dose of disbelief mixed with dismay. It didn't take long for Logan to understand their feelings as he watched Pastor Rowe trail behind them, sloshing water.

"Didn't work?" Logan asked.

Jem scowled. "Didn't work. He was at the bottom of the lake for hours while we had a nice picnic... and then like the force of evil he is, he got loose and showed up again."

"I tied him tightly. I used *heavy* rocks." Mrs. Dumphry looked baffled. "I think we're stuck with him."

"No," Jem breathed, but Logan heard his surrender.

"Put him to work and watch him closely."

"Work?" Pastor Rowe asked.

Jem looked to Logan, squinted, and then nodded. "We need a latrine dug. Come with me, *Clevis*."

Logan smiled hearing Pastor Rowe's first name and enjoyed the hostile but helpless expression on his face. They might be stuck with him, but he wasn't the big man anymore. He'd help with whatever they needed until they figured out a way to make the undead really dead.

Zoe would think this was comical, or quite possibly she would have run Pastor Rowe through with a sword every single morning just to be sure. Yeah, probably more with the stabbing than the laughing.

Zoe.

Logan lost his humor, felt his aches, the loudness of them, the way they reminded him of his weakness every time he thought to stand up and go after Zoe. She would be fighting, maybe—no, he couldn't think it. Couldn't think of bad endings when things between them had just begun.

"Drink some of this, Logan. We'll keep an eye on things and you will rest." Mrs. Daye's voice was kind, like she knew exactly what he was thinking. "I promised Zoe I would take care of you like you were my own child. I will. We survivors are all family now."

"We are. It's strange, you know?"

"What?"

"You looking after me."

Mrs. Daye's expression softened as she tried to understand. It took a few seconds and she whispered, "Because your mother left... because you've been without a mother for so long?"

Logan nodded, grateful she didn't make him say it. All these years later and it still stung.

Mrs. Daye brushed her hand on Logan's face. "Well, you have more mothers than you know what to do with now, and this one is going to force you to sleep. And that one..." She nodded toward Mrs. Rowe who was staring at them. "... is going to keep an eye on you while you do."

Mrs. Rowe moved closer, her face pale, still not over the shock of her strangely living dead husband. "I will watch over you, Logan, and keep you safe. You gave my kids a chance at life... I hope."

Mrs. Daye reached for Mrs. Rowe's hand while Logan patted her arm. "My kids and your kids are out in the world, and it is a dangerous world, but I'd still rather they be out there than here."

Mrs. Rowe nodded, while helping Mrs. Daye to pour the warm liquid into Logan's mouth, giving him not one chance to refuse. Within a few seconds, his brain grew hazy as his body drained of tension. Only one thought remained, a prayer in case the Great God Dunn was still listening. A prayer for Zoe.

*

Nate dodged a goofy grin on Darla's face when she looked at him carrying Cecily, whose head rested against his chest. He'd be a liar if he didn't admit that holding her and being this close was the answer to many, many prayers. And she really didn't seem to judge him for... well, anything. She seemed *attracted* to Devra's marks on his head, not disgusted. There was a look in her eyes that seemed like the old Cecily, but everything about her showed how much she'd been through and how much she'd changed.

"I think you can put her down now," Devra said, her eyebrow raised and challenging.

"Down?" Cecily asked.

"An experiment." Devra added for Nate alone, "*Sorry, but we need to know.*"

Nate pouted and then smiled. "*Thanks a lot.*"

He gently lowered Cecily, placing her feet on the ground

and holding the rest of her upright, while Finn, the immortal *nanny man*, lurked nearby as if Nate was going to watch the love of his life crumple to the ground while doing nothing. Whatever. Cecily clearly trusted Nate and never looked to her *supposed* true love for help.

Cecily rested her hands on his arms as she tested out her weight, understanding without being given any explanation about the nature of the experiment. She eased her weight onto her own legs, while lessening her hold on Nate. A second later, a smile broke forth as she stood without any assistance.

"How?" she asked, all of her focus on Devra.

"The middle of the earth is a very different place. Most wounds are healed by crossing the veil—not that I think yours are gone forever, but I thought you might be without pain. Hunger, age, time—it's all a muddle down here."

Cecily spun around, finally throwing a glance at Finn that faded quickly as she turned away again. Nate smirked at Finn just before Cecily turned to him, a dazzling smile on her face.

"I like it here," she declared while Darla skipped into her arms.

"Race ya."

Cecily laughed. "Maybe a little later. For now, I'd like some answers." She looked to Devra. "Do you have answers?"

Devra's expression drew shadows. "I have answers for you and a welcome to my current domain."

Cecily glanced around the cavern. "This is your home?"

"Not just here, but the underworld, yes."

Cecily tensed. "Are the Ezias down here? Will they try to infect us?"

"They are deeper—usually. And no, they will not or they will be severely punished. Over this domain, I have a great degree of power. Over the outside world, I have little."

Nate thought of Devra's power over the people of the Wild Wood. Of the thefts of all of the Oades' children.

"Yes, Nathaniel, you are right to question, and the time has come for answers."

Brody stepped forward, putting himself between Devra and Nate. "Don't tell him. He can't be trusted and you could be... *hurt*."

"You are good to me, Brody, just as you have always been, but Nathaniel has a right to know and Cecily and Finn, and their trusty Bear, have come a long way. For them to fight with us, it is right for them to know who I am and why I am here."

"Should I beat Nate soundly first, just to put him in a more respectful state of mind?" The other child soldiers laughed while Brody looked ready to kill Nate upon one word from Devra.

"No, the time has come to see if our work has any hope. If it doesn't, you will go back to your families to do what you can for them until the end of times comes."

"I will stay with you," Brody said. "Forever."

"As you wish." She turned to Finn. "Are you going to tell her, or am I?"

Finn looked decidedly uncomfortable and cast a worried glance at Cecily, who seemed confused.

"Tell me what?"

"It's not relevant—it *never* was."

Devra shook her head. "Just like a man—but it *is* relevant and it *always* was. And you left Annisha to find out *after* you married her and I paid the price for that."

"Annisha was always fair—to you and everyone else she ever judged."

"Then why was I banished to this place with this mission when my supposed compatriots weren't? Why was I banished at all? I did nothing to deserve this. Nothing but exist as a demon. And if Annisha was so fair, why were demons treated...?"

Finn pulsed with rage. "Devra, *really*, you can't think that Ranz and Delibrien didn't pay this high a price. If anything, you got the best end possible, and look how you've found a way to use that. You were given something to tend, a way to be redeemed. They weren't given that."

"You fool. I was left to anguish eternally in this place. Given a world to tend, but not the resources to do the job. I've had to steal children from the villages of the Wild Wood. All of these children are stolen and they know it, but they believe in this fight. And I've kept stealing them, even past what I needed, in the hopes that they would continue to live after the end comes." Indigo tears fell from her eyes. "They gift me with their trust after I've become this odious thing who lives in nightmares, all while I try to save them and the world that will soon abandon them." She brushed at her tears. "Tell her or I will."

"Tell me what?" Cecily asked, while the question, the knowledge about to come, seemed to weaken her.

Finn swallowed loudly enough to cause an echo in the chamber. "I was married—and divorced—before I married Annisha." He paused, his eyes veiled. "To Lady Devra."

✶

Millie fell to the ground as soon as she and Charity reached the main village filled with Grey Cloaks who did nothing but stare at the soggy, bedraggled hostages.

"*Your people are super friendly,*" Millie spat inside her head.

Oona looked at them, her eyes sad. "*They have their own struggles.*"

Millie didn't much care about that, but when she glanced around her, she did notice what she'd missed before—there were absolutely no children in the camp. "*Any suggestion on who might help us? Give us warm clothes?*"

"*Her.*" Oona pointed at the woman who had given them food when they first arrived.

When the woman noticed Millie and Charity, Millie said, "Could you help us? We're cold, hungry, and Charity hurt her ankle."

The woman said nothing but nodded, gestured to some of the other women who came near them, gathered them up, and helped them into a small hut. Most of the women left, but the one woman remained. Without a word, she filled a tub with hot water, helped them bathe and change into the soft grey clothing the rest of them wore. After she wrapped Charity's ankle in a poultice, she gave them hot stew and nodded for them to rest on her bed. Then she left.

Tired enough she almost fell asleep before closing her eyes, Millie struggled to stay awake long enough to look at Oona.

"*Sleep, Millie. I'll wake you when we need to go.*"

*

Dusty's eyes flashed to his sword that was smeared with blood... that wasn't his own—and it wasn't Grey's. Awesome. But the fight wasn't over. The beast's left head seemed madder than his right, but both hadn't let up and they'd been fighting for what seemed like hours, but might have been a few seconds.

The left head reeled back and then struck; the forehead of the beast connected with Dusty's chest, knocking the air out of him and sending him flying to the ground. Grey jumped forward to counter, but after a few seconds, he stumbled. Grey's blood drained down his cloak and would have been more obvious if it weren't grey on grey.

Dusty barely had time to gather a breath before his body flinched up and back into the fight. With Grey fading fast, he knew it was up to him to do this—that was just not a good feeling, but he wouldn't let his friend down again. Ever.

He raised his sword that seemed to weigh more than it had just a few minutes before and ran at the beast, clutching his dagger at the ready. When the right head struck, Dusty dodged and sent his sword into the chest the two heads shared, while using the dagger to slice at the left head's neck—his dagger becoming lodged in place.

The beast reared, its front hooves striking at the air close enough that Dusty felt the breeze they created. It took a few seconds to realize that while the creature became more enraged, Dusty was standing, gaping, and completely weaponless.

Crap was all he thought as the beast seemed set to lunge again, when it suddenly crumpled to the ground, grunted, and died.

Hmmph.

Dusty crept toward the nicely quiet, dead beast, leaning closer, his hand extended, waiting for some frightening flinch that didn't come as he extracted his sword and dagger. He wiped the blood away on his pant leg, looking more like a filthy, triumphant warrior than he'd ever imagined. After returning his weapons to their scabbards, he turned toward Grey lying helpless on the ground.

About to move toward him, Dusty froze when he heard a sound that was very much like the beast's, only a higher pitch. He turned and stared at the dead beast that was thankfully still dead, but movement from the corner of his vision had him backing up.

Dusty rushed toward Grey, gripped his arm, and dragged him up and over his shoulder, finding it easier than the last time.

"What is it?" Grey muttered, pain choking his words.

"Evil beast has a wife and *she's* not happy."

Dusty heard the pounding of her hooves as he lunged toward the space where the tree had been and felt the cool breeze as they fell through the veil into the underworld.

"So that would be the wrong door, I'm thinking," Grey said, sounding stronger.

Dusty set Grey down and looked at his shoulder, but the wound was gone. "You think?"

"Better luck next time, right?"

"I think I hate you."

Grey grinned. "Dusty the warrior."

Dusty beamed at him. "Well, maybe I don't hate you that much."

*

Zoe stood surrounded by the rebels who looked unsurprisingly like tired and wounded townsfolk. Her tales of the Crownlands, the enormity of what had become their fight, lived like an evil spirit amongst their group, stealing the hope that peace could be found if they just had the chance to explain.

"We should hide... make a life somewhere else," Mr. Pollak said, while others riled up.

"Are you kidding?" Mr. Daye demanded. "Do you really think we can find some out-of-the-way burg to hide in and raise our families? Dunlowe was the southernmost town in Stoughton—that didn't save us from anything. If what Zoe learned is true, they were starting at the bottom edge of Stoughton, with the intention of moving north, swallowing up the entire country with this new way of life—slavery. That is not something we can live with."

Mr. Pollak sputtered, "We aren't an army... we can't do this."

Jacoby stood. "We will do this. We have to. We need to fight for those who can't fight for themselves. We have to save the others..."

"Your daughter, for instance," a man from Darstel said. "Let's not pretend you don't have something in this fight."

Jacoby launched at the man and a second later they were brawling in the middle of the circle while everyone leapt to their feet, pulling and shouting and risking all of their lives with this nonsense.

Zoe nodded to Mindy who drew an arrow, strung it in her bow, dipped the tip into the fire, and shot it at the ground in the middle of everyone.

"Enough," Zoe said quietly. Everyone stilled. "Your pointless fighting could get us killed—could end any chances we have to help anyone, including ourselves. Jacoby, get off him. And whoever you are," she said to the other man, "knock it off. We don't have time for this."

Jacoby nodded to her, while the rest looked to her to continue.

Zoe turned to Mr. Daye. "What do you think?"

"I think you'll make the right choice for all of us."

"What?"

Jacoby moved closer, rubbing his jaw. "That is what we decided while you were gone—it's why we came for you, risking all of our lives for yours."

Zoe looked from Mr. Daye to Jacoby. "I don't understand."

"You're our leader—those soldiers knew it, just as we know it."

"I'm just a girl from Dunlowe. I'm not a soldier—Mindy would be better..."

Mindy laughed, a very strange and unfamiliar sound. "My first instinct is to shoot... *whoever*. I'm not a leader, but I will follow you into the fire any *where*, any *time*, any *day*. And before the others decided that we were coming for you, Heath, Jacoby, Mr. Daye, and I were already on our way. We see you. Those soldiers came for you and you alone. They know that you are the leader of this rebellion, Zoe Crane. So tell us where we're going."

A weight seemed to fall from the sky and land hard upon Zoe's shoulders. Could she do this? Could she lead? Why her? Why not her?

None of the people around her had been soldiers. They were farmers and blacksmiths; none of them knew anything about war. In this, she had more experience than they did. Something inside her quivered, but not for long before she looked at Mr.

Daye, who smiled at her as though she had made him the proudest man alive.

"Where are we going, Zoe?"

"We're going east. Now. We'll rest and attack the soldiers wherever we find them along the way."

"Along the way... where?" Jacoby asked.

"To kill the king."

✱

"You're not real," Morgan whispered over her parched throat, her eyes struggling to remain open, holding onto the false sight of her grandfather.

"Who is these days?"

It hurt to hear him—to see him—but she couldn't send him away. "I've missed you."

"Morgan, my dear, I've missed you too, but I made it back. I'm so very sorry it took so long."

Morgan's eyes tugged at her to close and she let them, the dryness growing painful. "I shouldn't talk to mirages... shouldn't give away my mind."

"But if you don't talk to mirages, how will you discover that they aren't mirages at all?"

"You aren't real—you died. I buried you."

"Ah, well, you did—or rather, you *think* you did."

Her eyes opened. "I buried you."

"You buried rocks, infected with a glamour."

Morgan shook her head. "You are a very strange mirage, you know that?"

"Morgan," he said, brushing his hand against her face,

feeling so very real. "Don't believe what your eyes tell you, only what your heart does."

Morgan flinched and sat up, staring at the man, remembering those words from the visions the Delphea trees gave her. She fought to swallow over nothing but a mucky kind of dryness. "I buried you. You died."

"I hated to do that to you, but my time was almost up and I found out that you might face this very test... and fail. Once I knew, I couldn't let it go, let *you* go. I sought out a man—a demon really—who could help me and he did. And here I am."

"But..." Morgan's brain stammered, giving her nothing but hurt. "You died and left me alone to face that horrible town. *Alone*. Always alone. How could you do that to me?"

"Honey, I had to. I simply had to."

"Why?"

Before he could answer, a strange shrieking came from the ground and the day turned to night as dark spirits blotted out the sky, surrounding Morgan, before they howled and launched at her.

18

A Portent of Things to Come

STEPHANIE APPROACHED THE CAMP and found it silent, eerily silent, before shouting broke out. The Commanders' chanting grew louder—chanting that meant they were about to start poisoning the world, like *that* was ever helpful. Sharp voices accused and warriors shouted. Stephanie hurried toward the ruckus, shoving soldiers out of the way until she found Lille clutching her side where her lavender blood flowed. A bloody dagger lay near her feet, and Duncan and Capria—the former leaders of the Protectors and Conquerors before Lille became queen and tore all that up—struggled against the soldiers, while Lille sought to calm the Commanders. Their chanting diminished and all eyes turned to Lille.

Into that abrupt silence, Stephanie blurted, "What is going on here?"

Lille cast a glance at her, her eyes narrow. "Where have you been?"

"Walking... I was bored."

The narrowness grew instead of lessening. Lille's eyes appraised Stephanie's appearance and Stephanie suddenly wondered if she looked like she'd spent several hours wrapped around the enemy. Was she mussed up? Her lips too red or puffy? Things she'd never had to worry about suddenly became stupidly important. Stephanie longed for the end of this charade when all of these people would know that she wasn't one of them or a duplicitous traitor, but a right and proper enemy.

"Duncan and Capria attempted to murder our queen." Oriel's hand twitched while holding a dagger to Duncan's neck.

"I need healing before we deal with this," Lille said. "Guard them."

Lille stumbled into the tent as the healers swarmed around her. Genovan looked helpless, though his glare at Stephanie told her that all of her mysteries probably weren't mysteries to him. But he did nothing, so something still eluded his understanding.

Stephanie shoved a little to get into Lille's tent but eventually made it, hanging to the back while the healers did their work. As soon as they finished and Lille looked less pained, Stephanie moved forward and sat on the mat beside Lille.

"You should go, Stephanie," Lille said, her words blaring her exhaustion.

"I thought I'd sit with you a while."

"I need to rest. This day and the ones to come..." Something in the usual spark inside Lille was waning.

"Is there something I can do for you?"

"*You?*" Lille shook her head. "It doesn't matter. We all make our choices and live with the consequences. I cannot say anything that will alter your course... you wear Daryn's soul—I should have known."

"What do you mean? What are you saying?"

Ranz's suddenly forceful presence appeared inside Stephanie.

"Drain her now... just to get her to sleep, for her not to say anything else."

A flash of an argument appeared in her thoughts, but she figured she'd provoked her jailers enough for one day. Ranz only asked that Lille be forced to sleep—something Lille herself wanted—so Stephanie drained Lille's energy until she faded into slumber.

"I don't much like your attitude, dearest."

"I am not terribly surprised, Ranz."

"But I think what you did to Thorne was brilliant." Ranz chuckled. *"No man should feel so entitled to a woman such as yourself."*

Stephanie let out a breath and felt the warmth of her connection to Ranz. If he would have sided with Thorne, treated Stephanie like chattel, it would have changed things between them.

"Dearest, there is some power in this tent. I wish to know what it is. Search through Lille's things."

Curiosity sparked along with that delicious feeling of doing something mischievous. Stephanie rooted through the clothes and weapons, before seeing a small pouch. She moved toward it, feeling something—an energy—radiating.

"Yes, dearest, that is the source. What's inside?"

Stephanie knelt on the ground and reached for the ties. Upon touching the leather string cinch, she felt an uneasy kind of tingling.

"I don't know about this, Ranz."

"We must know, dearest."

She tugged at the strings and the pouch opened, revealing

lavender petals, very much like the ones in the camp in the Wild Wood. A sweet fragrance drifted off of them that caused a pleasing lightheadedness. Stephanie felt instantly joyous.

"*Close it, dearest. Get out of here.*"

"But Ranz," she giggled. "It feels... wonderful."

"*You are speaking aloud. Silence.*"

Everything seemed suddenly funny and chuckles came from her mouth that inspired more laughter and a hiccup.

"*Dearest, get out of the tent. Clear your head.*"

Stephanie stared at the petals, yearning to touch them.

"*Don't touch them. Listen to me. Get out.*"

She giggled again and then swooned, while her hand reached for the petals, so pretty, so sparkly.

"*Stephanie, no!*"

Stephanie felt a great pull inside her as though Ranz was doing something, but he and his power felt distant. The only pull in the world came from the petals. Her fingers moved toward their beauty, finally touching one. She took it in her hand, feeling the pulsing that felt dangerous and alluring at the same time. Pulsing that she felt throughout her body... felt in Ranz's body... in Thorne's. The connection that sealed them now seared them.

The brand burned—no really *burned*—and Stephanie screamed, only no sound came. Her hand continued to move, but not of her own will, as the petal neared and then entered her mouth. Her body shuddered as she swallowed it. A fierce lavender glow lit her body on fire until the pain overwhelmed her and the world went dark, a lavender shade of dark.

*

Married. Finn had been *married* and *divorced* before Annisha. Married. Divorced. And he didn't tell Annisha until she was married to him, seeing and feeling all of his thoughts. Who would do something like that? Why?

I opened my mouth, but nothing came. Nothing. Not a single word, venomous or not.

"Cecily, it doesn't matter. Why would it? Why is it something I should have told you?"

Finn's pleading still elicited no words from me. I just stared, without many thoughts for him to feed on, except one: the feeling of support that came into my heart with the small pressure of Nate's hand on my shoulder.

"*Cecily...*"

I turned to Devra. "Is there a way to break the connection that allows Finn to hear all of my thoughts?"

"Of course." Devra turned to glare at Finn. "You didn't tell her? What you did? Why you did it? Why you refused to break your ties to Annisha, after promising to do it after she was gone? She didn't want Cecily's mind violated by your connection, and you promised, didn't you?"

"What?" I demanded.

"I... I wanted to protect her. I wanted to take care of her, to know when she needed me."

Devra was about to respond, but I held my hand up to stop her. "You wanted control. You wanted access. You wanted *me*."

"Of course, I want you. I love you."

My heart felt hollow, and the void felt like when I was ripped apart in the Source. "Did you promise Annisha to sever the bond so that you wouldn't have access to me?"

Finn lowered his head. "Yes, but then I couldn't—I just couldn't. I heard your first thoughts, I felt the connection. I couldn't give it up."

"But you should have. You didn't have the right to be in my head, not when I wasn't given a choice—when you *choose* to keep things from me. Marriages are only the beginning. I know almost *nothing* about you, other than that you claim to love me."

"I *do* love you."

"Then why would you keep your secrets?"

"Because there's so much you couldn't understand. You weren't there. You don't know who I was and what I suffered. I was afraid it would frighten you."

"You took that choice away from me. What is the big deal about you being married to Devra?"

Finn just stared, his eyes the eyes of a man staring at his worst nightmare.

Devra's voice turned soft. "To marry a higher demon, you must be at least part demon. Finn is more than half demon and still holds an allegiance to the demon clans."

"Demon?" I asked. "What does that mean?"

Finn's jaw clenched just before his words flew. "Even in Darienne, a place with wondrous variety and mostly equality, there are factions, divisions of our people, and immortals never forgive. A war was fought—demons were on the losing side when Darienne was first formed as a country, and they have paid the price since. Always lesser. Always suspect. Forced to live in separate towns or parts of towns. Forced to wear their demon marks openly so that all would know who—*what*—they are.

Only allowed in certain places, never near the royalty of our land."

"But you were friends with Britton, with Lille. Did they not know?"

Finn shook his head. "They never knew, but I suppose Britton does now."

"But Lille? She's your best friend."

"Yes, she *is* my best friend. Do you think I would ever hurt her? Do you think this lie has been easy to keep? Do you think I should be judged by what my great grandparents did in a time a million years ago?"

His hurt wounded me, but still, I kept away from him. "You never should have listened to my thoughts. Can't you see that? The violation? Annisha married you—she agreed to share her soul—and even then, you didn't know well enough to tell her who you really were. How did she react?"

"She punished me the first chance she got," Devra spat, "and the first ten years of their marriage were very hostile, until she forgave."

"Why didn't she tell Lille or the others who you were?"

Finn looked shocked. "Because she loved me!"

I barely thought about my words. "But I *don't*—I love the idea of you. A handsome man who seemed to love me and would always be there for me, who accepted all of the things I struggle with inside myself. A man who wouldn't turn on me like Nate did." I felt Nate's hand become tentative, so I placed my hand over his and looked up at him. "We're flawed, you and me. We have to learn and bump against our mistakes. But at least we're real." Nate smiled and I knew he felt my forgiveness. I turned back toward Finn. "I don't know you. I only know the little pieces you've given me. I was wrong to trust you so blindly, but then I didn't really have a choice, did I? You were always there. You forged a bond when I was at my weakest. That's over."

I looked to Finn's former wife. "Devra, how do I get him out of my head?"

"*Cecily, please. You won't hear my voice. You are weak and fragile of spirit right now. Let me be here for you.*"

"*I will miss this—I will.*" Tears slid down my cheeks. "*I will miss feeling so loved and taken care of, but this is wrong. I'm hiding in you. If you have access to my mind again, it will be because our love is real and I have chosen this commitment, not had it forced on me.*"

"Are you ready?" Devra asked.

"No, Lady Devra. Please. I'll do it." Finn backed away from us. "It is the only way I can recover even a tiny bit of my honor." Finn's eyes pierced me. "I am sorry, though apologizing for the gift of being close to you feels wrong."

He closed his eyes and a blue light swirled around him, growing brighter and brighter until a sudden flash burst through the caverns. The light blinded me for a few seconds before I saw Finn, lying on the ground, his body trembling.

I might have gone to him, comforted him, but my body stood still and watched his grief, knowing I was finally free to think whatever I wanted without regard to its effect on anyone else. I was finally free to figure out who I was now, beyond all of the forces—Pastor Rowe, Dunlowe, the mystics, Finn, Bay, the sevens, Nate, the Source, my family—who had pulled at me, who had defined my life since birth. I was finally free to be me, whoever that was.

*

Dusty squinted when a bright blue light seared the caverns, seeming to bounce off of the walls as it traveled past Dusty and Grey on through the dark recesses of the world.

Dusty looked to Grey. "What was that about?"

Grey shrugged. "No idea, but I think you're stalling."

"Are you sure it's time to pick another fight out in the world when we are perfectly—or possibly not at all—safe here?"

"My wound's gone—those gateways sure do the trick for healing wounds. Let's go."

"Why? What's the rush?"

Grey rubbed his hand over his face. "Something's coming, Dusty. I can't explain it. I just have the sense that there is somewhere we need to be. Somewhere that isn't here."

"But what if we get killed?"

Through a laugh, Grey said, "Who could kill such a fantastic fighting force as we are?"

"Ummm, lots and lots of creatures and now that you said that, you've jinxed us completely."

Grey looked around the darkness of the cavern, only a few lights near them remained lit. "We can stay if you want."

"Oh no. I'm not going to be the reason you get pouty and cry like a little girl."

"I will not..."

"Totally were gonna."

"Was not."

"Was so. Let's go down this one." Dusty pointed at the next corridor. "I definitely have absolutely no good feeling about it."

Grey beamed. "Perfect. Just what we were looking for."

*

Zoe sat in a tree watching the smoldering ruins of the town of Marsden, Jacoby's home. Not a single building remained of a town that had stood as long as Dunlowe, a town whose people—other than those like Jacoby who had escaped and come to Dunlowe—had been taken north to be sold. Jacoby had walked these roads with his wife and his daughter. Zoe glanced at Jacoby who stood watching her, awaiting an order that he would transmit to the others, all of whom were in position. She had a feeling about this town. Darstel, the town they had just come from, was nothing but ruins. No soldiers had troubled their way north, but Zoe felt that Marsden, the most northern of the rebel towns, would be the dividing line between a rebel uprising and an all-out war.

While she watched, leaning back against a thick tree covered in soft moss, she felt the fear that had been her constant companion since agreeing to be a leader, to be responsible for the lives and deaths of both the rebels and the soldiers she hoped would one day join their cause. But today was not the day when soldiers would believe that a rebel girl could lead a group of townsfolk and change the fate of a nation. Today was the day to start a brushfire, to grow a legend she'd have to pretend to be worthy of.

Zoe thought of Logan and what he would think of this lie she was going to fuel, but she knew he saw her the way the others did, not the way she saw herself. He wouldn't even think it was a lie. For her, knowing her love for him was made of such truth proved these lies wouldn't cost her too much.

A small movement in the trees beyond the ruins had Zoe

sitting up. She motioned to Jacoby who nodded, a wicked grin on his face and a lust for death in his eyes. He wasn't troubled with the plight of his enemies, and Zoe would have to take lessons because killing without hate was an impossible and soul-destroying thing. Jacoby motioned to Mindy and Heath. Mr. Daye. And the rest of the rebel forces.

Zoe leaned and struck her flint a couple times, igniting the metal bowl attached to the branch that now contained a small glowing flame. Moving into position, she drew her bow, arrow flaming, and aimed it directly for the soldier's heart. Better to die than to fail, she told herself, as the soldiers rushed out from behind trees to meet the rebel army.

As she ordered, her rebels shouted the name Zoe Crane to all who could hear, while her arrows protected them and lessened the force they would fight.

Just another day in an uprising, but for Zoe, a powerful one. A portent of things to come.

19

Tether

Stephanie felt her body before she found a way to open her eyes. Her breathing dragged in and out, and everything felt sore and groggy. What had happened? What...?

The petals. Something had happened with those petals... something had drugged her somehow.

"*Ranz, are you here?*"

Silence.

Her skin felt strange... almost naked—no, totally naked. She struggled with her eyes and her limbs, and after what seemed like much time negotiating, her eyes finally opened.

Stephanie saw trees, many branches crossing over her, linking with others. She was *outside*, not in Lille's tent anymore. In the woods. But she hadn't seen trees like this since she'd left Stoughton. She heard the rippling of a stream that drained into a pond. She glanced down and then bolted up when she found that she really was naked. Completely naked and outside. She glanced around for clothes, but there were none.

"*Ranz? What happened?*"

In the middle of her panic, she noticed something missing on her belly. Her brand—no Thorne's and Ranz's brand—was gone, her skin as pure as it had been before she'd ever met Ranz and fallen into this strange world of demons and Grey Cloaks, wars and power. She ran her fingers over her soft skin, too confused to know whether she should feel gratitude or tremendous loss. Ranz's intricate demon mark had been beautiful and Thorne's crest and her own small 's' were lovely, all of them giving her tangible proof of the connection that would bind them forever. *Forever* seemed a shoddy word now that the mark was gone.

Her heart fluttered, missing beats as she covered her naked body with her hands as best she could, but nothing made her feel as naked and vulnerable as the silence in her mind and the feeling that her connection to Ranz was gone—almost like it never existed at all.

A few tears fell and when one reached her arm, she realized that her golden skin had disappeared with her brand. Her golden skin that proved she was immortal, won after Cecily claimed immortality for the sevens in the bonfire in Dunlowe. No brand. No golden skin. No Ranz.

Stephanie Trench was *Stephanie Trench* again. A mortal girl. A girl with no power. A girl who was suddenly free of a future husband and an ugly demon.

Why didn't she feel any relief?

Once she calmed, Stephanie looked around the pond and found a wooden sign hanging from a tree that read in perfectly carved words *Secret Dunlowe Boys Only Fishing Club*. Below those words, letters—initials—were carved. LT. HC. JP. DD.

Stephanie moved to touch the letters, knowing exactly who they represented: Logan Trench, Heath Culver, Jem Payne, and Dusty Daye. Her fingers caressed Dusty's initials and then her eyes were drawn to words scratched into the tree that held the sign. *Zoe Crane was here with Mindy Samson on the day Dunlowe died. Long live the Dunlowe Uprising!*

Dunlowe was dead? There was an uprising? Zoe—the backstabbing hag—had been hanging out at a boys only fishing hole? But all of that seemed less important than not standing in a deserted fishing hole with no clothes on. She searched around the pond, spotting a wooden structure that covered some dry wood, boxes, a trunk, and some fishing supplies. Stephanie rifled through the first box and found nothing very helpful as burlap wasn't an acceptable solution. In the next box were some seeds and other dry goods, and the third was empty. Stephanie tugged the trunk forward and fought with the latch until it opened.

Her breath drew in when she saw the golden fabric of her favorite dress. Here? She instantly resolved not to care how her favorite dress—and shoes, as it turned out—ended up at the boys only fishing hole. Stephanie quickly dressed and hurried away from the pond toward her house. She hadn't known exactly where the fishing hole was, but she'd trailed Logan once—okay, actually she'd been spying on Dusty when he was fishing with Logan—but now she was certain and knew she could get back if anything happened.

Stephanie went the roundabout way to her house, just to make sure no one saw her, not ready to explain where she had been or what she'd done, when she had no idea what she was doing here. But when she neared her house, tears pushed out in a steady stream.

Charred ruins. Just a pile of ash remained of her beautiful house. She stumbled forward, clutching the black ash, clutching her home, dirtying her hands and not caring at all.

Zoe's words on the tree hit her. Dunlowe had died.

She brushed off her hands and hurried to the town proper but came to an abrupt stop when she saw the empty spaces where the town had lived and thrived. No schoolhouse. No worship hall. No Smyth Mercantile. Nothing remained but ashes... and mounds. Tall mounds, covered with dirt that caused her to shudder.

With weak, trembling legs, Stephanie ambled through what remained of Dunlowe, wishing for too many things to lock down. When she knew she'd had enough, more than she could handle, she headed back to the fishing hole, not certain what else to do, only knowing that the sun would set and there was wood for a fire, and fishing poles and fish.

Hunger clawed at her by the time she reached the fishing hole and she quickly went about making a fire, a difficult undertaking having never done it before. Watching others didn't seem to count as it turned out. The same was true for fishing, but her desperate belly kept her at the task until she caught a small fish, cleaned it as best she could, and cooked it over the small flames.

Her meal was not quite enough to satiate her hunger, but enough that she didn't want to go through the entire process again. Her restlessness turned to exhaustion and she crawled toward the trunk and dug through, finding a few of her other dresses that she could use as blankets. Stephanie's hand touched something in the darkness of the trunk that had her breath catching. She slowly brought it out and found the most incredible thing: her diary.

While her right hand remained on the book, her left hand covered her mouth and the choking sob that burst out. She hugged her diary like a best friend for a few seconds before positioning herself near the fire, making a bed out of her dresses, and laying back so that she could use the fire's light to read her journal, beginning at the middle when she was a teenager, not a little girl.

Dear Diary,

I love Dusty Daye, today, tomorrow, and forever...

Every day included more about Dusty than anyone or anything else. She read her thoughts about life, most of which seemed silly now, now that the world was so much larger than the life she had lived in Dunlowe. She read about her fear after Zoe turned against her and Pastor Rowe whipped Cecily. And then the entries ran out when the sevens were run out of Dunlowe.

These pages contained nothing at all about her complicated life as an immortal. Nothing about having her soul owned by a demon who looked disgusting. Nothing about being betrothed to a stranger who craved power and might never really love her. Nothing about making a choice to give Dusty up for the chance to be queen. A *chance*, not a certainty.

Dusty had been part of every day of her life, at least in her thoughts. She turned back to the little girl pages and found the inscription written by her mother, something she had refused to ever read again after the first time she read it as a girl—her mother, who had given her the beautiful leather-bound journal.

Dearest Stephanie,

I will be gone when you open this present and you may fill it with hateful words about the mother who couldn't remain with you.

But someday, my dearest girl, you will understand how complicated life is, how truly tragic it can be. Please know, I never wanted to leave you and your brothers, and your dear father, but sometimes we have no choice or the choices and the consequences are too dark to accept. I leave for you, dearest girl. I leave because I love you more than life itself. I leave to give you the chance I never had. Please take your chance and live a normal life. Adventure is all well and good, but nothing in this world is to be treasured like a simple, happy, loving life.

Love you with all my heart, my sweet girl.

Mom

Stephanie rested the journal against her chest and cried herself to sleep.

*

The shrieking filled Morgan's ears as she cringed from the dark spirits, her eyes staring at them, unable to pull away. Their wispy hands motioned and her body raised as they took control. She fought them, but they pulled her body up and held her, her arms and legs stretched out. Trapped. They swarmed around her, brushing against her. She tried to close her eyes, but they denied her. They moved closer and she struggled to close her mouth, but again they used whatever power they had to force her mouth to remain open.

They slithered against her skin and she heard their whispers, "Payment" as they moved into her mouth and into her eyes.

The violation of her body had her quivering, wishing to scream, but her voice was not her own.

"I am the payment," her grandfather said. "Back away from

her."

A flurry of anxious flapping surrounded her, like a thousand birds' wings all beating her, and then they moved away and stared at her grandfather, who stood proudly, but she saw the weariness in his shoulders.

"I am the reason she's vulnerable, the reason she can't fight back. I made the trade, so *I* will be the payment."

"Papaw, no!" Morgan cried the second the spirits freed her mouth to move.

He turned to her, his sadness plain. "I thought we'd have more time. I have so much to teach you, but the price always comes when it costs the most. I see that now."

"Not enough," the spirits said, their voices overlapping each other's. "Not with her so close... and draining of life. Not enough... we taste her weakness. Must have her."

"No!" her grandfather shouted. "The payment was for one. Just one. I *am* that one."

"But you aren't—not the only one. She gained the power from your bargain, she must pay."

"No. That wasn't the deal I made with the brokers. She made no deal—I did." His eyes caught hers and he looked so guilty her heart ached. "Take me."

"Papaw, what is this?"

"You would have died... many times over—a seer told me. I did this to save you, but I've cursed you in the process. Such is the way of bargaining magicks." He turned to the spirits. "The Ezias have honor when it suits them. You fight for a place in this world, for substance, for your king—to undo what was done to you. There has to be a way that I can help you, without robbing my granddaughter of her destiny."

"Her destiny was to die. She has no destiny now. We see that... we want her. The void inside her draws us in... we want to swallow her whole and use her, reap her body until there is nothing left and she is one of us."

"No!" Morgan fought to back away. "No, don't do this. I have a life, a destiny. A love."

"Love... yes, we *love* love. Tastes real. But you and your love are lost, strangers in the same prisons. You with no fate and he with a fate that is not his own. But power belongs to you both, power yours for the claiming—yes, we want your life, your power, feeds us. Hungry."

"The deal," her grandfather said. "Only the deal."

"A taste. An ounce. A tether," they sang and then something in them calmed, sounding more human. "We will let you guide her back. This barren land is not for her to fix. You, our marked, will be our envoy—since our others have been corrupted and betrayed our king—and we will help where we can. This dead ground kills you and kills our chances for real life, not shadow life."

"A taste, an ounce, a tether?" Morgan asked. "What does that mean?"

Her Papaw, the man she'd trusted more than anyone, walked toward her, shame blaring at her from his weary eyes. "I am so sorry, Morgan. I thought I could bear it alone—I didn't think this would happen to you. Maybe I should have let you go when it was your time..."

"When was my time?"

He placed his hands on her cheeks, cradling her face, while

her arms were still bound and stretched by the Ezias. "You were meant to die the day your parents died—you were meant to die instead of them, but I traded their lives for yours, a promise they forced me to make. You were given life, but a shadow passed across you that day that has never completely faded."

"My powers?"

"Given to you by a demon in a trade I made, a trade that brought us to this day."

Her lip quivered, thinking of the lives her parents could have lived, long lives, if only she had died instead of them. "Is this the reason I survived the Commanders' dead ground?"

"Yes. Their toxins steal destinies and kill the bodies that hold them."

"What do they mean—a taste, an ounce, a tether?"

"Honey, I don't want you to go through this—you've faced so much already. But I can't see another way. I should have known what a girl without a destiny would do to them."

"What? What do I do to them?"

"You are like a drug they will never get enough of... an addiction so strong, they cannot fight it—won't fight it."

"They said you could stay with me?"

A tear fell from his eye. "I will be here, but I will not own this body anymore. I will have all of my memories and I will be able to guide you some, but only according to their orders. For a while, as long as this earth threatens us, we will be allies, but that could change."

"You'll be like them one day?"

He nodded. "They will eat my emotions until they are gone and then they will eat my flesh, and yes, one day, I will be one of them."

"No!" She struggled to hold him.

"Free her!"

The spirits let go and Morgan fell into her grandfather's arms.

"Honey," he whispered, "I can't protect you from what you will endure."

"Just tell me," she pleaded.

"They will take a taste of your soul—it will be excruciating. They will take an ounce of your emotions, the richest ones first. You will never get them back, never be completely you again. And they will latch a tether to you so that they can enter you any time they wish, any time you call on them. You will be a conduit—you already are a conduit, but hopefully, they will allow me to explain that to you later. It is in their interests for you to know, so I think they will."

"If they are going to feed on me anyway, why don't I just surrender now?"

"No, they won't take more, not unless it is in trade for a deal you make. I know it is difficult to understand, but they *are* honoring their deal in their own way. Most never get a choice before their bodies are stolen. But don't make a deal with them and they won't take more than the taste and the ounce. The tether is to draw you in, so that when you need them, they can be there. They will help, but you will always have to pay... until—don't ask them for help. Let destiny—whatever that is and whatever it means—play out. Don't do as I've done. Don't let love cause you to cross the lines that cannot be uncrossed." He held her tightly. "I love you."

Morgan felt too overwhelmed and her shaking was too great to do much of anything but whisper, "I love you too," as the Ezias began to shriek and she was torn away from her grandfather, stretched out just as he was, as the dark spirits launched at them.

✶

"What are we doing here?" Charity whispered while Millie attempted to come up with a lie that sounded even close to plausible.

Nothing came to mind.

"*Tell her you overheard someone talking about a boat,*" Oona suggested.

"I heard someone talking about having a boat."

Charity looked confused in the moonlight. "So now you want to leave and risk getting lost at sea?"

"Maybe," Millie mumbled. "*Seriously, Oona, what are we doing here? I feel bad lying to Charity.*"

"*I'm a seer. I've been waiting for exactly this day, but even with that, it might not happen. The choice I thought would be made hasn't been.*" Oona looked crestfallen all of a sudden. "*So very long... so many pieces, all dependent on this one.*"

Oona seemed to see something happening that made her even more unhappy. "*I'm sorry. You can go back and go to bed.*"

Millie considered. "*No, you've waited a long time for this and all we are doing is hanging out here. We'll wait and see if what you want to happen happens. Okay?*"

A sweet look crossed Oona's ghostly face. "*Thanks, Millie.*"

✶

"Grey, wait," Dusty said, pulling him back. "I have a really bad feeling about this gateway. Let's go back."

"Are you sure?"

"Absolutely."

"Okay." Grey, just shy of the veil, backed away instantly. "The next one will be great."

"Thanks... for *listening*."

"Why do you sound surprised that I would listen?"

Dusty bit his lip. "I'm kind of a joke to people. A funny kid with floppy hair—not a man."

Dusty listened to his and Grey's footsteps as they walked back down the passage.

"If you want to be taken seriously, you must first take yourself seriously. Is that really who you want to be?"

"What do you mean?"

"Life makes people serious, but there's a choice too. I don't think you are less of anything because you laugh or have floppy hair—and you *do* have floppy hair. I think you are good and I like the way you see the world. I saw dark things in Ranz's cell, been through agonies that robbed me of my memories of any life beyond that cage. I could choose to wallow, but you make me want to laugh." Grey stopped and looked at Dusty, his grey eyes intense. "You are a good man and you don't need to change anything."

Dusty swallowed. "Thanks, Grey. Will you help me with something before we go out the next corridor?"

"Anything. Just ask."

20

Lineage

Under the strict orders and watchful eyes of Mrs. Daye and Mrs. Rowe, Logan had been sleeping, eating, or preparing to sleep and eat for days, but his body felt no better. His mood grew murky..er. Even having Jem force Pastor Rowe to dance for him wasn't helping anymore... or much anyway.

Days turned into nights and then into days again, and Logan felt like he'd never get better, never get stronger, never get off of his back. And it really ticked him off that Pastor Rowe as a dead person was more spry than he was. Rotten, rotten luck.

"I'm leaving," Logan announced and really meant it. He began to roll to push himself to his feet when a weight on his back gently pushed him back down.

Logan grimaced and moaned at the same time and gazed up at Mrs. Dumphry, the other enforcer of his recuperation.

"You are going to stay there and get strong or I am going to start teaching you everything you ignored in my class, and don't think I've forgotten anything, including that fourteen percent you earned on a test about agriculture. You *know* agriculture. Why did you fail?"

Logan turned red and looked away.

Mrs. Dumphry leaned closer, seeming to smell fear—though that might have been Logan's rankness after so many days without a bath. "Tell me, Logan Trench, or I will get Jem to make Pastor Rowe sing again."

Logan cringed. "Not that, anything but that." Lullabies from a madman had wrecked his sleep for days, but they had entertained all of the children who were just as bored as Logan was. Logan let out a breath. "I don't read."

"What?"

"I don't read."

"Can't read?" Mrs. Dumphry looked shocked.

"Just don't."

Mrs. Dumphry studied him in that way that always made him feel like a bug under a magnifying glass. She disappeared for a few minutes before returning with a book—he'd hoped they'd all been destroyed... bad luck all around.

She thrust the book in front of him. "Read this."

"Which part of *I don't read* do you not understand?"

Mrs. Dumphry moved closer. "Read the book, Logan, right now, otherwise I'm getting a stick and pretending it's a ruler—you are probably too injured to hit right now, so I'll have to hit Pastor Rowe instead."

"That doesn't really inspire me to want to read all that much."

"Read the book, Logan."

Mrs. Dumphry held the book open. A textbook—she'd saved a textbook from destruction, sadistic witch.

Logan stared at the words and felt the same weight crushing his heart that he always felt. He glanced away.

"I see," Mrs. Dumphry said. "Then we have work to do."

*

Nate walked with Cecily through the cavern to where the others gathered to hear Devra's tale, Cecily and Nate for the first time.

When Nate realized Cecily was staring at him, he turned his attention on her. "What?"

"Can I touch your marks?"

"I don't know... honestly. Let me ask Devra if it will hurt you." Nate focused. "*Will touching the marks hurt Cecily?*"

"*Having her touch you will hurt Finn, but you are not dangerous to anyone, unless you want to be.*"

Nate wasn't exactly sure what that meant. "It's okay."

Cecily studied him. "She's in your head? She's always been?"

"I guess so, but I never heard her before I came here."

Cecily shook her head, letting out a sigh.

"What?"

"All that time we spent together. Every kiss we shared, every hug, every walk around Dunlowe, it was never just us, was it? Finn and Devra—the former married couple—witnessed every private moment we ever shared."

Nate felt the weight of that disturbing reality and wondered if they would ever get free of these ties that had bound them, had stolen the normal lives they should have lived.

"I don't know," he said. "All of this is as much or more of a mystery to me than it is for you. I was a normal boy in Dunlowe. How I ended up *created* or whatever by a demon still boggles my mind. But I'm still glad not to be my father's son, so that's something."

"I wonder where he is and if he got what he wanted out of all of this," Cecily said quietly. "I just can't imagine that any of this really made him happy. Can happy people be that mean?"

"I don't know, but you didn't see him laughing as the soldiers beat every person in Dunlowe—even some of the kids."

Cecily shuddered.

"Sorry."

Cecily paused her walking and looked up at him, seeing him in that way of hers when her care seemed like a lasso that could trap him and hold him in the only place he ever wanted to be. She tentatively raised her hand and touched his marks, as tingling broke out in his body that had absolutely nothing to do with the marks and everything to do with her.

He caught Finn's glare and enjoyed it. Finn had had Cecily to himself for too long, even with her trip to the Source. It was time for a little competition.

"If Devra created you, does that mean you are a demon too? Are you immortal?"

Nate shrugged. "I have no idea." He paused abruptly, taking her hand. "Does it matter to you... what I am?"

"Nate, I have no idea who I am—*what* I am, now or in the future. I've been powerful and cruel, weak and kind, loving and hateful. You'll really have a hard time topping the things I've done."

"But does it matter if I am a demon?"

"I don't even know what that means, but I can't imagine that who your parents are can matter—I loved you when your dad beat me and destroyed my childhood. It's what we do with our lives, not where we come from, that matters."

"Thank you," Nate whispered. "The fact that you don't think Devra's marks are grotesque really helps me to come to terms with all of this."

Her face flushed. "Oh, I don't think they're grotesque at all." She looked away as they continued walking, her hand still in his.

"If you'll join me, I'll answer your questions," Devra called.

Cecily let Nate go, looking suddenly bashful, and walked with him to where the others were already seated. Nate sat and gestured for Cecily to sit next to him, while Darla leapt onto her lap and leaned against her as Cecily wrapped her arms around his sister.

"This tale is long and it is better to show some of it than to tell it all." Devra struck the ground and blue light flared, forming into a square that hung from nothing in the middle of the cavern, while the crowd sat in a circle around it.

"My history isn't really relevant..."

Finn grumbled something.

Devra ignored him. "But it is enough to know that two other higher demons and I were punished for our perceived crimes—only one of us was the true criminal, but I didn't actually know that until much later. And even he was driven to what he did by terrible circumstances. Annisha sentenced me to watch over the world, while living almost entirely inside the caverns. I can go out but only for very short periods of time. Longer and the weight of her sentence assails me."

"The sentence?" Cecily asked. "I thought she made a ruling and didn't have the power to actually *do* anything."

Devra squinted at Finn. "You've really glossed over a lot, haven't you?" Finn said nothing. "Others with power did help carry out her judgments, though I've come to believe that Annisha had much more power than she or Finn ever let on."

Cecily looked to Finn, but he was about as giving in knowledge as the cavern wall—at least the wall gave light.

"What happens to you if you stay outside the caverns for too long?" Nate asked.

"I sink into the ground and, without help, would be trapped there, alive forever, while attacked by a very specific kind of monster. You can see why being alone without my soldiers is a very dangerous thing for me. And without leaving, I can't really watch over the world, something I am compelled to do. My soldiers help me, bring me information, travel far and wide for the good of the world."

The blue screen hanging above the ground flickered and images spread across it. A woman walking toward a sword and falling upon it.

"Annisha," Cecily whispered, hugging Darla closer.

"Yes," Devra said. "Annisha died to begin a mission to determine the worth of the peoples of Stoughton who had long been the focus of a war between the Conquerors and the Protectors. But that wasn't why the mystics encouraged the plan. They wanted something else, something that couldn't be won while Annisha and Finn were around. While Lille was there. They fostered this war for their own ends, ends I still haven't determined.

"The moment Annisha went through the Source and became you, everything changed. You were powerful, more than anyone else, and that created a power vacuum. The world has gone mad ever since. The Ezias appearing above ground is just another symptom. I came to know that I would need an instrument in this fight and so went about the vile task of creating such a being."

Nate felt stung.

"No, Nathaniel, *you* are not vile, but to create you I had to deal with some nefarious types, work some magicks with the assistance of brokers, and owe some debts. Nothing is done without an exchange of goods and services, and the price is always high."

"Came to know?" Cecily asked, repeating Devra's words. "How did you know you would need an instrument?"

"A seer who uses the caverns came to me and told me that the world would end if I didn't follow her advice. I doubted, of course, but her gift was strong. She didn't just see the possibilities, she saw the choices being made in real-time, as we were talking. I was able to verify her portents and came to understand that she had a mission she was willing to die for. She told me I needed an instrument and then she told me I needed another." Devra smiled at Darla.

"Who is our father?" Nate asked. "My father—Pastor Rowe—said someone named Bayles came...?"

"Bayles? *Bay*?" Cecily demanded. "Is he their *father*?"

"Bayles was busy in all of this, but no, he wasn't their father. What his role was, I do not know."

"But *who* is our father?" Nate pressed.

Finn let out a curse. "Tell them it's not *relevant*, Lady Devra—you hypocrite. You've been listening to the boy's thoughts his entire life and you judge me."

"I did what I did to save the world, Finn. You did it to save yourself."

"My *father*," Nate said again, hearing his desperation.

Devra's face filled with compassion. "It's not that simple. You weren't made like a normal child, neither was Darla. Ideas like father or mother don't apply here. You were magically made. You are part of me. You are part of your mother. And you are part of a demon called Delibrien, who owed me a favor, and who isn't cursed to live underground—clever, clever man. I couldn't risk you suffering the same limitations I have."

"And Darla is the same?"

"Darla has one more component." Devra swallowed and glanced at Finn. "Something stolen by Finn and given to me."

"Please, tell us, Devra," Darla said.

"You don't know this?" Nate asked Darla.

"Only some, but not this." Her large green eyes looked worried. "Please, tell me who I am."

"Just like Nate, you are part of me, your mother, Delibrien... and *Cecily*."

Nate's eyes widened and he turned to stare at Cecily, whose face wore shock but her smile widened as she spun Darla around to look at her.

"I always knew... *something*. I felt you when I first heard you cry. I was willing to die to help you. And when we touched foreheads and I freed you just before the fire, I felt..."

"Wonder," Darla whispered. "Connection."

Cecily gripped Darla and rocked her back and forth. "I love you, Darla."

Darla cuddled into Cecily, answering Cecily's love in the most powerful way she could.

Devra's voice sounded strange. "You aren't angry at me, at Finn, at...?"

Cecily continued to rock Darla while very calmly saying, "To be angry would mean that I would change something, and Darla is beautiful and perfect, so no, I'm not angry..." Her voice faded for a moment and when it returned it was softer and more laced with sharp knives. "Darla is part of me as you have said, but she wears your demon mark. You have control over her, so I must tell you that if you hurt her, if she comes to any harm at all, the fate that awaits you will make treacherous demons quiver and cry for whatever beast spawned you."

Devra said nothing and just lowered her head.

"You are going to do nothing while that weakling threatens you?" Brody demanded.

Devra patted his arm to keep him in place. "If you think Cecily Daye is a weakling, you are seeing nothing of the true tale. Feel." Devra sent some emotion, some awareness, into Brody that had his eyes widening and his breath drawing in. He simply nodded, possibly having lost the power of speech— no great loss. Devra returned her focus to Cecily who looked curious about the exchange, but awaited an answer to her threat. "Cecily, I understand your feelings for her, but know that I don't have control over our fates. All of us may die and I assure you that if Darla comes to any harm, I will suffer with you. She's my child too."

Cecily cuddled Darla, while the force of her will seemed to fill the cavern, making the air feel too close. Nate felt the sliver of cold that always accompanied witnessing Cecily in her powerful state. He wondered what Devra had shown Brody, but didn't really think it was that much of a surprise that Cecily's strength transcended the limits of her body. Her weakness felt temporary, if that.

Darla, probably to keep peace, said, "It's time, Devra. Tell them why we're here."

*

Stephanie woke in the morning to a chill. The fire had died. Her journal lay against her chest like a blanket and she was still alone. She looked at her pale skin, checking to see if her brand was still gone. She wondered what she should do: follow the survivors who probably traveled north to fight in the Dunlowe Uprising—who were probably dead by now—or south to enter the Wild Wood, heading back to Darienne to find Ranz and Thorne and... *what?* Have them re-brand her, wander back into the frightening path of not being free to make her own choices?

They probably wouldn't want her like this. A simple common, mortal girl, the real Stephanie Trench.

Indecision warred. Could she ever happily live a simple life—not that remaining in Dunlowe seemed that simple anymore? But still, what did she want now that she was free to consider any possible path?

"That is what you are here to determine," a voice said, and Stephanie looked up, seeing a ghostly form with a lavender hue, shimmering and fading in and out. The girl looked strangely familiar.

"Who are you?"

"I am Daryn."

Stephanie flinched to her feet. "How is this possible?"

"I don't know... but I am here to tell you that this is your only chance to make a different choice. If not now, you will have to follow your choice until the end."

"So you mean I really could make a different choice? I could be free of Ranz and Thorne and immortality? I could come back here and live and die as a normal person?"

"Yes."

"I could have Dusty and be with him forever?"

"Possibly. He would have to make the same choice."

Stephanie thought for a minute. "You chose to get out—you killed yourself."

"To give us a chance at freedom and you wandered right back into their clutches. I get it—of course, I get it—but seeing it... hurts me."

"But I am you, in a way."

"You are, which means you are also the part of me that fell victim to vanity and greed and the poison those emotions make your soul drink. But you are also the part of me that just yearned to be loved, while busy pushing away everyone who tried."

"But Thorne loved you..."

Daryn turned petulant. "Thorne doesn't know the first thing about love, except love of power. Yes, he loved me in the only way his cold heart could, but it wasn't real love. Not like what Dusty feels for you... even now."

"Even now?"

"You are in his heart, as you have always been."

"But to have him, I have to be ordinary. I don't think I can..."

Daryn studied Stephanie's face, seeming to see things beyond what was there.

"What?" Stephanie asked.

"It's more."

"What is?"

"It is more than the legacy of me inside you that brings you to this place; something else lives in you. A legacy—a lineage—you don't even know you are part of."

Stephanie glared at Daryn. "What does that mean?"

Daryn shook her head. "I don't know completely—but one day you will. They are calling me back. You have until sunset to decide. Choose wisely, Stephanie. The path is dangerous either way, but only one road will give you any peace."

✶

Morgan couldn't move any part of her body, couldn't scream, as the Ezias pressed their way into her mouth, her nose, her eyes. Not just one, but what felt like thousands, all swirling through her, corrupting her veins, discovering her body and soul like desperate explorers. She wished her eyes would close so that she didn't have to see her grandfather suffering a worse fate. To her body, they would just trespass; to his, they would stake their claim and never leave.

As more and more of the Ezias infected her, she felt just how many different souls they were, the flavors of each different. Some sad. Some angry. None happy. All driven by an insatiable need. Their fervor sickened her.

"*Here,*" one called to the others, having found something that caused him to salivate. "*This one, this ounce, yes here.*"

But others refused him, calling their attentions to other parts of her body, other things they found that she couldn't see or understand. They argued for long enough that she was able to get more accustomed to this violation, not accepting it but her panic slowed.

"*Yes,*" they whispered. "*We aren't so bad.*"

"*Do what you've come to do and leave,*" she pleaded in her mind, still unable to close her mouth as other Ezias entered her.

"*The tastiest bits are often hard to find. Later you may learn to shield them better—better we find the best bits now.*"

They continued as though she weren't even there while she watched her grandfather's body trembling, his eyes weeping as bit by bit he lost himself to them.

"*Here,*" a female voice said and the others gathered around, all of them finally agreeing. "*This one, yes, this one.*"

They rapidly joined together and pulled at an emotion and as they took their ounce, Morgan saw what she was losing. A moment of elation and love when she looked at Dusty, the moment he arrived in the Wild Wood, the moment she knew he was safe and still cared for the sevens. All of the lovely feeling of that moment, the Ezias consumed with much gnashing and a terrible numbing. Only a second later, when she thought of that moment, she felt nothing. Emptiness. Indifference.

"*No! Please don't take any more!*"

"*We've had our ounce... and it was delicious. Now we shall take our taste.*"

Together, the Ezias, thousands of them, merged together and launched themselves at her core, her soul, and bashed through it, causing shuddering Morgan couldn't stop, nightmares that she knew she'd never be free of. They had trodden through her soul, leaving a wake of their hostile poison. Her grandfather had been right—her soul would never be pristine again, never the same, like defiling a worship hall, they had come and left a mark that could never be removed.

Their taste would last forever, and so would the tether they left tied to her soul, so they could stomp through her life again and again, preying on the weakness she knew they would find. The dream of strength and the chance to cast them out died the moment she saw her grandfather's eyes turn indifferent, his tears evaporating in the dry wind and his face turning hard.

He wasn't himself anymore and Morgan's faith turned to dust, knowing without being told that she was destined to become just like him. What other choice did a girl without a destiny have?

21

Beloved Child

MILLIE FELT SO GOOD about supporting Oona by remaining in the jungle, waiting for something to happen, right up until the rain came. It spat at her from the sky above, reminding her why she hated rain. Annoying. Drippy. Soggy. Miserable.

Millie turned to Charity who had a look on her face that said in a decided fashion that she thought Millie had lost the few marbles she had and wasn't going to say anything in an effort to keep Millie from sobbing into the mud. Millie turned to Oona, who grimaced, surely sensing Millie's decision to abandon this plan in three, two, one...

Oona's face suddenly became jubilant. She looked to Millie, hopping up and down. "*It's come. It's come.*" A sigh came from her that told a story of faith about to break that was now renewed.

"*What's come?*" Millie asked.

"*You're right—I should have said,* they've *come.*" Oona pointed at a tree that began to shimmer just as two men, one with his hand on the other's shoulder, walked out from behind the shiny rippling and stood before Millie and Charity.

"Well hello," the Grey Cloak said, while Millie and Charity took a step back. "You two are much prettier than the last creatures we met. Thanks for that."

A face peered at them from around the Grey Cloak's shoulder. A familiar face, though his hair was very different, very short.

"Millie! Charity!" Dusty raced around the Grey Cloak to swallow them up in a big hug that only a person like Dusty could give.

Charity sobbed and Millie felt tears on her face. Oona watched them, crying too, her hands covering her mouth. But Millie realized it wasn't Dusty's, Millie's, or Charity's happiness that touched Oona just then—though there was something mysterious in her eyes when she glanced at Dusty—it was the sight of the Grey Cloak, standing back watching Dusty's joy. Oona stared at him like she hadn't seen him in a thousand years, as though he was the dead who had come back to life.

"Oona, are you okay?"

She nodded. *"Better than okay. But please, I need you to be my voice as soon as we are in the caverns. And we should go... soon."*

"Is *he* safe?" Charity asked Dusty, pointing at the Grey Cloak.

"Definitely," Dusty said. "Grey, come meet my friends—they are like my sisters."

Grey smiled and walked closer, his friendly face making him not nearly as scary as the other Grey Cloak who looked remarkably like him—they even had the same marks on their foreheads.

"Grey, this is Millie Smyth and Charity Culver. They are from Dunlowe."

"So they will have more stories of Mrs. Dumphry, yes?"

Charity blurted a laugh. "Oh, we all have tons of stories about Mrs. Dumphry."

"Wonderful." Grey extended his hand to Millie, who tentatively reached and took hold, feeling brave. "Nice to meet you, Miss Millie."

"Your name is Grey?" Millie asked.

"It is now. Dusty named me because I seem to have forgotten my name... and a bunch of other things."

Oona whispered something in Millie's mind and while Millie still had Grey's hand in hers and felt his goodness, so like Dusty's, she said, "Your name is Reece Greysen, and you are the rightful king of the Grey Folk."

*

Bay watched Amanda's and Abigail's faces as their boat neared another shore they wouldn't be able to reach. They watched, their faces grim, as desert overtook the forests near the water, overtook the sand, and drove into the sea. The water steamed. Such a large ocean that would one day run dry.

"We'll find a place to reach land—I promise."

"We haven't yet," Abigail whispered, a haunted tone growing in her voice to match the look on her face. She stared at the water, and her face held no less horror. Over the days, she'd seemed more and more distant, more and more fixated on the water. "Please, Bay, we need to get away from the water—I need..."

"Abigail," Amanda blurted. "Stop whining. Seriously. We all want to reach the shore and find our friends. Bay can't make the world different and we're luckier than anyone trapped on that burned-up land."

Abigail's head hung down. "Sorry."

"Abigail, is something happening to you, something we can't see... or feel?" Bay asked.

Abigail's eyes came up, her shock staring at him. "I..." She paused. "I don't know."

Amanda's expression changed as she stared at her sister. "What's happening? Is something happening?"

"There's something pulling at me from the water. I don't like it. It feels dark... and forever."

Amanda wrapped her arms around Abigail. "Nothing's going to hurt you here, nothing at all. I won't let it."

Abigail nodded. "Okay," she said, but clearly didn't believe.

Screams suddenly echoed nearby, seeming to come from the water itself. Screams that reminded Bay of the Strait of Darienne, where the cararks live to kill, where the screams of the dead echo for an eternity.

Bay moved carefully to peer over the edge of the boat and saw the swish of the cararks' mighty bodies and long tails. When he looked up, Mortimer caught his doom.

Mortimer's arms encompassed the two girls. "We're going to be fine."

Yes, Bay thought, lies really are for the best right now.

*

The first shades of sunset were upon Stephanie and she still hadn't decided. She'd paced most of the day, feeling anxious, trapped. This choice wasn't a choice between *every* possibility, just two. And they both were troublesome. If she remained, she couldn't find Dusty. She'd be alone, heading north, hoping to find somebody she knew. Dunlowe was gone. Kilby and Darstel could be too. Her family could be dead, all of them.

The idea of it struck her. Her father could be buried in one of the mounds she'd tried not to see in Dunlowe. Her brothers could be dead. Everyone. And if she remained here, she would be mortal. She would grow old and have gnarled hands and wrinkles and eventually die.

Or she could go back to Darienne, have powers, be beautiful, immortal, and fight to be queen. Ranz and Thorne needed some work, but she would find a way to take control in the end; she knew herself well enough to know that.

But what if things went badly there? What would happen when her friends knew what she was? How alone would she feel when her only companions were Ranz and Thorne, who each wanted to use her for something? Could she really marry a man who didn't care as much about love as he did about power?

She slumped onto the ground, wrapping her arms around her knees. If she stayed, she could try to find Logan—he was certainly too strong to die. If only she could ask him what he thought about all of this, but then she knew... he loved Dunlowe and a normal life. He never wanted more than that. Dusty could have stayed in Dunlowe forever and been happy; he had a joyous spirit that would be happy anywhere. Cecily and Nate would have gotten married, probably started a family if she hadn't been a seven, if Pastor Rowe hadn't turned crazy. Cecily could have been happy here. Millie. Charity. Abigail. They could be happy here. Not Amanda, she would have left searching for adventure. And Morgan would have gone to one of the universities in the north. She needed to learn, always.

A calm settled over Stephanie's heart. Morgan knew what she was and what she needed. Amanda knew and lived it. Stephanie had to come to terms with who she really was... and it certainly wasn't a simple girl living a simple life in a town like Dunlowe.

She was grateful for this time and this choice and knew that her path might turn disastrously dark, but at least she knew now why she had chosen it: because it was who she was. Stephanie Trench was born for power and if it didn't come to her, she would fight for it.

Stephanie held her journal to her and then kissed it. She took off her dress and wrapped it around the journal, tucking it and everything else she had removed back into the sheltered spot, not sure why, but feeling a sense of closure with that act. She looked down at her body, seeing herself as she had been, one last time.

"You know my choice. I want to go back."

Lavender light flickered and a jolt later, Stephanie felt a sharp blade against her neck.

"She's a traitor, my queen!" someone shouted. "She was rifling through your things."

Stephanie looked down at her hands holding Lille's possessions, including the bag of petals that had started this journey. Oriel held the dagger at her neck. The sharp blade had already cut her and the feel of her blood trickling caused a shudder that proved even more painful. When Stephanie glanced up at Lille from her place on her knees, ready to explain that her curiosity had gotten the better of her, she found the queen's face hard.

"Imprison her with the others."

"What? Lille, what are you talking about?"

Lille's violet eyes flashed. "Traitors are everywhere around me. I can't trust anyone."

"I was just curious."

"You don't know what you did—you don't know."

"I'm sorry. Please, I'm sorry."

"Get her out of here," Queen Lille ordered. "And if she fights you, kill her."

*

Morgan fell to the ground when the Ezias left her body, shuddering and weeping for what she'd lost. Her tears sizzled on the desert floor and her hands clutched into the dirt, bloodying themselves for their efforts. The hard, cracked dirt wouldn't give. This life wouldn't bend, wouldn't cut her a break. Wouldn't let her be happy. She'd found a sister and a place. A family. Lille wouldn't want her now, and neither would the Delphea trees.

Defiled. Tainted forever. The taste of the Ezias lingered in her mouth, their poison now hers to drink forever. Her place... gone. No reason to climb to her feet and keep walking, no reason at all.

"We must go back," the beasts controlling her grandfather said.

"No."

"Yes. We—I..." He tested out the word *I* like it had a foreign sound. "I must be the envoy for the Ezias, must help with this desert problem. We know much, more than you or the queen. Let's go."

"No."

"Why?"

"I want to die... here. I want to end. I hate this life... I hate what you've done. I *hate*."

"Yes." He leaned down, giving her shade with his body. "So do we."

"What you did... what you took..."

"You still don't see," he, or *they*, said.

She looked up at him, pained by seeing her grandfather's face, knowing his body was no longer his. "What do you mean?"

"We took our ounce, our taste, and left a tether."

She grunted. "Yes—yes, I know. You stole from me a memory, a feeling, I can never get back."

His eyes locked with hers. "But you can make another. You can hug that man you love... and *feel*. We can take that if you make a trade, but you can make another, and another. You can feel everything, every single day. Make new memories, thrive. We can't. We can't make a new feeling—we can't feel *anything* on our own. The emptiness you feel in that one memory is all we have, all we are. You see us as parasites, stealing from the living. We see ourselves as trapped souls, yearning for hope that we were denied. A place to live... or even die. Anything other than to swirl aimlessly for an eternity, feeling nothing."

Morgan swallowed over her dry throat. "Were you ever real people?"

"As real as you are, but our tribe was cursed into becoming this plague upon the world."

"Why do you seem so different now that you are in my grandfather?"

"Because his long life was enough to truly feed us, to remind us of what it is like to be... human."

"Is he still in there?"

"Yes."

"What does he want me to do?"

"Live."

*

Zoe followed Jacoby—alone with him for the first time, though she knew Mindy and Heath were trailing them, the only two who knew where she was. More battles, more fighting. Their enemies seemed to know their plans, practically before they did. Mr. Daye, Mrs. Hardy, and Mr. Kent searched through the group, listening, watching—seeking out their traitor—but their work had come to nothing. Zoe had to do something, had to place herself in harm's way, to know at last whether Jacoby was the traitor. Mindy's suggestion was tempting, but randomly killing all the suspects was a bridge too far for Zoe, who still struggled with killing the enemy soldiers.

So, here she was, alone in the darkness with Jacoby as he led her to the place where his old life ended. When they left the cover of the trees, the moon shone down on the perfect place for a small home, a peaceful place on a hill surrounded by trees, with a stream running just fifty yards away. But there was no house, only ashes, most of which had blown away.

"We had a front porch and a swing," Jacoby whispered. "We sat there every night and watched the sun as it dipped below those trees. When we had Emmaline, the first thing we showed her was that porch swing."

Jacoby's ragged voice, so full of pain, pulled at Zoe, who

took a step and rested her hand on his shoulder.

"She's not going to remember me or her mother. She's just a little girl, nearing two. Blonde hair—always tied with a green ribbon—and big blue eyes. She won't know me. She won't know where she came from. She'll believe whatever they tell her, whoever they tell her she is—nothing more than a slave." His words choked out and grew more filled with naked anguish. "If I don't find her soon, she'll grow up. How will I be certain what she looks like, who she is? What if I can't find her because I can't remember what she looks like? What if I fail—what if she never knows who I am or that she had a mother and father who loved her?"

His tears fell and so did Zoe's. He might be a traitor, but this pain was real.

"What was Emmaline's room like?" Zoe asked, sniffling as she did.

"My wife painted suns and moons on the walls, and made a beautiful quilt that was bright and cheerful. Emmaline would never have known hardship if I had any power, but I couldn't help her." His voice grew more distant. "The soldiers were here when Cecily sent me back, after that stupid attack on the sevens and their families. If Cecily hadn't used her magic, they would have been long gone by the time I reached home."

"I wonder if Cecily knew."

"I don't think so," Jacoby said. "I think she would have stopped it. When I appeared back here, I raced up that hill as my wife fought the soldiers who were trying to get her to leave our baby behind. She fought so hard, and then one of the soldiers struck her and she fell. She was gone in an instant. I went mad and killed one of them and the other three caught me, dragged me to the cage they were building in town. I prayed for death, begged the soldiers for it, but they knew living would be the worst punishment. I saw Emmaline later in a wagon heading north with some women and children. She still had her green bow in her hair, a thick green bow with an *E* stitched into both ends... by her mother."

Zoe moved in front of Jacoby, blocking his view of the house that was no more and reached her arms around him, pulling him to her and holding him as he wept. Holding him as he said goodbye to the life that was gone. She felt his pain as though it were her own, as though this little blonde girl with a green bow was hers to mourn. It didn't make sense, but at that moment she didn't care, until she saw movement in the woods near them, the flash of a blade stealing the moon's reflection.

She shoved Jacoby away. "Traitor!"

*

Darla was part of me. I felt it—I'd *always* felt it, from the first moment I saw her and heard the beasts within her, torturing her. That brought my mind to a sudden stop.

"Devra, who hurt her?" I asked. "Who hurt Darla when she was a baby? You didn't, did you?"

Devra shook her head. "No, and I couldn't help her at that time, couldn't get to her. Pastor Rowe made many deals with all sorts of nefarious types. The house was shielded in some way, poison to those who might enter uninvited. I had to trust that you would save her."

"But who did it?"

Darla's hand rested on my face and I looked down at her. "Please don't ask," she whispered. "There are bigger things to worry about right now—you fixed it, you saved me. That's enough."

"I don't understand. You know who did it?"

"I think I figured it out, but it confuses everything. Let's worry about it later when the world isn't dying. Please."

Little sprite, I thought as I caressed her face. She could ask me for the world and I would give it. For her, I would let this go... for now.

"Fine." I looked to Devra. "Tell us what you fight for."

The shiny blue screen flickered and showed images of desert landscape, flashes from many places. Being in the caverns, I felt removed from the vulnerability I felt on the surface of the world, of the pain living in that growing barren space.

"The seer came to me and told me I would need instruments, so I created them. The seer told me to be ready for your arrival, and I was, and I made it in time. The seer has guided me to this place where I have an army ready to fight for the world, as well as the world's most beloved child here in this cavern."

I looked to Nate, then Finn, and back to Devra. "What do you mean *the world's most beloved child*? Darla?"

Devra's eyes eased from the same light blue as Finn's to deep indigo. "You. The seer said it, said all of this is about you... your connection to the Source."

"That's severed now. I'm not the most *beloved* anything. I'm just Cecily."

"Your connection is severed and the world is dying—don't you see?"

"No, I don't see. What do you mean?"

"What is your connection to the Source?" Devra asked. "The seer couldn't see that, didn't understand. We all know you gave up massive power to return, but something happened in the process to create this destruction. What is the connection?"

My mouth remained shut as I stared at Darla, but I didn't really see her. My thoughts rumbled about, pressing me to consider what I would do if anyone took her from me, if anyone killed her, if anyone drained her life. And then I saw what the outcome would be if *I* had to be the one to drain her, to kill her, to hurt her. I would die before I let that happen.

"Oh no..."

Devra moved closer. "Tell me. I've waited so long to understand what is happening, to know *why* I must do the things I've done. I've done it all because the seer told me to—to be a Keeper for the world as Annisha sentenced me—and I believe the seer still. She hasn't led me astray. *What* is your connection to the Source?"

Tears stopped my words as I fought to hold back a sob. The Source...

Finn's voice broke through the silence. "Cecily is the Source's daughter."

"No," Devra breathed while Nate said, "What?"

I nodded. "I am. I am her daughter and she had to do this to me to save all of the worlds she created... and now she's grieving for what she did to her child and this world is dying. I think the *Source* of all of us, of all of the worlds, is dying."

22

Legacy

CROSSING THE GATEWAY and finding Millie and Charity—and that they were okay—well, that was an awesome moment for Dusty, but finding out that Grey was supposed to be the king: super awesome. But Grey didn't seem to think so. His face stumbled through a variety of expressions, finally landing on a petulant kind of empty as he wandered a few feet away.

"Say it again," Grey pleaded with Millie.

"You are Reece Greysen, the rightful king of the Grey Folk."

Grey moved rapidly toward her, grabbing her arm, while she attempted to flinch from him. "How do you know?"

Millie looked about to piddle like a puppy and Dusty, wishing to avert that little adventure, tugged Grey back.

"You're scaring her, Grey."

"I am so very sorry," Grey said instantly. "Please forgive me."

Millie nodded, while perhaps tinkling a tiny bit. Millie became distracted for a second and then said, "We have to go now. Please take us to the caverns and then we will explain everything."

Charity muttered, "*We*? *I* don't know anything."

Millie grabbed Charity's hand. "You aren't part of the *we*

actually, but I'll finally tell you what I've been keeping from you since Dunlowe."

Charity smiled, hugging Millie. "Finally!"

"Everybody touch." Dusty led the way through the invisible doorway to the underworld.

Once on the other side, Dusty turned to check on the girls and found them wide eyed and staring at the caverns. "You get used to it and there's no better way to wander around the world—except there are a bunch of creatures down here, the wolves are particularly bad. Snakes are also not good. And there are some strange flapping creatures. But mostly, it's great. It would be nice to know where you're going to end up when you leave through a gateway though."

"I don't think that's going to be a problem." Millie cringed when a wolf's howl danced around the caverns, but she pulled herself together and studied Dusty. "You look different."

Dusty's brow crunched. "Oh, you mean the hair—yeah, well, we had a fight with a beast recently and my hair was a bit of a problem, falling in my eyes all the time."

"It's not just your hair; it's everything," Charity said.

"You look like a warrior," Millie added.

Okay, now Dusty was really glad they'd found the girls. He couldn't wait to see Cecily and be a... *man*. But right now he was too embarrassed to say very much and was very grateful to Grey—who after a smirk that made Dusty's face redden more—changed the subject.

"Will you tell me how you know me?"

Charity grunted. "Yes, Millie. Tell us about yourself... *finally*."

"We should sit."

Millie led the way to a large flat rock and attempted to brush it off to seriously limited results, before finally taking a seat. Once the others joined her, she fidgeted with her hands for a minute. "So, it's kinda like this, I can see *dead* people... and beasts."

*

Oriel roughly dragged Stephanie from Lille's tent and Stephanie allowed herself to be dragged. She felt disoriented from the journey... or maybe from the aftereffects of eating the petal. Either way, her body wasn't working right, didn't feel right at all. When she did get fed up with Oriel's hands on her, she reached for her power to drain Morgan's true love, but found none. She tried again and again, but felt nothing, no power.

She'd made her choice—she should have her power back. She definitely felt her brand just where it should be, under her dress that had thankfully been on her body when she returned.

Oriel shoved her into a wooden cage with Duncan and Capria, both of whom wore bruises from a beating. Would Stephanie be next? Surely not, only she didn't believe anything was certain now.

Stephanie leaned against the bars. "*Ranz?*" Nothing. "*Ranz? Are you there?*"

He wasn't, so she attempted to use the brand to reach Thorne, but didn't feel her connection to him at all.

"The fall from grace is always the best sight of all," Duncan said.

"They will kill you for this," Stephanie said.

Capria wore a strange look. Stephanie hadn't seen her much

since Lille ordered her south after she betrayed Lille and the rest of the Protectors in the Downs, just as Duncan had in allying with the Grey Cloaks and the mystics. Pieces finally fit. Duncan and Capria were on Stephanie's side... perhaps.

"Why did you do it?" Stephanie asked. "Why stab Lille now?"

"We are running out of time."

"Why?"

"One of our own is coming to finish things. These bodies are faltering." Capria looked to Duncan, while Stephanie studied them both, confused, but feeling danger as the two looked at her like wolves before a feast.

Duncan turned to Capria. "One chance, before her connection and power are restored."

"Just one," Capria said, nodding.

A second later, they leapt at Stephanie. Capria's hands reached for Stephanie's neck as Duncan punched her gut.

Stephanie fought for her power, while still helplessly trying to keep them at bay. But she had no power. They had her air—she couldn't call for help—and just like in the sea, she felt herself going under, only this time she wasn't ready to go without a fight.

*

"Read it, Logan. Right now," Mrs. Dumphry ordered while Logan considered violence.

"I can read, Mrs. Dumphry—it's not that."

"Then read it."

Logan ignored the tightness in his chest and looked at the

open page of the book Mrs. Dumphry held in front of him. "The Great God Dunn advocates learning for children, but that learning must always be tempered with character building and the refinement of morality coupled with an understanding of the eternal price of failure."

"Sheesh," Mrs. Dumphry choked. "No wonder you all hated me. Look at what we taught you: learn or *else*."

Under his breath, Logan added, "It might have had something to do with that ruler of yours."

Mrs. Dumphry grinned. "You know I saved it from destruction, don't you?"

Logan blanched, while Mrs. Dumphry laughed, looking less and less like an ogre all the time.

"Just kidding. But Logan, you read just fine. Why the struggle?"

Logan swallowed. "My mother. One night, we read together from a story she loved—I haven't thought about that story in forever, but I still remember that it was about a town so low to the sea that houses had to be built on stilts—and then I went to bed. When I woke, she was gone forever. Ever since then I read as little as possible, but I do remember loving it before she left. I remember reading to her almost every night. I'd tell her stories and she let me tuck her in. I felt so special then; when she left, she took that with her." He stopped talking before his voice gave out.

Mrs. Dumphry gently patted Logan's face. "I remember when your mother first moved to Dunlowe. Something had happened to her parents, something we weren't to ask about—Pastor Rowe said. We were all a lot younger then, but we did as

Pastor Rowe ordered, hardly ever questioning. Although now that I think about it, some people did question—your mother was one of them. She was nineteen then and madly in love with your father. Next to her beauty, your sister looks like a bug. Rosa held such a joy about the world that it shined out and made everyone feel more warm. I'd never seen a woman love her children more in all my life. When she left you all, there was much talk, but I think we were all afraid to ask the real question."

"Which was?" Logan pressed.

"Why so many people who questioned Pastor Rowe disappeared."

Now the tightness in his chest felt more pointed. "Jem, bring your slave over here."

Jem nodded and directed Pastor Rowe to stand before Logan and Mrs. Dumphry, who whispered to Logan, "Should I stab him a couple times just for fun?"

Mrs. Daye and Mrs. Rowe moved closer, while Logan shook his head just slightly to Mrs. Dumphry, keeping his eyes focused on Pastor Rowe. "Did you have anything to do with my mother leaving Dunlowe?"

The dead man became nervous, his beady eyes flashing from the watching faces and then to Jem who instantly understood.

"You will tell us the truth whenever anyone asks you a question."

Pastor Rowe looked like a fish on a hook. "I did and I didn't."

"Speak plainly," Logan growled. "Or we are going to see what happens if we cut you in pieces and tie them to trees all over Stoughton."

Pastor Rowe's hands clenched. "I made a deal—I made a bunch of deals. I didn't know what I was doing... clearly, since I'm currently a slave to my killer. But the deals all had prices and I didn't always know who instigated them. There are brokers of magicks, so you don't know who profits from the payments."

"What did that have to do with my mother leaving?"

"Everything. It turned out your mother wasn't from Stoughton at all and was hiding here. She was from somewhere across the seas. There was a bounty for her return and I set the trap that got her caught."

Logan picked up his dagger and launched it at Pastor Rowe. It stuck out of Pastor Rowe's chest while he stood there, looking annoyed.

"You can keep doing that all day; it is uncomfortable for me. But you can't kill me—you can't even wish me dead more than I already wish for it, Logan Trench."

"Don't count on it. You..."

A strange sizzling sound stole Logan's curse words.

"What is that?" Mrs. Rowe asked, glaring at her dead husband.

He held up his hands. "I have no idea. Is it just me or is the ground growing hot?"

Jem looked at the ground and then at Logan. "The ground *is* getting hot."

A scream came from someone in the crowd.

"We need to get everyone away," Mrs. Daye stammered, but her eyes fell on Logan. "But..."

"Just go!" Logan ordered.

"Like hell," Mrs. Dumphry spat. "Come on, *Clevis* Rowe,

put your back into it."

Jem hastily directed Pastor Rowe to one end of Logan's litter and together, while barking orders all around them, Jem, Pastor Rowe, Mrs. Daye, and Mrs. Dumphry lifted Logan—the useless—off of the ground and carried him to the north. Other wounded were carried or limped to keep up. The children ran ahead of everyone and townsfolk carried the babies. Logan was instantly free of the heat, but he could see in the faces around him the proof of their continued pain. When he glanced back, he saw what looked like a desert forming from what had been only seconds before a thick green growing space.

A scream brought his eyes to the group trailing them and as he watched, the sizzling earth sparked and a few townsfolk vanished before Logan could focus on who they were. Mrs. Smyth's face filled with terror and she let out a cry before her body turned into a flash of flame and a second later, nothing remained but a whiff of smoke.

"Run!" Logan cried as other townsfolk disappeared and all he could do was watch.

*

Nate sat just inches from Cecily but in his mind, he was miles away, struggling to deal with the fact that his lineage included some demons and a kind human, while Cecily was born of two good humans but was actually the Source's child. He'd heard from Cecily about her experiences in the Source, but nothing prepared him for the reality that his ex-girlfriend, the person he'd attempted to kill, was the child of a deity. Was Cecily a god?

Nate felt warmth in his mind—Devra's touch. "*I am feeling*

unsteady with this knowledge, just as you are. And I don't know the answer. The child of the Source is in this cavern, such a small distance from me. And yet, she is still just a young woman living as well as she can with the burdens she holds. For my part, the fact that the Source would believe Annisha's soul worthy of this gift shows a real want of judgment."

Nate didn't understand all that, but his heart and hopes faltered. He was a demon and she was a god. How could there be any chance for him... and her... for *them*?

Cecily caught him staring. "Why are you looking at me like that? Why are *all* of you looking at me like that?" She looked down at Darla. "Even you. Why?"

No one said anything for a few seconds and then Finn's voice echoed through the chamber. "They are feeling as I did when I first found out. You see, faith in general has faded from Darienne—it is the State, not religion, that guides us. The Source was believed to be a place, an empty one filled with energy that fueled the world, until you met *her*. In other countries like Stoughton, religion has been corrupted by leaders and much of the goodness removed, though the faithful and their struggles for decency are honorable. To be in the presence of the Source's child calls into question our worthiness to be here. Clearly, I wasn't worthy. The fact that I didn't know who you really were changes nothing. You aren't like anyone else alive—you stand apart."

"You're being ridiculous."

Nate, hating more than anything to agree with Finn, said, "No, he's not. We should be bowing to you, groveling at your feet, begging for forgiveness."

"Don't be stupid." Cecily grabbed Nate's hand, but he flinched away from her touch, causing hurt to shine at him from her eyes. "I'm me. That's all. The Source loved Annisha's soul, thought it perfect, and made me her own daughter. And then I almost destroyed worlds, so she took the power back. I'm not perfect and I'm beginning to wonder if Annisha really was." Cecily glanced from Devra, whose face turned hard, to Finn. "Was she perfect? Did she judge Devra more harshly because she's a demon, because of your lie, because you had been married to Devra?"

Finn looked sick as he whispered, "Yes to all counts. Annisha wasn't perfect. She hated demons and struggled every day we were together because she felt tainted for loving me. But she was mostly good—she was. She was mostly fair. When she sacrificed herself for this mission, it was partially in penance for her regrets about the things she'd done and to free the people of Darienne from her bigotry. She wanted them to have a clean slate, not revere her so much. That kind of legacy and reverence is a burden for anyone. Of course she wasn't perfect. She was flawed and struggled just like the rest of us."

Cecily's eyes filled with tears as she cradled Darla. "Oh no... no... was it Annisha who tortured Darla? Some legacy of her vengeance against you, Devra? Did she? Was it *me*?"

"I didn't know it would happen," Devra said softly. "I didn't know, and it didn't happen with Nate. I put just enough of me into him to have the connection, but mostly he is Delibrien and Mrs. Rowe. But I needed Darla to be stronger and I had limited resources, so she carries more of me, and when I combined her with part of you, some part of Annisha's sentence flared to life.

You see, part of her sentence was that my body would be as barren as she perceived my heart to be. I cannot have children from my body, but I had no idea that my sins—or her slanderous will—would hurt children brought about outside of my body. The monsters who clawed inside Darla's tender spirit are my future if I ever disobey Annisha's very powerful ruling." Tears filled Devra's eyes as she looked at Darla's wet face. "I am so sorry."

"We'll do better," Cecily breathed, rocking Darla. "We'll do better... if we live long enough."

*

Morgan walked beside the body of her grandfather, her steps shaky, her will absent. Her hand kept resting against the pocket of her dress, feeling the outline of her glasses. They had become her anchor, proof that somewhere inside her was the Morgan she had been. She tripped once and her grandfather's hand shot out to catch her.

Morgan thanked him before silencing herself, refusing to speak any more to the Ezias, though they continued to talk to her about the land and how beautiful it had been. They told her about the Deeper Reaches, the place somewhere in the middle of the earth, in the deepest layer, where they had won a domain of their own, thanks to a treacherous man who had come to guide them. They'd never had a king before, never had plans and a purpose—he gave that to them, unified them with a goal. He'd given them orders and then left them to obey. He'd ordered them not to contact him, but a rebellion came, severing the ties when he had been gone too long. A faction wanted to remain loyal to their king, while the others wanted him dead and the memory of their servitude obliterated.

"Which are you?" Morgan asked, her curiosity taking control.

"We are loyal to our king."

Morgan looked at him for a second before turning away to stare at the ground. "Does that mean...?"

"Yes. Our king instructed us to find you and take you as our own, but we think he will be pleased with this outcome."

"Who is your king and why would he want to hurt me?"

The Ezias said nothing for a few seconds before saying, "Give us another ounce, another taste, and we will tell you."

Morgan shook her head. "Never."

She felt the Ezias' eyes on her. "Lies do not become you. Face the truth. You will need us. You will see that we can be allies to you, and while you can make new memories, you will never wear out, as long as you never give too much at a time."

"Nothing is worth that—nothing."

"Then you lack imagination, which we know is not true. So that makes you a liar... or one who hasn't accepted the truth." He looked distant for a second and a swirl of Ezias appeared around him, all whispering too quickly for Morgan to understand.

"What is it?"

"Take my hand."

"Why?"

"I must show you the conduit. We don't have time to move slowly now."

"The conduit? My grandfather said something about that."

"He's urging you to listen, to do as I say, without argument."

Morgan squinted. "Sure he is." Knowing there was no way to know the truth, Morgan reached and took his hand.

A second later, she appeared in a cavern, hearing a familiar voice echoing off the walls.

"You see dead people?!!!"

But before she could ask anything, the world went dark for a second before she appeared again, this time in front of a cell—a cell that held Stephanie, who was being strangled by Capria and beaten by Duncan.

For the rest of her life—however long or short that might be—Morgan would always doubt her goodness because it took a *long* moment before she called for help.

23

Mostly Dead

Bay let out a breath as he saw his life, his death, all of the terrible and wonderful things he'd done play out in his mind as cararks circled the boat. Their huge bodies could wreck the wood like it were dry autumn leaves under a careless foot. He heard the screams of the dead, the deaths he had witnessed, carried in the cararks' bodies, blaring out and bringing him back to the lesser days of his life when winning meant more than living.

He looked at Abigail with her dark eyes trained on the water and Amanda, who seemed genuinely afraid, and wondered how he had ended up here, a guardian to these children. Where was his war? Where was the reckoning that had to come?

A carark swiped the boat and it lurched to one side. Mortimer and Bay grabbed Amanda and Abigail, ensuring they remained inside as the boat swayed greatly before finding its equilibrium.

"Don't let them take me," Abigail pleaded in Bay's arms, and he knew he would give himself for her, if the choice came—if he had that power.

Full circle. A good man, corrupted, had become a good man again. Could it be that simple?

"Bay," Mortimer grunted, and Bay turned to stare into the

distance at the head of a carark, moving swiftly toward them, aiming to ram them.

The moment was here. The chance to save them all, to save these girls. The choice.

But he couldn't do it—couldn't face it. No. Bay wouldn't have his chance at redemption—wouldn't use the one tool at his command that might save them—but at least their deaths would be quick.

Cecily, he thought, *I'm sorry I'm not a better man.*

✶

"A traitor?!" Jacoby stammered, staring at Zoe, his eyes squinting at her in the moonlight. "I'm not a traitor to you, Zoe. I would never do anything to hurt you. I'm your..."

"Shush," Zoe ordered as her mind stuttered over the meaning of his honesty, of who was the traitor if Jacoby wasn't. "We're not alone."

Jacoby spun to face the soldiers emerging from the woods, their swords reflecting the moon's beams. Jacoby and Zoe spread out, each grabbing for their weapons. There were so many—too many. Some carried loaded crossbows, a single arrow an ending. Zoe's strength faltered as she watched Mindy emerge from the woods with the soldiers, followed by Heath. Zoe's heart, her hope, her *everything*, fluttered and wished for death.

"It's time to die," the soldier at the lead said. "It really is too bad that the great and legendary Zoe Crane could be brought down by such simple betrayal."

Zoe had no words and lowered her dagger.

"Zoe, don't give up," Jacoby muttered, before looking at

Mindy and Heath. "What did you do? Why?"

"I did what I had to do," Heath blurted. "To save what was left of my family. I made Mindy understand—she understands now. She's on my side, the king's side."

Weariness—a brand new kind—washed through Zoe's body. "They kidnapped your family, killing townsfolk in the process, as part of a deal with you? To get you to betray me? *Us?*"

"Yeah," Heath said. "I didn't know that others would die, but yes, the soldiers helped my family. My dad was going to lose his leg if he didn't get to a doctor—we didn't have a doctor, not since Doc Forester died or got lost in Dunlowe. I couldn't lose any more of my family. You don't understand—you don't have anyone left to lose."

Zoe grimaced from the pain inspired by his words, from the narrow idea that having no one left to lose made her luckier in some way. He couldn't understand, not with a huge family, full of love. But Mindy could—Mindy who had no one left to lose either.

"You betrayed me," Zoe said to Mindy.

"It was you or Heath—what choice do I have?" Simple betrayal. "I told you I wouldn't make a good leader—*remember?*"

Zoe nodded, wondering at Mindy's tone and the confused slant of Heath's head. But instead of moving on that, Zoe looked at the soldiers. "Why don't you join us? Help us to free your families, to change the country. Do any of you really want me to die?"

"Yes," Mindy said. "They do. They *hate* you... because you still dare to hope and fight for a new future, while they are cowards who've already surrendered."

"Hey," a soldier said, while others muttered.

The leader said, "Let's finish this and meet up with the others."

"Others?" Zoe asked.

"They are attacking our rebels as we speak," Mindy said. "They are all going to die. What's *your* first instinct?"

Instinct? Not a good leader? The words mashed together inspired a memory. When Zoe had challenged the other rebels and said that Mindy would be the better leader, Mindy's words had been simple: *My first instinct is to shoot... whoever.*

Zoe caught the dark look in Mindy's eyes, even through the darkness. Heath or Zoe? Mindy's choice wasn't simple at all. In the defiant tilt of Mindy's chin, Zoe suddenly knew the real choice Mindy had made, and it wasn't for Heath. Friendship and loyalty over love—Zoe wondered if she would have made the same call as her heart broke for her friend who could never be a traitor.

"My first instinct is *exactly* the same as yours."

"Right," Mindy said, calm and seemingly at peace, before she shouted, "Now!"

Mindy punched Heath, knocking him out, while grabbing her bow. Jacoby and Zoe attacked the soldiers, keeping their attentions, while Mindy threaded her bow and went to work, thinning the herd of soldiers to a more manageable number. The fighting erupted into a state of chaos that Zoe could barely take in. Like in the tent with the three soldiers she'd killed, she fought as though her body itself were the weapon. Jacoby existed in a blur of violence and a few seconds later, the soldiers' bodies littered the ground in the same place where other soldiers had killed Jacoby's wife.

Mindy trembled as she loaded her bow, looking down at Heath's body sprawled on the ground. He began to stir, while she pointed an arrow at him.

"You're a traitor. You deserve to die."

Mindy's entire body shook, as Heath cried on the ground. "I did it to save my family—I thought you understood."

"You're really stupid enough to believe that the king will keep his promise? Yeah, he probably healed them so they would make better slaves."

Heath shook his head as his expression turned to confusion. "No, the king wouldn't do that."

"But he would do *this*? Kill Dunlowe? Kill kids? You picked the wrong side—you deserve a coward's death."

Zoe walked slowly to Mindy. "We have to go fight with our friends. Just leave him behind. You don't have to kill him."

"Remember, Zoe, you are all forgiveness and unity. I'm not."

Zoe patted her arm. "I'm your leader, and I'm telling you to let him go. There are so few of us left from Dunlowe, one day that number will be zero. I'd rather Heath survive to remember us."

Mindy slowly lowered her bow, her face wet with tears. "Let's go."

"Jacoby, make sure he doesn't follow."

Zoe heard the sound of a fist impacting with a traitor's head, but she couldn't care about that, only Mr. Daye and others who were fighting for their lives and the future of a country.

✶

Stephanie's air was gone; her body, still with traces of mortality, failed. Capria's hands at her throat tightened and Stephanie felt the end, but then as though in a dream, she heard Morgan's voice calling for help. Morgan? It couldn't be.

But Stephanie heard the soldiers gathering around, the door to the cage opened, and many hands dragged Capria and Duncan away from Stephanie. Morgan stood nearby—it had been her.

Stephanie tasted the wrongness of owing her life to the girl she'd tried to kill, but pushed that away. "Thank you," she choked out.

Morgan nodded, her eyes dark. "What are you doing in there? What did you do?"

"Morgan?" Oriel moved closer, taking Morgan in his arms, but only for a second before Morgan shoved him away and looked down. Oriel looked confused for a second and then his eyes wandered over Stephanie, Capria, and Duncan. "What's going on here?"

"Yes, what is going on?" Lille demanded, rushing up, intending to get to Morgan, but Oriel held up his hand to the queen, requesting she stop.

Oriel studied Morgan. "What is going on?"

"I believe I can be helpful in this matter," an older man said—an older man who looked exactly like Morgan's dead grandfather.

Oriel gaped. "Josiah? Is that you?"

"This is Josiah Hale's body, but he doesn't control it anymore."

Lille moved closer. "Who's Josiah...?" Her words tapered as

she stared more closely at Morgan. "Morgan, what's happened?"

Morgan raised her face to meet Lille's, but she looked uncomfortable, embarrassed maybe, or ashamed. "Josiah Hale is my grandfather. I thought he was dead, but he lived and now the Ezias control him."

Shocked gasps erupted and everyone moved away from Josiah, all weapons pulled from scabbards and pointed at him.

Josiah didn't seem worried. "I come as an envoy, to work with you."

Lille stood proudly, though her fear was plain to see. "Why would we work with you?"

"Because this barren land is a threat to us all."

Stephanie had held her tongue for long enough. "Fine, but can't we worry about the fact that Capria and Duncan tried to *kill* me?!"

"I believe I can assist with that also," Josiah said, without emotion.

Oriel ignored him and looked to Morgan. "Sweetheart, are you infected?"

Morgan bit her lip and shook her head. "No, but..." Tears fell and her body trembled. "But they... they were *inside* me. They took... something, but they didn't stay."

Lille covered her mouth and took a step away from Morgan.

Oriel remained still, showing no emotion at all for a few seconds. "Tell me something funny, Morgan."

"What?" she asked, looking like she'd lost her compass.

"Tell me something funny."

Morgan still didn't understand and Josiah said, "The Ezias have no sense of humor. He is testing you, though there isn't any need."

Oriel, Lille, the Commanders—everyone waited for Morgan, who looked worse than Stephanie had ever seen her look, to come up with something funny. Morgan failed, her trembling growing worse, her vulnerability and pain shouting at everyone, but no one did anything to help.

"Lock her up," Oriel said, his voice constricted, while Morgan shook her head and almost fell.

Stephanie felt the memories of her first time in Ranz's cell and whispered, "Morgan, think about Dusty—remember the time…"

Morgan nodded as she tried to control her crying. "Dusty… um… he was mad after Mrs. Dumphry picked on Cecily one day—he filled Mrs. Dumphry's desk with frogs, her wagon with worms, and hid manure in socks all around Mrs. Dumphry's house, even the chimney." Morgan blurted a laugh. "He kept adding more. She stank for months—Pastor Rowe…" Morgan laughed soundly. "… Pastor Rowe kept giving lessons about hygiene, while Dusty just sat there grinning."

Morgan's laugh turned to more tears as she hunched over. "I promise, I'm not infected… but that doesn't mean I'm not tainted."

Genovan and the Commanders moved closer. "She's not infected and if you don't stop making her cry, we are going to be angry." His arm surrounded Morgan, who leaned into him, accepting his help. "What about the matter at hand? Duncan? Capria?"

"They *are* infected," Josiah said, as Duncan and Capria shouted their denials, only to be silenced by ropes shoved into their mouths. "They have broken with our king and are acting in an alliance to destroy Lille. They have been infected for a long while, gathering information, controlling outcomes, searching for their moment to destroy you all. I believe they almost succeeded and would have if not for the Daye boy and the return of the Daye girl."

Shock covered Lille's face. "Capria was a friend... until she turned on me, on our cause."

"She didn't turn—neither did Duncan. They were infected and consumed."

"Is there any way to save Capria and Duncan?" Lille asked.

Josiah shook his head. "There is nothing left to save. They must be killed right now and with my help."

Oriel looked to Lille, who, after a pause, nodded. Oriel signaled to the soldiers holding Duncan and Capria. Stephanie shuddered at how quickly they were killed, while Josiah moved in, his hands on each of their chests. Dark spirits circled and shrieked as Capria's and Duncan's bodies quivered and jerked until the screaming stopped and all went quiet. Stephanie stared at the bodies that turned to dust before her eyes.

The silence felt uncomfortable when Stephanie realized everyone was staring at her.

Lille's voice was cold when she said, "And what are we going to do with you?"

*

Millie bit her lip as the others stared at her. She'd covered dead people, angry ghosts, why she loved her cat, and such. And then she'd gone into how Oona brought her to the place where

Dusty and Reece would be and at about that point, all of their eyes glassed over and Millie wasn't certain whether she should continue.

"*We need to continue. Things are getting desperate in the world.*"

"Oona says we need to keep talking and then get walking."

Grey stared at her. "You hear her right now... and she's really my niece?"

"She's right next to you. She loves you a lot. You were the best part of her childhood and then you were gone and her mother was killed. And then her father planned to kill her but she got away. She's only *mostly* dead, you know. Not completely dead. We're going to get her body and she's going to get back in it and then..."

"*There may not be time. Things are changing fast.*"

"We need to get moving—the world is dying, desert is covering it. Our friends are in trouble, and we need to do all we can." Millie looked to Oona. "That enough?"

"*Yes. My body will have to wait. Let's move... toward the only one who has even a prayer of fixing this.*"

Millie stood up, grateful that the others, though still a bit overwhelmed, stood with her and moved in the direction she led, following Oona. When Oona moved faster, Millie hurried to catch up and the others were soon running. Millie felt Oona's panic and knew she wanted more than anything to be back in her body. If she gave that up—even for a little while—it meant that things were *really* bad.

"Oona, can you see a chance for us? For everyone?"

"*I've never seen that—everything about the Source is hidden from me. That's why things change so much. We have to reach the others... we just have to try. Please run faster."*

"Come on!" Millie shouted and raced after Oona.

*

Morgan felt Genovan's support, but her weariness smothered her gratitude. The look in Oriel's eyes, the horror staring at her from Lille's face, had her leaning into Genovan, barely caring if she fell, only knowing that Genovan would never let that happen.

"And what are we going to do with you?" Lille asked, glaring at Stephanie.

Morgan didn't know or care at this moment what Stephanie had done, she only knew that Stephanie had helped her at one of the weakest moments of her life.

"Please don't hurt her," Morgan managed to say, but Lille cut her dead with a look.

"I can't trust anyone," Lille whispered. "Not Stephanie who almost got herself killed going through my things or..." She looked to Morgan. "... or you. The defilers have been inside you, have sullied you. I don't see how you can remain my heir."

"My queen," Oriel said. "Now is not the time, and *this* is not the place."

Lille seemed to suddenly understand how many people were hearing her talk about not having an heir. The mystics floated nearby, their faces glowing though they seemed uncomfortable after witnessing the executions of their former allies. But Morgan saw a triumphant glare in Ameel's eyes as the mystic smugly looked at the ruin Morgan had become.

Lille fumbled with the pouch tied to her waist and Morgan saw the hint of a lavender petal in Lille's hand. After a second,

Lille stood more erect. "I am sorry, Morgan, for doubting you. Of course, you are my heir, but things have changed. If you accept the changes, you will remain my sister, my heir, my only family." Her words seemed genuine, but Morgan felt a hardness that had never been there before.

"What changes?"

"I've never asked you to swear your allegiance to me and my rule. I will require that now."

"I'll do anything," Morgan said quickly. "Just tell me what to do."

"Kneel."

Genovan released Morgan and she moved forward, dropping to her knees in front of Lille.

"Swear to serve me, to obey every order, to love Darienne, and to be willing to give your life to preserve this country and my rule."

"I swear... to it all," Morgan stammered, staring at the ground.

"Okay then. Rise."

Morgan climbed to her feet, with Genovan stepping forward to ensure her legs held her. Morgan extended her hand to Lille, craving the connection of their palms and the songs of the Delphea trees. But Lille flinched away.

"No, Morgan, you mustn't ever touch me again. Not me, or Oriel, who is my chief protector and advisor. I can't have your taint touching him ever again—I might be polluted, disgraced forever."

If not for Genovan's arms, Morgan would have given up her struggle to stand. The hardness remained in Lille's eyes and

Morgan saw treachery growing. Oriel wouldn't even look at her, probably wishing he could bathe after touching her tarnished body.

Josiah stepped forward. "The desert is coming and you worry about minutia. What is an heir if none of us survive?"

"What are you saying?" Lille asked.

"I am saying the desert is here."

A second later, screams rose from the crowd and soldiers panicked, running like a herd of wild animals. Genovan grabbed Morgan and swung her onto his back as the Commanders formed a ring around the queen as they ran, leaving everything behind. Tents were trampled as the soldiers fled in the early morning light. When Morgan looked back, she saw smoke rising from the far end of the crowd and knew lives ended in that smoke.

When she turned toward the front, she caught Oriel's glance and saw confusion and disgust, warring with concern and love. Even now, even with death chasing them, she wondered which would win.

*

"What are we going to do now?" Darla asked me, but I was still reeling from all I'd learned about Annisha, Finn, me... the Source.

I thought of the Source's face, her wonder at actually meeting a person for the first time and feeling so awkward about it. I certainly hadn't been easy on her. Petulant and willful, lacking respect for her, but then I'd settled and felt the momentousness of meeting her, feeling her care for all of the worlds. How could that have faded so much? How could her feelings for me—about what she'd done to me—change her, unless my power poisoned her in some way? Could I have destroyed everything, even after trying so hard and giving so much?

And what would happen if I called my power back to me? Would it work? Was I as broken as I thought?

"What are you thinking?" Devra asked.

"I'm thinking everything."

"You can't contact the Source in some way?"

"No, not that I know of, but I thought..." I glanced over at Bear. "I thought my friend, Laura, sent Bear to me. I thought the butterflies I saw before the Ezias came were from her too. But if she could do something, she would have. She wouldn't just watch the world die—she'd be giving the Source a *what-for*. Something else must be happening... and I'm wondering if it is my fault."

I studied all of the hopeless faces. "You needed the instruments—the seer said so. What were they supposed to do?"

"She didn't say. I thought I'd see her again, but then she was just gone."

"Darla, what can you do?" I asked.

"I'm not sure exactly, only I feel pulled to push, to see what I can do, but I know what happened to you and I'm afraid."

I looked to Devra. "Will the desert strike us here?"

"Not so far, but I should tell you that Brody just checked on the veil between us and the Wild Wood, and *it's* gone."

"The veil is gone?"

"No, the *Wild Wood* is gone."

I leapt to my feet, setting Darla beside me. "While we've been in here worrying about all of this... the Wild Wood *died*?

All those trees... the people, the animals?"

"Our parents," Brody said solemnly.

"No," I breathed.

"Yes," Devra said. "I think my hope is at an end. I think..."

Footsteps echoed through the great cavern. Devra and her child soldiers and the rest of us stood as four people came around the corner.

"Dusty!" I cried as he ran toward me, seizing me in a gigantic hug. "What...?"

Millie, suddenly forceful, said, "There isn't time for talking and catching up. Oona says we need to move now or all of this is over."

"Oona?" I asked.

Hope lit Devra's face. "The seer."

Millie moved in front of me, her hands on my face. "Oona doesn't know everything, but she says this is on you... with Darla and Nate to help you. Either you will find a way or no one will. No one has the connection—no one has ever had the connection—to the Source like you do. Oona says you must think... you must do *something*."

Something? What *something*? My head was a blank chalkboard. Empty. How could it have come to this? The more they stared at me, searching for answers, the more desperate I became. This was on me. I had the power, *one* power, and a chill snaked through me.

"I have to go to the Source—I have to make her see reason."

"But how?" Dusty asked. "Unless you mean—no, just *no*."

"I have to, Dusty. There is only one way for me to get there."

"To die," Finn whispered.

I nodded. "I believe it's my turn. No long goodbyes, okay? There isn't time."

"Cecily," Millie said. "Oona says you have to take Darla and Nate with you."

Horror sparked a fire inside me. "No."

Darla's hand took hold of mine. "Let's go. I'm not scared. Let's go where all souls are home."

"Darla, no, I can't..."

Nate stood beside me, his eyes filled with anguish. "There is no other choice. Let's go on this adventure and see what we find."

After a long breath, I surrendered.

"Oona says she sees reasons for hope now that the decision is made."

"Dusty, take good care of Bear." I moved to hug Bear's head. "And get home to our parents when you can."

"No goodbyes, Cecily. Not ever. I think I will see you again. You just don't know how to stay dead."

"You will see me again, no matter what." Ignoring his orders, I reached and grabbed him, holding him to me. "You are the best thing about being alive. I love you."

I heard the tears in his heart when he said, "I love you too."

I turned to Nate and watched as Devra placed her hand on his neck, removing her mark.

"Won't I lose my mind now?" Nate asked.

"You don't belong to me anymore—you belong to something greater."

Devra removed Darla's brand from her neck, but the marks on their heads remained.

"I'm so honored to have brought you into the world to save it," Devra said. "Thank you."

Once Nate turned away from Devra, I reached for Nate's hand, as Darla's hand found mine; together we walked toward the passage.

Finn stepped in front of us. "Please, don't do this."

A strange calm—a fatalistic calm—that reminded me of when I decided to let the mystics torture me or when I helped the Source to destroy me, bloomed in my chest. "This is what I do."

"Can you forgive me?"

I said nothing—I honestly had no idea what to say. But whatever he saw in my eyes had him backing away with his head down. While I stared, Finn raised his head and his eyes were still filled with love, love that reflected back at him from my heart. Sure, he wasn't who I thought he was, but was that really all his fault or mine too, for believing a fairy story instead of giving him the chance to be real? Maybe he would have told me if he hadn't heard so often in my thoughts how perfect he was. I'd built the cage that he had to live in—I saw that now and wished he could hear my thoughts, but I'd robbed him of that. If I lived... if the future brought us back together somehow, we would have the chance to truly know each other as equals, to find out what love really meant.

But this was not the day for those fairy tales.

"Live, Cecily. Do it again. Come back to me," Dusty called as we walked up the tunnel and through the veil into the barren way.

24

The Meaning Struggle Gave

"You've got to let me go!" Logan shouted as more townsfolk vanished. "You'll die if you don't!"

"Then we'll die," Mrs. Dumphry spat. "Now stay still and shut up."

"The river." Mrs. Daye jerked her head toward the large river, leading to an even larger lake. "The river!" she shouted to the others. "Get to the river!"

The group moved like a herd of deer, all trekking to the river, running like they belonged in the woods rather than a town. And Logan remained still and silent, but horror lived in his soul. So many wounded had died. The earth betrayed them, just like the king of Stoughton. What could be next?

When they reached the river, he heard the anguish in their sighs, knowing their blistered feet stung them, even in the cool water. They didn't stop. They tripped and struggled, while walking in the river, marching in the direction the water flowed toward the lake.

"There," Jem said, pointing to a small island in the middle of the massive body of water. "Let's go."

"But Logan? The children?" Mrs. Rowe said, out of breath

and holding a baby.

"We need a raft," Mrs. Daye said. "Pastor Rowe, you won't die from the desert. We need you to make us a raft."

Pastor Rowe didn't look as disgusted as he normally did when given a task. He merely moved away from Logan's litter as soon as Mr. Payne moved to take his spot. Pastor Rowe gathered wood and handily built a raft, his skills seeming to be magnified by being dead. While desert surrounded them and the water below them steamed, Pastor Rowe worked until finally, he dragged the raft to the mouth of the river.

"The children first," Logan ordered, refusing to be moved about that.

Mrs. Dumphry nodded. "Yes, of course."

Most of the surviving adults—and there weren't many—helped the children onto the raft and, with Pastor Rowe's help, swam to the island while dragging and pushing the raft. Pastor Rowe guided the raft back and Logan's saviors settled him on the raft and went to work swimming toward the island.

What a useless idiot to have gotten shot with so many arrows. To have allowed all of these people to risk themselves and the others to die because he was too weak to help them.

Tears fell from his eyes as the people on the shore, including Abigail's little brothers, Robbie and Darryl, struggled to pull him safely onto the beach and then all of them collapsed. Logan rested his head back, hoping no one saw his tears, but then a hand patted his right hand and another his left, and he looked up to find Mrs. Daye's and Mrs. Dumphry's kind faces staring down at him like *moms*. It had been such a long time since he felt that kind of support.

"The river's gone," Jem said, "and the shore is steaming. We don't have long before it comes here."

"There's nowhere to go now," Mrs. Daye said, her voice calm. "We've done all we could do. We've fought this battle as well as we could. What happens now is out of our hands. I believe there is a higher power guiding us—I know it's hard to believe sometimes. We spend a lot of time messing up and getting in the way, but I believe there is love and purpose in this world. And hope. The courage that surrounds me right now proves we have triumphed, for each other and for all those who fell... here and in Dunlowe. Let's stare our end in the face, and be brave. Always."

Brave? Yes, Logan could be brave because Zoe knew what he felt for her, the feelings he'd hidden for so long. He didn't want to die, but he could go softly now, because she *knew*. No regrets. He'd been loved by the girl who was his world.

✶

Stephanie ran with the panicked crowd, racing without a plan from the desert trying to kill them. Morgan still rode on Genovan's back and Oriel and the other Commanders surrounded Lille as she fled, looking more like a frightened ant than a queen. Those in front came to a sudden stop and it took Stephanie a moment to understand why, to feel her place in this new cage.

The desert was in front of them. Behind them. All around them.

The mystics huddled together, shaking in their robes. Soldiers crowded together and the Commanders formed a wall near Lille that Stephanie lunged to get inside.

Lille turned to Josiah. "What can you do?"

"Not much—Morgan could though, but I think it is too late."

"What do you mean?" Lille demanded as more screams and more shoving rocked the crowd. Even the Commanders swayed under the pressure of so many bodies flung against them.

"Morgan is a conduit, but she has no idea how to use her power and the crowd is too large for her. Even saving some will take time and you don't have time."

Without a pause, Lille said, "What about just me?"

Lille looked shocked at her words, at her cold, raw need to survive, while Morgan studied her, shaking her head, her eyes grazing over the Commanders and Oriel, even Stephanie.

"It will take time," Josiah said.

Smoke rose over the crowd as more and more were consumed.

Lille looked to Genovan. "Put her down."

Genovan helped Morgan to the ground, but left a hand on her shoulder, his eyes revealing his distrust for his queen.

Lille moved toward Morgan. "You need to do what he says, learn fast and save us—save as many as you can."

More smoke, more cries, and Stephanie felt a flickering within her. Not Ranz. Not Thorne. Her own power. Someone pushed her and she saw how she would die if she did nothing. Trampled—suffocated—by the frightened soldiers, mystics, and fools, all clamoring for their lives. Greedy immortals always wanting more.

After the next person shoved her, Stephanie turned and knocked the man to the ground.

"Stephanie!" Lille called.

"You want me to try to save these miserable cowards until

Morgan can figure out what to do?" Stephanie demanded.

"Can you?"

"You wouldn't believe what I am capable of."

Stephanie drew her power to her, to deny the desert its claim, to steal from it its power to kill them all.

What had been a flicker became a deluge. Her power expanded, driving the desert back in inches that became feet until the soldiers could step away from each other. Once there was more space, she held the desert at bay.

"How long?" Lille asked.

"I don't know—not long. I suggest you hurry."

Lille barked orders at Morgan and Josiah, but Stephanie's focus turned them to whispers until Lille stood beside her. "Thank you, Stephanie."

"Glad you didn't kill me?"

Lille's eyes told a story with an unfinished ending. "Yes."

✳

To die for a cause had always seemed romantic. To hold Cecily's hand had always felt right. But to head toward certain death with his baby sister felt criminal. And yet Nate, Darla, and Cecily walked straight down the corridor and through the veil. Only a step later, the desert stole their lives in a painful flash.

A second after that, after a searing bright light, they stood in a dim, dank cavern with thousands of other people, all standing around looking afraid and disoriented.

"This is all wrong," Cecily whispered. "They should be resting. Come on, let's get to the Source."

Cecily moved through the massive crowd until a woman

called her name. Cecily turned, searching for the source and found Millie's mother, Mrs. Smyth.

"Cecily, did it get you too?"

"*It?*"

"The desert."

"It's killing people in Stoughton too?" Cecily asked.

"Yes—*me*. Tell me, is Millie okay?"

"She is, Mrs. Smyth. I just saw her and she is safe from the desert. She's been very brave."

Nate couldn't stop himself from stepping forward. "My mother... do you know if she's okay?"

"She was and I haven't seen her here. I'm taking care of our people, until we know what we're supposed to do. It's unsettling, but we're all together. Cecily, your mother hasn't arrived. She's still alive."

Cecily nodded, looking about to break apart with so many worries coming for her. "Thank you. We're here to help if we can, but we must go."

"Go, Cecily. All of Dunlowe believes in you."

Cecily just nodded, clearly afraid to say anything as her eyes watered.

Darla tugged her away. "Don't think of everyone right now. Just your mission. Find the Source and help her."

Cecily nodded to Darla and led the way through the crowd, heading for a dark hallway in the back. She rushed through, turning abruptly when she reached a room filled with dirt mounds, most of which had been trampled. Hands stuck out of some—*gruesome.*

Cecily shook her head. "This is all wrong. What if...?"

She didn't finish her sentence and bolted from the room, racing down one hallway and then another until she came to a stop at a strange looking doorway.

"It's all wrong," she whispered as she moved closer to the door, nudging at it to open.

It didn't.

Cecily kept trying, throwing herself against the door again and again, until she crumpled to the ground, weeping. Darla moved to comfort her, but Nate pulled his sister away.

"Why?" Darla pleaded.

"Just wait."

Darla scowled.

"Trust me... I know her."

*

Dusty watched Cecily leave with Nate and Darla. He just *watched*. After coming so far, fighting so hard, he was still just a kid brother after all. Finn hunched over, looking just as he had after Cecily had vanished on the way to the Downs—only he looked guiltier for some reason. The gorgeous dark-skinned woman seemed heartbroken, as though her children had just died. And the kids in the cavern wept.

Millie stood, not crying, and stared at Dusty.

"What?" he asked.

"There are other fights going on right now... other people in danger. What do you want to do?"

"Fight for them," Dusty said immediately and felt Grey's hand on his shoulder. "Who needs us most?"

Millie paused and then grimaced. "It's looking bad all over.

Oona says we won't have time to save everyone, but she knows how to save some."

"Lead the way, Millie. We're ready."

"We are," Devra added, while the kids suddenly looked more like warriors. "We'll save as many as we can, bring them here. Start again."

Millie nodded and took off down the cavern, looking fierce. Who would have thought? But then, no one was who they would have been before change comes. And once it does, old thoughts and decisions rattled loose. Dusty hated to admit it, but even with the wreck of the world and the sorrow that would come, he wouldn't go back and be who he was before—not for anything. Struggle gave meaning to everything. Even a kid like Dusty Daye.

*

Bay gripped Abigail's shoulders, holding her as they faced the end. The carark glided toward them, causing few ripples to reach the surface.

"I'm sorry, my little Amanda," Mortimer said, while hugging her.

"This isn't the end," Abigail whispered in a haunted voice. "This isn't the end."

Just a second before the carark hit their boat, another boat in their small armada shattered, wood flying in the air as screams disappeared below the water. A frenzy hit the cararks and they all raced toward the fallen. Another boat vanished. A few seconds later, another.

Then the cararks were simply gone, but before Bay could feel any hope, Mortimer pointed behind Bay, who turned and found a massive whirlpool building, already pulling at their boat.

"Row!" Bay shouted, and everyone in the remaining boats took to their oars.

They rowed, desperation in every movement, but the hopelessness of everything grew after they lost two boats to the chasm. They couldn't make any progress, could only hold the line, but their strength was fading. Their lives—their futures—draining away with the struggle.

Bay heard the screams as another boat vanished, and another, until there were only two boats—Keefe's and his own—and the end in sight. Amanda's hands looked like claws as she gripped the oar and fought with more force than any warrior alive for her life, her sister's life, but mostly for her best friend's life. Mortimer fought hard and Bay worried he'd rip his oar to pieces.

Abigail, without an oar to row, watched the whirlpool. She stared at it with an odd expression on her face, a mix of hatred and longing. In between her inner duel with the water, Abigail looked worriedly at Keefe in his boat, seeming to wish she were with him, seeming to feel the distance between them. Amanda wasn't the only one who had made a loyal friend of a beast, because Keefe stared, with concern in his eyes, right back at Abigail.

Bay focused on his rowing, his muscles burning and clenching, as they would until the end. Not one of them would ever surrender until death robbed them of the choice.

25

Try

Night fell as Logan and the others waited for the end, only they weren't waiting quietly. They were singing, loudly. Jem and his father filled the air with majestic voices, and Logan tainted every second of it with exuberant caterwauling. People laughed while the children mocked him.

They had a fire. They had fish. They had each other. No matter all else, this moment was worth living.

When Logan looked over at the steaming lake, seeing how much lower it was than just minutes before, he knew they wouldn't see the dawn. Strange how he missed seeing it, now that he knew he wouldn't. Strange how he wished he'd known and paid more attention to the last one he saw. Strange that he still believed there was a chance... for a miracle.

*

Zoe fought hard, with Jacoby and Mindy beside her, while all of the rebels clashed with the soldiers, no one willing to give in without a fight. In the middle of the battle, with friends' and enemies' bodies covering the ground, Zoe felt something. Heat beneath her feet. She heard a strange crackling. Without a word, the battle stopped and all those who remained standing stared at each other, and then at the ground, as the heat grew more intense, blistering.

"We have to get out of here," Zoe said, looking to Jacoby.

Jacoby nodded. "I know a place."

"Everyone," Zoe called, "no matter which side you're on, come with us!"

Zoe checked on the children, glad to see townsfolk and soldiers lifting them onto their backs before hurrying toward Zoe and Jacoby. Jacoby ran quickly back toward his property and from there up a hill where the ground grew rocky. Screams wrenched out in the morning air, tearing through the stillness. Birds with crazed cries flocked in the skies, darkening the day, while animals raced around them, howling in pain. Zoe's feet felt charred as though she were standing on hot coals as she ran up the steep hill and followed Jacoby into a cave.

As the soldiers and rebels hurried after them, Zoe shouted, "Get farther back! I don't know..." Zoe couldn't tell if her feet hurt from before or if the cave floor was as hot as the ground outside. She knelt down and felt the ground and lowered her head.

Jacoby knelt beside her, his hand resting on the ground next to hers. "Damn. Let's get them farther back... there's a stream."

Zoe stood up. "Everybody move! Back to the water."

Zoe rushed with the others, all coming to a stop in a stream not deep or wide enough to give her much comfort. Something shimmered along the cave wall, but she turned away from it, gathering a moment to find her strength.

She stepped to the front, where everyone could see her.

"We're friends and enemies, but we don't have to be. In this moment, we're just people who want to live. We just want to see our families again. To remember the simple moments that we took for granted. The moments when life was about more than death. I am honored to stand with you, no matter what comes—truly honored."

Zoe felt a hand on her shoulder and turned to see Mr. Daye staring down at her, smiling, proud. "You are magnificent, Zoe Crane. So much more than anyone thought you were or would ever be. Don't ever hide your greatness again. To do that is to deny the world its most amazing gifts. And you, dear girl, are certainly one of them."

Mr. Daye hugged her. Really hugged her. A warm and genuine hug just like she'd seen fathers give their children, only she didn't have that memory. She wasn't certain when her last hug from her parents happened, but it was too long ago to remember. As she melted against Mr. Daye, she savored the connection, the pure care, communicated in this seemingly ordinary gesture. Only it wasn't ordinary at all; it was the greatest treasure of her life. After a few seconds, she thought she should pull away and not be greedy, but when she tried, Mr. Daye held her more tightly, somehow knowing in the way dads did that she needed more.

When the heat below her feet flared, Mr. Daye tugged her deeper into the water and let her go, but grabbed hold of her hand. Jacoby took her other hand.

Let it come, she thought—there was no better ending than this one. Logan wasn't here, he was safe. And he knew he was loved. So let the end come.

*

Morgan watched as Stephanie's body began to shake under the pressure she exerted holding back the deadly desert. So much power... to *drain* power? That's what it had to be. What else—*who* else—could Stephanie drain? Morgan flashed back to how angry Stephanie had been when Morgan concealed her power, all while Stephanie concealed her own.

You wouldn't believe what I am capable of.

Morgan seriously doubted that, but Lille ordered Morgan to focus on the Ezias' instructions that came out in a monotonous stream as though there was no reason for panic.

Morgan nodded, hearing and understanding most, but felt dread for what was coming next, the reality of her life now.

Near the end of the instructions, the Ezias looked to Lille. "We will need a payment for the final clue to save you, since this doesn't save us. We came to try to stop the desert, not to save your lives."

"Payment?" Lille asked. "What are you talking about?"

Morgan shuddered, while the Ezias gazed down at her. "We will need five ounces and another taste of Morgan's soul."

"No!" Oriel shouted, pressing in but not touching Morgan.

Lille turned to Oriel. "She's already polluted—what does it matter?"

Morgan's mouth dropped open before stammering, "It matters... to me."

Lille's chin came up, reminding Morgan of Stephanie. "You swore to obey my orders, to serve me and Darienne. Prove it."

"Please don't ask this of me."

"I'm *not* asking." Lille turned to the Ezias. "That will take time, won't it? You can do it after?"

He nodded, his eyes locked with Morgan's.

She looked up at him, seeing flashes of images, feelings she might lose, wondering which would hurt the most. "What does my grandfather say to do?"

No compassion entered his eyes, but his voice softened. "He says words like *defiled* or *polluted* hide the reality of being a survivor. Nothing you ever go through can defile you unless you believe it to be so. He says that he is sorry for this, but believes that not having a destiny frees you to live your own life. You can choose to simply save yourself and remain whole, or you can save your friends, your love, and some of these immortals and pay a price. It really is up to you."

Stephanie grumbled, "It may be up to you, but unless you do something soon, there will be no choice to make."

Lille turned snotty and began to speak, but Oriel placed his hand on his queen's shoulder to stop her and looked at Morgan, his teal eyes sparkling in the bright sun. "Please, Morgan—please…"

Morgan turned to the Ezias and slowly nodded.

The Ezias gave her the final instructions and she concentrated to pull at the doorway she supposedly was, the conduit to another place.

"Hurry!" Stephanie cried, as screams rang out and the crowd pushed in.

*

It wouldn't open. The damned living door wouldn't open, wouldn't budge. I screamed and bashed at it and it wouldn't move.

I sank to the ground, crying for more things than I could count. For Millie's mother. For my family. For Dusty. For my death and Darla's and Nate's deaths—all of this. Even the afterlife was destroyed for us now. The Source who brought peace wouldn't. We would just exist in this half-life, without hope of an ending.

Sadness assailed me. Hopelessness. And then something flickered inside me: rage.

If this was to punish me... if this was to teach me and all of my puny kind about the value of the Source, then she was a cruel wretch. No. This was ridiculous. I'd given my power, I'd embraced a life of pain, in order to save worlds and now they were dying anyway.

I clamored to my feet and stood, my hands resting against the doors that used to be alive. If the Source wasn't going to help us, then there was no reason to hold back.

I let out a breath and focused, anger tinging every thought, every memory of my time in the Source, all of her great wisdom, all of her love. She wouldn't do this to people she loved.

Something swirled inside me and I slammed my hands into the door and it flinched open. I heard Nate say, "See, I told you," to Darla probably, but I was already walking through the small opening into the Source's domain, seeing in the first moment the changes that had come.

Everything that had once been living, vibrant and beautiful, was now dead. All of the plants husks, all of the animals rotting, even my goat. The blue globes that used to give light had burned out. The glass of the ceiling was a series of shatters that still managed to hold together. The sky above was an angry and violent swirl of grey and black.

I saw Laura's body as she lay face down in the dirty water that had been the glistening pond. My body refused to move, refused to exist in this moment where belief faded and emptiness grew. I turned back to the doorway where Nate and Darla stood and headed toward them.

"Where are you going?" Nate asked.

"Away."

"Away where? There's work to do here."

"No, it's over... it's all over." My body trembled as I felt the death in this chamber wash over me.

"No, Cecily," Darla pleaded. "Pick me up."

I stared at her, not understanding. "Why?"

"Just do it. Quick."

To deny Darla anything would be a struggle, even at the end of the world, so I reached and lifted her into my arms.

"Now what?"

She leaned her bald head against my face, Devra's mark touching my skin. The instant the marks touched me, my thoughts cleared. I could breathe.

"There's something in this room," Darla said. "Poison. I sense it, but I can't feel it. Something about Devra protects me."

Nate moved closer and I saw his marks glowing and swirling. "Me too. I don't feel what you feel. I still think there's hope, but I really want to get Laura out of that pond. So don't go anywhere, okay?"

I nodded, okay now, as he hurried toward Laura and gently pulled her body out of the muck, cradling her against him.

"Laura, honey, come back to us," he said, but her body remained still. *Dead*, but she'd been dead before.

I felt Darla cringe when I thought of seeing if her touch could help Laura, but before I could ask or move closer, Nate touched Laura's face to his head. My breath held, but nothing happened. She remained still. Covered in filth. The spark of her life gone.

"It's not over. We need to find the Source," Darla whispered. "She is where it all begins and ends."

I turned and walked through the garden—now a wasteland— seeing Britton's lifeless body awkwardly sprawled on the ground. A few more steps and even the hope Darla held faded when we saw the decomposing dry husk of the Source.

*

Nate watched as Cecily stood as still as a statue, her hand over her mouth. Not breathing. Darla glanced at him, her green eyes filled with horror.

Nate moved closer, seeing the dry, flaking shape of a person. "Is that...?"

"The Source," Cecily whispered.

"How can the Source die?"

Cecily said nothing, reverting to a person without a soul who would soon be just like Laura and Britton, void of life. Nate suddenly understood exactly why he and Darla needed to be in this place. This exact moment, only now that he was in it, he didn't know what to do. He and Darla weren't as affected by the grimness here. Devra had given them a gift, something born of her endurance to face an unending struggle without even the chance at redemption. Fortitude—yes, that was it. Mrs. Dumphry would have approved of his vocabulary. So he had this gift, but how to use it...

"Tell me about her," Nate said, moving between Cecily and the chunk of ash.

Cecily squinted at him, her internal rage simmering. "Why? What good can possibly come of it now? She made worlds and then she died. Enough."

Cecily turned away and Nate heard Darla say, "Tell me about her, Cecily. Tell me what she looked like." Darla stared up into Cecily's face and then cuddled against her, with her head underneath Cecily's chin. "Please, tell me."

Nate wasn't at all surprised that the conniving little sprite would be successful where he had failed.

"She was regal in a way that made Lille or Devra seem common. Her posture seemed stiff, her chin lofty. She seemed hard, not the way I see mothers to be, but she was the mother of everything. And I was the first person to ever see her, talk to her. I was awful. And at moments, I was wonderful. I broke myself and endured terrible pain... and now this."

"Cecily," Darla whispered.

"Yes."

"Do you really believe that all of her power would end?" Darla asked. "Do you think we aren't all connected? Do you think power can really be destroyed?"

Darla's words floated around them and Nate nodded to her when her questioning eyes turned to him for support.

When Cecily spoke, her words sounded haunted. "Power—real power—exists forever. I thought I severed the bonds to my power. I suffered... but just a few minutes ago, I got in here. I busted through the door." Her eyes flashed to Nate. "My power scares you... in the cave, you looked afraid. Why?"

"I still felt your power..."

"... because we were in the cave, right? Because I wasn't hurting?"

"No, because I felt your power intact. This is why I've flinched from you, why you terrify me. Part of me is a demon, Devra or the other one, and Annisha judged them harshly. My fear of you is the fear of a class of people used to suffering at the hands of others. I thought I was crazy, or a coward... and maybe I am, but now I understand. Like an instinct that keeps an animal alive and away from predators, my body feels the danger in yours. I feel it now. I felt it in the cave. I even felt it when the Ezias attacked you, when you thought you were at your weakest. You severed your bond to your power because that was what was asked of you, but the power is still yours."

Nate raised his hand and placed it lightly against her cheek. "I see you, Cecily. I know you, and I love you. This isn't over. Think. Your power is yours alone and when the Source took it, *this*—all of this—was the outcome. She took something that no longer belonged to her—it belonged to her child. Her child needs to step up and do what the Source couldn't."

Cecily looked over at the Source's body. "I don't know what to do."

Darla snuggled against Cecily's chest. "There's only one thing you have to do: *try*."

26

The Nature of Everything

When the water began to steam and then boil, Zoe flinched back, pulling Mr. Daye and Jacoby with her. She stepped onto the rock, feeling its heat. The other rebels and soldiers joined her on the ledge beyond the water. Not much space now and nowhere to run. They backed against the walls as the ground grew hotter. When it became cramped, Zoe looked to her left, seeing some space and tugged Mr. Daye and Jacoby to get them to move over—Jacoby held Mindy's hand, who moved with them but surrender already lived in her eyes—not wanting to let go of them for even a second. The fire in the ground could come and they would vanish and if Zoe wasn't holding onto them, she might experience her death a moment after theirs, and that moment seemed more frightening than anything she'd ever faced.

They stood quietly and she wished she could fill the silence, while knowing there was nothing that needed to be said. But that didn't mean they should go quietly.

"Mr. Daye, do you remember that song Mr. Payne sang with his family... the joyous one?"

Mr. Daye looked at her, his brow appearing to work hard

as he thought. "Days grow long, but never long enough... and mornings always come..." he said, and then more loudly, he sang it again, as the voices in the cave joined to fight against the coming darkness. Proud voices echoed through the cave, owning this moment, denying fear its place. They'd seen too much, done too much to quibble now.

While the others continued to sing, Jacoby said, "Zoe, I should have told you. I'm sorry."

Zoe looked up at Jacoby. "What?"

"I should have told you... but I didn't know how—didn't think you would believe me."

"Tell me now, Jacoby. We are friends, you and me—you can tell me anything."

He shook his head, looking up. "We *aren't* friends, Zoe." His face stared down at her. "We're *siblings*."

"What?"

"Our father was a rogue... he had a wife in Marsden and a wife in Dunlowe. I didn't know until the night I came to kill the sevens and anyone who would harbor them. I saw him. I saw you. I heard him yelling at his other wife, heard how they spoke of you. I watched you on the porch—I saw your shoulders shaking as they said such vile things. I ran to meet the others, almost late for the attack because of you, because I wanted to meet you and tell you he wasn't always like that. He was never like that to me and my mom. He was a good man—but he wasn't—and then he was dead before I could confront him. I watched him fall and die just as I arrived to do what I could for you and the people of Dunlowe—I came for you, led the others back to Dunlowe because of *you*. How I prayed that you still lived... and then to find that you not only lived but were the hero who saved us all. I promised myself to be good to you, to show you the support you always deserved. Please, forgive me. We're going to die, but please forgive me for not telling you the truth when it still mattered and for having a father who was good and kind when you had no one. Please..."

Zoe felt her lip trembling as she whispered, "I have a brother..."

He nodded. "... who loves you."

Zoe squeezed his hand, as tears fell from her eyes at the beauty, the stark and amazing beauty of this moment. With her eyes closed, she leaned the few inches that separated her from the cave wall, planning to rest against it, when, suddenly, she fell through it as though it were nothing more than a veil, dragging Jacoby, Mindy, and Mr. Daye with her.

*

Stephanie shook, her body as trembly and weak as a human's. It shouldn't be. She'd been strong as an immortal. She'd overcome her human weakness. She'd claimed her life. Sure, she could release the weight and let these people die. Let the mystics die—who might or might not be allies later. But for now, she would fight to hold on.

Her eyes caught the sight of Morgan's surrender to whatever price had to be paid to save the queen and some of her subjects. *Subjects*—a funny word given how much treachery lived in this crowd, and with a queen who so quickly offered up a terrible price to be paid by her supposed sister and heir.

The distress—the epic kind of sorrow—in Morgan's

eyes brought Stephanie no comfort, not when she knew that Lille and the others would see Stephanie as just as defiled by Ranz's ownership of her soul and by Thorne's brand. In truth, Stephanie felt more concern that this *supposed* taint of Morgan might empower her former sister seven to be a more fearful adversary. Stephanie shuddered under her burden remembering the moments of surrender, the time in her cell, the price she had paid to be where she was, and felt grief for Morgan's plight, no matter how this changed her story.

Watching Morgan's love for Oriel turned against her, used as a tool to control her, felt just like when Ranz used Dusty to control Stephanie. How similar the corruption was, how simple the tools of treachery. Stephanie suddenly wondered if there was a book somewhere that taught cruel beings how to gather power—if there were such a book, Stephanie definitely needed to read it.

The weight upon her threatened to break her and she screamed, "Hurry!"

Morgan's concentration looked as painful as Stephanie's burden and she felt closer to Morgan in this moment than ever before. In a flash Stephanie felt a larger plan and knew in a way that seemed too real to disbelieve that a greater war was coming. Not just for a nation, but for a world. A war the sevens would be part of, each claimed to preside over or be allied with different factions. The blueprint of this epic battle only burned in her mind for a second, but the aftereffect left her feeling like a pawn, more than ever. Not a pawn of Ranz or Thorne, but of fate.

Just as quickly as she knew that, she knew something else, something that changed everything. Almost like she'd summoned him, Ranz's awareness returned to her.

"*Oh, dearest, you are magnificent.*"

"*I am not your pawn, Ranz. You know what I know. Look in my mind and see what I see.*"

A second later, she felt his jolt of awareness as she used her power to drain *him*, while he sat in his cave prison, unable to do anything to protect himself.

"*Things have changed,*" he said. "*So what will you do with this knowledge, dearest? Kill me? Punish me as I have punished you?*"

"*No, Ranz, I want your guidance. I want you with me in this. Look at Lille, what she's doing to Morgan—at least you are honest about it.*"

"*I am.*"

"*If you really love me and respect me and treat me as your equal, I will be a loyal friend to you forever. If you cross me, I'll leave you as nothing more than a husk in a cavern with all your playthings in cages to watch you die.*"

She felt Ranz smile, sensed his pride. "*I can accept those terms, dearest. Loving you has never been a problem. Unlike most people in Darienne—including Lille—you never looked down on me, never treated me as less. When that viper Annisha imprisoned me, you—the soul inside you—carved a place for me, gave me this home, gave me a chance to exist beyond my prison. You were loyal when even my own kind turned on me.*"

"*Then why... did you treat me so badly, doubt me so much?*"

"*Because you could kill me. Control comes before trust. Now I have no control, but I trust, and I'm glad for the change in my circumstances, dearest—or would you rather me not call you* dearest *anymore?*"

Stephanie considered while her limbs began to fail.

"*No, Ranz, please call me* dearest *and be my family because I have none anymore.*"

"*Soon, you'll have something better... power.*"

"*If I survive...*"

"*If...*"

*

Bay's muscles locked up, but still he forced his limbs to move. To row. To fight against the swirling abyss. It couldn't be much longer—they'd held on and held on, like people who don't know how to surrender. Amanda grunted as she rowed. Was it time to tell them to let go, to order them to? Would they listen? Would Mortimer ever stop trying to save his best friend? Bay knew the answer: Mortimer would be rowing as the boat fell into the chasm and even then.

And still, Bay could save them all, but the price was too high. Facing the man he'd been and what he'd done was simply a harder road than dying with those he was proud to call friends.

A shout broke free and Bay watched as Keefe reached his limit, his hands becoming still as he looked over at Bay and nodded his goodbye.

A cry erupted in the front of Bay's boat. Bay's eyes struggled to let go of his last sight of his friend, but he did and found Abigail standing in the bow, her eyes filled with shock and overwhelming sadness, as though Keefe's death left too big a mark to recover from.

"Sit down, Abigail!" Amanda ordered, but no one could move without damning them all. No one could do anything as

Abigail's face went pale, as the war she'd seemed to fight since they first approached the water found its ending. A fatalistic blankness appeared on her face, as though a pawn finally accepted her place. She took one moment to stare at Amanda, her eyes widening as she seemed to see things the others couldn't. And then she dove over the edge of the boat, instantly carried away by the cruel water while Amanda cried out but never stopped rowing.

*

I looked around the wrecked room, my eyes flinching over the bodies strewn around it. The Source. Laura. Britton. I couldn't focus on them just now. I couldn't fight back the gloom inside me if I stared at them. I needed a smaller goal, just to get me started, so I looked over at one plant that was dry and brown, where I remembered it being fuchsia.

I focused, pushed my will, but the power wasn't in me. I couldn't find it, and the sights of the room overwhelmed my focus.

"Nate," I said softly. "I need your help."

"Anything."

"Please, put your arms around me." I meant to explain, but his arms surrounded me before I tried.

Darla in my arms and my body leaning against Nate allowed me to forget myself and close my eyes. I pulled my focus toward the power lurking and corrupting without a master, instead of staring at the destruction.

I took a deep breath and felt the power of Darla's marks touching my skin, while Nate's face rested against mine, the marks on his head sending power and peace in equal measure. Time seemed to stand still. And then like a mighty wind, I felt the wave of my power, of the Source's power, in this room, and my rage flickered as I reached for it and brought it home inside me.

My body trembled for a minute, but settled quickly, the power feeling relieved to have a direction, to be home at last. With my eyes still closed, I thought of a plant and its colorful flowers. I thought of the blue globes, seeing them lit. I thought of the pond, teal and sparkling. I thought of the purple stone path, covered with moss. I thought of the blue dragonflies, orange butterflies, and a golden frog seated on an emerald lily pad. I thought of greenery and plants of more colors and types than could ever live in a human's imagination. I thought of the sky above the windows and pictured it the stretch of blueness it had once been. I pictured the glass of the ceiling pure, not fractured.

I held all of the sights and then I heard the sounds and smiled.

"You're doing it, Cecily," Nate said, kissing my cheek. "Now for the hard stuff. Wake Laura."

I pictured Laura's face on the last day I'd seen her alive in Dunlowe and then flashed to seeing her on the day I gave away my power. I heard her laugh in my mind and wished to hear it now, but I heard nothing.

"Open your eyes," Laura said.

I opened them, but didn't see a smile or any warmth at all. Anguish stared at me from her eyes.

"I tried... to get her to bring you back, to share her power.

I tried, but she refused—she didn't want to burden you, and then it was too late. I felt millions die. Suns blew out and worlds vanished. And Dunlowe. Darienne. Lands across the sea. Places we never knew about. And here, the fields of dead are broken. Peace is gone."

"Do you still believe in me?" I whispered.

"Always."

"Then let's bring Britton and the Source back and fix this."

"That's just it. She made me promise—she begged me, made me swear that no one would bring her back. She's tired of her burdens, her cage here. She wanted to be free. She said others of her kind have fallen and that's what causes suns to burn out and worlds to drift into eternal darkness. She wants to be finished... she needs us to let her go."

"And let our world die?"

Laura looked at me, her face sad. "Unless you take her place."

"What? I can't do this."

"We'll help you," Nate said. "This won't be your burden alone."

"But I wasn't worthy of this—she took my power for a reason."

Laura shook her head. "She said that was a mistake. She said she didn't see. She wasn't always looking at the world. The moment she really paid attention to Annisha, was the moment of her death when her soul was pure. But the Source watched more after you were gone, wandered through time and space and found that Annisha wasn't some lofty perfect person. She was flawed just like everyone. The Source was so sorry for what she said, what she did. Please, Cecily, take her place, at least for now.

Save the worlds who need you, and we'll figure out everything else later."

"I don't know what to do."

"Britton will know more. He was here much longer than I was."

A second later, Britton held Laura, kissing her passionately enough that I covered Darla's eyes.

"Sorry," Britton muttered when he turned to me, but I was staring at the husk of the Source in the middle of her verdant garden.

"I can't leave her like that." A moment later, the orange table appeared and the Source's body, looking regal and whole again, lay on the top, completely still. "What do I do?"

*

While a strangely red moon shone down and a fire crackled as it gave some light, Logan felt heat through the wood and fabric of his litter and knew they were close to the end. Abigail's brothers sat on his stretcher with him, holding his hands, afraid but trying really hard not to show it. Their eyes held a strange and old starkness, just as they had since they realized their mother had vanished into smoke, killed by the desert. Mrs. Dumphry, Mrs. Rowe, and Mrs. Daye sat near each other talking about the past. Jem and his dad hummed softly after saying prayers that the two Payne girls who'd been stolen when Heath's family was taken would be okay, actually glad they weren't here to die. Logan heard Jem say, "At least Amanda will survive, no matter what happens to the rest of us." But Logan had his doubts about immortal girls surviving a burning world. Somehow, though, he knew Stephanie would find a way to survive—she was just that kind of girl.

Logan glanced at Pastor Rowe, who looked concerned. "What is it?" Logan asked, while the others turned their focus toward the pastor.

"I'm just wondering what happens to me. If you all die, will I be here forever feeling the awful grinding inside that I feel when I'm not near Jem? Or will it go away? I know you don't care, but..."

"You deserve that and worse," Mrs. Dumphry spat. "And it isn't that we don't care, it's that we're rooting for you to suffer more."

"I'm not," Jem said quietly. "We're going to die and I believe there will be peace. I believe I will be with my mother and brother again. I get to end. I know we're supposed to want to live forever, but I don't. I want a peaceful ending." He looked at Pastor Rowe. "I feel it, your disconnection from everyone. You exist but you don't. I don't wish this on even you."

"Nor do I," Mrs. Rowe said, uttering the first words she had spoken to her former husband. "Forgiveness won't make you a better man—I don't know that anything will, but through your scheming, I gave birth to two decent people. How can my heart hold any hatred when they live? I forgive you."

Pastor Rowe said nothing for a few minutes. "If some of you climb on top of me, you might live," he said in fractured words.

Everyone quickly glanced at the children. Robbie and Darryl. The Blake twins. Little Buddy Harrison. A few babies. What of the others gathered around? And who would tend to the children? How could they possibly choose who deserved life more?

The ground flared and the empty lake sizzled out.

Jem said, "If we're going to try, we need..."

Everyone scrambled to their feet as smoke began to rise from the ground, all eyes on Logan.

"Mrs. Daye, get on his back," Logan ordered. "You'll take as many kids as you can, but they need someone to watch over them."

Mrs. Daye shook her head, backing away. "Not me, someone else."

"Mrs. Daye, listen to me. If Cecily comes back and you are dead, she'll kill the world. Get on the stinky dead guy's back *right now.*"

Mrs. Daye made a face but complied and then children launched into her arms and some into Pastor Rowe's. They clung to his neck, his chest, his legs—nine of them and then another baby was handed up for Robbie to hold. Ten and a mom with enough love to tend to them all.

Everyone began to back away from the heat. Logan saw their fear and courage warring with each other.

And then he heard the damnedest thing.

"Mom, why are you performing circus tricks... on... *oooh*, Pastor Rowe, you've looked better."

Logan craned his neck to see the face that matched that voice. Dusty's hair was short and his posture proud—he looked like a warrior—but his smile shone exactly as it always had.

"Oh, my..." Mrs. Daye gushed, clearly wanting to hug her son and not be trapped by circus tricks. "Dusty, the ground is burning."

"I know. Climb down. We'll get you out of here."

*

Morgan took a breath, forcing her brain not to think about the price, the ounces, of letting the Ezias back into her body.

Lille's words haunted her. *She's already polluted—what does it matter?*

The nature of everything changed in that moment. Morgan would never again feel like Lille's beloved sister, her oasis in a world that had killed her family. Now she was just a piece of property the queen wielded, because Morgan had sworn an oath to a lying queen.

With no way out that would allow her to keep the one thing she still held, her honor, Morgan obeyed the Ezias' commands and used her body to open a conduit as the cries of the crowd grew, as thousands died.

When shimmering lights sailed out from Morgan's body and the doorway opened, Oriel and his queen rushed through the gateway, followed by mystics and soldiers shoving to get through. The Commanders entered, but Genovan stood beside Morgan, waiting for something.

"Gen, you have to go."

"Morgan, you aren't defiled, and if you are, you are not alone. Don't forget that."

Gen crossed the gateway as more and more crowded together, smashing each other to save their own lives, while Morgan was powerless to do anything but hold open the door.

Through the crowd of bodies, Morgan saw Stephanie fall to the ground. Soldiers and mystics trampled her as the death-laden smoke grew thicker.

"Save her! She saved you!" Morgan cried, but no one

listened and after a few minutes, Stephanie's broken body didn't even flinch anymore. Morgan turned to the Ezias, still standing beside her. "Please, save her."

"That will cost you."

Morgan shuddered, almost losing hold of the doorway. "How much?"

"Five more ounces."

Ten ounces and another taste. Tears fell as she nodded to the Ezias who mowed through the crowd, sending bodies flying as he reached Stephanie, taking her into his arms and walking toward Morgan.

After a flurry of rushing bodies, Morgan suddenly stood alone in the thick smoke with only the Ezias standing in front of her, Stephanie in his arms.

"We can go through now," he said.

"What do you mean?"

"It's over."

Morgan squinted through the smoke that soon cleared when a warm breeze hit it and saw the meaning of his words. The desert had won. Thousands upon thousands had died, many good, while Morgan had to doubt the worth of the survivors when looking at Stephanie's broken body.

"Going through the gateway will heal her. Come."

Morgan nodded and a flash later, she stood inside a cavern, surrounded by pain and dreading the price of saving so many questionable lives.

27

Truth

Cecily, still holding Darla, and Britton talked quickly while Nate stood nearby, his focus on Laura, who after a minute noticed him staring and moved closer, wrapping her arms around him.

"She's not a silly chicken anymore," Laura whispered while still in his embrace.

"She never really was."

Laura pulled back and studied Nate's face. "You look so different, but good."

"I'm better now. I have a purpose."

"What's that?"

"To help the Source in any way I can."

Laura's eyes flickered to Cecily. "It's unsettling, but it is as it was always meant to be. She's special. The Source broke her and Cecily broke herself, but it was the Source who stumbled, while Cecily simply continued. It's what she does."

"It is, and I'm grateful for it. You know, you look good too. Love suits you."

A flush came to Laura's face. "It was worth dying to meet him."

"Who knows, maybe the Source will give you back your lives... and all the people who died in this mess," Nate said and Cecily turned abruptly toward him, her face hard.

"No, I mustn't."

Nate saw Cecily's tension radiating. "Why?"

"My mistake before was acting without thinking, without considering the ripples. I can't walk in here and start reversing the rules. I need time to think and consider—all who died, and who are probably still dying, must stay dead... including Laura and Britton, and you and Darla. I'm *sorry*." The weight of her words pushed at her, but her will turned to steel before his eyes. "I must be wise... now."

Britton tugged her arm. "Cecily, work to be done. Less people dying is better."

Cecily followed Britton's lead as he pulled her away and kept talking about all he knew, while Laura kept her focus on Nate.

"Are you okay?" Laura asked.

"Other than my mother, almost everyone I care about in the world is already here. It is so good to see you."

"She needs us, you know? The other Source's biggest mistake was not relying on anyone, not having friends. Cecily will never live that life. I believe there is a reason I am here and you are here... and Darla. Look how Darla soothes Cecily, without saying a word." Laura nudged his shoulder. "I was always rooting for you against that Finn character."

Nate laughed. "Well, I don't know if she will ever love me again, but fate did a nice job of removing the competition."

"Nate, Laura, I need you," the Source called and her friends immediately answered.

*

Dusty felt like a hero, showing up, saving his mom and all of the wounded and the kids, just in the nick of time. Saving Logan—yup, Dusty was going to use that for a long, long time. All of the survivors—Dusty tried really hard not to notice how few there were—were safely in the caverns, a job well done. At the moment when he was about to ask what had happened to everyone, Millie tugged Dusty's arm.

"What is it?" he asked.

"Oona says she really wants us to do something else—this one will be beautiful too."

"Millie, you tell Oona…"

Millie smiled. "She can hear you, Dusty."

Dusty looked around at nothing and said, "Oona, thank you. I can't see what you look like or hug you right now, but I owe you… *huge*. My mom—I can't thank you enough for helping me to save her. I'm not sure I'll ever see Cecily again, but my mom…" Dusty didn't even mind the girly tears lining up, because he meant what he was saying as he watched his mother ensure Logan was okay, although Logan stood burly strong again. The caverns had done their work on him and everyone else.

Millie glanced at the air next to her. "I think Oona is blushing because of you."

Dusty smiled.

"Okay, now she's mad at me, but she says we need to go right now and to bring your mom and Logan."

Dusty looked around for Grey and found him waiting just a few feet away, ready for the next mission. Finn and Devra hung back a little bit, but they were ready.

"Logan, Mom, let's go. We'll be coming back here."

Dusty took off following Millie who dashed along the middle of the cave. Time was wonky in the caverns and he never knew how long he'd been running, but after a long while, he heard urgent talking and when they rounded the corner, his mother let out a cry before launching herself into his father's arms.

Dusty smiled, but he didn't rush toward anyone. His eyes focused on Logan, who froze and didn't appear to be breathing when he saw Zoe, who stood just as frozen, her eyes just as locked on Logan. Dusty had seen passionate embraces and loving relationships. Finn and Cecily. Nate and Cecily. Dusty himself had experienced them with Stephanie, but in seeing Zoe and Logan, Dusty finally saw what was lacking in his own relationship with Stephanie. He couldn't think of a word—maybe he'd ask Mrs. Dumphry later—but he felt it. Between his mother and father, there was love, worn openly only because it shined out of both of them. Between Zoe and Logan, there was *truth*.

After many long seconds of just gazing at each other, Zoe and Logan walked calmly toward each other and embraced in a way that seemed more like a marriage than any Dusty had seen.

Millie patted his arm. "Beautiful, huh? Oona is very happy... but she says there's something else to see and it won't be easy for you. Will you come?"

"I'll follow Oona to the ends of the earth—which might have just happened."

"Oona says *no*. She can't see everything, especially in the Source, but she says that whatever Cecily, Nate, and Darla did worked. The world is coming around, but we need to go if we are to see it. She says Reece—or Grey, if you like—has a choice to make. Finn should come too... and Charity."

Dusty hurried away, leaving enough of Devra's child soldiers to guide the people of Stoughton—both the men in soldiers' uniforms and the townsfolk—to the group of wounded and the children they'd left behind.

Dusty called to Millie, "How much farther?"

"Oona says *just around the next corner*... but she always says that and she's always lying."

✱

As quickly as the whirlpool appeared, it vanished. Their lone boat rocked lightly in the calm seas and they all just sat there breathing and grieving. Keefe. Abigail. So many other friends and comrades, brave fighters who deserved a better end than to be bested by a strange phenomenon in the suddenly treacherous world. Or a friend who wouldn't face his past in order to save them.

"Can we go to the shore now please?" Amanda whispered.

Mortimer looked to Amanda. "What about the burning dirt?"

Amanda shrugged. "I don't care about the dirt or anything else."

"Now, now." Mortimer carefully scooped Amanda into his arms and held her while she sobbed for Abigail.

Bay looked to the shore and saw that the water wasn't sizzling. "I think it's over."

"I can't risk Amanda."

"Easy there, Mortimer. I'll go first."

Bay swayed when he stood on the desert land, but wasn't harmed. The heat had come and gone. The others joined him, Amanda riding on Mortimer's shoulders, as far from the dirt as she could get. When they'd walked a few yards, Bay stopped abruptly when he saw Finn, Dusty, Millie, Charity, a Grey Cloak with his hood pulled down, and *Lady Devra* standing beside some dried shrubs that used to be the hedgerows.

Mortimer set Amanda down and she rushed toward her sisters, gathering them to her, while sharing her sad news. Tears fell, and then Bay heard the words that shot directly to his heart. "Cecily is gone too, and we don't think she's coming back."

Finn seemed as unprepared to hear those words as Bay was.

"We don't have time for this right now, but there will be time later," Millie said, motioning for the rest to follow.

Bay walked next to Finn. "What happened to Cecily? Where did Lady Devra come from and who is the Grey Cloak?"

"Later... if I think about all of it now, I won't be able to face... *anything*."

Bay nodded, feeling as though the desert had won. Had stolen their hearts and their dreams and left nothing but broken men and women to walk the earth.

*

Morgan watched the much smaller crowd mill around the cavern, different factions already forming. Stephanie stood near her, healed of her wounds, but wearing an uncertain look as her eyes locked with Morgan's.

"You saved me—why did you do that?" Stephanie asked softly.

"Because you deserved to be saved—you certainly deserved better than to be trampled by the same people you tried to help."

Stephanie's face wrinkled as she fought herself for words. "I... —will you pay a higher price or was the price the same?"

Morgan just swallowed.

"You gave away more of yourself, didn't you? For *me*?"

Morgan nodded, while she felt the Ezias beginning to swarm just out of view, felt a tug on the tether within her.

"It's really bad, what happens to you?"

Morgan nodded.

"Morgan, I..."

Just then, Lille raced toward Stephanie. "Thank you, Stephanie—thank you so much. I was so wrong to have locked you up. You've saved the future of Darienne. I can't thank you enough." Lille reached out impulsively and hugged Stephanie.

Morgan felt the slight, worse than a blade puncturing her.

Stephanie gripped Lille's arms and held her away. "It was Morgan who..."

Lille's voice turned cold. "Morgan did her duty and nothing more." Her warmth returned as she looked to Stephanie. "Come, we have much to talk about. Your future in Darienne... how much you are going to love living in the palace in Cloud City—so much to talk about."

Stephanie took a few steps, but stopped as the blaring whines of the Grey Cloaks' instruments sounded, while everyone cringed from their powerful volume echoing through the caverns. The sounds of footsteps clamored and within a few seconds, a large force of Grey Cloaks surrounded the much smaller group of a hundred or so survivors. It only took a moment for the mystics to join the new arrivals.

Stephanie rushed back to Morgan, placing her hand gently on Morgan's face. "No matter what you think of me after this day, I want you to know that I won't forget what you did or the price you'll pay. And if you are ever willing to break your allegiance, you have a place in this world."

*

The Grey Cloaks stormed toward Lille's forces, Thorne at their lead, and Stephanie shuddered, thinking about Morgan's regret for saving her when she knew the truth about Stephanie, a truth that was coming... very soon.

"*You've won, dearest,*" Ranz said. "*Stop worrying about Morgan and celebrate. Thorne is going to kill them all.*"

"No," Stephanie breathed.

"*No? What do you mean? We can end all of it right now, dearest. You will be queen. They will be dead.*"

Stephanie's heart skipped a beat as this possible future played out before her eyes. She stared at the death in Thorne's eyes, seeing clearly the murder he was capable of.

"*You will be queen,*" Ranz pressed.

"*I just saved them—I could have just killed them.*"

"*You could have—why didn't you?*"

The question lingered, but something else pushed at her mind, pulsing through her as she stared at Thorne and a series of passionate memories seared her mind. Things that had been just beyond her grasp when she'd been in Thorne's arms, feeling how accustomed he was to having her there. How entitled he seemed. What was misty at first became solid in her mind. Thorne had

had his hands on her... been *with* her.

But how?

This battle was on the edge of breaking out, but Stephanie's mind became trapped in memories she hadn't experienced and realities she wasn't prepared for.

"*Ranz, did Thorne rape me when I wasn't in my body... when you trapped me in my cell?*"

Ranz said nothing for a few seconds, allowing Stephanie to remember how sore her body had been after her punishment in Ranz's cell, how sore in places she'd never been sore. She remembered the dark bruises coloring her wrist.

Her stomach dropped as she came to understand what had taken place in the process of branding her.

"*Answer me, Ranz, or I'll drain you right now.*"

"*It was the only way, dea—*" He thankfully stopped before uttering the term of endearment that would have gotten him killed. "*You had to be his, otherwise he could have lost you to a passionate night with Dusty.*"

"*Dusty would never have done that, never taken something from me knowing that it might bring shame to me—bring consequences I wasn't prepared for.*"

"*To forge this alliance, a price had to be paid.*"

Yes, the sevens often had to pay prices, didn't they? Cecily. Morgan. Stephanie. A thought occurred that had Stephanie flinching. "*Were you...?*"

"*No, I wasn't there. I pulled part of your consciousness back into your body. You were not harmed or hurt. You felt pleasure.*"

"*Not harmed? Are you insane? You and Thorne raped me... and you say there is no harm. You took away my choice—you stole my innocence."*

"*Then kill me, dearest. You have the power.*"

Lille and Thorne shouted at each other, while the Commanders and mystics prepared to do battle. Stephanie ignored them and their hostile words and thought back to the choice she'd made to remain in Darienne rather than a simple life in Dunlowe. She felt the cracks splintering her resolve.

But Stephanie wouldn't get another chance to go back, to make another choice, and even knowing what she now knew about those she had allied herself with, she still couldn't imagine not owning her choices, her mistakes, and she certainly couldn't imagine giving up her place on the throne.

Stephanie stuffed down her hurt, her childhood, and resolved to be more treacherous than those who thought they owned her. Ranz could hear every one of her thoughts, and she gloried in it, not having to hide her bitter soul from him. He would accept her as she was and never judge her for her lust for power. To serve that need in her heart, she forced herself to endure.

But she also knew as she stared at Thorne that Dusty Daye would be the only boy she would ever love.

The sight of Dusty and Finn, Millie and Charity—both dressed like Grey Cloaks—Amanda, Bay, and some others running toward the about-to-happen war, sent shivers through her heart because Dusty's presence, her relief that he still lived, would make what she had to do that much harder.

✶

Dusty charged toward the battle about to erupt in the caverns, not believing his eyes. The desert had almost killed them, so few survived out of the thousands who had lived before the desert had come and yet, they were already preparing to fight. It was like they weren't even grateful to survive. Immortals sure were *stupid* sometimes.

And then he saw Stephanie and his heart leapt. She was alive... and beautiful, though she wore a tortured expression as she walked toward the Grey Cloaks.

"Stephanie, no!" Dusty yelled, but she turned and held her hand up to stop him.

"Dusty, no. This is what I have to do."

She moved in between the leader of the Grey Cloaks and Lille, all swords and daggers aimed at her from both sides.

The leader of the Grey Cloaks barked something at her and the look she gave him had him taking a step back. She whispered something and he scowled. When she turned back to Lille, her eyes carried wisps of sadness but no uncertainty.

"This battle isn't going to happen. The Grey Cloaks are going to leave and you are going to continue south to Cloud City."

"How?" Lille stammered. "Why would they listen to you?"

Stephanie stood up, her bearing as proud as Lille's. "Because I am their queen, and one day, you will bow to me or I will send you to meet your parents and your brother. I will rule Darienne, but I don't want my rule to come from this stupid moment when I saved you all. So I guess I will save you again." Stephanie turned to Morgan, her voice softer, a hint of kindness in her eyes. "Remember what I said, Morgan."

Morgan walked forward, her eyes squinting at Stephanie. Dusty watched her, his mind stumbling over how horrible Morgan looked, sickly even, with dark circles under her eyes. Dusty moved toward her, but Millie held him in place, whispering, "Oona says wait. Morgan will need you soon."

Morgan stood before Stephanie, her eyes glancing from the leader of the Grey Cloaks, who looked remarkably like his brother Reece, to Stephanie. "Why?"

Stephanie's boldness faded. "Because we all have to be who we are—*this* is who I am."

"But he tried to kill me in the Downs."

"I know."

"Is he the one who stabbed me when I tried to rescue Bay and the others?"

Stephanie hedged.

Morgan grabbed Stephanie's arm. "Please, tell me. I saved your life—just tell me the truth."

Stephanie, though clearly stronger at that moment, didn't pull away from Morgan or lash out at all. "It was... *me*. I did it. I'm sor—"

Morgan released her and stepped back, her hand covering her mouth, as her eyes grew watery and a tear seeped down her pale cheek.

Dusty looked to Millie. "Please."

"Wait," Millie whispered.

Stephanie's and Morgan's eyes remained tied together, and Stephanie said, "I'm sorry. You saved my life and I tried to take yours. But I owe you a debt now, and I *will* repay you."

"Don't bother," Morgan whispered as her head sunk forward and her shoulders slumped. She turned and walked beyond the crowd.

Dusty wanted to follow her, but the sight of Bay moving

toward Stephanie kept him in place.

"Don't do this," Bay said. "You can still make another choice. Even now. Even after what you did to Morgan—don't go down this road. You don't know the price to your soul—I do, I've been where you are. Your family will forgive you."

For just a moment, Stephanie really seemed to consider his words, her eyes still holding on to the path that led to Morgan. Then her expression changed, as though she'd weighed all her options and made her choice. Bay shook his head and moved away, seeming to be trapped in dark memories.

Millie grumbled something Dusty couldn't make out and lurched around him to face off with Stephanie. "You disgusting harpy! How could you do that to Morgan? And what about Charity and me?" Millie pointed at the leader of the Grey Cloaks. "He's the one who kidnapped us to take us to an island to be your *servants*. *You* told us to stay in our tent. You've been working with them all along. I always knew you were a snotty good-for-nothing vixen, but now I know that you are nothing but a filthy traitor."

Stephanie sealed off her emotions and became the haughty princess they all knew, not a shade of doubt or regret in her anymore. "Millie, you are nothing but a sniveling coward and that's all you'll ever be. I am a queen, married to Thorne Greysen of the Grey Folk. Eventually we have to stop lying to ourselves and embrace who we really are. Bad luck for you."

"I am *not* a coward, Stephanie Greysen." Millie stood tall. "And you are *not* a queen. You married the wrong *brother*. This is Reece Greysen." Millie pointed at Grey, who pulled back his hood. "He was stolen and crammed in a cell for thousands of years by a treacherous demon named Ranz with the help of Daryn. Reece is a good man and the rightful king of the Grey Folk."

"How do you know this?" Thorne Greysen—Grey's crappy brother—demanded.

Millie smiled at him. "Your daughter says *hi*."

"*Oona*? Oona lives?"

"And she's coming for you, you piece of..."

Grey set his hand on Millie's shoulder in support. "Leave the caverns, brother. Take your *wife* and your Grey Folk with you, but know I am coming for my kingdom. I don't much like what you've done with it since I've been away. There is a reckoning coming."

Thorne looked unsettled, but bravado flared. "I'm ready when you are, you doddering, screaming fool, crying for your love in a heap on your cell floor. You'll never be anything other than Ranz's chattel to me—never anything other than *Two*."

Dusty prepared to launch at Thorne, but Grey smiled and winked at him. To Thorne, Grey said, "And you'll never know what love is, how the memory of one person can be the key to your soul. You'll never know respect and wonder for life. And you will never have friends, because one as treacherous as you must always watch his back... even from his new wife." Grey turned to Stephanie. "You had the love of a good man, and you chose unwisely and now you are married to a monster." Conflict raged in Stephanie's eyes. "He killed his last wife and plotted to kill his daughter. Watch your back."

Thorne and Grey glared at each other for a second before Grey said something in the Grey Cloak's language that sounded appropriately hateful. Thorne's hand gripped his blade even tighter, before he spat something back. Grey simply smiled at him and nodded.

Thorne grabbed Stephanie's hand roughly enough that she flinched. Her eyes turned venomous and something happened that had Thorne ripping his hand away.

Good for Stephanie, Dusty thought, but then he saw a wave of something overcome Stephanie. She looked about to fall.

Thorne leaned closer, whispering something as indecision blared on Stephanie's face.

"Say you understand," Thorne said, loud enough to hear.

Stephanie looked to Dusty for just a second. Hope and fear and love and loss flinched through her eyes like many flashes of lightning, all hitting at once. Then she turned back to Thorne. "I understand."

"We are leaving," Thorne said under his breath.

She nodded to him but paused, looking once more at Dusty.

Just so they were completely clear, Dusty said, "Goodbye, *Mrs.* Greysen. You aren't at all the person I thought you were."

Stephanie flinched worse than when Thorne had hurt her and turned, following her husband and all his soul-deep ugliness away from the family—and the boy—who would have loved her forever.

28

Always

Morgan couldn't find an emotion in her body—couldn't *feel* anything. This taste of sudden indifference brought an ounce of compassion for the Ezias. She tried to summon something, any feeling, but the knowledge that Stephanie had stabbed her in the back and almost ended the lives of Bay, Lille, Finn, Charity, Amanda, Mortimer, and Abigail left her hollow. Morgan stared around her at the faces of the would-be dead—all except Abigail, who was missing, probably somewhere safe. Bay's eyes caught Morgan's, but he quickly looked away, seeming disgusted by the sight of her. Oriel. Lille. Now, Bay. Who would be next?

Lille stood with Reece, their eyes locked, seeing nothing but each other. Millie and Dusty stared at them, joyous at the sight of the reunited couple.

Morgan heard Reece say, "What happens now?"

"I have absolutely no idea." Lille smiled up at him, giddy and young, all the world hers.

Good, Morgan thought, Lille had her love back. She really wouldn't need a sister anymore. Morgan let out a small grunt. *Sister?* No, Morgan knew the truth. She was nothing more than a subject, a pawn.

"It's time, isn't it? To pay?" Morgan asked the Ezias.

"They are anxious for it." Her grandfather's occupied body looked around the cavern. "This seems very public though."

"I can't hide my shame from anyone."

Morgan felt a touch on her shoulder and turned, staring up at Dusty, seeing worry in his kind blue eyes.

"Don't touch her, Dusty. She's been defiled by the Ezias," Lille called.

Dusty frowned at Lille. "*Defiled*? Like she has *cooties* or something?"

"I order you not to touch her—it's for the best."

Dusty chuckled. "Glad you're not the boss of me, Lille."

"Cecily wouldn't want you to be tainted."

Dusty leveled a glare that had Reece looking uncomfortable, as though he didn't know whether to be on Lille's side or Dusty's. "That's the thing. Cecily liked—no *loved*—Morgan more than she liked you, so I know exactly what she would want me to do. But *thanks* for thinking of me."

Dusty moved even closer, lowering his head until it was level with Morgan's. "Hey there," he said softly. "Been a rough week, huh?"

A small smile emerged, a new memory, an emotion. She nodded her head, fighting tears.

"That's all right. It's been a rough one for me too, but have I got stories for you about wolves and two-headed she-beasts. And you've got stories for me, too, huh?"

"Lille's right," Morgan said. "I am *tainted*, polluted."

Dusty smiled and the sun lived in his eyes. "Silly, you're *Morgan*, the smartest girl in Dunlowe who can be pretty stupid sometimes."

He leaned forward, his arms holding her tightly as she cried, grateful for his touch, more now than ever, now that touch would be more rare than ever before.

"What's going on with you and Oriel?" Dusty whispered.

"He's obeying our queen—he'll never touch me again. I swore an allegiance to her, Dusty—I'm trapped here."

"Everything changes, and we'll all be okay."

"Cecily? Is Cecily...?"

She felt Dusty sigh.

"Nate?!" Charity blurted and Dusty released Morgan, but pulled her to his side, keeping her close.

Nate walked directly to Dusty, ignoring almost everyone, but giving a smile to the dark-skinned woman with indigo hair who moved closer. Nate's bald head was covered with strange marks and his eyes looked different, older.

"Is she okay?" Dusty asked.

"She is."

"Where?"

"The Source."

"And the Source?"

Pride shone on Nate's face. "Cecily *is* the Source. She sent me to tell you so that you wouldn't expect her to come home."

"I knew she wasn't coming home."

"She's still trying to repair the damage done to so many worlds caused by the former Source's death. Cecily saved the world—the desert won't kill you now—but she wanted you to know that she won't be acting on events that happen here. She's afraid that without limits to her power—which there are none—

she could damage things. She is going to learn and study, and she regrets that she won't be able to help in the coming struggle." Nate turned to Lille. "You are the Queen of Darienne, yes?"

Lille nodded.

"The Source charges you with a task."

"Anything," Lille said.

"Cecily said you have in your possession petals that can be used to heal the land, but they will not heal all of it. Desert will be part of every continent now as a reminder to treasure the gifts of life that the earth gives. She said to tell you that the Delphea groves will live again and they will be as they have always been, charged with guiding the course of the world." He smiled less formally and said, "She also said to say 'Who's the little apricot now?'"

Lille smiled, but looked wistful. "Please tell her *thank you*. I wouldn't have a land to be queen of if she hadn't taken on this burden. I'm just beginning to understand the burden of being queen—I can't even imagine the burden of being the Source. What she had to give up..." Lille glanced to Finn who stared at the ground. "Please tell her we love her... always."

"I will."

Morgan felt emotions trembling within her. "Nate, are you with her... wherever the Source is?"

"I am, with Laura, Britton, and my sister, Darla. We will take care of her—I promise. We all willingly serve her and love her. There is nothing we won't do for her." He turned to Dusty and his eyes became full. "She loves you best, Dusty, and being apart from you is the greatest price she's had to pay. She's resolved not to interfere in the course of this world, but please, take good care of yourself. She can't have the detachment the former Source had—she loves too much for that. So please, don't get hurt, or this desert may seem like a town fair next to the tidal wave that might wash over all of the worlds."

Reece stepped toward Dusty. "We'll take care of him and be his family. And he has parents too, waiting for him in the caverns."

"I must go." He turned to Devra. "Thank you for doing all that you've done. You saved the world—without your actions, your commitment to Annisha's sentence, all would have died in hundreds, maybe thousands, of worlds. Cecily sends you her blessings and releases you from your sentence. All of it."

Devra's hand moved to her belly, a question in her eyes.

Nate nodded. "Even that is possible now. Darla says *thank you* too."

"Take good care of her."

"Take your child soldiers to the Delphea grove that will appear in the Wild Wood when Lille completes her work. They will find their families sheltered there. The trees saved them."

"Thank you."

Nate looked again to Dusty. "Please tell my mother what has become of her children. Tell her that we learned everything about being decent from her."

"I will. Thanks for letting us know—it would have been so hard to be trapped, wondering forever what had happened."

"That's exactly what your sister said."

Dusty fumbled some words but finally muttered, "But she's not my sister anymore. She's the *Source*."

"There is absolutely no reason she can't be both."

Nate vanished and Dusty slumped, pulling Morgan back into his arms, needing her this time.

Over his shoulder, she saw her grandfather nod that it was time.

"Dusty, there's something I have to do—something awful. Will you come with me?"

"Always."

*

Zoe looked around the cavern where everyone rested—soldiers and the reunited townsfolk. It seemed the gateway had healed the wounds of all those who survived, but not the exhaustion from so much fighting and loss. Logan held Zoe's hand and for the longest time, they simply stared at each other, but then she pulled away, kissing him and moving toward where Mindy sat, alone, her body bent like it had been broken in half. Jem and Logan moved closer, joining Zoe in kneeling in front of Mindy. Jacoby followed, standing slightly back.

"Why?" Mindy said without looking up. "Heath was with us since the beginning. How could he do it?"

"To save his family—that's why," Zoe said.

"At the cost of all of us and hope for the future? Your life was worth less than his family's lives." Her eyes locked with Zoe's. "I will fight with you forever. I will die for you. I *believe*. You are going to change the world."

"I hope so—I'll certainly try. And maybe Heath will come around some day."

"I think he's dead."

"Then we'll save his family in honor of the price he was

willing to pay for them."

Jacoby added, "Remember, Mindy, you saved Zoe. You saved me. Everyone would have died if you hadn't done what you did. You are a hero."

"No, not today. I'm just sad and broken today. But give me a day, and I will be the bravest, toughest fighter you've ever seen."

Zoe tentatively reached and held Mindy, whispering, "You already are."

When Zoe stepped away from Mindy, one of the young people who followed the dark-skinned demon woman approached Zoe, and Zoe moved toward him, listening, before turning to the crowd, all of whom quieted to hear what she had to say.

"The desert isn't deadly anymore, thanks to Cecily Daye's sacrifice. The land will be mostly healed very soon. I wish I could say the same for our country. The deserts probably killed more than our war, but our war isn't even close to ending. To the soldiers here, we will give you safe passage back to your land, but I would ask you to consider fighting with us. A country that enslaves its people, leads by fear, kills without regard to life— isn't a country that should stand. People should be free to live their lives in peace. To raise their families in peace." She glanced at Jacoby, who nodded to her. "My niece is a captive, being taken into a life of slavery. That isn't something I will allow, not for her, not for any of your families. I know many of you had no choice but to become soldiers. I know many of you have families who are enslaved. I am Zoe Crane, and I swear to you that I am going to fight for this country, as long as it takes, as much as it costs, until the end."

She grinned at them. "And I will be alive at the end and the king won't be. That is my promise to you."

A soldier was the first to stand and cheer, soon joined by others, until everyone chanted the name Zoe Crane.

Logan moved toward her, a smile a mile wide on his face. He leaned and said into her ear over the cacophony of chanting, "Apparently, my girl is a hero."

Zoe looked up at him, her heart in her throat. "Do you have a problem with that?"

He turned cocky. "Only the *Crane* part, because I'm still thinking Zoe *Trench* has a really heroic ring to it."

In answer, Zoe stood on her tiptoes and kissed him soundly.

*

Dusty stood with Morgan and her *possessed* grandfather, still not completely certain what was really happening, only knowing Morgan couldn't handle too many questions.

Genovan approached them. "I have to go with the queen on her mission to restore the land." He looked to Dusty. "Will you watch over Morgan for the Commanders?"

"Of course," Dusty said, just as Morgan blurted, "Your duty is to the queen, not to me."

Genovan placed his dark hands under Morgan's chin, raising it so she had to stare at him, keeping her eyes from hugging the ground. "Morgan, this is just the beginning. I think Lille will remember what you mean to her. She is new to her duties, but holds some old hatreds and ideas. The Ezias were a scourge on Darienne for a long time and the infected were killed instantly, as is often done to those who are a threat."

"Like the Commanders?" Morgan asked.

"Yes, they *tried*, and just like the Commanders, the Ezias are hard—if not impossible—to kill once they have fully become. She won't kill you, but you know, she might..."

"Use me. Force me... to..."

Genovan nodded. "The Commanders feel your plight and are here for you. Besides, with Cecily gone forever, caring for you will help with our grief. Please, allow us to do as our hearts compel us."

"I'm very grateful." Morgan brushed a tear away with the back of her hand.

"And I will look after her while you're gone," Dusty added.

"Then she is in good hands with a warrior like you."

Dusty beamed. "I've changed, haven't I?"

Winking at Morgan, Genovan said, "We'll just have to take some time to determine what exactly you've changed into."

Genovan walked away, and Morgan's grandfather stepped forward. "Their anxiousness grows. When the fervor is great, it will be harder on you."

"I'm ready," Morgan said. She looked to Dusty. "You'll come?"

"Of course. I just need to do one thing." Dusty motioned to Millie. After waiting for the Commanders and Lille, Oriel, and Reece to follow Devra to a doorway, Millie hurried over. "I am going with Morgan for a little while. If you and Grey want to go free Oona, I'd love to meet her when..."

"If you have something to do..." Morgan stammered, but Dusty squeezed her hand.

"Stop, just stop. I'm coming with you."

Dusty turned back to Millie, who smiled sadly. "Oona says you are doing exactly as you should, and she'd rather wait until you can come. And she'd be honored if Morgan would come too."

Morgan studied Millie's face. "Are you okay? You look..."

Millie nodded. "I'm fine. It's just... after we bring Oona back, will you both come with me to see my father again? My mother didn't survive."

Dusty and Morgan both hugged Millie. "Of course."

Millie stayed with Charity and Amanda, while Dusty walked with Morgan as they followed her grandfather to a secluded cave near the large cavern. Dusty kept her hand in his and forced himself to be strong, to understand that if this was something that could be fought, the Commanders would have fought.

She didn't need a warrior right now. She needed a friend.

Her grandfather stopped, gesturing toward the ground. Morgan nodded and released Dusty's hand, taking a place on the cave floor, her hands clenched into fists.

"Can I do something?" Dusty asked.

Morgan shook her head. "Just being here is enough." She turned to her grandfather. "Please, let's get this over with."

He nodded, without compassion.

A second later dark spirits flew out of everywhere, including Morgan. They swarmed around and Dusty fought the urge to bat them away like evil gnats. They swirled and swirled and then dove into Morgan, through her eyes, her nose, her mouth, seizing her while her body lay still and a terrible whimper came from within her. They formed a writhing shell around her outsides while they did whatever they did to her insides.

Long minutes passed. Some of the longest minutes of Dusty's life, just like watching Cecily tortured by the mystics back in the Wild Wood. And when it ended, Morgan wept as though her soul had been drained. She tried to rise but slumped back down.

Dusty ignored her grandfather and took a place beside her on the ground, pulling her body against his, her back against his chest, wrapping his arms around her.

"Dusty," she cried. "They steal *you* from me."

Dusty's throat grew almost too tight to speak, but he forced his way past. "What do you mean? *I'm* right here."

"Every single feeling they take, every single emotion… they are all of you—my memories of you are what they steal, what they consume like food. It's all you."

Tears pressed at him. "You know what, Morgan?"

"What?"

"We'll make more, you and me. We'll make so many memories that they will never get the upper hand. I'm prepared to be ridiculous to make these memories worth snacking on."

Dusty won an exasperated sort of laugh from Morgan.

"Only you," she chuckled.

"Thank goodness there's no one like me."

Morgan struggled for a second and Dusty helped her to turn over so that they stared at each other, face to face. Morgan put her hand on Dusty's cheek. "Thank you." She moved her thumb, caressing him softly. "She made the wrong choice."

Dusty bit his lip, but then asked, "Which one? They both abandoned me."

"Well, one saved the world and the other is bent on owning

it, so you guess which one."

"Stephanie Greysen?"

"She made the wrong choice."

"Maybe she did, maybe she didn't. We all have to follow our own paths—that's what I'm trying to tell myself."

Morgan laughed softly.

"What?"

"It's a good thing Cecily's gone."

"Why?"

"Because she would be *very* upset that you cut off your floppy hair."

Dusty laughed but then grew serious. "But do *you* like it?"

Morgan ran her hand over his hair in a way that felt nice. "I love it. We all have to change sometime."

"I'm just glad you're changing back."

Morgan looked confused. "What do you mean?"

"Your hair is brown again, the color it should be. And your skin isn't gold and isn't as pale as Lille's anymore."

"And my eyes?"

"One is green, one is brown, just the way they should be."

"Yes," Morgan said softly. "Just the way they should be."

She reached into her pocket, pulling out her glasses and placing them on her face, while Dusty smiled, finding a moment that was right in a world that had too much wrong.

29

The Deep East

Morgan dared to smile and even sigh as she rode on Dusty's back to rejoin the group, after he had given her time to collect herself. The warmth of his body and his spirit brought light back into her, made hope possible. Even with Morgan's trust in Dusty, she still feared he'd turn away from her, seeing her violation by the Ezias. But he hadn't and now they would make new memories to replace the ones the Ezias consumed.

Dusty's care for her cushioned the blow of Lille's return from her mission—she never even looked to see if Morgan was okay.

Millie seemed anxious for their return and Dusty hurried toward her.

"Is Oona okay?" Dusty asked.

"She is—she doesn't mean to be a bother, but it's been such a long time."

Dusty looked around and then shouted, "Grey, come on! Oona's waiting."

Reece talked to Lille for a second before kissing her hand and joining Dusty, Millie, Morgan, Charity, and the demon Devra, who introduced herself to Morgan and shook her hand, not asking why she rode on Dusty's back.

They walked a long way in the caverns, it was hard to know how long or how far, until they reached a passage that led through a more and more narrow corridor leading to a room that brightened at their approach, brighter than anywhere in the caverns. The walls were completely made of the rock lights. In the middle of the room sat a pile of rocks, covering something that shimmered... something grey.

"Are you okay to stand now?" Dusty asked.

"Yes."

"We'll help her," Millie said, and Charity and Millie put their arms around Morgan's waist, keeping her balanced on her weak legs.

Dusty joined Grey in lifting the rocks off of the pile one by one, their pace quickening as they competed with each other until only the shiny grey cocoon could be seen.

"Have you got Morgan?" Millie asked Charity, who nodded, but Devra, without a word, took Millie's place.

Millie approached the cocoon and knelt beside it, placing her hand on it and extending her other hand into the air next to her. A moment later the cocoon moved.

"Dusty, help me." Millie tore at the fabric that enclosed what turned out to be a lovely grey girl, who looked to be about their ages.

Dusty's eyes went wide at her beauty and he placed his hand gently behind her neck, helping her to sit as she stared at him, love and wonder flowing out of her... and toward him.

"Oona?" Dusty whispered.

"Yes, Dusty. I've been waiting so long to meet you."

"Me too," he stammered, turning red.

For a few seconds, they stared at each other and the sight was the most beautiful thing Morgan had ever seen. Dusty deserved to find happiness with a girl who could appreciate just how wonderful he was. And Morgan would be his friend and she was more grateful for that than anything in her life.

∗

Stephanie felt woozy but didn't know why. All of the faces around her—Dusty, the sevens, Lille, Finn, Bay, the Commanders, soldiers—seemed underwater, everything blurring and swirling as she fought to keep her feet below her and her sight from giving out.

Fury and satisfaction lived in Thorne's eyes as he glared at her, leaning closer. "You used your power against me." His words low, deadly, words only she could hear. "You think I would tie myself to a woman powerful enough to kill me, without having a leash to keep her bound?"

Stephanie shook her head, not understanding.

"We are married, you and I. Bound to each other forever—or until death *possibly*. Our fates are one. You use your power on me, my brand will poison you. Feel that, Stephanie?"

The brand seared her and a wave of dizziness almost took her to the ground.

"That is the force of my power, a power you better accept. I will punish you fiercely for your failure today. But make no mistake, there is no life or crown for you without me." More loudly, he commanded, "Say you understand."

With every moment, every memory, she'd shared with Dusty flashing through her mind, Stephanie closed the door to the life she'd thought she'd live and submitted to a future defined by her immortal *husband*.

"I understand."

Stephanie felt the sting of Dusty's goodbye, the way he called her Mrs. Greysen. But he lived, and that was enough.

She followed Thorne out of the caverns, to the sea, and onto a ship that would take her to her new life. Thorne's rage at her had a life of its own, and she tasted only disgust to be married to the man who raped her—to be bound to him forever. All in all, the trip reminded her of her cell in Ranz's cave. But the sea was gentle, the wind fair, and she stood on the deck looking out at the water, choosing to find something about this moment that wasn't dreadful.

But thoughts of Morgan seeped into her tiny peaceful moment. Then Dusty. Her father. Her brothers. Her mother. The sevens. Everything and everyone that was gone from her life forever ganged up on her, stealing every chance of finding a moment of solace.

"*Ranz?*"

Nothing.

"*Ranz, please, I know you're there.*"

Still nothing.

"*Ranz, I'm lonely. Please.*"

She felt him sigh before saying, "*Dearest, I'm so sorry, but I am not allowed to talk to you without Thorne's permission. Not anymore. This is part of the deal I made, though it hurts me more than you would understand.*"

"*But why...? How could you abandon me now?*"

"*To make you queen, I would give up anything—Thorne*

is making me prove that."

"But why?"

"*The transition time between your old life and your new one will be brutal, and relying on me will keep you from embracing your future. It is time to find out who you really are. I'm sorry it will be so violent for you...*"

"Violent?"

"*And painful. But I promise by the end of your training, you will be ready to claim your crown.*"

"But what did I do wrong?"

"*You flinched, dearest. You aren't ready to win. You failed us and now you must pay.*"

"But, Ranz, please..."

She felt him closing a door inside her, disappearing behind it, and leaving her completely alone.

Stephanie swallowed over the hurt and cringed from the violence and pain that was coming, and did nothing to stop her tears from meeting the sea.

✶

My tears hit the pond in *my* garden, obscuring my view of whatever I wished to see. Darla sat in my lap, watching with me. Britton and Laura worked in the mound room, easing all of the millions of recently dead into their new homes, where I would give them peace. I could have done it for them, but Britton ordered me to rest for a bit and breathe. All this power was overwhelming, and he was good and wise and I would listen.

Nate returned from his visit to the caverns—which Darla and I had watched—and joined us, moving where I could lean against him.

"You did well. Thank you," I said.

"I'm sorry you couldn't go."

"The Source trapped herself here for a reason and until I understand what that was, I must comply."

"They all love you."

"And I love them... in a different way than the Source ever could. I belong there, but I can feel it, I belong here too."

"And Darla and I belong wherever you are."

"Yes, please. Nate, you know..."

"Cec—my Lady Source, *whatever* we call you now, don't worry about relationships or anything else right now. I am happy to serve you in any way I can."

"Thank you, and you call me Cecily."

"I'm not sure I can."

"Try hard, otherwise I'll turn you into a toad and you can entertain Darla and me on a lily pad for a while."

Darla giggled in my arms. "Do it! It'll be fun."

Nate laughed and I took a deep healing breath, knowing there would be no time to heal the fractures from Annisha's life or my own. I had to simply shore them up and move forward with my burdens, burdens made easier by Nate and Darla, Laura and Britton.

I shook loose all of the thoughts that gave me pain and watched in the pond the beautiful and tragic sights on the world I loved best.

I watched the survivors from Stoughton cling together and keep each other strong. I watched soldiers joining Zoe's rebellion. I watched my sister sevens as they rushed toward what remained of their families. Jem spun Amanda around and their father crowded in. I reached into the mound in which Mrs. Payne rested and gave her the warmth and beauty of her family, not waking her, just easing her into the healing that would come. Millie hugged her father as they wept for Mrs. Smyth who hadn't gone into a mound yet—had firmly refused—and was helping Laura and Britton guide the others to their resting places. Charity found no one from her large family and stumbled over the answers to questions she shouldn't have had to ask. The truth wrecked her heart but gave a direction to her future.

I looked on Pastor Rowe, the dead man who still lived, as he watched everyone, feeling disconnected and out of place. But the townsfolk didn't forget him; Jem called him over to tell everyone how all of the children and wounded would have died if not for Pastor Rowe. The pastor looked even more uncertain with Jem's praise, and Zoe kept her wary eyes open but her gratitude still lived as she looked up into Logan's face. Theirs was a beautiful love and Zoe would forever be my regret as Devra was Annisha's. How unkind I was to such an amazing soul. Perhaps one day I would be able to make it up to her, but I was relieved she now had a brother who adored her as much as she adored him.

"I wronged her so much," Nate said quietly.

"You and me both."

A smile grew on my face watching Reece Greysen, Dusty's best friend, march toward Mrs. Dumphry with open arms, while she gave him a timid look and backed away. He ignored her apprehension and lifted her into an enormous bear hug while she blushed and then giggled like a school girl.

Abigail's little brothers refused to believe that Abigail was really gone and I remembered when they had boldly stood in front of Pastor Rowe, fighting for my life when few others would. A smile bloomed in my heart. The boys were wise beyond their years, I thought as I turned our view to where Abigail lay on a beach, exhausted, having used powers she didn't know she had—and forming an alliance that would carry a high price—to drag Keefe out of the turbulent sea and to the shore. Oona would know soon and lead Abigail's brothers to the sister they believed in more than anything, before Abigail would have to say goodbye again.

But Oona was busy just then being introduced to my parents, who surrounded her with love and gratitude, while Bear softly nuzzled her cheek. I couldn't feel anything but wonder at a world that took and gave so much. I felt Oona's courage, saw the treacherous path she had walked to reach Dusty and to save the world. Oona and Devra, without them, no one would be alive right now.

I stared at Dusty, carrying Morgan on his back, forcing her to laugh, to build new memories that might be stolen soon by the fate that seemed cruel by every measure. But I couldn't see all ends, only I knew Morgan was important, that not having a destiny freed her to live in a way no one else could, to master fate in a way unheard of on any of my worlds. I worried about her though, and pained for her.

Nate tightened his hold on me and whispered, "Show me Lille and the petals—I want to see the world reborn, and Cassa and Jaden... please."

"What do you say?" I teased.

"Please, *Cecily*."

"Thank you." I showed him the view of Lille dropping lavender petals on the ground. Just a few brought ripples of wondrous color to the world as the desert was swallowed by lush green and gold grasses, rolling hills, and deep forests. The few petals dropped in Darienne brought a sea of changes that washed up the continent and into the Wild Wood, made new and more verdant than ever. The Delphea groves burst to life, more of them than had ever been, more watchful and empowered stewards for the world.

Inside the grove stood the hundreds of villagers from the Wild Wood, and Devra emerged from the caverns bringing home the children she had stolen. The children would have a choice to remain with their families or continue with Devra's work, because even released from her sentence, I felt her commitment to the world, to Nate and Darla, and to me. She quietly removed her marks from the villagers and from the children. I felt Nate's joy at seeing the Oades reunited with their children, a community put back together. I felt their wonder at learning that their children's efforts and success at saving the world had inspired the Delphea groves to offer safe passage to their families.

Devra looked distant for a moment and then looked up into the sky, seeming to stare directly at me, and Nate and Darla. The indigo tattoos on their heads shone more brightly.

"I am one of your instruments on this earth, Source, loyal to you alone. I will never stop honoring Annisha's ruling, though I will come out of the darkness to better serve the world. I am here when you need me. And I am honored that children of mine were born to serve you."

The smile she gave me brought a kind a healing to my

heart that I couldn't explain, so I broke the rules and whispered, "*Thank you*," into her head. She looked grateful and full of joy. She nodded to us and went back to her work, while apprehension grew in my gut.

"You're dreading it—just look already," Nate said.

I nodded and turned the view to Finn, who stood with Bay, both of them pictures of brokenness. The Commanders stood nearby, looking lost, the only survivors who genuinely wished they'd died. Genovan seemed disconnected, even from his brothers, at that moment. The three of them were the price of my leaving and there was nothing I could do or say to help them just now, because what they needed most was to let me go, let go of all of the possibility I represented in their lives. I was not of their world anymore, and though it made me sad and even knowing Bay's and Finn's crimes, I could see the purpose to all of this. Finn and Bay had been defined by wars and love for too long—so long they couldn't even see who they were anymore, what their own purposes were. If I'd remained in the world, they would have helped me. Now they were free—and forced—to find their own fights, and even knowing as I did what that could mean for their futures, I saw the need for it.

Because what I knew now was that there were mounds for the dead where they would find peace, but that was not the only possible ending. Eternal fires burned in the Source where dark souls dwelled... forever. The Source had owned vengeance in her heart and I wondered if I had enough to keep those fires lit or whether the dark souls needed more kindness than even the gentle ones did. But I would do as the Source did until I better understood. My heart still ached at seeing Finn, Bay, and the

Commanders so haggard. If darkness had its way, it would claim them soon.

Thinking of darkness, I turned our view to Stephanie and watched her wedding to a treacherous man who might meet the fires of the Source one day—he might be reason enough to keep them burning. I watched Stephanie as she made her vows. When Thorne Greysen leaned to kiss her, she took a step back and slapped him, intending to storm away. But her husband had other plans and grabbed her, stealing the kiss that sealed them forever, while his people cheered. I felt her anguish and isolation, the vile pain seething through her at the violation of her body. I sensed the demon Ranz within her—no longer her master, more like her hostage at this point. Her soul grew murky as girlish dreams were corrupted by greed, jealousy, and envy, by pride and coldness—all cages that would deny her the real love that could have saved her. Of all my sisters, I knew I would weep most for Stephanie. That I might have saved her... that I could have, that I could even now, brought tightness to my chest.

"Have faith, Cecily," Darla whispered, seeming to feel my heartbreak. "It isn't over yet, and even she may find a way to redeem herself one day. And yes, I do feel your heartbreak. I've always felt you as much as you felt me, and now we are even more connected."

I kissed Darla's head. "Would you let me do something... it might seem odd?"

"Anything," Darla said, while Nate added, "What?"

"I love your demon marks, but Devra shouldn't be able to have power over you here and she very possibly might. I don't wish to completely remove your link to her though."

"What do you want to do?" Nate asked, grinning in a way that confused me.

"I want to add my own mark—is that strange?"

His smile grew as he shook his head. "No, go ahead."

Darla elbowed him in the ribs and looked embarrassed for him, while I had no idea what was going on. Darla looked up at me. "I'd like that... as long as its pretty like Devra's."

I focused and turned Devra's deep indigo marks to gold, severing the link of the color, but leaving the design intact, while adding a delicate silver vine that wound through and around the openings in Devra's intricate marks.

"Well, how does it look?" Darla asked.

"See for yourself," I said, tilting my head toward the water.

She glanced at the pond, now turned into a perfectly still mirror and I watched her smile widen. Darla turned back to me and threw her arms around my shoulders.

"I love you, Cecily."

"I love you too, Darla. Are you going to tell me why Nate is still looking so goofy?"

"She better not," he warned, but his smile made his threat sound silly.

Darla moved her head to whisper in my ear. "He likes that you've claimed him and me. No matter what happens, we're family forever."

"Yes, we are," I said, my words fumbling over the tears I felt coming, as my eyes caught Nate's and I felt so many things for him I'd thought were dead. "*Forever.*"

Trapped in that moment, looking at my future with Darla and Nate that no one could ever take from me, I felt the beautiful part of true power. Much was a burden, but this... this *forever* was mine to treasure. Darla and Nate couldn't die and leave me, they'd already died *for* me. I didn't even dream that our paths would be easy, but we would be together, whatever that meant for Nate and me.

"Quit with the lovey eyes," Darla said. "I want to see the other places, either on our world or one of the other worlds... the ones you saved."

"Very well."

I cuddled Darla close and turned back toward our little pond and showed her a place on our world that we'd never known existed—I showed her the Deep East. Her eyes stared in awe as the petals that touched the earth in Darienne worked to heal a place on the other side of the world. Desert turned back into green lands that were low to the water. Upon a bluff stood a woman staring out at the sea, a woman who clearly yearned for something—or someone—who existed across the water.

I felt her longing and knew exactly who she yearned for. I wondered whether fate would conspire to give her what she wanted and also wondered what the price would be for her if her prayers were answered. But I pulled away and showed Darla other places, reminding myself that the wants in every heart weren't for me to solve. I was the Source. I gave them the world. Fate and chance would have to give them the rest.

The End

Coming Soon...

Through *The Wild Wood* and *The Downs*, Cecily Daye and the sevens followed a shared path, sometimes fleeing and sometimes embracing their fates, but in *The Barren Way*, their paths separated, maybe forever.

Cecily, still reeling from the cost of following her destiny, will face trials greater than any she has known, with consequences that bring peril to more souls—some dearer to her than her own—than she has ever imagined.

Divided, the six other girls must find their own ways through the challenges that have engulfed their world and the families they left behind, while also being pulled toward their own destinies that are fraught with danger and violence, love and hope, friendship and goodbyes.

But Cecily and the former sevens face the same question: will peace ever be possible after they've done so many dark things just to survive?

For now, they must continue toward the place where answers will be found. They must...

enter

THE
DEEP
EAST

Acknowledgements

So many people play a role in my life and my goals. I am extremely grateful for all of the love and support that surrounds me, both personally and professionally.

Special thanks go to:

My parents

My Critique/Edit Brigade: Kasie, Chelsea, Mom, Kat, Tawny, Michelle, Jodi, Margaret, and Sandy

Allison Leonard of Studio127 Photography

Brian and Margaret

Chelsea, Jodi, Frankie, and Ang

Beth, Leslie, and Karla

Carrie Deem, Mary K. Donovan, Dr. Heather Heap, and the students of Mill Creek High School

Michelle Sambas, Kim Davis, and the students of London High School

Kathy and Connie

Ari, Connor, Brenna, and my Squishy (love you, Ellie!)

Katie and Ryan

Dr. Jessie Sams, Leslie Hill, and Stephen F. Austin State University, for including my writing and characters in an amazing fictional language class. I loved every minute of it! The Grey Folk salute you (not sure if that is such a great thing). :)

I would also like to thank Dr. B and all of the vets, vet techs (especially Eilene), and receptionists who have taken such amazing care of my pups throughout the past six years (including handfeeding my little guy when I was out of town) and have been so amazingly supportive of my writing adventure. Thanks for making me feel like a rock star every time I drop by.

The Barren Way Playlist

Thanks to all of the artists whose music helped me to write this book. I couldn't have done it without you!

Dark Was the Night — Blind Willie Johnson (This is the only song that is on every playlist for every story I've ever written.)
Say Goodbye (I Won't Even) — Adaline
Thinking About You — Big Scary
Love Never Fails — Brandon Heath
Just the Way You Are — Bruno Mars
Kingdom Come, *Go*, and *Poison and Wine* — The Civil Wars
Shine — David Gray
The Broken Ones — Dia Frampton
Life Boat — Early Morning Rebel
Superman — Five for Fighting
What the Water Gave Me; *Never Let Me Go*; *No Light, No Light*; *Leave My Body*; and *Swimming* — Florence + The Machine
I Can Barely Say — The Fray
Holding a Heart — Girl Named Toby
Demons — Imagine Dragons (Thanks Heather!)
Keep Breathing, *This Is War*, *Ghost*, *Keep Warm*, *End of the World*, and *Always You* — Ingrid Michaelson
Rain (Setting Out in The Leaf Boat) — The Innocence Mission
Down and *Echo* — Jason Walker
Way to the Future, *Closest I Get*, and *Lost and Found* — Katie Herzig
Without You — Lana Del Rey
Follow You (With Brandon Heath) — Leeland
Lay Your Head Down — Peter Bradley Adams
Welcome Home — Radical Face
Kite Song — Rosie Thomas
Like the Sun — RyanDan
Breathe Again and *Lie to Me* — Sara Bareilles
Broken (feat. Amy Lee) — Seether
Give Me Strength — Snow Patrol
Times — Tenth Avenue North
River Flows in You — Yiruma
Skin — Zola Jesus

Books by Julie Anne Nelson

<u>The Sevens Series</u>
The Wild Wood (book 1)
The Downs (book 2)
The Barren Way (book 3)
The Deep East (book 4) coming December 2013

*For more information about
Julie Anne Nelson, upcoming release dates,
contests, and story extras,
go to...*

www.julieannenelson.com